THEY DARED TO BE DIFFERENT IN A FIERCE, UNFORGIVING WORLD...

TEKAKWITHA—she would witness savagery that would drive her away from her campfires toward eternal light, a miracle worker armed with the genius of faith and the power of pure love.

QUORENTA—an outcast among her own people, she practiced the black arts—and took to her heart and hearth the orphaned Tekakwitha, the child born to become legend.

KRYN—handsome halfbreed, he was driven to prove himself a braver, stronger, truer Mohawk than all the rest—until a miracle led him from the Clan of the Turtle to the white man's God.

JEROME—Indian warrior and rebel who first planted the seed of faith in Tekakwitha's heart—at the cost of his life.

PERE CLAUDE CHAUCHETIERE—French aristocrat and Jesuit, he dreamed of martyrdom in the New World, never imagining that destiny had other plans, that his greatest triumph—and trial—would come from the innocent girl who tormented his heart and soul, the one they called...

LILY OF THE MOHAWKS

LILY
OF
THE MOHAWKS

Jack Casey

BANTAM BOOKS
TORONTO · NEW YORK · LONDON · SYDNEY · AUCKLAND

This story,
about the purest of hearts,
is for June.

LILY OF THE MOHAWKS
A Bantam Book / September 1984

ISBN 0-553-24420-5

Published simultaneously in the United States and Canada

Bantam Books are published by Bantam Books, Inc. Its trade-
mark, consisting of the words "Bantam Books" and the por-
trayal of a rooster, is Registered in U.S. Patent and Trademark
Office and in other countries. Marca Registrada. Bantam
Books, Inc., 666 Fifth Avenue, New York, New York 10103.

PRINTED IN THE UNITED STATES OF AMERICA
H   0 9 8 7 6 5 4 3 2 1

Contents

THE IROQUOIS CONFEDERACY
AND EUROPEAN COLONIES -- 1663
"The Land From Which All Rivers Flow"

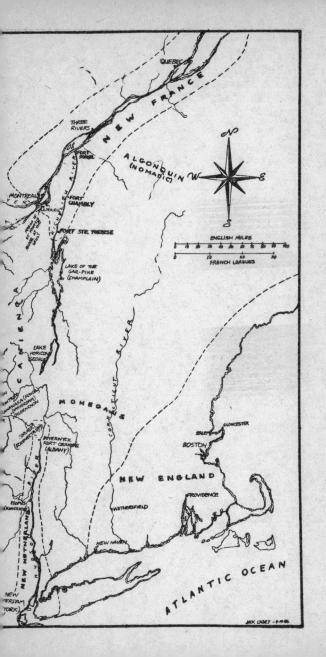

Prologue

As Europeans greedy for new lands pushed inland from the Atlantic coast, they ran headlong into a proud, strong, unified native culture, The People of the Great Longhouse. By 1650 these natives had not evolved past the Stone Age, yet a sophisticated political system united their five separate nations into a League for mutual benefit—trade, protection, and domestic peace.

The "Iroquois," as the French called them, were taller than other natives. Except for their darker skin, early writers tell us, the Iroquois resembled Europeans, young Europeans, for the forest life kept them trim and athletic. Fond of oratory, they conducted themselves in council, one Jesuit wrote, "like Roman senators." They hunted for their meat—deer, bear, moose, and bobcat. They planted crops—corn, squash, and tobacco. They built walled towns, "castles" the English termed them, and lived in bark longhouses, four, five, six families side by side around separate hearth fires.

Long before the white man's arrival, this race had seized the high ground of the continent. Down from their land river networks flowed in all directions—the St. Lawrence, Mohawk–Hudson, Susquehanna, Delaware, the Ohio–Mississippi—highways for their swift bark canoes to speed them to trade, treaty talks, and war.

All three European nations, Holland, England, and France, tried to befriend the Iroquois. Holland was successful and trade through the Dutch East India Company flourished. Britain was more successful. The five Iroquois nations, the Seneca, Cayuga, Onondaga, Oneida, and Mohawk, served as England's allies for over a century. France succeeded only occasionally in making peace.

From 1609, when Samuel de Champlain fired upon an Iroquois hunting party, until 1760, when the Iroquois helped

1

the British drive France from Canada, the great League hated the French and attacked them often. The French kings sought to end the warfare and secure a lucrative trade in pelts. Louis XIV sent Jesuit missionaries to make inroads, to soften the culture toward France. Then he soaked the native villages with brandy to seduce hunters from hunting, women from planting, warriors from waging war.

While the king and his ministers used these missionaries for political ends, the "blackrobes" themselves were very sincere, dedicated men. They truly loved the native people, and believed they could save them from devil worship by bringing them the "good news" of Christ's gospel. The courage of these Jesuits remains unsurpassed in human history. Starved, beaten, burned, emasculated, tortured, and bitten, they sang hymns till death and forgave their torturers in the manner of Christ: "Forgive them, Father, for they know not what they do." Captured by the Iroquois, Father Isaac Jogues, whose thumb was gnawed off, escaped back to France where he was honored as a hero and the Queen Mother kissed his mutilated hand. Yet he insisted on returning to New France, then journeyed as envoy to the same Iroquois, the Mohawks, who had enslaved him. He was murdered shortly thereafter in the easternmost village of the League, Ossernenon, where this story begins.

Ten years after Jogues's murder, a young girl was born at Ossernenon, and this is a story of her life. Orphaned by a smallpox plague, she grew up alone, retiring, introspective and shy. She thrilled at the legend of Hiawatha, the great chief who formed the League to bring peace to all men, yet all about her she saw feuds, massacres, torture and the debility brought by the white man's alcohol. Only Kryn, the half-breed war chief, embodied the traditional values of her people, she believed, and upon him she fixed all her admiration and hope for the future of her race.

Tekakwitha loved Kryn from afar. She loved him for his wisdom, his discipline, his courage in battle, his stoicism, and for his compassion. Like him, she came to believe the white man's religion would deliver her from the vices and decadence of her people. She converted to Christianity against her uncle's wishes, and she took the name "Catherine" after Catherine of Alexandria, a virgin she admired in the priest's book on the saints. She fled to be with Kryn and with other Christians at the Mission of St. Francis Xavier at LaPrairie, on the river bank opposite Montreal. The Jesuits ministering to the mission marvelled that she had remained chaste among pagans where young girls lost their virginity about their seventh year. They lauded her piety, her holiness, and her influence on converted natives in the letters they wrote. She died three years after arriving at the mission, and her people regarded her as a saint, praying to her for spiritual guidance and emulating her example.

Hundreds of miracles were reported due to her intercession. High-ranking French officials were cured of gout, of paralysis and hearing loss by praying to her. Two priests of the mission wrote biographies, and it is from them we have drawn the skeleton of our story. For the next eighty years Kateri's reputation spread throughout New France by word of mouth. Among her people she became a folk hero. To the French she represented the highest attainments of the Iroquois character under missionary guidance.

When the English captured Canada during the French and Indian War, they drove the Jesuits out. Nearly a century passed until they returned in 1848, and the story of Kateri Tekakwitha, long forgotten, was revived. Since then, a slow but steady effort has been undertaken to canonize the young Iroquois maiden in the Roman Catholic Church, to make her the first native American saint. She was beatified in 1980, one step away from canonization, and her "cause" is now being actively pursued in Rome.

Kateri Tekakwitha's appellation, "Lily of the Mohawks," illustrates the many cultures battling for mastery during her lifetime. "Mohawk" is an English word adopted from the Algonquin word for "man-eater," and refers to Iroquois cannibalism. The "Mohawks," in their own language, were called the "Canienga," People of the Land of Flint, because of the rocky headlands of their nation. I have used "Canienga" throughout the book in referring to the people known to other generations as the fierce "Mohawks." The "Lily," a flower symbolizing chastity, refers to the emblem of the French royal family, the fleur-de-lis. According to legend, an angel gave King Clovis a lily at his baptism to signify purity, and it passed into use on the royal standard and coat of arms. French Jesuits, laboring against terrible odds in so wild and warlike a land, saw their efforts flower in Kateri Tekakwitha— a lily had sprung from ground soaked with the tears of many captives and the blood of martyrs.

Today Kateri Tekakwitha, "Lily of the Mohawks," is revered for her many graces and favors by Catholics and non-Catholics alike. In the saga of the settling of America, she lives in twilight, on the periphery of the white man's frontier. She speaks eloquently to us today in our more jaded scientific age: Why did she leave her culture for the Christian mission? What struggles did she win in conquering native impulse and superstition? What example does she serve to women of all ages and races and times?

I have peered carefully into the past and have written as truthful a story as I could. I have come to know and admire and, yes, love her and her mentor the heroic Kryn. I invite you to enter this time, the seventeenth century, and this place, the Land From Which All Rivers Flow. I invite you to meet and come to understand a lonely, courageous young woman with a gift of poetry who transcended the pagan brutality of her culture, and who allowed nothing, not mandatory marriage or the customary role of women, or even the spiritual failings of her priest, to keep her from where her heart and her soul led. Kateri's story, I believe, is universal, and in that belief I offer this volume.

JACK CASEY

Troy
January 23, 1984

AWAKENINGS

Ossernenon, Land of Flint
1663

1

The old woman dwelt apart and for this was called mad. Outside the palisade, beyond humps of the maize plantation, down a path into the forest, down again into a ravine of dripping rock and moss, she lived alone. Her bark hut covered a stone grotto, and in this dim, birdless place, half underground, half above, Quorenta practiced black arts. Her *orenda*, her aura, was most powerful. She fashioned spells and brewed the potions White Adder, the albino magician, used. Some children mocked her, threw mud and stones when she entered the common field to collect her maize; others feared her, claiming one look of her eye turned people into stone like the stone giants of northern legend.

Long before, Quorenta had been destined to become grand matriarch of the most powerful *ohwachira*, family, of the Turtle Clan in the nation of the Canienga, the People of the Land of Flint. But she bore no children. Her husband divorced her. Over the years, instead of adopting captives and orphans as other barren women did, she withdrew in disgrace, mulling upon her destiny, isolating herself to a far corner of the longhouse, then to a hut outside the palisade, then to the ravine. At her mother's death, rule of the *ohwachira* fell to her younger sister.

Quorenta ministered to girls during puberty rites. She alone visited them in their first flow of blood when, declared unclean, they were sent beyond the palisade. She helped them build huts, catch fish and turtles and rabbits to eat; she gave them herbs and potions for cramps. She counseled them on how to live two lives—an outer life of duty, joy, and nurturing in longhouse and village, and an inner life of sorrow and stoic endurance of famine, death, plague, and war.

One ray of hope had entered her life. Three years

before, fur traders from Quebec had infected Ossernenon with a plague. Putrefying corpses lay in village lanes, and the wailing of women and groaning of men filled the town day and night.

In his longhouse, the great chief Tsantongowa and his three wives were dying. Ministering to the sick, Quorenta found among the soot and tangled skins a child of four summers, a girl, suffering, but still able to scream. She brought the child outside the palisade to her own hut, which remained uncontaminated since she had few visitors. The little girl recovered—due to potions and charms and the sweatings and cold baths—and when autumn came, the plague subsided. The dead were buried, and the village rallied to face the onslaught of winter. Tsantongowa—the child's father—her mother, and baby brother had all died.

Quorenta appeared before the Women's Council and begged to keep the orphan, Tekakwitha. She promised even to reenter the village. No, the Women's Council ruled, blood was far stronger than affection. The orphan's family reclaimed her; she was fostered to Tonedetta, Chief Iowerano's barren wife. But with the girl's parents an essential love had died. Smallpox had dimmed the child's sight, making her shy and uncertain. Her retiring ways seemed sullen, and her stepparents lavished affection on the more active children in their longhouse, ignoring her except to assign her chores and begrudge her food. And so, seeking a parent's love, Tekakwitha often stole outside the palisade, through the maize fields, and down the ravine to visit the outcast who had saved her life.

One autumn noontide, the little girl walked her accustomed path past lazy sunflowers above cornstalks and swelling pumpkins. A certain stretch of the path always terrified her where it dipped into the shade of an oak tree. The girl closed her eyes, murmured a charm to keep evil away, then ran past the frightening place. Soon she arrived at Quorenta's door.

"See, Aunt, see what I've made," she said, producing a doll of corn husks.

"Ah, yes." The old woman grunted and turned from her stirring. "You have fashioned a little Tekakwitha to be your companion just as you are mine. Oh, how beautiful you have made her! Eyes of wampum shell, but this hair—is it from your uncle's array of scalps?"

"No, Aunt!" The girl was shocked by the notion she

could even touch Iowerano's scalps. "It is my own, see?" She held up her shortened braid.

"Ah, then," said the old witch as she rolled her eyes, "you must not let your Tekakwitha fall into any hands that hate you or envy you. They can work evil magic if they possess strands of your hair."

"I won't allow the others near it." The girl held the doll to her cheek and rocked it as women rocked their crying babies. "They are skinning dogs for the feast tonight. Have you visited the pit?"

"Sit here by me, Tekakwitha." The woman gathered her buckskin skirt, and the girl hunched down. "Yes, I have seen the pit, and it is a noble one. When the feast begins, will you be my companion?"

Tekakwitha frowned, held the doll at an arm's length. "Mama says I must shun you tonight, that you will bear the bones of your ancestors by yourself, apart from the procession." She paused thoughtfully. "She said something else, too, Aunt."

Quorenta peered down quizzically. Large eyes burned in her dark, thick face, gray hair greased with bear tallow shone, and a necklace of wolf teeth and gleaming stones reflected the fire. "Yes?"

"She said, Aunt, that you caused the plague that took my real mama."

Quorenta dropped her eyes and gazed into the fire. "Do you believe her?"

"People say such terrible things about you!" the girl cried, shaking off a sob. "I want to live here with you. I don't want to live with them." She turned back, holding the doll very tightly. "You'd never bring a plague upon my mama and papa . . . would you?"

Quorenta removed the earthenware kettle from the fire and busied herself. "I do not have that power, little one."

"Then tell me, who did it?"

The old woman stroked Tekakwitha's hair softly and spoke to comfort her. "My little one grows weary of fables and the tale of the enchanted moccasins. Seven summers you have seen, and the quietest of hungers stirs within. You shall be an old and wise matriarch and rule over a vast *ohwachira*. You shall give birth to chieftains and wise men of the council fire." She pulled herself to her feet. "Let us walk in the sun."

Out through the bearskin flaps she led the girl. They walked together past a creek tumbling down the ravine.

"It is the white man who brought the disease, little one, the white man who brings all that is evil."

"The iron-makers?" Tekakwitha asked, referring to the Dutch.

"No, not the iron-makers, but other white men to the north, men of a different tongue with different *manitous*, different gods, from the iron-makers. The iron-makers do not bother with us other than trading. These others brought the disease with their blackrobes and their sacred cups. They attempt to change our customs. They bring whiskey, so that our men will hand over the skins of beaver and deer and elk and otter for shiny beads and a few hatchets."

"And what is the whiskey?"

"Ah, my little one, since the great plague, the council at Onondaga has ruled no whiskey will be permitted. It is a magic potion that brings great joy and hilarity at first, then anger, violence, bloodshed. It makes brother kill brother, man kill wife. Men would rather drink it than hunt. I have seen villages suffering from this whiskey, the hungry children crying, the sacred wampum belts desecrated. Like their plague, the white man's whiskey destroys the Canienga from within." She pointed to her large belly.

"It is good we have driven them out," the girl said, more to the doll than to the old woman.

Quorenta paused to think, her eyes gazing high into the pine. "My mother was a great matriarch. She remembered a time before white men settled in this land, when the traditions of the League were strong, when war was waged with the bow, when captives' thumbs were cut off so they could never again pull a bowstring. Yes, it was a better time before the guns and the powder and the liquor and the plagues, before our people were cheated and corrupted. Your father, Tekakwitha, was a brave chief who sought to drive the white man from this land. Tonight when you remove his bones from the earth, you must do him great honor. Wrap his bones in the finest of skins, and array chestnuts and the mandrake root about them. Lay pine boughs and beaver skins in the pit, then place the bones very tenderly there."

"Yes," said the girl with reverence, "but I reserve the finer skins for my mother."

Quorenta closed her eyes and groaned.

"What is it, Aunt?" she asked with alarm.

"Your mother does not deserve better than your father, Tekakwitha."

"Why?" Quorenta walked on in silence. A wind stirred the high boughs and a thrush piped as the sun shone through, upon the carpet of pine needles. Tekakwitha trembled. "Why?" she asked again. "Tell me, Aunt, was my mother disgraced? My foster mother forbids any word about her. Tell me!"

"You are young, Tekakwitha," the woman said sternly. "You are young, but you have a glimmering of wisdom. You may grow to be honored among us, the mother of many warriors, but you will never live out your mother's disgrace."

"What did she do?" the girl implored.

"She was not Canienga. She was Algonquin. Your father took her during a raid upon a tribe near the great northern river. She was but one of his wives, his concubine."

"You have told me this before. Many women, children, too, are taken in war and made members of the Canienga and the People of the Great Longhouse. There is no disgrace."

"Yes, but your mother was Christian!" Quorenta said this with such hatred, the girl felt deeply shamed. "She believed in the white man's god, and she tried, even among us, to convince others of his powers. Until she died, she never gave up the beliefs of the white man and the blackrobes. Your father, Tekakwitha, loved her very deeply, and her beliefs turned him greatly. Before your mother entered this village, your father was betrothed to Tonedetta."

"To my stepmother?"

"Yes. When he brought an Algonquin woman back as a trophy of war, Tonedetta's love for him became bitter. She married Iowerano instead and urged that Iowerano lead the clan. Yet your father's counsel and bravery far outshone Iowerano's, and until his death he was chief. That is why Tonedetta hates your true mother so, and why she treats you beneath the other children of her longhouse. That is also why your uncle Iowerano will not accept you as his daughter."

Tekakwitha would not look into Quorenta's eyes. Despair and shame filled her. She hugged the doll made of corn husks, suddenly the only certainty in her life. With much effort she held back her tears.

"But I am Canienga!" she cried.

"That you must prove, little one," Quorenta said softly.

"I will!" Tekakwitha blurted. She suddenly wanted to hurt Quorenta who was forbidden in the procession. "I will bear the bones of my father and brother in the procession tonight, and I will hurl the bones of my mother into the pit for slaves and captives and whites!"

Clasping the doll, she ran from the old woman's side. Desperately she clambered up the ravine into the cornfield where green stalks swayed, and she entered the forest on the far edge to find refuge and solitude.

2

She often walked in the dim, virgin forest to soothe her anger or bruised pride after a scolding or an insult or a quarrel. The songs of birds, the sweet pine, the squirrels and chipmunks—nature eased away her care. She knew she would never walk here again, for today was different, far different. Iowerano, after occupying this headland for ten years, had ordered the village moved a day's walk upriver. All who had died here—her father, mother, and baby brother—must be buried in a common grave near the old village so their spirits would rest. The move unsettled Tekakwitha deeply.

She removed her moccasins and dipped her feet into a brook. The cold water and soft mud were soothing. She walked again. After some distance she stepped up to a bank of moss and fern and dropped her moccasins and the husk doll to the ground. Impatiently she sat, arms folded on her knees, annoyed that the forest had not calmed her troubles today. A deep sadness filled her, and the sight of squirrels and frogs and swallows brought no joy.

Many times Quorenta had spoken of the great Hiawatha. How Tekakwitha wished she'd lived long ago when the famed chief united the five nations! Urging that all men are brothers, he'd pictured the five nations as five families occupying the same longhouse: Canienga, Oneida, Onondaga, Cayuga, and Seneca. Hiawatha offered all nations the Great Peace, a peace that spread like a blanket of first snow over the entire world. Hiawatha taught that the majestic pine tree was a symbol of the League's unity—five roots holding the tree firm with an eagle perched on a high limb, scanning the land, vigilant for the peace.

Then the Onondaga chief, Atotarho —The Entangled One — summoned the Thunderbird who carried off Hiawatha's daughter in its talons of fire. Tekakwitha had thrilled each time Quorenta told the legend, her voice growing thick, her fingers knotting like claws. Tekakwitha imagined the great wings flapping, forests and rivers and mountains falling away, the chief's daughter screaming in pain and fear, the Thunderbird bearing her from her loving mother and father. How the father missed the daughter! Hiawatha left his nation, paddled along rivers, over lakes, through swamps. And at home, The Entangled One, his hair a mass of writhing snakes, set brother upon brother, murdering and torturing and scalping each other.

Alone, Hiawatha had traveled the mountains and ridges of the Land From Which All Rivers Flow. Tekakwitha pictured him, alone, always alone, battling high waves in his canoe, slaying deer and elk for food and skins, huddling by his wigwam fire in a blizzard. How Tekakwitha wished she'd lived at that time when the five nations needed unifying, so she might aid great Hiawatha. He would not have wasted time in petty squabbles as the villagers did today. Tekakwitha longed to be with him back in the time of legends, wished to share with him the pure feelings of her heart, yet she felt low and despicable. Her mother, a Christian! Never would the great Bringer of Peace notice the daughter of a Christian—a race that brought whiskey and war and disease! Yet she wished it could be so.

Yesterday the other children had thrown stones and mud at her. "Stranger," they called her, for she would not play with them. "Stranger, stay away." And one among them cried she was the child of Quorenta, the bat feeder, and should be killed. And they laughed, chasing her until she reached her longhouse. Tonedetta, her foster mother scattered the crowd, but scolded her severely. "You are different," she told the girl. "You should remain inside."

Tekakwitha now stretched and raked her fingers and her toes through the moss. A sunbeam slanted through the fragrant pines. She felt alive here, alone in the woods, and suddenly she laughed. She laughed, knowing that she was different and, being different, was also free from the villagers, from their demands, from their disputes. She laughed because Hiawatha had traveled alone for years on his quest for peace, and he never needed them! The children who called her names, the foster mother who scolded, no, not even her secret friend Quorenta—she didn't need them! But suddenly the memory of her mother stopped the laughter. The disgrace! She buried her face in her buckskin sleeves.

She remembered how once, in the dead of winter when the ancient women talked quietly with no emotion, her mother had held her, a young child bundled in fragrant otter skin, and had tenderly but firmly denied her the nipple the baby brother sucked. Tekakwitha remembered the strong arm beneath her bottom, the firm chest and smooth chin of her father as he carried her to the canoe to join the fishing party, and the deep resonating of his laughter. She remembered a warm web of love and holding and joy around the low hearthfire or out in the broad daylight harvest, a warm web of belonging and laughter. Her father was the greatest of all, solid as the earth, unmoveable, she remembered, and her mother was warm as the sun, bounteous and nurturing. Then came the plague.

With her eyes closed to daydream, the earth fell away, and the sun hid behind clouds. Like Hiawatha's daughter, she was borne off by a pair of talons. Now the rivers were dry. Now the corn sang no song. There was no joy in the village, only duty. No playmates, only ridicule. Only when the elders spoke of the time before the white man did she feel a warm sense of tradition and sacred custom, of dignity and pride. Comparing the time of Hiawatha with her own, she felt cheated. When comparing her parents with her foster parents, she felt terribly alone and abandoned. But now even all that was changing. Tonight she'd dig up the bones of her parents and her brother, deposit them in the vast common grave, then trail behind the villagers to a new location across the river and higher up, at the base of long, boiling rapids. And tomorrow, as if swept away in that boiling water, every last familiar thing would be gone.

Her heart ached with uncertainty, and she held the cornhusk doll tightly. Quorenta had accused the head chief, Iowerano, of cowardice. He was removing the village of the Turtle Clan upriver, away from the Dutch. "As the tortoise draws in his head at approaching danger, so too does Iowerano move us farther into the Land From Which All Rivers Flow. He is afraid."

And yet, Iowerano had explained the move to his braves thus: "The soil is depleted and the bones of our dead know it is time they come together in the common pit. I have scouted a site where the river flows—not broad and placid as it does here—but wild and rocky. The place is far better fortified. Trouble is brewing among the whites. The English toward the rising sun battle with both the Dutch to the south and the French to the north. This new site, Kanawaka—At the Rapids—will allow us better to protect the eastern gate of the great League."

The white men's wars, the white men's gunpowder, the white men's ways—all these corrupted her people. Tekakwitha had never seen a white. Squat, low-bred, pale of skin, they were described as having eyes of pale green—Iowerano even possessed a scalp of hair the color of corn silk!—she despised them. Why did they war? Why did they not forge a league as great Hiawatha had and meet at a summer council to negotiate their differences?

Tekakwitha felt proud to be Canienga. The confusing emotions of her mother's disgrace, her own orphan's presence in the chief's household, and the unsettling move upriver melted away like morning mist, and she lifted her eyes up and fastened her gaze upon an ancient pine where the sun shone. Like Hiawatha's pine, its roots—the five nations—radiated from the trunk, holding it fast in the earth. No base nomads were her people! Her people built palisades and villages—they did not wander half-naked, half-starved through the forest like the Algonquin. Her people planted and harvested maize; they did not chase the herds northward, nor eat the bark of trees. But above all, her people held traditions sacred—the wampum belts handed from chief to chief, the Dance of the Green Corn, the Dream Feast, the First Planting, and tonight, the Feast of the Dead.

Comforted now, Tekakwitha rose from the bed of moss. Tonight, with all the dignity of the festival, she'd rebury the bones of her father and her brother. She pulled on her moccasins and, with a lighter heart, returned to the village.

3

White Adder, the magic one, white of hair and skin, pink of eye, danced with tortoiseshell rattles, often breaking into eloquent song. In the center of the village the six large families of the Turtle Clan had assembled. A gray-haired matron from each family, wearing embroidered skins and plaited braids, presided over the feast. Roast dog was served on bark dishes, and sagamite, a corn porridge flavored with savory bear bacon, was ladled from the kettles.

Tekakwitha was late, and as she approached the cluster of her cousins and uncles and aunts, Tonedetta scolded her. "You've been playing with that doll and have nearly missed the feast. Here, Pouter, take meat." Brusquely her foster mother thrust a bark dish forward.

Composed by her long walk in the wood, Tekakwitha ate quietly, watching the joyful bustle of the village. Stacks of maize, furs, planting sticks, kettles, and woven mats were piled in front of the longhouses, ready for the move. Young, marriageable women, hair plaited with shells, buckskin tunics embroidered with porcupine quills, now sat eating demurely and looking askance at the young hunters who vied for their attention.

Tekakwitha's eye wandered until she saw Kryn. The tall, powerful warrior was joshing with younger men of his family. Many times she had watched Kryn deftly skin a bear he'd killed. Many times had she sat near the circle of his boy admirers as he told tales of conquering the Hurons—a nation polluted by Christian ways. Working upon her embroidery, pretending not to listen, she heard Kryn's tales of battling swollen, icy rivers in his bark canoe, of meeting the claws and teeth and burning eyes of wolf and panther and bear . . . and of peaceful fishing at night on the northern lakes. She took comfort in the deep, calm modulations of his voice, in his quiet acceptance of danger and fortune and pain and hunger. She took pride, too, that Kryn, as she herself, was only half Canienga.

16

A Dutch fur trader had lain with the eldest daughter of the matriarch. Before the pale-skinned babe appeared, the Dutchman returned to his people. The bastard child was adopted, and because his mother's line was noble, he was given a slight claim to chieftainship. However, though his skin soon bronzed as dark as any Canienga's, his pale blue eyes testified evermore to white man's blood. Partly from shame of this, partly from a stubborn determination to overcome the stigma of his birth, Kryn never decorated his flesh with the tattoos and paint others used. He kept, too, his father's Dutch name, Kryn. His bravery in the hunt and in battle earned him a leadership role in the clan, a role Iowerano resented. Kryn claimed—and this endeared him to Tekakwitha—that her father Tsantongowa, Great Beaver, had taught him the use of javelin and bow and arrow. Was he suggesting that she, too, could prove herself, despite her Christian mother? Tekakwitha now wondered. Yet, it was Kryn's quiet, placid nature that drew her most strongly to him. When searching for an embodiment of the great Hiawatha, she always pictured Kryn.

Suddenly, startling her, White Adder leapt into the circle, barking and hissing, then launching into song. "Far beyond the fiery lake of the sunset," he cried, gesturing dramatically, "they have wandered their lonely roads, and now the spirits of our ancestors hunt the spirits of deer and bear in summer glades—even when the cold breath of winter steals upon us here." White Adder thrust his face near Tekakwitha's and opened his eyes wide to frighten her. The fine blue paint upon his cheeks heightened the pink of his eyes. Tekakwitha shrank back.

"There, in the happy land, my pretty one, strawberries, the jewel of our summer, grow big as pumpkins, and sweet maple syrup flows from trees like blood from wounds. Butterflies painted in exquisite colors grow large as you, my pretty one," he said, fluttering his fingers at another child. "And there walk the noble warriors who've passed through dark lands of mists and serpents, there proudly walk the noble matrons of our clan, listening to the songs of birds sweeter than any we know, while deer and bear, beaver and otter, wolf and wildcat live as brothers."

White Adder spun away, sprang into the air, and shook his rattles menacingly. "But tonight we open their graves where their ghosts still dwell, moldering in the earth, flesh and robes eaten by worms; tonight we call forth the long procession of ghosts who lurk outside the palisade at night envying our fire, our warm food, our brotherhood, ghosts who lurk in the fog and rain, who dance only on the breast of snow when northern lights glimmer. And we will honor those who have fallen to evil spirits, to conspiracies of the cold, evil, heartless one, for we too will fall one day and go under the earth."

"Well spoken!" Iowerano cried, and he offered White Adder a roasted dog's leg. The magician snatched it, sank his teeth into the flesh, then wiped the grease upon his long white hair. He spun in a dance, then leapt from the circle, progressing to another family group to earn more applause and meat.

As the sun's waning rays pierced tall stands of pine and evening breezes breathed of tranquility, a procession of women, moaning, wailing, punctuating their low chants with loud shrieks, passed through the gate of the palisade, across the fields of cornstalks, and into a thicket of briars and bushes that surrounded the cemetery.

The women knelt, then sprawled upon the graves, kicking and pounding the earth with their fists, wailing in high, eerie pitches. At a signal from Sirenta, eldest matriarch of the Turtle Clan, they raised up again and began digging with small wooden hoes. Tenderly, with much care and love, they pulled the bones of their fathers and mothers, their grandmothers and sisters, brothers and grandfathers from the clay. Hair still clung to skulls and leathery flesh encased the bones. Corpses buried only weeks before were unearthed, still putrefying and flyblown, and as the sun set and the evening star gleamed, the moaning, chanting women scraped the bones free of flesh, combed the long black hair of the skulls, and placed the cleaned bones into new robes of beaver and deer.

Women with many dead relatives were helped by others of their family. Linawato, a cousin of Tekakwitha, seeing her fall behind, crawled to her and whispered, "I shall clean these bones for you." She began peeling dried flesh from a rib cage.

"No," Tekakwitha whispered—talking during the sacred rite was forbidden. "That is my ill luck. I must prepare it."

"Yes?" asked Linawato. "And who is it?"

"My mother," Tekakwitha said in shame.

"Here then," the cousin offered, "let us trade," and Linawato cleaned the baby brother's bones.

When the bones had been wrapped in fur and darkness was full, the procession of women threaded back to the village. Met by the men, who'd stoked one huge bonfire from the six cooking fires, they passed through the western gate in a torchlit line, beyond the far cornfields, until at last they reached a large pit with scaffolding above it. There hung many hatchets, kettles, robes, war clubs, bows, and spears. The new moon rose in the clear midsummer sky, and wolves howled in the heart of the forest.

The six large family groups ranged round the pit and opened their fur bundles. With vines and strings of wampum shell they wrapped the bones together, children aiding their mothers. Then Sirenta, matriarch of ninety summers, sang a dirge.

> "Out from the earth have we all come. Through wombs of our mothers we pass into this world. We live, we plant, we bear other warriors and mothers of warriors, then we die. Through the wombs of our graves we pass into the next world. For many years has the Clan of the Turtle dwelt upon the hill of Ossernenon. Through summers of plenty, gifts of god Teharonhiawagon, and through winters of famine, the spite of Tawiskaron, we have dwelt together. But now the corn is stunted in the field, our waters are defiled, and the palisade, once stout and strong, creaks in the wind.
>
> "As we move now a day's journey to Kawanaka, the place of white water, let us return the bones of our ancestors—our wise and nurturing mothers, our fierce and eloquent fathers—together into the earth. And with a song of joy, let us cover over this place so their ghosts may sleep peacefully here where they dwelt."

A cry of approval went up. In the torchlight, the men and women climbed through the scaffolding and tenderly laid the gifts—hatchets and kettles and robes—upon the fresh earth of the pit. When all was ready, they brought the bundles of bones wrapped in fur and arranged them with much care among the gifts.

At a distance from her stepmother, Tekakwitha lay the bones of her father and her brother upon the soft deer robe. She'd strung a necklace of clam shells around her father's skull, a mark of honor to a great chief. She laid the bones of her brother upon a blanket of fern, arms crossed beneath his skull, legs to either side. Then, fighting back tears, she placed the cornhusk doll between the bones of her father and her brother.

"Keep this little Tekakwitha with you, great chief Tsantongowa," she sobbed, arranging chestnuts and sacred roots about the robes. "Keep her safe in your protection near little Arintato. Keep her here, the orphan who lives now as a ghost in Iowerano's longhouse in the village of the Turtle Clan of the People of Flint." Tekakwitha smoothed the chief's locks upon the deerskin, then sat back to take a last look at her doll between the large and small skulls.

A signal was called. Tekakwitha scrambled to the top of the earthwork as men hurled timber from the scaffolding into the pit. Bags containing bones of slaves, captives, and outlaws were opened, and the bones were hurled randomly into the center of the pit.

Tekakwitha loosened the thong of the robe that held her mother's bones. Desperately she repressed fond memories of her mother, the warm flesh of her embrace, the loving voice, the smile that beamed like a spring sun. Bones were all that remained, bones and disgrace. And grieving, tears of shame scalding her cheeks, she hurled the bones into the center. Higher burned the fire as warriors waved torches in the wind, then hurled them into the pit. The solemnity turned to a wild joy. The girl hung her head. While others danced and sang that their relatives had found final rest, the orphan mourned her loss and her disgrace.

Cracking and groaning, the scaffolding tottered and fell. Torches flew in after it. All the villagers began to fill the pit. Upon the forest wall played the shadows of this great toil as new torches were lit. As the earthworks diminished, the hole was filled in, and children danced upon the common grave, singing in joy:

> *The sun passes overhead,*
> *Lighting the bright, green forest.*
> *In dead of night the moon*
> *Guides us upon our way.*

> *"We dance and sing and feast*
> *Until the sickness strikes.*
> *How beautiful is the world!*
> *It is a pity I must die."*

4

Tekakwitha retreated into a grove of scrub pine. The dancing and singing, the rattles and elkskin drums, the sweating warriors painted in fantastic design and the wailing women filled her heart with troubled feelings even as the cool, dark forest was filled with shadows and piercing screams. She felt apart from it, as she felt apart when war captives screamed and sang their death songs in the torturing. She wished to run off, but wolves and bears and wildcats prowled the western ridges, and the hated whites hemmed in the land on the other three sides.

Not wanting to join the orgy of farewell that would rage in the village, Tekakwitha lagged behind the returning procession. She breathed in deeply the cool, fragrant wind, and she paused to listen to the owls hooting and the bats flicking overhead. Suddenly she heard her name in the wind, "Tekakwitha! Tekakwitha!" Her breath halted, her flesh tingled; it is a spirit calling me, she thought. "Here, Tekakwitha. Join me." From the brush along the trail a great black bulk suddenly rose, and a hand reached out and touched her shoulder. The girl cried out. "Be quiet," the whispering voice said. "Come with me."

To her relief she recognized the hair and gleaming eyes of Quorenta. "How did you come here?"

"I have been waiting for you." The old woman led her into the brush, then escorted her along a hidden path. "Together we shall watch the festivities from outside the palisade."

The din of singing and yelling and the flickering of torchlight soon disappeared. Quorenta and Tekakwitha walked along a side trail and emerged into a cornfield.

"See how they dance and sing," Quorenta said. "Their joy shall be short, though." She and the girl crept closer to the wall of stout logs, and they sat, peering in through a space as the procession again occupied the village.

"Will this move upriver bring us luck?"

"No, little one." The old woman caressed Tekakwitha's hair. "Upon the shell of a turtle the world was created by an otter who dredged mud from the bottomless lake. And so does our clan hold the turtle sacred. Yet now, with whites in our world, the turtle no longer bears us afloat boldly. Now, like the turtle, Iowerano moves upriver, retreating from the white man as the turtle draws in its head. The Turtle Clan grows meek."

"Yet the soil fails and the waters are no longer clean here."

"There are other reasons for that." The woman held the girl closer. "Twenty summers ago, Iowerano captured many Hurons and three whites—one of them a blackrobe."

"A blackrobe?"

"A magician among his own people. This blackrobe was called Jogues, but he escaped among the Dutch, leaving a silver cup and dish buried in the land. This caused worms to attack our corn that summer. During the winter, many of us went on the hunt like the nomads and bark-eaters, so we might survive."

"And yet, the village remained here at this site?"

"Yes. The chiefs and the matriarchs wished to prove the white man's magic was weak, that we could prosper despite it. Two summers later, the blackrobe, a brave man in the torture when we chewed off his fingers, returned from across the sea. Iowerano made peace and asked him to remove the silver cup and dish from the earth so the corn might grow tall and plentiful. But before he did, a visiting chief of the Wolf Clan with a grudge against the French buried his tomahawk in the blackrobe's skull. We threw his body to the dogs, and we impaled his head upon the northern gate as a warning to all French."

"Did that break the spell?" Tekakwitha asked. Within the palisade a shout went up, and the flames of the bonfire rolled to the sky. Sweaty, naked forms danced in glee.

"For a time. Two summers later another famine struck. It was then the summer council decided to wage war on the Hurons far to the setting sun. They massacred as many Hurons as geese fill the sky in the time of changing leaves.

They tortured and killed three blackrobes—one was the man whose golden scalp hangs in Iowerano's collection."

"Then was the evil curse undone?"

Quorenta laughed a low, menacing laugh. "No, for afterward the plague that bore off your parents came. And because the cup is still buried in this ground, our soil is impoverished by droughts and locusts and worms."

"Then surely our move away will cure it?"

"Yours is the hope of the child. Mine is the wisdom of watching many winters. Our clan may move farther westward into the Land of Flint, but until the cup and dish are dug up and destroyed, our passing through this gate toward war will be futile, and French warriors will find nothing to bar their way."

"But is there no hope?"

"Only one. Yet the council at Onondaga when the fifty chiefs come together will not consider it. We must attack the northern whites, the French. Even now they progress into the Lake of the Gar-Pike. We must drive them down into the broad river, and from there out into the sea. But our chiefs sit like the Women's Council, smoking their pipes, unwilling to wage the necessary war."

"But chiefs can recruit war parties without the council's ruling."

"Yes, but it will take many, many warriors to drive out the French. Only one warrior proves brave enough to do so."

"Here in the Turtle Clan?"

"Yes. Only Kryn can lead such a band. If he were to depart, his followers would ridicule those who remain at home, and many others would rally to join him."

Tekakwitha thrilled to hear Kryn's name. Yes, she felt, he would be the savior of their people, and of the other four nations in the League. She saw him before her, tall, handsome, powerfully built, his hair plucked into a comb on top of his head. He'd defy Iowerano and the other chiefs of the council, for he held the respect of the warriors and did not rule by title alone.

"Kryn has been upriver seeing to the building of our new village," Tekakwitha offered. "They say he has braced the walls within far stronger than these and that he digs great ditches around the outside."

"He is wise," Quorenta said. "Being half white, he learns from the white man. Yet his heart is all Canienga."

Again Tekakwitha thrilled hearing his name. "Karitha, Kryn's wife, and my aunt Tegonhat are best friends. I longed for Tegonhat to adopt me when she married Shining Cliff, but he fell in battle before a baby came and so they never dug a hearthfire together. Kryn ignores this custom of waiting for a baby—he took Karitha as his wife despite her barrenness because of her skill in trading with the whites." Her eyes brightened with an idea. "I will ask Tegonhat to persuade Karitha! She will adopt me and so have a daughter! I will live with Kryn in his longhouse!"

"No!" Quorenta said sharply. "That is not possible!"

"Why?"

"Because you are not moving with them."

Tekakwitha frowned, not understanding. Inside the palisade, the celebration continued, naked bodies writhing and mating and dancing in the firelight.

"Many are the times you spoke to me about remaining in the ravine," Quorenta continued. "You pledged that if presented the chance, you'd live with me. Now you have that chance."

The girl's heart sank. The ceremony deep in the forest, laying the bones of her father, brother, and mother to final rest, the imminent move—all had unsettled her. But the tale of the curse of the blackrobe's cup and the suggestion Kryn might save the clan had caused her to think ahead. Not move with her people? She'd not miss the other children. She'd not miss her foster mother or Iowerano's distant presence. But could she turn her back on this new beginning for her people only to guard potions and charms in a smoky hut?

"I must go with the rest, Aunt," she said timidly.

"But with the bones buried you are free now. You may go where you wish."

Tekakwitha hung her head. Gone were the regrets she'd felt before, gone, strangely enough, with Quorenta's tales. "I wish to accompany the village," she said. Quorenta did not respond. Plaintively the girl spoke again: "Often have you told me of the great Hiawatha forming the League that binds the People of the Great Longhouse. You have filled me with respect for my people even while I have hated them in the village. I have longed to journey back to the time of Hiawatha, yet wishes often do not come true." Her choice—to abandon her old friend and move with the villagers—proved difficult to explain. "My, my mother was Christian, and so I am not descended from a great *ohwachira*. Yes, and they call me 'pouter' and 'outcast' in the village. But, dear Aunt, half of me still is Canienga. Like me, Kryn is only half Canienga, and see how he benefits our clan! I must go upriver with the clan, Aunt, I *must*!"

"You will leave me to myself, then?"

Tekakwitha leaned to embrace the woman, but Quorenta held her off.

"You will leave me to myself, then?"

The choice seemed most difficult. "Why cannot you come with us?"

"I am an outcast. You are an orphan. We are alike." Quorenta's arm fell from her shoulder. Suddenly an explosion of flame lit up the night, and White Adder, who had secretly thrown gunpowder into the fire, leapt high, screaming and dancing.

"White Adder will need your potions, Aunt," Tekakwitha said as she turned. "Aunt? Aunt?" During the momentary eruption, Quorenta had disappeared. "Aunt!" Tekakwitha cried. "Don't leave me! Aunt!" Her eyes scanned the brush where the lurid firelight played, but the only movement was foliage waving in a gentle wind. Alone she sat, watching the wild celebration of her people, and doubt ran deeply about the correctness of her decision.

5

In the crisp morning, Ossernenon's twoscore warriors wended down the hill and lashed bundles of skins, pottery, hatchets, spears, and kettles into the fleet of gray, elm bark canoes. Women and children emptied the longhouses of everything useful. Along the path upriver lay heaps of pelts and valuables waiting for the great migration.

In the council house, Iowerano folded sacred wampum belts carefully and wrapped them in doeskin. This winter the tribe would add rows of memory shells to commemorate the Feast of the Dead and the migration and construction of the new village.

When all was ready, Chief Iowerano called an assembly at the western gate. All villagers clustered about him in anticipation, and he quelled their voices by raising his arms. "Long have the fires of our council and our hearths burned at Ossernenon." His deep, eloquent voice intoned these words with much ceremony. His gestures were slow and dignified; gravely he nodded, his head topped by the antlers of his office. "Long have the fires of autumn nights burned low while mothers and wives have awaited the return of the war party. Long have fires burned brightly in feasts to Aireskou while we have caressed prisoners through the night until dawn." The chief motioned toward the sun.

"Now let fire expel all evil *okies* from among us. Let it destroy the useless thoughts and deeds even as it destroys palisade and abandoned longhouse so to make room for the new, the vigorous and the strong. And finally," the chief said, as he received a torch from White Adder, "let it fasten in our minds the knowledge that all things grow, bloom, and thrive, then faltering with age, sink back into the earth." Ceremoniously the chief touched the fire to a heap of corn husks and the blaze crackled, spat, and climbed up pine pitch smeared upon the gateposts.

The Turtle Clan of the Canienga threaded away—men down the hill to the laden canoes, women along the ridge toward the ford, leading children and dogs to await the emptied canoes that would carry them across the river. Black smoke billowed and rolled forth from the abandoned town, and one by one, the longhouses blazed, then fiery skeletons collapsed in showers of sparks and black smoke.

Day after day the sun and moon and stars spun above the meandering river. In chill, foggy mornings, activity at the new site began long before sunrise. Kettles were slung, sagamite was stirred and spooned onto bark plates, corn cakes were baked in the ash of the fires. Then work continued with vigor, and the new town rose.

Kryn had designed stronger fortifications based upon fortresses of whites he had seen. Long, sturdy trunks of oak—the height of three men—were fastened into the earth. In an alternating pattern, one pole straight, the next leaning inward, the third leaning out, then the fourth straight, men lashed the trunks with rope woven from root fibers. This alternating pattern gave the wall far greater stability during a seige and also allowed spaces for arrows to be shot.

At about the height of a man, they erected a scaffold of poles and bark around the inside perimeter. They placed bark tanks strategically: during a seige, they would fill the tanks with water so burning arrows might be extinguished before setting the palisade ablaze. Outside the wall, they cleared the ground and heaped up earth. Thus, any advancing war party would rise into view before crossing the open ground to the palisade.

Within the wall, women worked to frame, cover, and furnish the twelve longhouses. Saplings, set six paces apart, were bent until they joined at the center. Lashed together, then ribbed with other saplings, they made a frame shaped like an inverted canoe, and bark plates were fastened as a covering. Inside, the women constructed sleeping shelves at waist height, and they dug hearthfires—five or six to a house—and lined them with stone.

Each *ohwachira*, a large, extended family of four or five generations, was composed of ten or twelve smaller family groups. These smaller families—father, mother, children, and perhaps an uncle or aunt—ate and slept together around the individual hearths. Grandparents and great-grandparents kept their own hearths, and the entire extended family was ruled by the oldest woman descended in a direct line from the previous matriarch. She named the chief. She voted in the Women's Council. She banished outlaws from the village. Both marriage and divorce were casual ceremonies, men living in their own *ohwachira* until they fathered a child, only then setting up housekeeping at a hearth. After divorce, children remained with their mothers. Family lines followed through the mothers so that lineage might be assured in a village where polygamy and orgies were frequent.

By autumn the new village at Kanawaka was complete. Many journeys back to Ossernenon brought canoes of maize and pumpkins to the new village to store for winter. Hunters ranged in the virgin forest and brought bear, deer, elk, and moose daily to provide meat and skins. With survival assured for the winter, Kryn's thoughts turned to trade. Perhaps by heredity from his trader father, perhaps because he enjoyed taking advantage of the whites through guile, Kryn conducted much of the Turtle Clan's trading with the Dutch. Pelts—tied into bundles, loaded into canoes, floated downriver to Corlaer or Beverwyck—were exchanged for kettles, hatchets, scissors, cloth, glass beads, and shiny metal trinkets that the villagers valued greatly.

At the Dutch patroon's town of Beverwyck also stood the

governor's stockade, Fort Orange, manned by a detachment of helmeted soldiers. Within the stockade, a stout magazine of stone had been built to store gunpowder, cannonballs, muskets, and musket balls. Sometimes, despite protests from the French and English, the Dutch traded muskets, powder, and shot for pelts. Their motive was twofold: Weapons and ammunition brought far higher prices than the trinkets, and with their Iroquois allies supplied with guns, the Dutch feared neither French nor English, nor did they fear so much the roaming bands of Algonquins that fell upon their settlements like wolves in winter.

When the geese filled the air with honking and their V formations flew southward across the sky, Kryn, Arosen, Ringtail, and Diving Otter collected pelts from each longhouse. As Kryn sorted through the piles on the shore by his canoe, he came upon a pelt deftly embroidered with warriors chasing a bear.

"Which woman executed this?" he asked.

"I do not know," Arosen answered. "That came either from Otsiketa's wife or from the longhouse of Enita's *ohwachira*."

"I know of no one in either longhouse capable of doing such fine work," Kryn said. "Yet, I have a buyer for embroidery," he mused. "Take this back, Arosen, and find out whose hand has crafted such designs."

Kryn lashed the remaining bundles of pelts to the ribwork of the two canoes and climbed the hill to his longhouse. Karitha, his wife, had taken corn from a common store and was grinding it in a stump mortar. As always, Karitha would accompany Kryn on his trading expeditions to advise on kettles and beads. In the dim longhouse, Kryn wrapped up dried bear bacon, crab apples, and ground corn and stowed the food with his flint and iron. As he was closing his hempen bag, he peered up, surprised to see Iowerano in the doorway.

Iowerano held out the dressed skin. "You wish to know who executed this. I must first know why."

"You needn't be so suspicious of me, Cold Wind," Kryn said. "I only offer to bring the woman upon my trading expedition."

Iowerano grunted. "You do nothing if it is not for profit. Tell me, what will this woman be called upon to do?"

"If it is Tonedetta, your foremost wife, I take back my offer," Kryn said. "She and Karitha do not often see with similar eyes."

"What reward will there be for such embroidery as this?" Iowerano asked suspiciously.

"I go as a trader from the entire village," Kryn said, turning away. "I will return with hatchets and kettles and iron needles and fish hooks and such."

"There is more here than that." Iowerano's thick face scowled impatiently.

Kryn motioned for Arosen to carry his hempen bag down to the canoe. "Smoke with me," Kryn said, as he waved the chief in. Iowerano squatted down, produced his pipe, and together they smoked in an attitude of considering important business.

"The chief at Fort Orange," Kryn explained, "has just ended a quarrel with the chief of Manhattoes far downriver. The chief of Fort Orange wishes to send across the sea to his great father a sample of our embroidery."

"You understand the ways of these strangers far better than I," Iowerano said to insult the half-breed.

Kryn shrugged. "In trade, one must only supply what will be bought."

Iowerano considered. "The hand that stitched this belongs to the daughter of Tsantongowa, Great Beaver, who died in the plague. The girl is now under my protection." Iowerano did not mention that the girl was causing discord in his longhouse. "I will let her accompany you, even though the river will freeze and you will be returning on snowshoes" —he grunted and held up his finger—"provided you return with a musket for me."

Kryn shook his head. "The Dutch have not traded guns with us since we refused their gin." He smiled. "I make no promises, Cold Wind, ever."

"Very well, then," Iowerano said, thumping his chest with bravado, "I will make the promise. I will allow the girl to accompany you. Then you will see that your side is fulfilled."

Kryn considered. "I will try, just as I will try to be back at Kanawaka before the river freezes."

Late in the night the small band set out from below the turgid pools of white water. By sunrise they reached the Dutch settlement, Corlaer, which the Algonquins called Schenectady. By midmorning they beached the canoes above the great cascade Cohoes, and portaged the two large vessels along black cliffs where water gushed in a delta of white veins down to the wide, brown river flowing south. It was early evening when they again set their canoes in the water and rode the pull of the tide to Fort Orange.

Lights glimmered in windows of the thirty cottages on either side of the river, as they beached their canoes on the mud flat. Kryn and Arosen immediately climbed the hill to the fort, entered the fortified gate, and knocked at the door of the patroon's agent to inform him they had set up camp nearby. Karitha, Tekakwitha, and the two other youths—Diving Otter and Ringtail—cut saplings and erected a wigwam of skins. Karitha kindled a low fire and together they sat within, awaiting Kryn's return.

"What is the white man like?" asked Tekakwitha, gazing thoughtfully at the fire. The day's long journey had filled her with many new sights. The lights through glass windows were the capping wonder.

"The white man is a fool," Karitha said.

"How? His fort seems larger, stronger than ours. His fire at night gazes out into the darkness as if through eyes."

Karitha pitched a twig into the fire. "Our canoe glides as a petal upon the water." She demonstrated with her hand. "It bends to the demand of the current. Wild reeds caress it in the shallows. But the white man hammers great wooden craft, bigger than our palisade, and he mounts white wings to spirit them along with the wind. These floating towns must lie far from shore and cannot enter streams and lakes." Karitha slung the kettle and put in handfuls of dried corn. The youths left for water. She continued. "The Canienga takes the deer and stag and bear for his sustenance, for robes and blankets. He eats of these creatures and so becomes fleet and brave and strong. The white man slaughters fat, dumb beasts that live close by him, tame boars and the bison that he milks, and so he becomes as dull and sluggish as his beasts." Karitha bared her teeth in contempt.

"The Canienga puts up his town in the midst of forests and lays out plantations nearby. Game and corn and squash and wood for the fire are all at hand. When the area is depleted, the Canienga move to a new location and build their longhouses and palisades together. But the white man cuts back the forest. For him it holds a strange darkness, a fear. He builds houses so they will last forever. He seeks permanence and will not allow that all things pass."

Karitha narrowed her eyes and dropped her voice. "But the white man is a fool worst of all because he hopes to change the Canienga. He creates greed where there was none. He creates vanity where before there was self-respect and cooperation. He poisons us with his liquor so evil deeds abound. He sees no gods in the rivers, in the forest, in the sun, and so he denies they are there. He shows no respect for the People of the Great Longhouse. He invades our land, corrupts our people, calls more and more of his brothers to join him." Karitha looked up with cold determination. "We must teach him respect."

Karitha's contempt, joined with Quorenta's strong words of midsummer and this journey into the heart of the white man's land, now caused Tekakwitha to dwell upon the matter with the concentration she usually saved for embroidery.

"Perhaps we may correct the white man's mind," she suggested. "Perhaps he may come to see the beauty of our lakes and rivers, the usefulness of our maize, our longhouses, our canoes, and customs. Can we not open his eyes to the god of pine, the god of flint, the god of the lakes, not even to the fierce sun-god Aireskou?"

"The white man twists everything to suit himself," Karitha answered. "You are wise, little one, to suggest the white man and Canienga might share. But, as a river only flows one way, the white man draws all he can use from us and gives nothing back."

"But why?" the girl persisted.

Karitha considered a long moment before speaking. She answered slowly. "The white man despises the world about him and so seeks to conquer it. He is blind to beauty and so makes representations—not of forest or cascade or deer or sun—but of his own cities and his people. He shuts out the stars with his roofs of wood and slate. He lights his rooms with small torches and stokes fires into blazes that would shame the Canienga."

The youths returned with water, and Karitha stirred the dried corn into a paste, then added cubes of bear bacon, suet, and dried fish.

"The worst among the whites, though, are the blackrobes. Before Kryn and the League obliterated the Huron nation, the blackrobes had taught the Huron to hate their world, to abandon warfare, to forget pleasures of the Eat-All Feast and even copulation. The blackrobes weakened the Hurons and made them easy prey. The blackrobes taught the Huron to project all thoughts and hopes and desires into a world beyond the clouds where the white man's only god sits and metes out punishment. In their world after death, there are no spirits of deer or bear, no fruits to eat, no maize. How stupid!

"The blackrobes show bravery and are admired for how well they withstand the torture. But they seek to make women of our warriors, to break up the longhouses and the *ohwachiras*, to replace the fierce Aireskou with their god, a meek victim of torture who died upon a scaffold very long ago."

The flap of the wigwam opened and Kryn entered with Arosen. He squatted upon his heels. "All is ready," he said, his blue eyes flashing with excitement. "The chief of this town is calling a council for the morning, and I have no doubt we will get what we seek. The great chief of the Dutch, One-Legged Man, is here."

"That is good," Karitha said with determination. "We will do in winter what the great sachems failed to accomplish at Onondaga when the corn was ripe." She served the porridge upon bark plates, and Kryn ate his hungrily.

"Your *orenda* is that of a man," Kryn joked. "You strengthen your will and your courage, and no sympathy or compassion will sway you."

Karitha made a fist. "We will strike as the fiercest of north winds, our hearts and blood frozen like the lakes and rivers, our purpose clear and bright as midwinter sun." These words revealed a direction, a violent one, to Karitha's hatred. But Tekakwitha felt too young and insignificant to ask what Karitha meant.

"Karitha speaks like an orator in the great council house at Onondaga," Kryn said pleasantly to Tekakwitha. Awed by Kryn's presence, unsettled by the mirth of his blue eyes, she sat a little apart from the circle at the fire. "And you, peaceful one," he said, touching her cheek, "I spoke to the white man's chief and showed him your work. He and his wife were deeply impressed. They wish you to embroider a buckskin vest and skirt so they may send them across the sea to their great chief."

"I hope my work pleases them," Tekakwitha said quietly, hesitantly.

After eating, she wrapped herself in her fragrant otter

robe and lay awake, deliciously tired, gazing through the center hole of the wigwam at the autumn stars that seemed so ominously different here in the land of the whites.

6

Next day, the sun rose into a sky without clouds. Great flocks of geese stretched from the horizon in V formation. Along the mud flats where Kryn had camped, frost gleamed on reeds and cattails, on the stockade on the hill, on shingles of farmers' cottages and barns, and on the weather vane atop the steeple of the Dutch church.

After the trading party had breakfasted and answered to morning's necessities, the three youths went fishing, Karitha headed for the docks with a bundle of pelts to trade, and Kryn and Tekakwitha climbed the wagon ruts through Beverwyck to Fort Orange, the stockade on the hill.

"So many of those beasts!" the girl observed as they entered Parrel Street. "They look like small moose, only so much uglier. And that—" she said, pointing to a horse-drawn wagon, "a canoe to pass through village lanes on spinning legs." Tekakwitha then observed the women's starched bonnets. "They carry nothing upon their heads but wings." She gaped at the tall houses, the glass windows, the brick and stone chimneys reaching for the sky. When she saw a windmill, its sails and groaning arms turning in the breeze, she uttered a cry. "Wings upon spinning arms." Flagstones had been laid in the square before the house of the patroon's agent, and the clacking of wooden shoes upon the stone startled her.

"How does Tekakwitha like the white man's town?" asked Kryn laughing.

"It is very busy."

Along the street, boys halted games of marbles; women in dirndls carrying baskets on their arms turned; the plump keeper of the ale house folded his arms and puffed upon his clay pipe; merchants stood in the doorways of their dim shops. All paused to gawk at the tall, buckskinned figure of Kryn, hair bristled high in a rooster's comb, and his small companion in a buckskin skirt, her hair braided with beads. At their intent gaze she grew timid and held Kryn's arm.

"It is a frightening place," she said. "A place of wings and many spinning things. The whiteness of their clothing dazzles my eyes." A wagon approached and Kryn pulled the girl out of the way. "Those beasts bear all the burdens," Tekakwitha said. "The women don't even carry cradleboards!"

Kryn smiled. "The white man is not fond of using his back and so fashions many machines."

Just then, the bell rang in the church steeple and a flurry of pigeons and swallows rose over the slate roofs. Tekakwitha clutched Kryn in terror. He whisked her playfully into the air then set her down. "It is just the tongue of the white man's god telling those who live under roofs how short the shadows have grown. It is the proper time for our visit."

Kryn knocked upon the spiked oaken door and was admitted. He turned the girl over to an old woman who led Tekakwitha, faltering, terrified, up the oddest ladder she had ever climbed—a staircase—into a room overlooking the street, the plaza, and the church.

Kryn entered a long, low room with men ranged around a table smoking clay pipes. Brant Van Slictenhorst, the patroon's agent, greeted Kryn and motioned him to a chair. Unaccustomed to the furniture, Kryn sat bolt upright, his forearms resting on the arms of the chair as if on the gunwales of his canoe.

"Governor Stuyvesant is pleased you have come," Van Slictenhorst said in the traders' language—a hybrid of Dutch and Iroquois. Kryn nodded. "The French from the northern river incite the Mohegans, the Leni-Lenape, and even the neutral Manhattans to scalp our people and burn their homes," the agent said. "Just this summer—in this year of Christ 1663, no less!—they massacred our settlement at Esopus and carried off our women and children. This grieves Governor Stuyvesant very deeply. He will be grateful if the People of the Great Longhouse will aid him in gaining peace."

Kryn scanned the table of small men in starched white collars and dark, pointed beards. Behind them the tall governor paced back and forth before the window, his hands folded behind his back, a scowl on his face, and the thudding of his wooden leg on the floorboards dull and monotonous. Kryn considered. How different was this from a smoky council at Onondaga with the chiefs of the five nations in their antler headdresses. He bared his teeth in a sarcastic smile. "One-Legged Man wishes the People of the Longhouse to be both his arm and his war club?" The agent nodded. "And One-Legged Man and his traders will sit home like women, awaiting the outcome of our well-planned raids?" The agent nodded again. Kryn bared his teeth. "When One-Legged Man sees two wolves lurking near his door, he wisely sets them at each other's throat so he may sleep secure in his home."

Governor Stuyvesant stopped suddenly and, his thin lip twitching, snapped at Van Slictenhorst in Dutch: "This Mohawk bastard has a haughty air about him. Give the heathen a glass of gin. We'll loosen him up."

"With all due respect, sir," the agent said, "this is merely a formality among the Iroquois in negotiations. They scout the terrain completely, so to speak, before entering unknown lands. He is just cautious of being ambushed, sir." Van Slictenhorst turned to Kryn. "Do you know of the great battles waging between our nations across the sea? The French call us heretics and burn us at the stake for not following their blackrobes. They strip us of our land and enslave our youths. They ravish our women. Their king says he represents the sun and so indulges in every vice imaginable."

Kryn held up his hand. "It is the custom in the council house to allow each chief to speak as long as he needs. Yet the People of the Longhouse do not allow fools into their council. You speak as a fool, Little Chief. What happens far over the sea is of no concern to my people. Little Chief and One-Legged Man should be wise enough to see that white men on all sides are grasping at our land." Kryn pointed to the parchment map. "The white man believes our land is flat and by drawing lines he may possess it." He seized the map from the table, crumpled it in his strong hand and slapped it down upon the table. "Our land is not flat," he said, pointing to the peaks and valleys the wrinkles formed. "Our land," he pointed to the highest folds of the map, "cleaves the clouds and water pours downward in all directions. The whites do not know the peaks and valleys of the Land From Which All Rivers Flow, yet they wish to take it from us. You as much as the French." He snarled in disgust. "Only a fool accuses others of his own crimes."

Van Slictenhorst's discomposure was felt by the other

eight gentlemen, even though they did not know what Kryn was saying.

"Bring in some gin," Stuyvesant ordered. "We'll reduce this heathen bastard to his proper stature."

"Please!" Van Slictenhorst pleaded. "He understands much of what you say. Do not offend him or all is lost."

"I come as an envoy of my nation," Kryn said, folding his arms, glaring at them across the table. "There is today much turmoil within our League. The elders advise us to sit patiently and allow the white man's wars to weaken him so that he cannot remain in our land. Then, they say, we may again take up hatchet and war club against all of you. Others say not to align with any nation of whites for the other two white nations will fall in together and work to drive the People of the Longhouse out.

"Yet, when thunder shakes the earth and clouds blacken the sun, there exists a strong fear among us, a fear that inaction will serve us worst of all. While the council usually rules about wars we wish to undertake, this summer all nations were not unanimous in wanting war. Therefore it falls back upon the clans and the war chiefs to decide whether to mount raiding parties. I wish to do so, upon my own word, with my own braves. The French have built forts up the river toward the Lake of the Gar-Pike, the northern lake they name Champlain. They now threaten us at both the eastern and the western doors of the Great Longhouse. I plan to drive them down to the great northern river. When the wise sachems see my success, we will mount a vast campaign and drive them forever from our land."

"That is indeed a wise plan," Van Slictenhorst said, and he spent a few minutes describing how the Canienga would drive the French back to the St. Lawrence. The governor and advisors nodded gravely and judiciously smoked their pipes.

"Ask him if he has the same plan for the English," Stuyvesant said, his eyes flashing with interest.

Van Slictenhorst put the question to Kryn. Kryn replied, "We have the same plan for all whites."

This news threw the assembled Dutch into agitated conversation.

"But what of the peace between us?" the patroon's agent asked above the talk. Kryn waited patiently until all was quiet.

"The white man's peace is the stealth of the thief. He

steals farther and farther up our river valleys. He seeks an assurance of peace only to mask his true intent." Carefully he gripped the arms of his chair. "I will not lie to Little Chief or One-Legged Man. So long as English and French steal into our homeland seeking to force us out, we will be at peace with the Dutch. The Dutch do not threaten us as severely as the others. But when the hawks are gone, the thrush ranges farther from its nest. The Canienga will watch the thrush with the eye of an eagle."

Kryn glared as the agent relayed his words. They angered Stuyvesant. "This is what comes of doing business with murdering savages!" he muttered.

"You've told us this, but you still ask our help," the agent said. "Why should we help you?"

"You began this parley by asking my help," Kryn reminded him. "This is why I have come today. We will be friends until the Dutch again show their greed." He fixed Stuyvesant with a steady eye. "One-Legged Man has mentioned gin. While the council at Onondaga cannot make up its mind about taking to the warpath, it remains firm in outlawing traders who come into the Great Longhouse with casks of gin. I am outraged the one-legged chief of the Dutch has suggested gin either for myself or for my people. Gin infects us, poisons us, makes us crawl like animals. It is clear that One-Legged Man harbors the same evil intent as the French with their brandy and the English with their rum."

Van Slictenhorst repeated this to Stuyvesant. Stuyvesant muttered a curse and looked away.

"I have come to tell you I will fix my hatchet in the war pole," Kryn said. "I will mount a winter raid upon the French."

"But winter is not the season—" the agent blurted.

"Yes," Kryn interrupted, holding up his hand. "So also do the French believe. They will not be expecting us. We will steal upon their villages and massacre them and burn them in their beds. I come before you today to ask for guns. In the three clans of the Canienga—Turtle, Bear, and Wolf—only thirty-two warriors of the entire hundred and eight have guns. I asked you in the summer, Little Chief, to secure as many as possible from One-Legged Man. I have brought pelts enough to buy fifty at the price agreed upon."

Van Slictenhorst repeated this to Stuyvesant. Stuyvesant stood up and paced back and forth before the window. His wooden leg inlaid with silver made a hollow sound upon the floorboards.

"Tell this red bastard what I say word for word," he instructed the agent, his head bent, his finger to his temple. "The French are harrying us everywhere. At home in the Low Countries, the legions of Louis the Fourteenth wreak havoc, turn our villages and castles into smoking ruins. We must open the dikes and flood our fields to stop their advance.

"Here the Papist bastards incite the savages against us and the massacres have caused fear so great that homesteaders leave their farms and seek shelter in the forts. We are becoming so weak, the English in Wethersfield and Boston are turning greedy eyes upon our great port of New Amsterdam. They seek to capture all river valleys from Acadia to Virginia, and with these ports, they will rule far inland. We must stop them.

"Tell this haughty bastard that if he can hold the French to the Saint Lawrence Valley, if he can burn the three forts along the Richelieu River, if he can check their movement up Lake Champlain, we will withstand British advances to the east."

Van Slictenhorst repeated this. Kryn nodded, folded his arms over his chest and asked: "How many guns?"

Stuyvesant scowled disgustedly, then conferred with Van Slictenhorst.

"The ship lies at anchor in the tidal basin," the agent relayed. "You say you have skins enough for fifty. The governor says you may take seventy guns." Kryn nodded with approval. "And two hundredweight of shot and twelve casks of powder."

"In addition to the pelts I have brought," Kryn asked, wary of the governor's bargain, "what must we pay?"

Again, agent and governor conferred.

"You will return in spring," Van Slictenhorst said, "and you will pay us the scalps of seventy French soldiers." Two at the table, understanding the pidgin Dutch, gasped. Stuyvesant nodded gravely from the windowsill.

"This will leave many scalps for trophies," Kryn said boldly. "It is the wisest bargain," he said, arising, "when both parties benefit."

7

Wide-eyed and tight-lipped with fear, Tekakwitha followed the fat Vrouw Vanderdonk from room to room. The tall *kasten*—wooden chests—the bed closets, the high hearths with swinging kettle arms astonished her. The glass, the porcelain, the polished brass dazzled her with reflected light, as bright as sunlight upon a brook. The strong, competing odors of lye and vitriol, herbs and spices annoyed her, yet she found a comforting aroma in carded wool.

From a great bin two spinsters drew the wool, twining it between their fingers, then feeding it into another marvel, the spinning wheel. As the yarn collected on a bobbin, it was gathered into skeins, ready for dyeing. Vrouw Vanderdonk, mother hen of the household, displayed the wonders of the dyeing pots, all the time aching to remove the ashes and beargrease on the little girl with a scrub brush and soap.

It was at the loom in the basement that the girl uttered her first words in the house. "The pattern," she said in Iroquois, "lives as an *okie* of the cloth," and she wove her fingers together to demonstrate. The good vrouw humored her, but Tekakwitha persisted. "The design from here," she said, pointing to her temple, "becomes the cloth itself." Still the woman did not understand.

"Yes, child," she answered in Flemish, "the fabric is very pretty. It is a bedcover she is weaving."

Tekakwitha stared, enchanted with the process. In her village, the pelt was skinned, cured by rubbing with moss and the brains of deer, then presented to her for embroidering. She dyed her porcupine quills and her ligaments and sewed her pattern upon it. She had seen fabric from the white settlements and often had wondered how design merged with texture so inseparably that decoration was the essence of the cloth itself, not a mere addition. Seeing now the fabric taking shape upon intricate machinery, she thought the whites were clever magicians for capturing the spirit, the *okie*, of a design and causing both fabric and design to take shape together.

"The design in my village of a bird, a deer, a tree, also lives beyond the sight," the girl said with the excitement of uncovering some profound yet simple truth. "To this day I have only sewn as others have done. Now I see how *okies* may be captured."

"Yes, child," the woman said, "the fabric is very pretty indeed." And the girl, unable to communicate her great revelation, withdrew her excitement and followed Vrouw Vanderdonk down to the kitchen for chocolate. Tekakwitha squirmed uncomfortably on the white man's chair. She took the delft cup, fearful the hot sweet liquid was the hated liquor, and she stared with wide brown eyes at a young kitchen maid who trembled in fear by the hearth.

When finished with the one-legged governor and the patroon's agent, Kryn sent for the girl. "She's been ever so nice," the vrouw said, "not at all a savage. You have a very well-behaved daughter."

"She is not my daughter," Kryn said through Van Slictenhorst. "She is the one who embroiders such fine patterns upon the skins." The woman expressed great surprise, then curiosity to see Tekakwitha's work.

Promising to return next day, Kryn led the girl out into the sunny courtyard, across the flagstone square and down the street through the fortress gates. As they passed along, Tekakwitha spoke of the confusion and activity of the white man's world, the winged and spinning things, the beasts of burden, the metal tongue of the white man's god, even the revelation she'd had watching the loom, a revelation that taught her a new manner of embroidering garments and moccasins. But Kryn paid little attention. His mind was filled with thoughts of blood and war.

To accommodate the unexpected size of his cargo, Kryn chose a great elm the following morning, and with his hatchet and knife, he peeled off a ring of bark about the height of two men. While Tekakwitha stitched in the sunlight near the wigwam, Kryn and Karitha and Arosen sewed the bark into a canoe with strands of root and creepers. They split saplings and ribbed the inside, lashing the ribs to the gunwale, and athwart the gunwales they lashed three braces of strong white oak. They worked quickly and surely, mixing pine sap from the forest with bear tallow they'd brought along, and with this, they smeared and sealed tight the seams.

Late that night, when the lights had blinked out in the

homesteads along the riverbanks and when the town crier had made his rounds in the fort, Karitha, Kryn, and Arosen each paddled a canoe to the bulky ship that lay at anchor some distance below Fort Orange and Beverwyck. There, Flemish sailors loaded their cargo.

Alone now, for the two other lads had not yet returned, Tekakwitha worked by the dim light of the fire. Since her discovery of how white men formed decorative designs, the girl's mind delved into thoughts, observations, remembrances. New ways of seeing old objects occurred to her. Weaving the dyed strips of sinew in and out in imitation of the loom, she worked with care, but with a speed and sureness that far outstripped her past work. She delighted in the supple new figures that appeared in her work. Dogs and deer and warriors and maize, the sun and moon and stars enchanted her.

She had just completed the suit of clothing for the patroon's agent and had begun embroidering moccasins when she heard footfalls and voices outside the wigwam. She hoped it was Kryn and Karitha, but a strident laugh caused her to shiver. She'd heard such a laugh late at night in the longhouse.

"Kryn? Kryn?" she called.

"No, little sister, it is we," and another peal of laughter made her shudder. The two youths, Diving Otter and Ringtail, entered the wigwam.

"I am glad you have come," she said. "I have been alone since Kryn left to load the new canoe. He was cross you weren't here to help."

"It is not good for you to be alone," Diving Otter said, and he grinned at Ringtail. "We are here now." His voice carried an odd note that conjured fear in the girl. "We shall keep you from being alone."

Tekakwitha tried to remain calm. She wrapped up her work, stirred the embers with a stick and announced, "I am weary. Now that you are here, you may await Kryn's return. I will sleep."

Ringtail produced a flask from inside his vest, and taking a long swallow, he passed it to Diving Otter. They laughed defiantly.

"Kryn will be very displeased if he finds liquor among us," Tekakwitha warned.

"We shall call you Complaining Crow," Diving Otter announced, "for you will caw to him and he will be angry."

"She will not caw," Ringtail said, "for she knows a punishment awaits her if she does."

"No punishment of yours can influence my actions." The girl spoke boldly. "You two with your swaggering and boasting, must you kindle your courage with the white man's liquor? Oh, no, you do not frighten me."

"That we shall see!" cried Ringtail. He seized her wrist and pulled her to her feet. Laughing, the strong youth spun her about and pressed his hand over her protesting mouth. "Though small, she is a strong little bitch. Help me, friend, and we shall see what she carries beneath her skirt."

Diving Otter cried out and sprang forward. "It cannot be what our sisters have! She has not yet passed through the first bleeding. And yet..." He grabbed Tekakwitha's kicking legs and tried to part her thighs.

Terrified, the girl bit the hand that held her mouth. Her cry of fury was muted. She spun left and right to avoid the hand probing up her thigh beneath the long skirt.

"Come, little sister, we shall teach you the dark pleasure."

"She scratches!" Ringtail cried. Her sharp nails sought his eyes. "Pin her wrists, friend! She is wild like a briar patch."

Diving Otter laughed drunkenly. "Not beneath the skirt."

As she felt his hand reach its goal, Tekakwitha screamed, kicking and clawing desperately. "No! No! No!" She thrashed, unspeakable horror filling her—a memory of bodies sweating in the firelight, clasped in lewd contortions, the groans of men, the women's dirge of pleasure, the panting, twisted forms, buttocks locking, breasts shimmying, throats bared, eyes rolled back, teeth gnashing. The vision overwhelmed her with dread, and she threw open her eyes to see Diving Otter, loincloth ripped aside, pulling at himself, a maddened gleam in his eye. With one hand, she groped the face of Ringtail, gouging his eye. He cried out and dropped his grip.

"She has the claws of the wildcat. She blinds me!"

"The little bitch!" Diving Otter spat at the fire. "We'll teach her." He picked up a stick of firewood and slapped it in his hand.

Speechless with fear, Tekakwitha pulled her skirts tightly about her thighs, and with wild eyes, backed along the wall of the wigwam.

"Cover the door, Ringtail," Diving Otter directed. "We'll take her in here." His sneer spread as he reached for the gin bottle and, watching her carefully, took a long swallow. Tekakwitha backed around the perimeter of the wigwam until she faced Ringtail who blocked the entrance. Trembling with fear, she looked slowly from one to the other. "Try for the outside, little sister. Try!" Ringtail whispered hoarsely. He laughed.

With a dry throat and a spinning head, Tekakwitha crouched down, eyes flat with mute hatred, slow, catlike movements belying her racing heart. Ringtail bared his teeth in a sneer. He accepted the bottle from Diving Otter and, striking the stance of a fearless warrior, swallowed from it.

Suddenly a shower of embers and ash erupted. With bare hands, Tekakwitha hurled the campfire at them, and as they groped, coughing and cursing, she darted through the door. In cold moonlight she ran until her lungs ached and a sharp pain pierced her side. Despite the raw, wintry air, she waded into a nearby marsh to wait for Kryn, and shivering in fear, she watched the river glide by in the moonlight while dogs howled balefully at wolves and the iron tongue of the white man's god tolled the hours.

8

Kryn's anger smoldered in his eyes when the frightened, shivering girl blurted out her story. He moored the canoe to a sapling and walked slowly, calmly to the tent.

"My fine warriors," he called, shaking them from their stupor, "you have brought great honor to the Canienga by visiting the storehouse of the traders and accepting the bottle of their hospitality. It is noble of you, too, to pay such compliment to a small orphan girl, a maiden. Come, brave ones, whose courage needs only liquor to feed it"—roughly he pulled them to their feet—"come and find the rest due great warriors after returning from a campaign." Into the night he dragged them, assuring them with grim sarcasm their help with the guns in portage next morning was all that obstructed a much longer sleep, a sleep to last all winter and beyond.

Arosen stoked the fire and discarded the rest of the

liquor. Karitha tried to comfort the shivering, terrified girl, yet grew somewhat impatient when Tekakwitha withdrew and responded hardly at all to her kind words. It was only when Kryn returned to the wigwam and spoke to her in his soft, deep voice that Tekakwitha stopped shaking and allowed Karitha to wrap her in a rug of otter skins.

"I have secured those dogs," Kryn said, "who entered our wigwam, the wigwam of humans, by mistake. You shall be safe."

Yet the girl was besieged by horrible nightmares. The path to Quorenta's hut loomed in her dreams, the place in the shade of the oak tree. She murmured and tossed through the night. Red, burning eyes and the snarling fangs of the wolf filled her dreams. She ran, but he pursued, growling, panting. When she fell to the earth with exhaustion, the mud sprang alive with frogs and water snakes, and she groped through the shameful slime to find her feet, to be off again, running, fleeing from the hot eyes and breath of the wolf. And while she fled all night in terror through a swamp of shadowy horrors, the two youths, naked, staked to the mud flat, awaited the chill embrace of the advancing tide.

At dawn, Kryn went again to the stockade to deliver the commissioned embroidery. Vrouw Vanderdonk exclaimed with delight at the intricacy and variety of the bear, deer, maize, sun, and fish designs. Well paid with six bolts of cloth, two kettles, and thirty-one hatchets, Kryn returned to the canoes. The two youths were stoic—anxious to show the night caused no ill effects—and they proved cooperative in dismantling the wigwam and arranging cargo to balance the canoes. Then, facing the northeast wind, they paddled and portaged homeward.

Great fuss attended their return to Kanawaka the following day. Women pestered Karitha and Tekakwitha for needles and the "knives that meet each other"—scissors—and fabric from the white man's loom. Children squealed as Kryn doled out Dutch sugar candy, and warriors clustered about, each anxious to be awarded a gun.

Iowerano, though, dampened the excitement somewhat. "Before these guns be passed out," he told Kryn, "we must confer."

"Let us go to your hearth fire," Kryn said to avoid the questioning looks of the warriors.

In their fur robes, the two chiefs climbed the hill. A line of women chattering excitedly carried bundles from the canoes up the hill. Within the palisade Kryn and Iowerano entered the chief's longhouse, which was hung with tapestries woven of corn husks. Iowerano produced tobacco, and they filled and lit their pipes. Kryn reported on his meeting with the Dutch.

"I see the craft of the one-legged man here," Iowerano said at length, considering each word. "Into our hands he places his iron weapons and says, 'Brother, protect yourself,' while he means 'Protect me.' And even as we follow the path of war, he grasps another handful of our land, and his timid, cowering settlers arrive who clear more forest, shoot more deer, net more fish than they need, who clog our rivers with wooden boats and erect towns never meant for moving. I do not like acting as his slave."

"Last summer," Kryn responded, "when I was trading at Fort Orange, news came of the massacre at Esopus, farther down the great river. The Mohegans had scalped white men and took away women and children as is the custom. But these whites sent up wailing such as I have never heard except to accompany the death of a great chief. Immediately I seized the opportunity to ask for guns so we might better punish the Mohegans who had promised nevermore to campaign against us or the Dutch. But more than that, I sought guns to punish the French. I bargained with Little Chief, and he framed a fair deal, for it is said, As the weasel senses the snare, her panic causes rashness.

"These Dutch are women, Iowerano. They tend the fire and build the home and prepare much food, but they have no stomach for war. The Mohegans, though, defy us. They must pay. Much respect did we win when we burned and tomahawked the entire Huron nation twelve summers ago. Then did all tribes say, 'The People of the Longhouse must be appeased, else they will come against us and wreak what they wrought against the Hurons.' But of late they say this no longer. And the French bluecoats encourage them—even now challenging us by clearing the land for a fourth outpost at the mouth of the northern lake."

"We discussed all this in the council house last summer," Iowerano protested. "Your blood is too hot, Kryn. The peace we enjoyed these last few summers has allowed us to strengthen our towns, bring new warriors and hunters to manhood, recover much from the white man's plague that weakened us so. Good has the peace been, so good that fifty wise sachems ruled it should continue at least another summer."

"Yes," Kryn said abruptly. "So they ruled while sitting about the council fire in the center of our land. And outside in the forest, the fox and bear, the wolf and eagle laugh us to scorn. 'See the women,' they say, 'pounding corn into meal even while soldiers march against them.' No, Iowerano, I cannot agree with this decision. Reason and peace always guide the People of the Longhouse, but the law of the white man, whatever tongue he speaks, is the law of the wildcat in marking and patrolling his precinct. We must strike. Last summer's raid at Esopus was encouraged by the French to turn both Dutch and Canienga eyes elsewhere while they steal down the great lake they call Champlain—this insult cannot be borne. I shall bury my hatchet in the war pole and lead a party against the Mohegans on the Burnt Hills."

"But not against the white man?" Iowerano asked.

"Your logic battles with itself," Kryn said wryly. "You complain of the advance of the Dutch, yet you decry taking arms against the French. You complain of those who have shown us nothing but friendship, yet you seek to put off a war against those who will build wooden war ships upon the northern lake to scatter our bark canoes before them like frightened birds." Kryn smiled. "In the dead of winter, as the French soldier huddles like a widow near his fire, Canienga and Oneida and Onondaga will strike their forts and drive the French from our territory."

"Have you asked the aid of other war chiefs? The Wolf and Bear clans?"

"Let us first caress some Mohegans. For it is said, Until the fire burns sufficiently hot, the kettle will not boil." Kryn's blue eyes danced with mirth. "We must heat the blood of our warriors."

9

The frost set in and the river froze. The villagers readied for winter. High upon its headland the new village rose strong and proud, but the riverbank was deserted, bark canoes upturned upon the shore. Within the village rumors blew strong and unpredictable like gales of the new winter. Kryn, many said, was hunting and wouldn't return until spring. Kryn, others said, had secretly recruited a scalping party and was attacking the French. Kryn, still others said, had journeyed westward to the Oneida and the Onondaga to gain their support.

One evening, an entire month after her return from Fort Orange, Tekakwitha had retreated to a dim corner of Iowerano's longhouse when Arosen's cry caused all Kanawaka to bristle. "Kryn returns! Prepare the way! He brings twelve captives who need caressing tonight!"

Instantly preparations began—rattles and drums were snatched from pegs, clubs and planting sticks were seized, knives and war clubs were taken up.

"Come, cousin," Linawato said to Tekakwitha, "we shall have great sport tonight."

"You may enjoy the sport for both of us," Tekakwitha replied.

"But these are Kryn's prisoners! It will offend him if we do not entertain them properly."

"I wish to remain within."

The bearskin flap of the door opened and Tonedetta entered. "Be up and out, Tekakwitha!" she said. "There'll be no shirking tonight."

Obediently, the girl rose and followed her cousin and foster mother outside. Stretching from the western gate of the town into the forest, two lines of villagers waited impatiently. Some beat on their drums, others shook their rattles in anticipation. In the center of the village, men were stoking the fire under a great iron cauldron which hung from a tripod.

"The war kettle!" someone shouted. In the center of the twelve bark huts, White Adder pranced and sprang, calling out to the sun god, Aireskou.

Reluctantly, Tekakwitha took her place in the line. Children around her bragged how they'd strike and punish the captives, and they boldly wielded sticks and iron rods and flint knives.

Light faded under the cold cloud cover, and bleached cornstalks, lately dusted with snow, rustled in the wind. A triumphant scream pierced the quiet. "Kryn arrives!"

Despite her hatred of the approaching ceremony, Tekakwitha's heart thrilled to the announcement—Kryn was returning victorious! Cloaked in a long, gray, elk robe, Kryn stepped from the forest. A roar sailed up against the clouds, a roar punctuated by the rattles and drums. Kryn held up his arms. All fell silent.

"Into Kanawaka I lead the first captives this new village has seen." He spoke in a deep, oratorical voice. "I ask you to spare no effort in welcoming them, for their deaths will assure our victory."

A resounding cheer rang out, and the rattles and drums sizzled with nervous energy. Iowerano stepped forward and embraced Kryn ceremoniously. With the agreement of the Bear and Wolf clans, Iowerano saw prestige to be gained by supporting the attack, prestige and glory the half-breed Kryn must share with him.

Iowerano silenced the crowd by raising his arms. "Brave is this warrior chief," he called, "and his campaign has been rewarded with captives. Yet this short campaign heralds great things for the future. Kryn will lead our warriors against the French, and when he returns, he will bring with him the scalps of bluecoats and blackrobes!" Shouts erupted from every throat; the drumbeats grew more savage, the rattles more insistent.

"Lead forth the captives!" Kryn called out, and a warrior brought forth a young Mohegan already covered with welts and burns. The warrior jerked upon the bark halter around the captive's neck, and the young captive hesitantly advanced, his hands tied behind his back. The crowd cheered and pressed forward, brandishing clubs and rods and knives.

As this first captive entered the gauntlet, he sprinted past his guard until the bark halter nearly strangled him. Yet he maintained his stance. The crowd surged forward, lashing him with clubs and planting sticks, slashing at his skin with knives. The children, too, ran forward, beating his shins and thighs and genitals with sticks, pounding on his feet with rocks. Only as he reached the palisade gate, where the gauntlet ended, did the beating cease, and the young man staggered, bloody and faint, into the village.

Next there emerged from the forest a young woman, naked, breasts and thighs excoriated and burned from previous tortures. A shrill scream rang out from the women, and they elbowed forward to welcome her. She entered the gauntlet, head down, resigned. The Canienga women jabbed her with sticks, struck blows on her scalp, pulled at her hair, flailed at her breasts and buttocks with knives. Again the children ran out, many thrusting sticks between her thighs from the front and behind. The woman reeled under incessant blows and fell to the ground. Then the crowd pounced, raining blows upon her as she lay defenseless, unable to ward off the blows with her mutilated hands. Only with difficulty did her captor push away the villagers and drag her to her feet. As she entered the village gate, the violence temporarily ceased, and she stumbled, dazed and bleeding, toward the scaffold in the center.

The fire beneath the kettle had been banked, and now the kettle was boiling. Forms passed back and forth before it. In its lurid light, the young Mohegan and the woman were tied to stakes on the scaffold, then were set upon by kneeling village women who gnawed at their fingers.

Tekakwitha turned away, sickened by the sight, frightened by the mad scramble of the villagers and their impatience, now registered with rattles and drums, to attack the next captive. She put her fist to her mouth and bit her finger to keep from crying out. She looked for Kryn and saw him standing at the head of the line, arms folded, watching the procession. The next captive to emerge from the forest was a girl of about ten summers. The din of rattles and drums and calls for her to enter and be welcomed terrified Tekakwitha, yet the young girl, bruised and burned, looked down the gauntlet with loathing and spite.

Suddenly Iowerano stepped forward, his arms held high. He called to his sister, Tegonhat, and the woman went to him.

"The chief rescues the girl," an old woman whispered close by Tekakwitha, "to keep as his concubine."

"Let this one pass unharmed," the chief called down the line, and Iowerano's sister, Tegonhat, shielding the girl, entered the gauntlet and walked unmolested toward the village gate. Seeing her chance to escape the brutal spectacle, Tekakwitha darted from the line of villagers.

"Tegonhat!" she called above the din. "Tegonhat! I will join you. I will accompany you to our longhouse, and I will watch over the girl so you may return to the welcoming."

"Very well," the woman said, placing her other arm over Tekakwitha's shoulder, "come with us."

A warrior bearing torches passed them, and suddenly the bloodthirsty crowd erupted again as an old man, shriveled and naked, entered the line to receive his welcome. The crowd pressed forward.

The woman and two girls entered the dim longhouse. Expertly Tegonhat lashed the concubine's wrists to the chief's sleeping shelf. Tekakwitha climbed upon her own sleeping shelf opposite and pulled a bear robe over herself so only her head was visible.

"I will guard this girl," Tekakwitha said. "The chief has spoken. I will allow no one to take her."

"That is good," Tegonhat said. "But should you wish to join in the festivities, I will watch for some time."

"It has been so long since our village was privileged to honor such captives," Tekakwitha said, "and you are much more experienced than I. You should remain at the scaffold to see how bravely they all meet death."

"If you wish to join us," Tegonhat repeated, "find me and I will watch for some time."

"Be sure the prisoners have fitting deaths," Tekakwitha said, "and the war kettle boils with their bravery. Aireskou thirsts for blood tonight."

"Yes," Tegonhat said, and her eyes beamed in the low light of the fire. "You speak well." She turned and left the longhouse. Tekakwitha looked over at the captive, and for many long moments, the two girls' eyes locked.

"You have been saved," Tekakwitha said at last. The Mohegan maid said nothing. "I will see that no one harms you." The girl stared with loathing at her. Tekakwitha desperately wanted her to say something, anything, even an angry explosion or a curse. But the girl simply stared, her eyes holding a bitter knowledge that unnerved Tekakwitha. "It may not be too bad," she said in a tone she used for pet racoons. "If Iowerano enjoys the dark pleasure, he will spare you." With mute hatred the girl stared. "I understand," Tekakwitha offered softly.

A roar went up in the center of the village, and Tekakwitha shuddered. She looked toward the door, then back to the girl. The girl's eyes never wavered. Tekakwitha was suddenly startled with knowledge of what the girl was thinking. "No," she said, "I am not his concubine! He's my foster father. Oh, no!" she insisted, for it seemed very important suddenly to have this girl perceive the truth. "No!"

With fear she met the girl's accusing stare. Screams from the torturing rose from the scaffold outside, and in the girl's eyes the low flames of the hearth fire burned. Tekakwitha was seized with terror. Dimly she remembered the path to Quorenta's hut by the great oak tree. She remembered another concubine long ago, the screams of a young girl, and blood, blood everywhere, and herself running, running until her lungs were raw, until the strong arms of Kryn caught her and held her closely. Breathing heavily, she now stared at the mute concubine and her fear deepened to despair—Kryn had watched the procession of prisoners with satisfaction. He would be no comfort tonight. And suddenly the hatred in the other girl's eye was what she herself felt.

10

Upon the scaffold an orgy of torture raged. The Mohegan warriors and women, tied by hands and thighs to stakes, screamed and sang their death songs. Like demons Canienga women chewed the captives' fingers and thumbs. The men tied bark belts smeared with pitch around the prisoners' waists, then lit them with coals. Iowerano, to heighten his enjoyment of the torture, heated a necklace of iron hatchets in the fire until red-hot, then hung it around the bravest warrior's neck.

Beneath the scaffold, the villagers danced in the firelight, frenzied by the torture and screams. White Adder leapt, yelling spells and curses, urging the villagers on. Canienga warriors thrust burning sticks into the mouths and rectums and vaginas of the Mohegans. Canienga women hacked off fingers and testicles with clam shells. A warrior plucked out the eyes of the bravest captive and replaced them with burning coals. The stench of burning flesh and singed hair mingled with the screams of the victims, but over all rode the death song of the bravest. He had been composing it since puberty. Defiantly, in the face of pain and mutilation, he kept on with his proud death chant. In tribute to his own courage, he sang of the bears he'd killed, the rapids he'd navigated, the hunger and pain he'd endured. He sang to his sun god of the battles he'd fought, the men he'd slain, the children he'd fathered.

Finally, as the other captives slumped into stupors and were tomahawked for their weakness, Iowerano stepped upon the scaffold. Wearing the antlers of his office, he spread his arms, and his long bearskin robe swung open to reveal his loincloth.

"This is the bravest of the captives taken from his hunting party upon the burnt hills," the chief called. A knife flashed in his hand. "At the rising of the sun, O god Aireskou, our warriors will set off toward the polar star to drive the French from our land. Let them eat the heart and drink the blood of this brave one so their own thirst for blood will be unquenchable!" He brandished the knife. The crowd surged forward. "Let them eat first this heart, then from the war kettle, and so be bold and unflinching in this winter attack."

The villagers screamed in one hoarse voice, and Iowerano turned, plunged the knife between the Mohegan's ribs and with his hand drew out the palpitating heart. In a renewed frenzy, the crowd pushed forward, hands reaching up. Iowerano held the heart over them, blood flowing through his fingers onto their faces and outstretched arms. Then Kryn stepped forward, hacked a piece of the heart and ate it. Wildly the crowd cheered. Other warriors performed the same rite and the palpitations ceased. When the last morsel of the heart remained, Iowerano consumed it, then hoarsely signaled.

Now the villagers mounted the scaffold and hacked apart the slumped bodies with tomahawks. Hurling arms and thighs and feet and torsos into the war kettle, they cried out their joy, and White Adder summoned the sun-god Aireskou to witness and to grant them strength. As the kettle frothed red with blood, the Canienga danced with abandon, anxious for the cannibal feast that would complete their rite. And as they danced, snow began to fall, softly, silently, then thicker, harder, whipped and swirled by chance winds.

By dawn, knee-deep snow covered the bloody scaffold, the longhouses, the ramparts of the palisade, the lanes of the village where dogs prowled for meat, the plantation of withered stalks, and beyond, the deep and silent forest. Snow covered the kettle where the cannibal feast had boiled. Muffled sounds of men packing muskets and satchels of food and snowshoes awakened children, who rushed out with joy and wonder into the snow.

Kryn had dispatched runners westward to the Bear and Wolf clans of the Canienga nation, then farther west through rocky defiles, through valleys and mountain spurs to the nations of the Oneida and Onondaga, inviting them to join the war party at the Lake of the Gar-Pike.

"Soon will all lakes and rivers be icebound," Kryn's message ran. "When the northern lights glimmer, the People of the Longhouse, like an eagle with talons bared, will swoop down upon the French and drive them from the land."

With the snow still pelting, Kryn and forty-one warriors assembled near the scaffold, their hempen satchels filled with ground maize, dried bear meat, tobacco, powder and shot. War clubs were in their belts; their hands held bows and arrows. Every warrior but Kryn had painted his face with blues and reds and ochres. All tied on their snowshoes, shouldered their packs, and turned their eyes northward. Dressed only in loincloths, leggings, and fur robes, they waited grimly until Kryn gave the signal. Then they set off, gliding upon the breast of the snow into the teeth of the howling blizzard.

SPIRITUAL EXERCISES

Jesuit Seminary, Montmartre
1655

1

Paris spread along the Seine in a profusion of elegance and poverty. There were the grand homes of ancient families tracing their lineage back to Charlemagne's twelve paladins, the elegant estates and palace of young Louis XIV, the gracious spires and buttresses of Notre Dame upon its island in the river, and all about like a flooding and ebbing sea, there were the filth and squalor of the poor.

On the periphery of the teeming metropolis, a square, massive structure of gray limestone had been erected, topped by a belfry and cross. Its purpose—to instruct and train and send forth elite soldiers of Christ, the Jesuits.

Apart from the city, the Jesuit seminary stood, yet its distance from the city, the nation, and the empire of man could not be measured in French leagues. Out from the seminary came brilliant men who heard the confessions of kings and rajahs and yellow-skinned emperors. Out came humble men who cared for the poor and downtrodden of the city, the peasants tilling the fields of lords. Out from this house walked men in black robes who forsook family, ambition, wealth, and even the pure delight of study to brave shipwreck, starvation, and murder while spreading the word of Christ through forests, deserts, and jungles.

Yes, even while the gray limestone walls of the seminary stood at the periphery of Paris, perhaps the most civilized city in the world, the spare interior belonged to a kingdom not of this world. Men were trained here in the rigors of Loyola, their souls and wills strengthened by study, meditation, and, periodically, the spiritual exercises. Within this fortress, the soldiers of Christ were grilled and tested, probed and scrutinized by wise lieutenants who found and eliminated any lingering human weakness. On a raw November afternoon, in a small cell in the great stone honeycomb, a young

57

man lay facedown upon the floor, guided by his spiritual adviser into the wilderness of his own soul.

"Whither you lead," he had pledged each day during the month-long spiritual exercises, "there I will follow."

The young man, Claude Chauchetiere, a slender, handsome son of a petty noble of Vienne, had entered the seminary at the bidding of his uncle, Pere Auguste Chauchetiere, S.J. Many young female eyes had turned when Claude entered the Parisian salons four summers before. His smoldering brown eyes, his patrician profile, his full, sensuous lips, and the grace of his walk had filled the dreams of young girls. Yet society was not for him. Theater, opera, lavish soirees and balls seemed trivial occupations of trivial minds. While prone to the intrigues of love four summers before and a sender and receiver of billets-doux, Claude had suddenly, mysteriously abandoned the search for a wife among the coquettes. Many gossips in provincial Poitiers whispered he had fallen and sinned, that his passionate nature, horrified by the disgrace to himself and his family, had seized upon his uncle's priestly way of life. The rumormongers of his village gossiped that to expiate the sin he entered the seminary and pledged his will, his soul, and his life to the spreading of Christ's word.

In the cold cell this November afternoon, Claude Chauchetiere listened to the aged priest's words, and he allowed his imagination free rein.

"Depart from me, ye cursed, into the everlasting fire which was prepared for the devil and his fallen angels!" the priest said. "We'll consider now the horrors that sinners will meet at the Last Judgment. In the name of the Father, and of the Son, and of the Holy Ghost. Amen."

The priest cleared his throat and settled into the chair, his head resting upon his right hand. "Far in the bowels of the earth lies the infernal pit. Screaming and kicking helplessly, souls of the damned fall into this burning lake, this bottomless, shoreless lake where, goaded by the hot spikes of fiends, they forever crawl through choking, sulfurous smoke. Let us meditate: What meets their eyes?

"Demons, hideous demons exhibiting shapes of our earthly beasts. Bedlam reigns. One has the face of a cat, an ass's ears, the talons of an eagle, and a goat's cloven hooves. Another has the scaly head of a viper, shallow of eye, quick of tongue, as well as the trunk of a dog and the black paws of a Moor's monkey. Nor are the demons immune to the flames.

In leprous, suppurating sores they ooze noxious matter. Such colors, too, hideous reds and purples, and gleaming, mucous blues, such colors are lit startlingly by explosions and sudden eruptions of flame.

"And the damned souls, though still human in shape, have undergone horrible changes. All hair has been burned away. Within their skulls their brains boil. Their eyes gleam with unearthly light like lime burning in the kiln, and tongues, swollen and black, distort the imprecations of their parched throats. Nor is there any rest. In seizures these damned souls thrash and claw mimicking carnal sins. Their charred flesh falls away to be replaced by tender new skin that soon reddens, blisters, and falls away again. Yes, these are the sights of hell.

"And what of the smells and tastes?" The priest coughed, then adjusted his position. "Into the pit of hell pour all the foul sewers of earth. In a torrent continually flow scum and poison and excrement, and as this burns, great black and yellow clouds of smoke scorch all noses and throats. Bitter residue remains upon the tongue, a taste fouler than vitriol, burning like lye.

"And the sounds? Though constant screaming and prayers for water and salvation, though the horrible tumult of curses and vile words echo ceaselessly in the vault of hell, ears remain particularly acute. They hear the demon's hot iron upon flesh; they hear the scurrying of fiendish hooves and claws; they distinguish each plea, each recrimination, and they hear the sobbing of despair, the hissing of falling tears. My son, no ship of galley slaves, no madhouse, no dungeon, no Inquisition chamber compares to the utterances of such pain and despair.

"Yes, my son, but the sights and sounds, the tastes and smells of that infernal region comprise not one part in a hundred, nay, not one-tenth of a part in a hundred of the sufferings endured. For true suffering, as martyrs show us vividly, is not suffering of the flesh. Never. It is suffering of the heart and of the soul. These damned ones know their sufferings will never ever ease, never cease, never. They count years, nay, they count entire centuries numerous as the stars of heaven, as grains of sand upon the beach, as drops of rain in the sea, yes, but even by combining all this time they will not approach one fleeting moment of eternity. And this causes their souls to despair.

"Yet, what weighs heavier still is the profound loss each feels by the absence of God. Excluded are they from the sustaining love of the Almighty. Eternally they will relive their sins, knowing such misdeeds can never be rectified. Each thief will know again the quickening pleasure of stealth and possession of another's goods. Each fornicator will feel the damp, guilty pleasure and the gratification of selfish lust." Claude shuddered at this example. "And in reliving the pleasure of his sins, each soul will suddenly be stabbed in conscience. 'If only,' the conscience will cry out, 'If only..., If only...' Yes, each will cry, 'Always I had the opportunity to seek the Lord's forgiveness, but did I genuflect? Did I bow? Did I beat my breast and as a penitent seek His all-saving grace? No!"

The priest coughed again, and his breath formed a steam cloud in the cold room.

"Far in the center of this vast bedlam, surrounded by a loud, pressing throng of demons with knobbed faces, demons covered in fur and feathers and scales, far upon a mountaintop in this vast volcano of flame, upon a throne of smoke and burning brimstone, sits Satan. His bat wings drape over the arms of his ebony throne. His fierce red eyes watch with demonic scrutiny. Satan, once Lucifer, God's beautiful bearer of light, now Prince of Darkness, gloats that he has seduced men from the right paths by infecting them with pride. Yes, my son, pride. Pride that the urges of the flesh deserve to be gratified over the wishes of Our Father. Pride that our actions have not been discovered, that our wills are greater than the Almighty's. Pride that our crimes are so heinous, the Lord can never forgive them.

"Let me leave you now, my son, with a parting thought. We are but men, poor, deluded men with many faults, subject to our passions. Humility alone binds us together, permits us to love our neighbors and ourselves, allows us, my son, to be saved."

The priest raised his hand, and while making the sign of the cross in the air, he whispered, "In the name of the Father, and of the Son, and of the Holy Ghost. Amen."

Stiffly he pulled himself out of the chair, stepped over the novice, and opened the thick oaken door of the cell. "God be with you, my son," he whispered, and he pulled the door closed with a dull thud.

Alone, immured—virtually entombed—Claude lay facedown upon the stone floor. Time seemed to have stopped. The November chill numbed him, and his shallow breathing caused the illusion that the walls were expanding and contracting. Not since childhood had he been as terrified as during his first week of the exercises. The wheezing, tired voice of the old priest wove a spell, and the imaginings, strong and tangible, posed true horrors that men of common sight could not see.

Claude remembered the gypsy's caravan, the young, dark-skinned woman swaying her hips to the melancholy strains of a violin. He remembered her soft, damp hand leading him to her wagon, the same hand held out for the gold he tendered. He remembered her dress passing over her full breasts, her belly, her wide hips, then falling past her thighs. He remembered the hot abandon, the growling, the fitful straining, her strong thrusts, and then the disgust, the utter disgust as he lay spent upon her. Yes, he remembered that first night with the gypsy and the many nights he returned to her for more.

Young, impressionable, passionate, he realized only now what horrors his surrender might have earned him in hell had he not repented. Wretchedly he squirmed on the stone of his chamber, at last confronting his weakness and his sin. The sulfurous smoke, the eternal burning, the hideous shapes, the gloating Satan again played through his mind. He felt nauseous. The gypsy with her laughter, her smell, had been an agent of the fiend. The old priest had opened his mind to truth, truth far greater than libraries held. He knew now how close he had been to damnation, and shivering in the November chill, he offered a prayer of thanksgiving that he had been lured back from the brink, that his mind and heart had been opened to the true path of salvation.

As he lay, allowing his thoughts to run freely, the Angelus bell tolled in the cloister yard, and reverberated in the stone vault of his chamber. Kneeling up, he crawled to his bed, and he folded his hands and prayed: "The Angel of God came unto Mary, and she conceived of the Holy Ghost..."

2

"... and after Christ had fasted forty days in the desert, the demon took Him to a high cliff overlooking all the kingdoms of the earth. 'All this I will give to you,' said the demon, 'if you bow down and adore me.' In the name of the Father, and of the Son, and of the Holy Ghost. Amen."

The bell tolled midnight. The candle flickered. The priest pinched the flame with his thumb and finger and plunged the room into darkness. Claude stood against the wall this night, his fourteenth in the spiritual exercises.

Fatigued by daily fasting and silence, Claude had relinquished logic, human sympathy, compassion, and commonplace thought. His imagination, led by the old priest's words, dwelt now in a spiritual realm. Life and even existence itself were no longer mere organic facts, cycles of growing and withering. Human existence now was a pitted battle, promising supreme delights as the spoils of victory and untold horrors as the punishment for defeat.

"While the battle is for sway of the entire world," the priest said, "it is waged within each human heart, each human soul. Consider Christ in the garden."

Claude saw Christ praying in the Garden of Gethsemane as depicted on the altar triptych in the chapel of his father's château. His imagination brought the painting to life—an olive grove, silver in the moonlight, crickets chirping, and the Savior, kneeling, imploring his Almighty Father to save him from the cross. "I pray," He said, "that you remove this bitter chalice so I need not drink from it." So violent was His agony that drops of blood started from His pores. "Your will and not mine be done." In the soft wind, Claude felt the tremors of Christ's fear—the calm, silent night only heightening the violence of Christ's private agony.

Claude saw, too, what Christ foresaw at that moment, the whipping, the bloody crown of thorns, the bearing of the cross through a shrill, reviling crowd, his human flesh kicked, whipped, spat on. Claude felt the indignity of being stripped naked, the unspeakable pain of nails hammered through his flesh, the piercing of the Roman spear, and the surrender to death. Vividly Claude saw and heard and felt these things, and honestly he asked himself if he could accept the destiny of crucifixion: His zealous nature said yes; his flesh recoiled in horror.

"Many have been the martyrs sent forth by our Society," the priest said. "They have followed Christ unto death, butchered by the yellow men of the Jappos, devoured by blacks of Africa, scalped and burned by the red men of New France. They all repeated Christ's words of the garden, 'Your will and not mine be done.' Yes, they went forth and met their destiny. What changed them from victim to victor? What earned them a heavenly seat and our earthly reverence? Not death—that is what we all must meet. No. They triumphed, each of them, when in the midst of torture and flames, they spoke Christ's words, 'Father, forgive them, for they know not what they do.'"

Claude thought of Isaac Jogues, a Jesuit captured a dozen years before by the Mohawks, the easternmost tribe of the Iroquois, the fiercest natives of New France. Claude had read Jogues's letters to the Provincial Superior and to the Superior General. The red men and women had gnawed his fingers, sawed his left thumb off with a clam shell. They had whipped and burned him with savage, inexplicable cruelty, and reduced him to a crippled slave. Yet, when Jogues was rescued and brought back to Paris, he spurned the praise of the Queen Mother herself; he cared nothing for the admiration of other Jesuits who were secure in their teaching and advisory posts; he longed only to return to New France, to continue his mission, even though death awaited him. "I go and I will not return," Jogues wrote from Quebec when he ventured again into the heathen heart of Iroquois lands. He had been finally tomahawked, scalped, his head impaled on a pole, his body cast to the dogs. What force drove him?

"Read upon the lives of the men of Loyola," the priest whispered. "Each was tempted, as was Christ, to bow and adore the earth and the demon and to receive whole kingdoms for a reward. As Christ in the garden, each agonized over the choice to go forth and meet his destiny or turn and save his base human flesh. And each of the great men went forth, suffered, and forgave. In the name of the Father, and of the Son, and of the Holy Ghost. Amen."

Stiffly the priest rose and left the novice to his meditation. At the closing of the door, Claude slumped upon his bed, exhausted. Yet his mind was still keen. He lay, considering the choice before him and the terms of the transaction. Could he go forth, knowing terrible tortures and death awaited? From where did the martyrs draw their strength and courage? From faith? Or was the source truly divine?

He examined his character. He'd joined the order to expiate a sin. His first stirrings of piety had been prompted by strong contrition. The horrors of hell had reinforced his choice, comforted him, but now he found his motives tainted, weakened by an outgrowth of pride. Yes, pride, he thought, regretting his pride of intellect, his pride in the singing during mass, his pride in keeping free of sodomy and solitary vice that others fell prey to within the stone walls of the seminary.

Then from his memory, the dark, limpid eyes of the gypsy woman stabbed at him. He had returned night after night to embrace her, to enjoy the damp and greedy thrill of her loins. Then, during a time of reckoning, when rumor with its wagging tongue ran riot through the village that the Comte Chauchetière's younger son was consorting with gypsies, he had turned in his guilt to the Jesuits. And in staunching the wound of his guilt, he saw now that he had been prideful of his virtue and had encouraged the eyes of others to watch him atone.

Yes, he saw now, his faith was imperfect. He possessed none of the courage of Jogues who passed among the savages with his cross and chalice to face certain death. His nature was flawed. What could he do? The years of his remaining study stretched before him like the cold, quiet cells along a hall of the cloister. "I must be vigilant," he whispered. "I must elect to follow as a soldier of Christ, and He will give me courage." And as his mind put aside the knowledge of his imperfection, Claude sought comfort in the rhythms of prayer:

"Our Father, who art in heaven, hallowed be Thy name. Thy kingdom come, Thy will be done, on earth as it is in heaven. . . ."

3

"Through the intercession of Blessed Mary, ever virgin, we beseech Our Lord to allow us entry into the Kingdom of God. In the name of the Father, and of the Son, and of the Holy Ghost. Amen."

Claude knelt, six days later, facing the stone wall. Cold, pure light, reflected from new-fallen snow, flooded through the northern window of his chamber.

"Consider, my son, the pure vessel, the House of Ivory whom the Deity chose to mother His only begotten son. No earthly honors, no wordly riches were hers, only the distinction of a pure heart and untainted flesh."

The priest fell silent. Claude considered his own tainted flesh. Purity in thought and deed, a life devoid of pollution, complication, scandal, these comforts were his wish when he joined the order. Yet the spiritual exercises brought his sin up again and again, forced him to confront it where it lurked in the private chamber of his heart, to relive it in the hope he might triumph over it. As the priest spoke, Claude turned his thoughts to the Virgin.

He envisioned a faint landscape, shimmering in the sun. Olive and cypress trees, dusted with white, stretched along the road to a village where white-washed domes quivered in heat mirages. Donkeys brayed and children cried. The landscape of opal and topaz gasped in the suffocating heat. The maiden gazed from her window, a hand idle on the sill, a veil over her face. In his vision, the heat, the dust, the languid afternoon, became inextricably bound with Mary's virginity.

Claude threw his eyes open, and like a splash of cold water, the sight of his own chamber illuminated by cold, clear light, flooded upon him. Carefully he catalogued the room—the wooden bed, the coarse straw tick, the crucifix above the bed, the basin with its thin crust of ice. Blessed, radiant light flooded in from the peaked window, and this gladdened his heart, his mind, his soul.

The priest stirred. "Yes, Mary, ever virgin, Mary the Madonna, Mary the Sorrowful Mother at last was assumed bodily into heaven. Through her intercession, my son, our founder Ignatius Loyola underwent his spiritual progress and recorded his struggles in these spiritual exercises. It is the beatified and radiant virgin who guides us and counsels us and provides the warmth to complement the light of intellectual endeavors.

"I ask you now, my son, to meditate upon Mary, triumphant over life and death. I ask you to reach out and touch the hem of her robe as she is borne up from this earth to take her place at Christ's side."

Claude gently closed his eyes and surrendered himself to a sweet, sunlit vision. Before him appeared the hem of a blue cloak, and as he watched, the robe became iridescent. Cool light and a gentle warmth emanated from the robe, and a sweet harmony played upon the wind. Well-being, comfort, and maternal love caressed him, and like a small child he

looked to see the face from which such love came. Wisps of
cloud swept about the presence above him, and as he concen-
trated, the clouds seemed to part. He heard faint harmony, a
whisper, and he peered still higher. The radiant face of the
virgin smiled down at him, a face familiar to his dreams.
Blond curls fell from a coronet set with stars. Her pale blue
eyes sparkled with unearthly joy, and her full, pink lips
parted. She spoke: "Come to me."

Swooning with rapture, Claude fell back upon his heels
and stretched out his arms. He bathed his fatigued, fasting,
troubled spirit in the joy that emanated from this vision. All
discomfort—his aching knees, his hunger, his attenuated
nerves—vanished. Claude sighed and clasped his arms about
himself. And each word quivering with new meaning, he
prayed:

"Hail, Mary, full of grace. The Lord is with you. Blessed
are you among women, and blessed is the offspring of your
womb, Jesus."

4

Claude sat, hands folded in his lap, looking in wonder
about him. The priest had departed for the last time. His
body, thinner now, trembled with new vibrancy. All desire
was purged by the spiritual exercises. He was completely,
utterly at peace. Slowly, carefully, Claude scanned the chamber. Ordinary objects—the basin, his hairbrush, the knotted
whipping cincture upon the iron spike—radiated goodness.
The whole, good, harmonious world had opened to him at
last. He listened, smiling inwardly, to the harmonious bark of
a dog, to the soft chiming of a distant bell, to the bold
pounding of his own heart. Like grace came rays of sun
bursting through his lattice, and in that light he luxuriated,
his heart happy, his soul complete.

In the following weeks and months, Claude's new serenity infused his strict life as a novice with hope and joy. The
demeanor of a Jesuit—dignified, patrician, careful—changed
his bearing, and even the facial expressions of a Jesuit—aloof,

thoughtful, grave—became the sole attitude Claude displayed to the world.

Yet as months lengthened into a year, then two, the inner turbulence returned, the war between forces of darkness and forces of light, each battling for possession of his soul. At night, lewd, enticing visions of the gypsy infected his sleep. Claude felt the silky, tantalizing touch of a hand, then lips and tongue. The moans, deep in her throat, reverberated through him, and his entire flesh trembled upon the verge of explosion...

Starting up in bed, Claude scanned in amazement the dry austerity of his chamber. With a towel he mopped sweat from his brow, and he lay back, waiting for his heart to slow. He brought forth the image of the virgin, fair-haired, blue-eyed. The quiet sanctity of her presence, her pale, chaste lips, her unblemished skin, her robes of cloud and sky comforted him. From another life he knew her. Now he prayed for her to intercede, to free him of the darker visions. "In the dark night of the soul," he murmured, and he spoke her name, "Mary!" And he took the knotted whipping cincture from the spike, bared his back, and administered such punishment as his flesh required.

5

Claude Chauchetière's visions were so vivid, so much a part of his ascetic life in the seminary, he was surprised to find in his contemporaries a dullness, a laziness that kept them from exploring their own souls in like manner during the spiritual exercises. This disappointed him. The practical side of his nature saw value in recording his visions, and so, even though against the rules, he secretly began a journal—hadn't Loyola, the order's founder? he reasoned—and there he poured out his innermost thoughts and feelings. The journal became his true confessor, though he did tell his sins in the dining hall each Saturday. He wrote of his dreams; he wrote of his doubts and his spiritual turmoil. As the journal became a talisman in his quest for truth and salvation, so then did the vision of the Blessed Virgin become his solace.

"Holy Virgin, embrace me," he wrote. "Allow me to recline my head upon your breast. May your breath, sweeter than the spices of the Indies, caress my ears, my nostrils, my lips. May your soft hand ease my brow. In the folds of your garment may I bury my eyes, weary with long study, and may I kiss the hem of your robe."

In a march of months and years he continued Loyola's rigors of study, prayer, meditation, and discipline. But each day he went to his journal with all the hungers and thirsts of his parched flesh, and freely, with no effort at all, his quill crossed the pages in love poetry to the Virgin. She became his ideal of perfection. He described her slender hands, her golden hair under a halo of sunbeams, her clear, pale eyes, her full lips, and her small white feet crushing the rearing head of the serpent. To avoid detection, he hid the book in a cranny behind his bed. Sitting in the refectory or kneeling in the chapel, he felt secure knowing it was there, and the possibility of being caught even tantalized him. Shortly after his ordination, he wrote:

We read today of Brebeuf and Lalemant, slain by the savage Iroquois in the land of the Hurons. Theirs was a mission so sacred and noble and pure— to bring the primitive children of the forest to Jesus Christ, to instruct them out of their superstition and illuminate the path to salvation. Yet how it ended for them! It would have been easier, it seems, to bring the word of God to Satan in the bowels of hell. What scenes of horror Père Ragueneau described! Men of pure motive, imparting the doctrine of the meek and forgiving Lord, brutally tortured with fire and iron not even ten years ago. Hoping to bring many souls to Jesus, these men stood in danger of losing their own to cowardice and fear. I am in mind of Christ's agony "take from me this cup, O Father." Their prayers to Him were answered, and with superhuman courage, they withstood the burning hatchets, the amputation of hands, the plucked-out eyes and red coals inserted. Yes, they withstood, and they forgave. And I must pace the halls of this cloister for four more years of study, meditating, contemplating the lives of these great men with no outlet for action!

'Oh, Blessed Mother of my vision! You incite me to action. I long like a worthy knight to arm myself, go forth, and bring your holy message to the infidel savage. And as the knight dedicates his courage and the spoils of his quest to his lady fair, so will I consecrate my heart, my will, and my soul to you. For you I pledge to exhaust the very last of my strength, and if flames ever envelop my dying eyes, it will be your vision of blue robes and cool, ethereal light that will guide me from this earth.'

6

In the last year of his studies, Père Claude Chauchetière became an outrider. From the bastion of the Montmartre seminary, Claude rode out to tutor nobles' sons in logic, mathematics, theology, and Latin and to counsel the patriarchs and matrons of France's great families in spiritual matters. His sincerity and zeal were noted by many, and they conveyed such to the Father Superior.

His uncle, a Jesuit and a confessor at the court of Louis XIV, called for him one summer afternoon, and they drove the eight leagues to Versailles in a coach. Cranes swung blocks of pink marble and white limestone into the air. Wagon trains of quarried stone, shrubbery, wine casks, carpets, chandeliers, and furniture, wended along the road. Armies of masons labored upon scaffolds. Teams and drivers dredged the earth, and already the lines of what would be walks, symmetrical gardens, and parks were being laid out by royal architects and engineers.

"I have heard much praise about you from Father Superior," Père Auguste Chauchetière said. "You have avoided youthful folly and are a credit to the order."

Claude felt uncomfortable. "I thank you for mentioning this, Uncle, but it is no less than a member of the Society should strive for."

"Of course, of course." A smile lit the older man's eye. "But service to God, and service to the Society can be performed by guiding secular affairs too, Père Claude. Cardinal Richelieu and the late Cardinal Mazarin have not found a counterpart at this young king's court. Louis Fourteenth vows to rule France himself. Yet, the king is a sensualist." The priest waved his arm out the coach window toward the monumental scale of construction. "He is particularly prey to the vice of lust, and he keeps pretty courtesans. He is vain, proud of his witty speech, his horsemanship, his dancing. He listens to counsel, yet makes his own decisions. Any aid the Society can extend to this young king will serve God above all, France's destiny as well, and Loyola's ideals most humbly."

"I do not see, Uncle, the burning importance of meddling in temporal affairs. Our task is to save souls."

The elder priest sighed. The coach turned into a broad drive and the horses pranced proudly toward the Court Royale. Ornate red brick outbuildings with blue slate roofs framed the château beyond.

"You have studied many years, Claude, but your education is not complete. You must learn about politics and the struggle for dominance." Again the priest waved his arm out of the coach window.

"I fail to see the relevance, Uncle."

"Look across to England. A hundred and thirty years ago, Henry the Eighth dissolved and looted all monasteries. The loss to the Church cannot be measured. Our Society has never established a toehold in England, and these heretics continue to harry us at all posts around the world."

"But of what heavenly value is worldly wealth and power?" Claude protested.

"Yes," said the elder priest, "I see now how sincere and youthful your motives are. I shall speak to Father Superior to remedy this lack in your education."

Père Claude grew impatient. "The ideal of Loyola is my standard," he said. "*Ad Majorem Gloriam Dei*—for the greater glory of God. This mention of worldly goals pollutes our vows. It lends credence to rumors that we own silver mines in Mexico, silk factories in China, that we trade and lend money as usurers, that we conspire with warlords, that we plot the overthrow of kings—"

"Here, we have arrived," the uncle said. "Let us enter Versailles. You will learn much from your short time here." And, summoning the footman to follow with their bags, the two Jesuits in black robes passed through the high iron gate.

* * *

For three exhausting days, Claude watched the strenuous pursuit of pleasure at Louis XIV's court: hunting, gambling, dancing, feasts in the paneled dining hall, a cotillion in the ballroom where chandeliers lit the graciously outfitted assembly and violin music bathed the room with sad, sweet melodies. Skeptically Claude watched the mannered quadrilles, the ladies alluring the men, the gossip and the passing of billets-doux. He witnessed excesses of food and drink; the flirting and suggestive whispers made him blush.

At the cotillion, the king himself danced. Younger than Claude, Louis cut a fine, manly figure, his dark, knowing gaze looking deeply into the ladies' eyes, his luxuriant black curls falling upon the gold satin of his coat.

With athletic skill, he pirouetted, spun, and vaulted. His impeccable grace displayed a masculine vigor that set ladies whispering behind their fans. His eyes fired with the exercise. And when the piece was finished, he bowed to their polite applause and left for the Royal Apartments. Claude tried not to imagine the revelry that would ensue.

The next morning, he was summoned to hear confessions in a side room of the Queen's apartment so that the entire court might receive communion at an afternoon Mass celebrating the Blessed Virgin's bodily assumption into heaven.

Claude spent the morning absolving petty nobles of their petty sins: gluttony, sloth, calumny, drunkenness, lust—sins of commission; sins of omission—missing Mass, long absences from the Blessed Sacrament, failure to fast or to do proper penance. Though used to the sins of the wealthy, Claude despised the attitude of the court: their sorrow, their longing for forgiveness, their contrition were all so insincere! He balked at granting absolution. And each time he whispered, "Go and sin no more," his cynicism disrobed the nobles of their pomp and strutting airs, and he saw them as weak-willed creatures, their souls sluggish, sleeping.

Despite the general order for a fast to be maintained, a servant brought Père Claude a luncheon of trout and mayonnaise and a glass of dry white wine.

"A fast is to be maintained until Mass this evening," he protested.

"This is merely hors d'oeuvre, Père."

"Are others breaking fast at this time?"

"The rigors of prayer and penance do take their toll,

Père. A luncheon prevents unseemly fainting during the service."

"Take this away," the priest said curtly.

The next penitent was a woman in a gown of red silk brocade. She wore a black veil over her face, and her golden hair had been piled in braided twists, one hank falling gracefully upon her shoulder. As Père Claude drew in her sweet perfume, an involuntary shudder passed through him.

She knelt, made the sign of the cross, and said in a bold voice, "Bless me, Father, for I have sinned grievously in thought, word, and deed. My sins are so numerous I cannot count them, and as is customary to a woman of my station, I will commit them willingly again and again. Yet, I wish to be forgiven today, for the Assumption was a feast celebrated by my mother, and I wish to keep holy her memory."

"I assume your sins are sins of the flesh?"

"Yes, Père. I am a courtesan and at the whim of the king and his ministers."

"Do you take pleasure in such things?"

"Yes, Père. I do." She spoke slowly, but with courage. "Afterward, I feel calm, purified. My conscience bothers me on no account. I am often at a loss to explain why such pleasure is outlawed. Yet, of course, I bow to the will of the Church in spiritual matters."

"Please describe these revels so I may see the depth of your sinning." Père Claude closed his eyes to hear the woman. By articulating her sins, she would suffer the shame of them and so aspire to contrition. He could tolerate her lurid descriptions of lust only by knowing it was forgiveness she truly sought.

"Very well, Père." The woman bowed her head. "The king is much enamored with the female parts. When we are called to the revels, ladies-in-waiting adorn our bellies and thighs with all manner of lingerie to draw attention to our lower regions. Indeed, some courtesans shave there; others fasten golden rings into their lips; others draw nightingales or flowers upon their thighs. This pleases the king very much, and he sends us many gifts of jewels and gowns."

Claude felt uncomfortable hearing her soft whisper, smelling her perfume. He longed to see her face, yet was oddly pleased she had worn the veil.

"The king is exceedingly virile—able in a night to have

seven women for himself alone. He devises games of dalliance that increase pleasure, that divert attention from mere copulation into other acts."

"Have you ever lain with the King?"

"Oh yes, Père. Many times."

"And do you afterward seek to confess and return to a state of grace?"

The courtesan was silent. Then she whispered, "No, Père." She paused for a long moment. "Only once have I felt disgust and remorse, once when the king ordered me to copulate with a hunchbacked dwarf. All other times I have enjoyed the pleasures, looked forward to them."

"The way you have chosen to live your life gravely displeases the Lord," Père Claude said. "Confession is a way to purge your sins upon occasion, but an effort to change your life must accompany any sincere desire for forgiveness."

"And yet, Père," she pleaded, "it is said a Jesuit is first a man and secondly a priest." She touched his thigh with her hand, and the shock it produced caused her to laugh. She clasped his thigh more strongly. Père Claude groaned, reached down, and with a trembling hand, peeled her fingers, one by one, off his cassock.

"Your sin has so polluted your soul that you now entice others and tempt them to damnation."

"No, Père, I only ask for compassion, for understanding," she pleaded quietly. "I am contrite, but I cannot promise to reform." She slowly lifted her veil.

In horror Claude gasped. He clutched the arms of his chair, his eyes bulged. The room pitched about him like a ship upon a stormy sea. He attempted to emit a scream, but like a man drowning, his voice faltered.

"I have been called beautiful by many men," she said, scowling.

"I...I...," Père Claude stammered to speak, emotion strangling his words.

"Please, Père, if I have distressed you so, I am sorry, so very sorry."

His knuckles whitened, his throat clogged. Looking up at him was the very face he had long prayed to in his visions of the Blessed Virgin. The face was indeed very beautiful. Clear, wide blue eyes innocently gazed at him; her full lips, pale and chaste, appeared so pure they couldn't utter words to describe such deeds as she had in truth performed. Every feature was the same as he had lingered upon in his midnight reveries of the Virgin. "Who . . . who are you?" he gasped.

"I am called Diana." She frowned, trying to understand.

"No, no," Père Claude said impatiently, perceiving a mystery of enormous proportion. "Who were you before?"

"Why . . . why . . . ?" she stammered. The question invaded her privacy.

"Monique," Claude whispered hoarsely, pointing his finger. "Monique de Biencourt."

Now the woman expressed disbelief. Her eyes started out, and she clutched her throat. "Who are you?"

Père Claude closed his eyes, leaned his head back upon the chair and swallowed. Like the hot wind from a burning city, his thoughts rushed over him, and he remembered odd snatches of conversation, old vistas, small insignificant scenarios, and his mind ached, his soul cried out.

"I am Claude Chauchetière," he whispered, his tongue thick and sluggish.

"I do not know you!" she protested. "I have known many men, but not you!"

"No," he groaned, "you don't remember. You wouldn't." Sick with shame, he covered his face, then he looked down upon the eyes and the lips so very familiar to him. "I met you in the salon of Madame Madeline de Gallieres. Her daughter Henriette was being presented to society that summer. I made an advance, and you cut me with a vicious insult. You said, 'I never speak to rubes who dance like swine.'"

Flustered and speechless, Diana allowed the veil to drop.

"You attracted everyone's eye with your beauty, wit, your handsome fortune, but I was merely a provincial in ill-fitting clothes. And now!" He groaned.

"Shall we continue?" the woman said sarcastically. "Or will you withhold forgiveness?"

"Did you marry?"

"Of course I married!" She grew impatient. "I married well. I bore three sons. I lay awake at night. I carried on affairs of the heart with silly youths, and then I was caught, turned out, dis-possessed. Such is the merciful treatment male hypocrites dole out." Her voice swelled with anger. "And this, this is how I avenge myself."

Haughtily, Diana pushed herself to her feet, collected her skirts about her, and left the room. And Claude lay his head back upon the chair, open-eyed, speechless.

STRUGGLES FOR MASTERY

*New France
Winter 1663—64*

1

She watched green and blue and red needles of light in the skies of winter nights, and she imagined that battles far in the north had sent up such gleamings, battles between Kryn and the hated French for sway over the entire world. Her life was drudgery—fetching wood and water, curing and combing hides, tending the pot of sagamite, and minding toddlers who both cheered and disrupted the longhouse with their play.

Tekakwitha, now in her eighth year, wished the war to be over, wished with every fiber, and in her naiveté, encouraged by White Adder's superstitions, she believed her wish could aid Kryn's victorious return. She wandered in the crystalline woods, trees cracking with cold, and she marveled how dead and frigid nature had grown. It seemed her own life, her expectations, her joys were likewise frozen into impassivity, but her will strained, and she longed for a task to busy herself. Yet the days shortened, the wind blew deadly cold from the north, and snow fell and accumulated in drifts higher than the palisade.

Far to the north in sparse shelter on an island upon a frozen lake, another Canienga was even more impatient—not that the war would be over, but that it would begin. Soon after reaching the island, a usual meeting place for war parties from the central and two eastern nations of the Iroquois League, warriors from the Wolf and Bear clans joined him. Then messengers on snowshoes from the Oneida and the Onondaga reached Kryn. "Wait," they told him, "our chiefs have decided to accompany you on your brave raid." And Kryn waited. For days Kryn waited. For weeks Kryn waited. His warriors, their blood hot to attack, soon grew impatient, then bitter, then cynical, muttering that the attack would not take place at all.

Next, the Scarred One, war chief of the Oneida, arrived

with eighty-two warriors. His men, also anxious for battle, progressed through the same frames of mind as had Kryn's warriors. "Wait," new messengers told both chiefs, "the Onondaga will come."

Finally, Garacontie, aged chief of the Onondaga, was seen on dogsled, crossing the breast of the frozen lake. With him he brought a hundred and twenty-three warriors.

"As our numbers grow stronger," Kryn observed sardonically to Arosen, "our spirit wanes."

By virtue of his age, Garacontie called a council and the chiefs voted two to one to delay the attack until spring. To uphold the democratic spirit of the League's negotiations, Kryn agreed to wait, and his stern expression never hinted of the impatience within. The chiefs' argument was sound: The Cayuga and the Seneca, the League's two western nations were at that time plodding over the frozen wastes of Lake Ontario and in springtime would come down the swift St. Lawrence River while the three eastern nations fell upon the French forts on the Richelieu River below Lake Champlain. Together, the five nations could then swoop down in a planned attack upon Montreal, Three Rivers, and Quebec, massacring and burning those cities of stone and driving the French forever from their land.

Yet Kryn saw his expedition losing its element of surprise—a key element in Iroquois attacks when they were outnumbered five to one. With pride and the arrogance of many victories, Garacontie assured the Scarred One and Kryn that the League's courage and ferocity would conquer all, even if the whites were forewarned. Privately Kryn remarked, "I don't need *could* and *would* and *should*; I need action!" Reluctantly he bowed to the will of the other chiefs, and he watched ruefully as his warriors, apart from their women, far from their supplies of corn, relying upon the hunt for food, eventually lost all interest in the attack.

2

Early in March 1664, before the ice broke and the waters flowed, two French bushrangers captured a Mohegan in the forests along the St. Lawrence. The Mohegan had been hunting. As the two Frenchmen escorted their prize toward Montreal, a band of friendly Algonquins joined in. They spoke with the Mohegan, silent until then, and the information they extracted sent a shudder through all of New France—six to seven hundred Iroquois were poised to attack at the first thaw.

Not since the Iroquois obliterated the great Huron nation fourteen years before had such a war party been amassed. Tales were told in the streets, in the trading posts, after mass on the steps of Quebec's cathedral. Huron eyewitnesses stepped forward to offer accounts of Iroquois butchery that succeeded in fanning the flames of panic. Barriers went up, walls were strengthened, escape routes planned, seminaries and cloisters fortified. Chivalrously the Jesuits of Quebec left their strong stone house, and the Ursuline nuns and the nuns of the Hôtel Dieu, the Hospital of God, moved in.

Sharpened barricades, cannon, stone walls—every conceivable means of defense was employed. And with lips whispering prayers, fingers counting rosary beads, the three French cities waited. They waited through days expecting evening attacks; they waited through evenings expecting night attacks; and they waited through long dark nights expecting dawn attacks. A week, then two, then three and four passed. No Iroquois came. Had the Mohegan lied? Unlikely, since two Algonquins were later captured, and during torture, they confirmed the Mohegan's story. Maddeningly the bishop, the governor, the priests and nuns and brothers, the merchants, the tradesmen, the craftsmen, and the farmers all waited for the fatal blow. The river thawed, the birds returned, buds appeared on the trees, but still no Iroquois attacked.

The answer, unlikely—no, incredible—slowly came to light. At Montreal, a young Frenchman, Adam Daulac, acting in the highest tradition of chivalry, recruited a band of sixteen men—locksmiths, limeburners, farmers, soldiers. They attended Mass the morning of the equinox, March 21st, commending their souls into the hands of the Lord, and they received the sacraments in the small stone chapel for the last time. As the ciborium and chalice went from man to man and the body and blood of Christ were placed upon each tongue, the men pledged to fight until death. The transubstantiated bread and wine gave them courage and sealed their destiny. After Mass, each wrote his will and filed it with the notary public. In the spirit of medieval chivalry, they armed themselves, fortified their canoes with ammunition and food, and embarked from the shore of cheering townspeople. Daulac's plan was that instead of awaiting the attack, his small band would ambush the Seneca and Cayuga as their flotillas came down the river toward Montreal.

The small band battled the raging spring river upstream for ten days. At last they reached Long Sault, a full mile of ragged falls, and where the white water paused in a hollowed bay, they beached their canoes and took possession of a ruined fort hastily built by an Algonquin hunting party years before. Three days later, the small party of whites was joined by four Christian Algonquins and forty Christian Hurons who'd learned of the expedition at Montreal and set out to avenge themselves upon the Iroquois. Together the men, white and red, slung their kettles and offered prayers to the Christian god in three different tongues.

A week later, scouts excitedly announced Iroquois canoes. Daulac ordered the breastworks readied, and trees were felled, stones rolled together, earth heaped up. Now Daulac, his blond hair flashing in the spring sun, ordered his men to ready for the ambush, and he set four musketeers in the brush where the canoes would land.

Down the foaming river came the first gray elm-bark canoe, steered by skilled hands, leaping and plunging. The canoe entered the calm pool, and the five warriors landed. Immediately four shots rang out. The surprised Iroquois dived into the canoe for their weapons and were shot. One escaped upriver and he ran through the underbrush to warn the others.

"Now they'll lay a full siege," Daulac observed laconically. He and his men continued to improve their crude fort with limbs and stone and mud. The roar of the impatient water filled their ears as they worked, weapons loaded, waiting for the advance. Soon, above the thundering of the swollen river, a scream went up, followed by a chorus of war whoops. The noise sent panic shivering through the small band. His blood hot for battle, Daulac made the sign of the cross and led his men, their faces twitching, eyes glancing upriver, in the Ave Maria and the Pater Noster. Down the white water came canoes of elm and birch bark. Five canoes of fierce savages, faces painted hideous blues and whites and greens, eyes keenly scanning boulders, brawny arms working paddles, entered the pool where their brothers had been shot. Despite more musket fire, all landed.

"Ave Maria, gratia plena..." murmured the French, cocking the flintlocks of their arquebuses.

Suddenly, the thirty screaming Iroquois came running, brandishing guns and tomahawks. Daulac cried hoarsely, "Do not fire till they are upon us!" Men twitched, lying on the packed earth, lips trembling with prayer. Then Daulac cried "Fire!" The arquebuses spoke. Half the attacking band fell. The rest still advanced. While the French reloaded, the Algonquins and Hurons aimed carefully with their bows and sent four more down. One massive Iroquois caught an arrow in the shoulder, and he ripped it out and hurled it at the fort. Again the men aimed and fired, and eight Iroquois dropped. The remaining finally stopped, turned, and ran back toward the river.

"They will bring the entire force upon us now," Daulac observed. "Let us further strengthen our wall and so further strengthen our hearts." At his direction, the men sunk a ring of poles within the outer wall, and filled this intervening space with stones to the height of a man. They left twenty loopholes, each to be manned by three guns and bows so a constant volley of fire would pour out in all directions from the circular fort. They hadn't quite finished when piercing, furious screams went up once more.

On came the Iroquois in long furs, crouching from tree to tree. Many brandished torches of blazing birchbark, bark they had ripped from French canoes. Some ran into the clearing to burn the palisade but such a steady fire met them, they recoiled and gave way.

"We will hold them, mon ami!" cried a freeholder to Daulac, raising his musket. "We will!"

"They are regrouping," Daulac observed with no emotion.

On again they came, shrill cries drowning the roar of the cascade; yet the drunkenness of battle filled the French with elation. Calling to each other, they fired in quick succession. Again the Iroquois were driven back.

"We have shot their chief!" Daulac cried, peering out from between the palisades. "Let us show them we'll accept no quarter." He and two others scaled the wall, cautiously advanced to the battleground and dragged the corpse of the Seneca chief inside.

"What will you do with it?" asked a young soldier.

"Offer its eyes to the birds," Daulac said. With a hatchet he hacked off the chief's head. Three men threw the body back over the palisade wall. Sitting on another's shoulder, Daulac impaled the bleeding head upon the highest pike of the fort.

A howl of rage went up from the Iroquois. Immediately Leaping Salmon sent three runners overland toward the Lake of the Gar-Pike. "Summon Kryn," he instructed. "Convince Garacontie to forsake the campaign downriver. Instead, they must portage their canoes overland, then embark down a creek that feeds this river, and so join us in this fight. We shall teach the white man of the Iroquois' wrath." Now building a fort of their own, Leaping Salmon's warriors shook rattles and beat skin drums to summon Aireskou. They did not attack again that day. As night fell, their fires burned angrily in the forest, and the waterfall thundered restlessly.

For four days Seneca and Cayuga warriors harried the Christians who chanted prayers while discharging their guns. Constantly the Iroquois taunted Christian Hurons to desert the whites, calling: "Come out, brothers, and you too will feast upon the white man's flesh when we overrun his ramparts. Three hundred warriors led by Garacontie and Kryn will soon arrive. They have taken three forts upon the salmon river. The whites in their stone cities cannot withstand our onslaught." But the Christian Indians did not go over.

Within the fort, hunger and thirst afflicted the small band. With no water, they choked and retched on their provisions of parched cornmeal. Three times a daring soldier braved Iroquois muskets to run to the river and fill a waterskin, but shared around, this water only tantalized their thirst. Daulac dug a hole in the center of the fort, and the men greedily sipped the muddy water seeping through clay.

Days passed. They caught rain one night in their hats, but it did little to ease their thirst.

"They refuse to attack," his men groaned. "They have summoned reinforcements, and they laugh at us starving here."

"Come out, come out," the Iroquois taunted. Starving, reeling with thirst, some of the Hurons deserted. Daulac himself could not refrain from shooting at the deserters as they ran for the forest.

Meanwhile, Kryn had arrived with reinforcements. He

sat with the chiefs. "We have waited through the winter, and this wait has cost us the campaign against the stone cities. We can wait a few more days." The others agreed.

In a delirium of thirst and hunger and fatigue, the seventeen whites and twenty-eight red men waited inside the fort through blustery April days and endless windy nights. "When will they attack?" the men demanded of each other. "Those demons laugh us to scorn."

"You are women!" Daulac screamed at the Iroquois. "Your chief's head grins at you from the pole, and you sit at your fires letting hunger perform your murder." Yet for days no taunt had effect.

Finally, at dawn upon the seventh morning after Kryn's reinforcements arrived, a blood-chilling scream rose from seven hundred throats. "The others have come," Daulac observed sardonically. "Let us make ourselves ready to die." And he and his men knelt on the trampled earth and offered prayers for salvation.

The battle began. Daulac's blond mane was everywhere as he encouraged his men. "By the oaths we swore to the virgin," he cried, running from loophole to loophole, "we will win our martyrdom today!" Grimly the men bit their cracked lips. Some knelt and prayed. "My friends, the battle will soon be over!" Daulac yelled, his musket to the sky. "Let His will be done!" Tears of emotion rolled down his shaggy cheek. For days they had chewed their leather clothes for sustenance and had sipped their own urine to moisten their parched throats. Dizzy with fatigue, they now braced themselves at the loopholes, awaiting the onslaught of all five nations.

The deserting Hurons were brought to Kryn, Garacontie, Leaping Salmon, and Scarred One to describe the inside of the fort. "We shall surround them," said Kryn, drawing in the dirt, "as the rising water surrounds the island and drowns it in the river. Let us be bold"—he looked up to the other chiefs—"but also cautious."

At a signal, the warriors ranged themselves through the forest. Cautiously they advanced, firing, jumping from side to side, using trees for cover. In the center, tongues of flame licked from every loophole of the wood and stone circle. Busily Daulac and his men filled their large muskets with stones and metal scraps to take down two and three Iroquois at a shot.

Slowly, steadily, the warriors advanced, falling in the

gunsmoke as if in a dream, screams of pain and rage erupting, the prayers of Daulac and his men rising above the din. Then miraculously, with the Iroquois fifty yards from the perimeter of his fort, Daulac's persistence won. The Iroquois broke and ran.

For three more days only the crackling of skirmish fire sounded against the roar of the falls. Within the fort, the French prayed with split lips and swollen tongues that their martyrdom be speedy. Kryn held council with the other chiefs around a fire. A stiff, changing wind blew smoke as it left their pipes.

"Let us leave these whites here," said the Scarred One, "and finish our campaign in the lower valley." The wrangling and smoking had filled many hours, patient, well-considered hours, while the French starved.

"We will lose all honor," said Leaping Salmon. "Elk Horn's head grins at us still from the pole where birds have stripped it."

"I cast my lot with Leaping Salmon," said Kryn. "An army advances from victory to victory and leaves nothing behind standing."

"What do you propose?" asked the Scarred One of Garacontie.

"The strength of our League is in its unity," the old chief said, interlocking his withered fingers. "We must avenge Elk Horn."

"We shall propose to our warriors that they draw lots and those winning shall advance on the front line." Kryn squinted through the forest to the fort. The French were saving what powder they had left. "Let us prepare shields and torches, and let nothing be left undone."

Industriously, the determined Iroquois split logs and lashed them into large shields. They twisted torches of bark together and smeared them with pine pitch. Then at dawn of the fourth morning, this army attacked slowly from all sides.

Fire spat from each loophole at the advancing hordes that swam in hideous array before their eyes. "They are coming!" a weary scout called, his voice cracking. The ragged, weakened soldiers, eyes red, lips blistered, sleepwalked to their stations. "Courage!" Daulac cried, possessed. "We win our martyrdom today!"

As the screaming red men reached the wall, Daulac crammed a large gun with powder, plugged the muzzle, lit a fuse, then hurled the grenade high to land in the swarm of Iroquois. But it hit the top of a pole and fell back into their midst, killing two whites and crippling another. The din of screaming was soon joined by the sound of hatchets chopping at the base of the palisade, and smoke rolled up as the Iroquois touched fire to the logs. In the confusion of the exploding grenade, Kryn and his Canienga took six loopholes and thrust their guns in, firing upon the fort.

Crouching low, Daulac screamed, "Stand your ground! Hold them to the very last!" With a battering ram, the Onondaga made a breach in the burning palisade. Screaming, wielding tomahawks and war clubs, they swarmed in, murdering the French they met. The Oneida, Cayuga, Seneca, and Canienga swarmed over the wall, hastily slitting throats and scalping the French and Algonquins. Reverently the Seneca took down the skull of their chief Elk Horn, picked clean by carrion birds.

Still four French, armed now with only knives and swords, attacked the Iroquois, and despairing of taking live captives, the Iroquois shot them dead. A cry of defiance and victory rumbled in hundreds of throats, then burst like a wind of fire into the air. Defiantly they danced, their blood hot, and birds of prey watched from the shadow of the forest. Searching the pile of tangled corpses, the Iroquois found two whites still breathing. Hastily they built fires and roasted the men in cannibal offering to Aireskou. And ruefully Kryn folded his arms, set his jaw, and watched the victory fires burn far into the night. So few had held off so many for so long. Why continue his campaign against the stone cities?

3

She had pleaded for the fine elk skin. It came from a buck so noble that its antlers were taken to make a new ceremonial headdress for Iowerano. Fine long hair, golden as sun streaming through rain clouds, tufted with white markings— the finely-dressed hide would have fetched a fair price in the lowlands among the whites.

In the communal sharing of property, no one begrudged

Tekakwitha the skin, yet many wondered what use she'd put it to. "I wish to work embroidery," she answered. "I will make a robe." This allayed further questions. On the cured side of the skin, Tekakwitha sewed with new skill, patterns never seen by the Canienga. She sewed with the inner eye gained during her visit to Beverwyck with Kryn that previous autumn, and she cured the sinew and the porcupine quill with new tinctures to bring even more stunning colors to the robe. She worked on it on a small island upriver from Kanawaka, and each evening she stowed the hide in a hollow trunk so no one might find it.

"Where do you venture, Pouter?" asked Tonedetta each morning.

"I go into the forest," the girl said. "I lay snares for rabbits, yet they are too wily and elude me."

"You lie. You visit Quorenta, the mad woman," her foster mother said.

"Oh no, Aunt, that is so far away—nearly a day's walk. Perhaps today I shall catch game to brighten our kettle tonight."

One morning, Linawato asked if she might accompany her cousin. Tonedetta ordered Tekakwitha to take her along, and sullenly Tekakwitha led the younger girl out of the palisade.

"Where shall we go?" asked Linawato.

"Where do you wish? I will not show you my special place."

"You have a special place?" Linawato asked. "Where is it?"

Tekakwitha changed the subject. "Let us try to catch a hare." The two girls, bundled in long buckskin skirts and high leggings and jackets with hoods of wolf hide, sat on a stump in the snowy cornfield. "I wish to do nothing special today," Tekakwitha complained. "Why did you want to accompany me?"

"My sister, Piping Thrush, has begun the bleeding, and my other sisters have helped in building the hut. I wanted to ask you about Quorenta, the old hag who visits during the rites. What secrets does she tell?"

"She is not a hag." Tekakwitha folded her arms and scowled upriver toward her island. She looked downriver and saw a fishing party on the ice, boys laughing. "All the men have gone to war," she observed.

"And what has this to do with Quorenta?"

Tekakwitha frowned. "Quorenta comforts the cramps that seize a woman's vitals when the blood loosens. She chants spells and administers herbs. She feeds them in that hour when they are disgraced and sent from the camps of men. She is a true friend."

"Let us go and find her. You know her well. My sister, Piping Thrush, shall need her soon."

Tekakwitha kicked the snow with her snowshoe. "You know so very little."

"Yes?"

"Yes. Quorenta will find your sister. She has the magic for such things, even as White Adder locates water with a wand. We are but girls still. We cannot meddle in such things." Disgustedly she turned away.

"What then shall we do?"

"You go back to the longhouse and tend to your sick uncle."

"He is better. White Adder cured him by flailing the skin from his arms and by sucking and spitting blood from his neck."

"Then go help the women prepare the hut for your sister."

Linawato hung her head. "I am too young. No, Tekakwitha, take me where you go each day, for it gives you such great peace that you smile inwardly and sometimes you sing when you return. Do you visit Quorenta?"

"No!" Tekakwitha said impatiently. She scowled at her cousin, then considered with a set lip. "Very well, I shall show you, but you must tell no one." Linawato beamed.

Tekakwitha took her cousin by the hand, and they threaded up the frozen course of the river, across the windswept ice above the falls to the island—a clump of barren trees shivering under the lash of the north wind. Tekakwitha led Linawato up a sharp escarpment of shale, then down to a sheltered dell where pine trees grew plentifully.

"It is here I come," she said.

"It is indeed a beautiful place," Linawato said, looking about. "Why do you never bring your cousins with you away from the village where we can play?"

"My cousins?" Tekakwitha asked in surprise. "All of them but you mock me. I enjoy the wind by myself."

"And what do you do? Scan the clouds for shapes?"

"I work." Tekakwitha pulled back her hood to display

braids plaited with shell and colored porcupine quills. She pulled the quills from her hair and squinted at her cousin. "You must tell no one! No one!" She held the quills in the other girl's face, and Linawato, bewildered, asked, "What do you do with those?"

"You must tell no one," Tekakwitha said more intently. "Do you promise?"

"I promise," the other said hesitantly.

"Do you promise upon the common grave at Ossernenon?"

"I promise," said the girl more firmly, her curiosity winning.

"If you ever tell, I shall show I am Canienga," Tekakwitha threatened.

"I will never tell."

"Follow me, then." The girl led the way to the wall of the defile. A large fallen log lay nearby, and she pulled out leaves and stones, then reached in the entire length of her arm and pulled out the elk skin. Carefully, smoothing it tenderly, she spread it across her lap. The softness of the fur soothed her, and she seemed to forget the other's presence.

"What is that?"

Tekakwitha looked up. "It is a robe."

"I can see that. But why do you not bring the robe into the village and sew it among the other women who talk of village matters while they work and keep informed? Why do you hide it here?"

To answer, Tekakwitha turned the robe over, and the cousin gasped in awe when she saw the embroidered patterns. "What are those?"

"These are patterns I have carried within and have now sewn into the robe."

"I have never seen their like among our people! They start out of the skin! They live! The deer run! The men paddle! The birds fly! Where did you learn such embroidery?"

"In the fortress of the white man. They have wondrous machines that weave *okies* into cloth. I sew all day in this manner for it gives me great pleasure."

"Here, Tekakwitha, a deer eats the grass! It is so real!"

"No, Linawato," Tekakwitha fell silent, and stroked with her thumb the texture of the embroidered picture. She spoke quietly, almost to herself. "The doe nibbles wintergreen, and within explodes the mint. Startled, she raises her head, chewing the cool mint while new sunlight bursts upon the brook."

"I have never heard that fable."

"It is not a fable," Tekakwitha replied impatiently. Needing to explain annoyed her.

"And this one?"

Tekakwitha smiled, for it was her favorite. "Yes, this one was conjured by thinking of Quorenta. About it I say: In the mushroom night where rats scurry, the damp gleams in lazy moonlight. And the owl, watcher always wakeful, flexes a single talon."

"Nor have I heard that one. Where have you gained such wondrous fables? From White Adder?"

"I did not gain these from White Adder. I have thought long while working them into the skin. I wish the robe to be beautiful."

"It is," said Linawato. "And this?"

Gently, Tekakwitha stroked the next picture, as if its texture communicated through her fingertips. "Salmon, long and sleek, leap and plunge and race and leap still higher; their broad heads know but one direction—up. Furious, lashing, they strain higher in the naked sun toward the spawning. After, the banks lie strewn with wet, naked corpses, a feast for flies and maggots."

"You must bring this into the village!" Linawato said. "You have composed oratory for each picture. It would greatly please your uncle to see this and to hear you speak."

"No!" Tekakwitha said firmly.

"But you must! Iowerano would be pleased to own such a robe!"

Tekakwitha snatched it from the other's hand. "It is not for him!"

"And who is it for? You still are too young to take a husband. Yet why else do you work so very hard?"

"Look then at these women in the field while the longhouse speaks its night wisdom." Tekakwitha motioned to another scene, ignoring the question. "About it I say: Women cry and groan at night; they grind their teeth in pain. But they giggle together as they plant the maize. And seed husks break to a warm sun. And men, fishing, fall silent upon the cold stream."

"And what explanation is that?" Linawato asked. "Who is this for?"

"I was mistaken to bring you here," Tekakwitha said in anger. "You do not see through my eyes. You cannot. I have worked alone upon this robe but for one purpose."

"Your riddles darken more than they light, Tekakwitha. I see no enjoyment in working alone on this island with no one near. I enjoy the mortar grinding, the women talking of affairs of the village, for then I feel welcome and more than a child. I do not understand all this."

"Perhaps this picture will explain." Tekakwitha displayed yet another. "With hatchet buried in the war post, men grow bold and dance the pantomime. They howl war songs and fall upon their shadows with clubs and hatchets. But in the forest lie the bones of two brave stags, antlers locked, gleaming, barren, white." She looked into the other's eye. "Do you understand now?"

"No. Why do you hide so many things from common sight?"

"You must seal your lips. If you tell, then I will cast a spell with Quorenta, and White Adder shall be your first husband."

"I promise."

"It is a present, a victory robe I have sewn."

"But you have no brave on the expedition."

Tekakwitha buried her face in the fragrant skin, and with pleasure she stroked her cheek with the long fur. "I have sewn it for the greatest chief of the Canienga, for Kryn. He will lead our men to rid the land of the cursed whites who infect us, who bring their liquor, who ridicule our beliefs, our tales, our customs, who rape our women and cheat our trappers. Kryn will conquer. And when he returns, this will be his victory robe."

"You wish to marry Kryn?" Linawato asked in disbe-lief.

"He is the best of men, even though half white," Tekakwitha replied dreamily. "He hardly knows me, yet I know he will be the savior of the Canienga for he sees things others don't."

"You are silly to think he will pay you attention with Karitha by his side," Linawato scoffed.

"Admiration and respect do not wish to grasp and hold," Tekakwitha answered, stowing the robe once again into the hollow trunk. After again pledging Linawato to secrecy, she led her from the dell.

4

Kanawaka bustled with news of Kryn's return. Women plaited their hair with wampum shells and baked corn cakes in the ash under hearth fires. The finest robes were spread upon the sleeping shelves to welcome the warriors, and anticipation set the women to giggling.

Toward sunset near the Day of the Longest Sun, Kryn's party broke from the forest. Runners had announced their approach, and along the path into the palisade, women and old men and children waited to receive them. Iowerano stepped forward.

"Welcome, brother." He placed his hand upon Kryn's shoulder. "Long and difficult has been your journey into the land of the whites. An Oneida party informed us yesterday of the difficulties you faced. With your fate is the fate of the Canienga tied, and we grieve that the expedition, so grand in aim, did not succeed. Yet soon will the council fire burn at Onondaga. Soon will the fifty sachems sit once more to discuss how best to impose the peace of Hiawatha with tomahawk and gun. Let us, therefore, not look behind at the obstacles that blocked our path. Let us look ahead to see what difficulties we shall face and thus be far better prepared to elude them. Welcome, Kryn. Let us eat quietly this evening, and retire to our beds."

"Iowerano speaks well," Kryn said. "It is wise not to turn backward and waste precious daylight in examining hardships passed. It is wise to learn again the pleasure of our wives, to bounce upon our laps the children who have grown so since last we saw them. It is wise to rest, Iowerano. Yet, I made a pact with the one-legged man among the Dutch, so tomorrow I shall journey to the fort where pelts are traded, and I shall sit again in council."

The two chiefs embraced, and with much joy the women, till then craning to spy their mates, pressed forward. Loud were the welcomes and the laughter of their reunion.

Loud, too, was the bereaved wailing of women who had lost their husbands, who collected their children and returned sadly home.

Stunned by the defeat she never foresaw, Tekakwitha sought a quiet corner of the new cornfield, and she lay upon the ground among rustling stalks in the warm summer night and looked up at the stars. Kryn's demeanor unsettled her. The future of her people was terribly uncertain. She was partly to blame, she told herself. When the river was breaking up and enormous floes jammed and buckled and climbed the banks, she had visited Quorenta to get a potion so the victory robe would assure Kryn's success. Quorenta, cackling that only the strongest magic could help the Canienga now, gave the girl a potion, and Tekakwitha applied it to the embroidered picture of a warrior falling upon a white man. Perhaps Quorenta had prepared the wrong potion, Tekakwitha reasoned, or else she herself had administered it improperly. When spells failed, it was usually due to such oversights. Looking out into the summer sky, the stars fell away into the soft, boundless heavens, and her flesh tingled with anxiety. What would she do with the victory robe, her work of so many months? She stood, brushed soil from her long skirt, and reentered the palisade.

As Tekakwitha passed through the alleys among the longhouses, she heard groans of the dark pleasure within, and she heard laughter, and she heard the soft weeping of widows. She passed before Kryn's longhouse and glanced within. Cross-legged, Kryn sat upon the earthen floor talking with Karitha. In his hands he held the blond scalp of a white man. Tekakwitha moved away. Kryn sensed her presence. "Who stops to peer into my home?" he said playfully. "Come in, little owl, it is dark outside and we have food for you."

Bashfully the girl entered.

"Why it is the one who stitches upon doeskin—the little beauty from Iowerano's house who accompanied us to the settlement of iron-workers. Sit beside me if you wish to hear of the bravest whites we have ever encountered, if you wish to learn a lesson in how pride—not determination, but pride—caused the worthiest expedition to fail." Kryn stroked the golden hair of the scalp. He fixed her with his intense blue eyes. "Why so shy? What wondrous patterns have you sewn lately?"

"Since you left," Tekakwitha said hopefully, with suppressed emotion, "my thoughts have followed your steps through the forests of snow, across the frozen lake, and down the river to the three cities of stone. My thoughts, as if peering into the bubbling spring and seeing reflections, have watched you and other warriors tomahawk whites and burn them in their homes for their arrogant incursions into our land." She peered up into Kryn's kind face. He smiled to dispel her disappointment. "Yet now I find my thoughts took an erring path. I could not foresee the band of whites that ambushed the Seneca and Cayuga."

Playfully, Kryn tugged at her braid, and he winked. "None of us can see into the future with accuracy, little one," he said. "Do not be troubled."

"And yet," Tekakwitha said impatiently, "and yet..."

"Look at this fine scalp," Kryn said. "It once crowned the head of the bravest white ever to fight our people. So crafty, so determined, so courageous was he that he held six hundred warriors at bay for many days."

"I was so certain of your victory!" Tekakwitha protested.

Kryn teased her. "You want bears to sprout wings and take to the air like birds? You want fish to leap and bound like deer over the snow? The future of anything," he said, "can never be certain. Only the past that falls behind us day after day can boast of certainty."

His words hurt her deeply. In vivid detail the images she had sewn upon the elk robe came again into her mind, and she saw now that by sewing such patterns, she had in fact wanted what could not be. She listened then to the story of the battle for the small fort at Long Sault, and late into the night she sat close to Kryn, comforted by his strong voice.

Next day, as Kryn loaded his canoe with pelts of the small animals the women had trapped during the winter, as he put the bundle of scalps into the canoe and loaded his provisions of corn and dried bear bacon, Tekakwitha watched him with a heavy heart, remembering another such journey. Bidding her good-bye, Kryn and Karitha paddled into the current and soon were moving rapidly toward the bend in the river that would hide them from her sight. Watching them go, she felt a keen sense of loss, a new emptiness that brought a sob welling into her throat. Tears came to her eyes, and ashamed at betraying her emotion, she turned away from the river to pick her way up the trail by the waterfall.

The river was much lower now. Removing her clothes in

the shade of lofty pine trees, Tekakwitha waded into the
water, and swam across the stiff current to her island. Reaching
the shore, she pulled herself out among lily pads and ferns
and cautiously stole through the underbrush and over the
rocky ridge to the clump of stunted pine. She removed the
robe from its hollow trunk and spread it under the small
pines, then she lay upon it, allowing the fur and the gentle
summer wind to caress and comfort her. Her flesh tingled.
She felt a sensitivity in her nipples—small and hard—and she
remembered, with the fur soft against her buttocks and
thighs, sitting next to the mighty Kryn, listening to his deep,
manly voice tell of slaughter and courage and the dangers he
had braved.

Then, vowing to accomplish the task she set for herself,
she kindled a fire in the pine needles, and slowly, gaining
much peace of mind, she burned the victory robe.

5

Some of the warriors, late in returning from the north,
detoured through the Dutch settlement Corlaer. Some had
pelts to trade from hunting. One had a French powder horn
of fine workmanship from the imperial army of Louis XIV.
Many had silver and gold coins they had rifled from the
pockets of the white soldiers. Parading through the cluster of
thatched huts and barns, these bronze-colored warriors, still
painted hideously, drew much attention from the plump
burghers and vrouws.

An enterprising gentleman approached them cautiously,
showing deference to their muskets and war clubs and hatchets. "Does the chief have anything with which we may make
a trade?" The fierce grin he received from the tall warrior did
little to reassure him, but he pulled a watch from his pocket.
He held the watch of finely-worked gold in front of the
warrior's eye. Gingerly he touched the warrior's hand and
said, "Come with me."

It was evening, and under the oaks that stood before the
small thatched homes, wives and daughters were milking
cows. The warriors followed the gentleman to his home, and

he opened a cask of gin to make the bargaining more enjoyable. Late that night, the good vrouws tightly locked both the top and bottom panels of their doors. They banked the fire, checked on the children, then huddled in sleeping closets, trying to ignore the piercing shrieks and howls of the drunken Canienga. By morning the traders had everything of worth the Indians carried except their weapons, and the small band of warriors left the settlement, each man in his canoe with a cask of gin.

Great praise was heaped upon these noble fellows when they unloaded their cargo at Kanawaka. The defeat caused the men to ignore the laws of the council. Those not happy with the gin said nothing against it. Even Iowerano helped carry the casks up the path from the river. With hoots and howls of joy the men broke into the casks and drank gin from gourd cups as quickly as water. By midafternoon the women, too, drank with violent thirsts. Mad glee and hilarity reigned.

Men and women stumbled through the streets, falling down on the ground like wounded animals, laughing uncontrollably. Squeals of delight filled the cornfields where the men chased the women, then caught, undressed, and mounted them. Without regard to *ohwachira* or matrimony, warriors fornicated with the drunken, laughing women, then with lust abated, returned to the gin casks. By nightfall, no kettles had been slung, no food prepared. Some dried eel was passed around to chew. Crying children were sent into the fields to pick roots and berries. Still the orgy raged. Young girls barely past puberty, displayed themselves wantonly, calling lewd words to the men, then screamed like panthers when mounted. As the soft wind swelled with rain clouds, the cries grew louder, less happy, more desperate and demanding. Then the last cask was opened, quickly drunk, then smashed with a war club.

Now the tone of the gathering abruptly changed. Insults filled the air. Women were beaten, clothing torn from their breasts, their buttocks. Grinding their teeth, the drunken weeping women were raped by insatiable warriors. Children screaming in fear and hunger were thrown upon the ground, out of homes. One violent warrior, slapping a woman about the longhouse, kicked the fire, and sparks ignited the dry lashings and the furs of his sleeping shelf. The four other families in various stages of sleep and undress jostled out of the longhouse, now in smoke and flame. The brittle house burned high into the night, spitting sparks, threatening the entire village.

Everywhere men prowled looking for more gin. Some drunken youths paddled back to Corlaer to buy more. Women who'd lost husbands, grief heightened by alcohol, wailed and pulled their hair and ripped their clothing and covered their faces with ashes. Fights erupted between staggering warriors, and tomahawks solved disagreements with blood. Screaming, bleeding men fought over women, while the cowering women screamed for one to murder the other. Guns went off. One happy old man threatened to shoot the moon from the turbulent sky and blew off his hand in the attempt.

Throughout the long night, the failure of the great expedition fanned flames of bitterness and shame in the warriors' hearts and the gin encouraged violence and lust.

"Come here," Iowerano said gruffly, seizing his concubine by the wrist. In the flickering light of the longhouse, groans and grunts and the clasping, clawing hands terrified Tekakwitha. Again she saw the oak tree towering over the path to Quorenta's hut, and she heard screams, horrible screams, and her breath came in gasps as she remembered running that day so long ago, running until she felt she'd faint. Quietly so no one would notice, Tekakwitha rose from her sleeping shelf and went out into the night.

The cool, dark pine forest breathed ever so softly. The carpet and the canopy of the forest were alive with small night creatures, and a moon through the tall pines cast a calming light while storm clouds built and obscured it now and then. Where was Kryn? Kryn was gone. Flames leapt higher from the burning longhouse, casting weird shadows of men and dogs and women around the palisade. The path to the old woman's house—where was Kryn? The memory, so ancient, so buried, yet grizzly, terrifying, caused her to gulp for air. Kryn! She gasped and clutched her throat. Where was Kryn?

6

Kryn declined the pipe. He folded his arms and stared ahead. Smoke hung lazily in the room as the burghers pondered the ramifications of the battle of Long Sault. Impatiently, Van Slictenhorst snapped off a piece of the stem, stuck the pipe in his mouth, and lit it himself.

"Governor Stuyvesant will be very displeased," he said to Kryn. "A mere twenty scalps. The whole League of the Longhouse held at bay by fifty men." He shook his head. "With each ship entering the harbor of New Amsterdam, we hear outrages of the French in our homeland. Their legions and their Jesuits undo us at home, in the West Indies, and here. Already they cheat us out of furs by debauching the tribes with brandy. We must check their expansion down through the northern lakes."

"Their warriors are very brave men," Kryn said. "Unlike other whites we have fought, these men would not surrender, even though the odds were so hopeless." He stroked the long, blond scalp of Adam Daulac. "The People of the Longhouse admire such courage, for it is the test of a warrior how he dies. Brave, too, were the blackrobes the French sent to us years ago—courageous, tolerant of the worst pain. Perhaps if the one-legged man had twenty such warriors, he would not require the League of the Great Longhouse to wage his wars."

"And yet, many were the Canienga," Van Slictenhorst said with irony.

"The Canienga do not attack like the whites," Kryn answered. "The Canienga steal through forests like morning fog. Their canoes glide noiselessly over the lake. They strike with lightning speed and retreat into the forest where no white can follow or survive. The whites march with drums and muster troops together for large campaigns. We made a grave mistake: We allowed the thinking of the whites to pollute our strategy."

"What will you do different in the future?" Pieter Schuyler, Mayor of Beverwyck, asked. "We feel the French bushrangers and fur traders are provoking the Mohegans to attack Corlaer soon, then Beverwyck and Esopus this autumn." Van Slictenhorst translated.

"Arm yourselves," Kryn said. "Strengthen your redoubts, train your men not to sow in the fields like women, but to fight and have courage. I am setting out for the Onondaga Council soon. All our nations assemble there, and this summer we shall discuss the invasion of the French cities. I shall insist that the Canienga, Keeper of the Eastern Gate, lead the next invasion. Have you more guns?"

This rather blunt statement caught the patroon's agent off guard. "I . . . I am not sure. I must, I must ask Governor Stuyvesant. He will be greatly angered that so few scalps have been brought back and that as you slunk through the forest in retreat, the French began building a fort at the mouth of the great lake."

Kryn's blue eyes flashed, his naked arms rippled as he rose from the uncomfortable white man's chair. "One-Legged Man, by marrying his purpose to ours, has made one great mistake. He should ship us more weapons of iron—hatchets and guns. It is a marriage now, but it can be put aside if One-Legged Man so wishes. Otherwise, he must remember that he and you are the wives who stay at home and till the field, but the Canienga are the husbands—who hunt, plan strategy, wage war. It is not proper for the wife to tell the husband how to act, for among our people a blow of the tomahawk saves many words."

Kryn turned from the room, leaving the men of Fort Orange, Greenen Bosch, and Beverwyck to huddle in apprehension. Kryn walked out into the fine sunny day, crossed the green where horses and sheep grazed, and he began plotting how to convince Iowerano to agree to an autumn campaign against the French when he sat with the sachems at Onondaga.

He paddled home with Karitha next morning, up the broad, placid surface of the river, then through defiles into the western river, and around waterfalls now quieted by the summer drought, then upon the dark, silent breast of the western river, winking at night with the light of stars.

"Before we journey to Onondaga, we shall fish in the mountains," Kryn told his wife. "I require the peace of catching the sturgeon to put battle screams and the Dutch man's cowardice out of my ears." They pulled the canoe onto the gravel shore where a spring freshet entered the river near Kanawaka. "Lately I have thought often that we should have aligned ourselves with the brave French who go singing to their death and not with the cowardly men of the lower valley. Warriors, not traders, deserve the friendship of the Canienga."

"I hear no one," Karitha said, and her nose, attentive as a doe's, drew in the air. "Some evil *okie* has taken possession here," she said. Together they climbed the hill. Through the cornfields where pumpkin vines were already winding, up to the high stockade with its four bastions, and into the village they passed, but they recognized little of it. Three of the twelve longhouses lay in heaps of ash. Fires burned low for green wood had been gathered, and smoke hung in a pall over the village. Everywhere through the town abject men and women lay groaning, staring in dull disbelief. Children wailed. Young warriors stumbled and fell, retching on the earth. Even the dogs, kicked and whipped during the two-day debauch, sulked in the alleys between the houses. The sharp smell of ash mingled with the stenches of blood and excrement.

"Where is Iowerano?" Kryn demanded of Eagle Talon, a burly warrior now prostrate after his binge.

"I do not know."

"How did this happen?"

Eagle Talon groaned. "We brought the firewater from Corlaer."

"Dutch!" Kryn said with the force of a curse. "Where is Iowerano?"

"I do not know."

"After fighting so poorly in the manner of whites," Kryn said disgustedly, "our brave warriors imitate them and hide their disgrace in liquor, even after liquor is outlawed by the fifty chiefs. Where are all the men?"

"White Adder is drawing the evil *okies* from a boy who was stricken mad," groaned the man.

Kryn hauled Eagle Talon to his feet. "You will go and kindle a fire at the longhouse by our landfall at the foot of the rapids. We will summon all men there, and afterward, the women."

"I will," the warrior said, and holding his head, he moved off toward the river.

Kryn stalked through the village listening for the chanting of White Adder. At last he heard yips and howls of the albino, and he pulled the bear robe of a door aside and stepped into the longhouse. No one noticed Kryn. In the center of the longhouse a boy had been suspended by the ankles. Barely conscious, his arms were roped to stakes driven into the earth. In a dervish dance, White Adder leapt, screaming through the fire, and he whipped the boy with willow branches and applied live coals to his flanks and arms.

"Tawiskaron!" White Adder howled. "Into this boy you have sent an *okie* quick and poisonous as a viper. I spy you, little devil, infecting this boy's dreams, forcing him to talk in your gibberish, to thrash and chew his tongue and roll his eyes far back into his head to watch your evil work. But my magic is stronger! See!" White Adder pulled upon one rawhide rope and from the ground came one of the stakes. Attached to it was the heart of a dog, a glistening brownish red. "And see!" he cried, pulling the other. The liver and kidneys of the dog were attached. Proudly White Adder displayed the gleaming organs to the assembled who sat mystified at the cure. "Out from his body have I flogged and burned the little devil," White Adder bragged, "down the cords and into the earth has he run—"

"Stop!" Kryn called. In surprise, all heads turned. "Cut down the boy!"

"The magic is working!" White Adder glared at the war chief.

"Cut him down, or I will."

"Yet," White Adder said to the crowd, "the war chief is correct. So quickly has my magic worked, we may allow this boy to lie prone and rest." He directed two of the men to cut him down, then he said, "We must burn these organs to destroy the *okies*. Do not touch any with your hands, lest the *okies* pass through your skin and afflict you."

"Hear me! Hear me, all!" Kryn called, extending his arms in front of them. "The only evil *okies* I find in the Turtle Clan of the People of Flint lie in the white man's liquor. I am half white," he said, and thrummed his chest in disgust, "yet even my Canienga blood gets so heated by firewater I carry no longer the grave demeanor of a chief. I erupt in rage and violence and visit injuries upon those of my longhouse."

Kryn paced theatrically into the center of the group. "We are all brothers and sisters, all sprung from the same Great Turtle upon whose shell the world was formed. Together we plant. Together we live. Together we hold the Land From Which All Rivers Flow. The white man wishes to exterminate us—never mind whether it is the Dutch agent or the angry one-legged man or the blackrobe with his shining talisman of his torture victim on crossed poles. The whites grasp at our hunting lands. If we allow them to use a shad or salmon stream, they build houses, then saw wood to make more houses; they clear the forests so the beaver leaves, and the deer and moose and elk retreat farther from our hunters. We must resist the white man, and to resist him, we must be strong. Let us strengthen ourselves by thinking of our forefathers and the peace of Hiawatha spread by the tomahawk. Let us purify ourselves from the failure of this grand campaign and from the poison of this liquor."

Kryn's voice rose with sudden anger. "We must remove our minds and hearts from the white man's world. Yet he is everywhere. Iowerano allowed a Dutchman to construct Corlaer. Visits of these whites are far more frequent than before, and we have even moved up the river! The Frenchman will build his huge war canoes with heavy muskets so he can control the northern lake." Kryn brought his fist down into his palm. "We must stop him!" Gravely the assembled nodded. "We must turn our eyes from the seductions of his trinkets, his metal tools. We must not smoke the peace pipe, nor make marks upon the skins of sheep that cheat us of our land. Most of all we must shun his liquor. We must dive upon him like the eagle upon the mouse. We must enter his towns and drag him sleeping into the street and murder him. We must salt the land with his tears and blood so no crops will grow. We must drive him from our land like a stray dog. Yes, we must keep foremost in our minds the wisdom of our mothers and our fathers."

Kryn had worked himself into a high emotional pitch while the others listened more intently than they'd listened to the witch doctor. "Our League, proceeding from the clear eyes of Hiawatha, shall always hold these lands," Kryn cried. "And we will strike fear into the heart that even hopes we will forsake them!"

In a lower tone of voice, Kryn continued. "Eagle Talon now kindles a fire in the longhouse by the river. Let us steam the evil *okies* from our flesh. Then we will journey into the northern mountains and fish for ten days before we leave for the council fire at Onondaga. Follow me now. We shall enter the vapor and emerge again strong and cleansed and whole."

Kryn pushed aside the curtain, and in a file, the able-bodied men followed him out.

White Adder sulked, mumbling to himself. "If my healing is interrupted, how can it ever work?"

"Kryn needs no magic," one of the women said.

"I should say not," another said, adding a giggle.

"Did you see how he stepped in and took control?" asked the first.

The second, a merry sort, laughed. "I have been saving

dreams of Kryn for the Dream Feast when we have the right to demand what we see in our dreams."

Many of the women nodded assent.

"Even in defeat watch how he bears himself," another said.

"I do, I do," the second woman said.

"Shush!" hissed the first, and her eyes indicated the door. Five heads turned to see Karitha standing in the doorway, and great was their embarrassment.

"We women shall likewise sit in the steam," Karitha said, "and clean the evil vapors from our minds." And she turned and left them. Many of the women burst into laughter. Some insulted Karitha from envy. "The barren one," they called out to her. Others contorted their faces.

From her hiding place between sleeping shelves, Tekakwitha watched and listened. During the heat and riot of the drunken orgy, she had longed for Kryn to save her. Her heart had thrilled when Kryn ended White Adder's "cure" of the epileptic boy, when he led the men to the sweating house. Yet even as she cast him in the role of Hiawatha, the great peacemaker and first weaver of wampum belts, the remarks of the women troubled her. Some possessiveness, some envy, some desire filled her also.

The others would not claim Kryn, she told herself, for they could not know how deeply Kryn's thoughts ran. He would not even notice them. Yet, again the women's gossip began. They talked of the dark pleasure and of Kryn. Though many expressed desire, none could claim she had ever possessed him. Uncomfortable, wanting to escape the suggestive talk, yet having strong curiosity to learn how the dark pleasure turned their thinking, Tekakwitha sat quietly in the shadows. And she luxuriated in feeling that her regard for Kryn was superior to their animal cravings. "No," she told herself each time one of the women made an observation, "he is not like that, Kryn is not like that at all."

7

The rapids sounded calming, cleansing within the house of steam. Cobblestones, heated in the blaze outside, were dropped into a small pool in the middle of the floor, and steam billowed forth in great white clouds. The men sat naked, their bronze flesh glistening in the ruby light from a torch of birch bark. The curtain opened periodically, and on bark platters the men brought new stones, red hot, and lowered them, hissing into the water. The men drank much water drawn from the river in a leather bucket, and to purify their flesh completely, they refrained from eating.

Alternately sweating, then plunging into a whirlpool at the foot of the rapids, then napping upon a soft carpet of pine needles, the men soon felt the debilitating effects of the alcohol pass. Exhausted, susceptible to Kryn's persuasion, they became like repentent children. And Kryn was relentless. Whether standing naked among the squatting men in the sombre red shadows of the sweating house, his words like a chant, or whether bathing in the whirlpool, his words breezy and hopeful as the water that churned and the sun that rose upon a glorious summer day, Kryn was convincing.

"We have been the war club and the arm for the Dutch against the French of the north. We have adopted the white man's guns into our warfare. Because stealth is not needed when armed with such weaponry, we have begun adopting his methods of attack. Vital to our interest is stopping the French, forcing them down the mighty river and out to sea. We shall make them a lost race in our land. And then we shall do the same with the Dutch who even now eye our rich hunting ground of Saratoga, who look with greed upon the rich valley of Schoharie."

Kryn addressed the men together, and he sat with them, talking man-to-man. He wanted to reshape their thinking, to replace the sorrow and disgrace of their failed campaign with a purified sense of purpose. He needed to gain wide support for his plan so that at the Council Fire at Onondaga, the

105

entire League would vote to harry French territory. And he wanted also to dissolve much of their support for the Dutch.

And while Kryn, the half-breed war chief, led the men from the sweating house, Karitha collected the women and led them there likewise to purify themselves. And while Kryn sought to return dignity and order to Kanawaka, Iowerano, the legitimate chief, lay in his longhouse, alternately sleeping and fornicating, a victim of the gin.

And Tekakwitha, entrusted with six children while their mothers entered the sweating house and the rain began, tried not to watch. But her eyes were drawn in horror as the passing effects of alcohol turned the chief into an insatiable beast and Tonedetta and two concubines submitted in turn to his whims of coitus and sodomy.

8

Tekakwitha begged to accompany the fishing party. "I shall keep the fire burning while the men fish," she earnestly told Tonedetta as they walked through the palisade gates with a load of wood. "And I will dry the fish and smoke it so we will be well provided on our journey to Onondaga."

"I see no good in associating with Kryn," Tonedetta said. "He is an upstart. He ignores true authority and merely wishes to impose his half-breed will upon the entire Canienga."

"The maize is only just ripening, Aunt, and the squash and pumpkins swell with summer rain. I do nothing but embroider moccasins and wedding dresses for those who pass through the rites of womanhood." Excitedly she gestured. "I can turn my stitches on the shore of the northern lake as well as here. Oh, please, Aunt!" In the last year, Tekakwitha had stopped calling her foster mother Mama, and now called her Aunt with much formality.

"I shall ask Iowerano."

"No!" Tekakwitha's eyes filled with tears. "He will never allow me to go! He trusts me not at all. You have authority in the matter of children. You needn't turn to him for approval." She followed her aunt into the longhouse.

Tonedetta turned and scowled, weighing the benefit of

ridding her longhouse of the orphan's presence against the possible wrath of Iowerano. She dropped her load of wood. "Very well," she said finally, "you may go."

Tekakwitha leapt up and ran from the longhouse. Excited to be accompanying the men on their expedition, to be so near Kryn, she sought the forest and danced in the sunlight, singing the bright song of the thrush:

> "Your song in the tree
> Full of air and sunlight
> Washed over me as I sat by the water
> And gladdened my heart.
>
> "White clouds in the sun
> Rolled to the horizon
> As my song joined the others
> Of birds on the wing."

They departed before the sun rose, a fleet of twenty canoes. Only three other women accompanied the expedition, and these were widows whom the men could not touch. Ten days of abstinence, Kryn believed, would purge the men of the disgrace of their defeat, and the serenity of catching fish would rejuvenate them for the Onondaga council. Tekakwitha and the three widows would quietly tend to the domestic needs of the men without interference. Down to the lower river, then against its current they paddled, carrying their canoes around steep falls that thundered with rainbow spray against split rock. They veered eastward from the river, and toward evening, after a day's portage, came upon the placid lake, alive with the loon's mournful call. Before dark, they struck camp in a stand of virgin pine, quickly throwing up tents of hide and bark. The women slung the kettles and boiled sagamite. They'd brought no red meat with them for Kryn wanted to purify the men further by eating nothing but the white flesh of water creatures.

Wearily the men ate and quietly conversed about the journey, about fish lurking under the waves, about bats skittish above the lake, darting past the face of the moon. The lake's great, breathing benevolence caused the men to speak in whispers. It blew the embers of the fire higher, made stars twinkle and moonlight dance upon the water. Tekakwitha drew her knees to her chin, hugged herself, and drank in the clean, delightful wind that stoked the embers, and she listened to the men's talk, empty now of bloodlust and war. From the deep heart of the forest breathed a peace she had never before known, free from tussling and mating of the longhouse, free from children wailing, free from the bustle and gossip of the cornfield, free from the leaping, screeching White Adder.

She only dozed that night, comforted by the closeness of Kryn, by the soughing pine and the gentle lapping of the lake upon the shore. Now and again a feeding trout or bass broke the surface, and the noise startled her awake, interrupting dream images stealing up this tranquil night like vapor. She nuzzled again into her doeskin robe, and gave herself over to fine thoughts of silver fish and frogs croaking along the edge of her dreams.

Next day, the warriors left before dawn. They paddled away into the mist. Slowly the fog left the lake, stealing like white *okies* into the great clefts of the mountains, revealing blue and gray headlands receding up the lake. That first morning was overcast. Tekakwitha accompanied Moneta, the young widow who'd taught her to sew, on a hunt for frogs and turtles in the marsh along the southern cup of the lake. To purify their flesh, the men would eat turtles this night, consuming the totem of their clan, and meditating, they'd call upon the great turtle, mother of the entire world, to protect and guide them in all things.

Squealing with delight, the two chased bullfrogs, then snatched them up, wriggling and slimy, and thrust them alive into leather bags. They rigged nooses and hung bait, then dangled the nooses over the lair of aged turtles. As these scaly beasts reached out to snap at the red bait, they pulled the nooses shut, hauling the unsuspecting turtles from the water.

After much good sport, Moneta and Tekakwitha had enough to carry back to camp. They returned together while chilly, oppressive fog hung in mountain ravines. Driftwood lay on the beach in gnarled shapes. As Tekakwitha paused to make water, Moneta turned away, scanning the lake for returning bark canoes.

"They have not come back," Moneta said when again the girl joined her. Both carried turtles, hung like war trophies, and frogs still leapt in the leather bags at their sides.

"Tell me . . ." Tekakwitha said, then paused.

"Yes?"

"You were married to Watchful Bear, a warrior of reknown who perished in the last expedition."

"Yes?"

"Can you tell me, Moneta, what the dark pleasure is like?"

The woman laughed, and her face cracked, and she giggled, then laughed still louder. Ashamed, Tekakwitha hung her head and walked on.

"Little one," the woman said, "let us sit upon that rock. And let us watch for the men here, and I will tell you."

They sat upon a large, protruding stone among brambles at the edge of the beach, and they looked out upon the placid surface beneath the ceiling of mist, while they scratched their toes in the sand.

"The dark pleasure," Moneta said, "begins in different ways. Into the heart it steals when chance words are traded among girls about a certain hunter, sometimes the one to whom we are betrothed. Soon the hunter arrives in our dreams, stirring currents of warmth and comfort below the belly between the thighs. It is only with difficulty we learn to bring the dark pleasure to the sleeping shelf when men mount us. Yet once the secret is learned, the pleasure is boundless, and we long for the sleeping shelf even while working in the fields."

She sighed and stroked Tekakwitha's hair. "My little sister, you shall never know the pleasure my husband Watchful Bear brought me! He was an older warrior, experienced in the ways of women. Yet, at first I did not love him. I submitted because refusing the betrothal would bring great disgrace upon my *ohwachira*. I had fastened my heart upon another man, and even during the tortures, when the victims sang and all appeared happenstance, I stood close to this other so he would mount me. But it never came to pass. And yet, Watchful Bear learned my secret, and after two summers, the dark pleasure crept over me. I learned to keep the other warrior in my mind while surrendering to my husband. And so, often does it happen, as you will learn when you plant and hoe with the women," she said and clasped the girl's hand, "that we separate the image of our fathers or young hunters or fierce warriors from the lower regions. We dream of other men and allow these dreams to give us pleasure when in union with our husbands. This is the dark pleasure that even now stirs within you."

"And who was the one who filled your thoughts?" Tekakwitha asked.

Moneta giggled. "That is as sacred as my medicine—unique to each of us and secret."

"I believe I know," Tekakwitha said, glumly.

Moneta frowned. "No one can ever know!"

"And yet I do," the girl said.

"We must return," Moneta said quickly.

"It is he, is it not?" Tekakwitha whispered.

Moneta, bending to shoulder again the straps of the bags and turtles, looked up in surprise. "Who?"

"Kryn!"

"No!" said Moneta quickly. "It is not him! He is a half-breed! No, it is not Kryn! Never! Forget what I have said! I spoke with a loose, foolish tongue! The lot of women is never frivolous, always fraught with pain, with suffering! Kryn? Ha! He married the stern Karitha! He made his choice! He holds forth no warmth, but learns from her the tight lips, the aloof bearing! Kryn!" And Moneta laughed harshly as she shouldered the turtles and the leather bags of frogs and left prints in the sand far ahead of the confused girl struggling along behind her.

Each evening the flotilla of canoes glided toward camp over the placid water. Fragrant smoke trailed off among the pines, and the men, soothed by a day of fishing, unloaded their catch in the quiet of the summer night. Murmuring about events of the day, the men ate sagamite and fish—their only meal—then drank sparingly from the lake. Afterward they smoked around the fire. Tekakwitha listened intently as Kryn told thrilling tales of the campaigns to subjugate the Hurons, the Tobacco Nations of the Ottawa Valley, the Erie, the Susquehanna, and the Nation of the Cat. Other warriors remembered, nodded their heads judiciously, added an anecdote or an observation, then Kryn continued.

"It was always foremost in our minds," he said, and his words trailed off over the lake, "to control the passage of furs to the whites. For we knew, both at the Council Fire and in our individual clans, the whites needed furs to survive in this land. If we alone controlled the trading, then we alone controlled the whites."

Sitting beyond the circle of warriors as the shadows flickered, Tekakwitha heard in Kryn's words new thoughts of warfare and struggle, tribes far off conquered by the People of the Longhouse, and the mastery all men strove to gain. In the lazy breeze, the thrilling exploits told so softly mingled with her very personal feelings: Kryn would establish the People of the Longhouse once again as masters of the nomad Algonquins and the towns of white men. Her thoughts grew more personal. Perhaps Kryn would take her from Iowerano's longhouse into his own. Tekakwitha breathed deeply and a shudder passed through her, leaving a delicious, tingling sensation. She thought of Moneta and her words about the dark pleasure. She looked at Kryn. Cross-legged he sat, his muscular, yet supple arms gesturing casually as he talked, his stern jaw set, his mouth occasionally relaxing with humor, his hair in its fine rooster comb, and the skin he never painted. Just then, sensing her eyes, Kryn looked at her. Seized with panic at the intense blue of his eyes, Tekakwitha dropped her gaze, turned her head, and blushed with shame at her thoughts.

Late that night she heard the racoons enter camp to steal morsels of food. The day's catch hung far out on limbs in leather bags, and the racoons did not touch the dried, smoked fish upon racks. They came to pilfer the heads and entrails. Tekakwitha listened to their soft movements, for she could not sleep. She lay upon her robe gazing at the wigwam where Kryn slept, longing for the safety and security of his longhouse.

By day, she dried the fish, hanging fillets over fires built with green wood. Lazily the smoke cured the flesh of the pike and the lake trout, the sturgeon and bass. When needed, she helped mend nets of wild hemp and linden bark, which men weighted with stones in feeder streams to snare brook trout. The work soothed her, and she chatted with the other women. But each afternoon, as the women idly turned the fish on the racks, Tekakwitha stole into the forest to a place she'd found between two mossy boulders. Among ferns at their base, she drew out an otter's skin, and she embroidered her patterns.

On the day before they were to depart, the men spent the morning hours on the lake, then returned at the time of the shortest shadow to break camp. The women loaded the heaps of dried fish into the canoes. The men took down the temporary huts, for the night would be clear, and lashed the

furs in the canoes. Kryn stood in the middle of the camp
directing the men when Tekakwitha timidly approached him.

"I have something I wish to give you, Chief," she said,
holding the present behind her back.

Kryn smiled. "Ah, little one, you perform the work of
three squaws, and you never giggle or gossip in the way
others do." He stroked her braided hair. "You are indeed a
fine one to bring upon such expeditions."

"I am grateful," she said, handing him the embroidered
pelt.

"What fine work!" Kryn exclaimed, examining the fur
more closely. "I have never seen its like! Is this the pike?"

"Yes," the girl said. "Lurking in the watergrass, the pike
awaits the minnow, and minnows, unsuspecting, flash silver
in the sun."

"Who has taught you?" Kryn asked.

Bashfully Tekakwitha stared at the ground. "I have listened
to the men talk around the fire."

"And this one?"

"Sad is the cry of the loon, and feeding trout trouble the
waters; yet fishermen sleep well in the shower of stars."

"Indeed, you are eloquent as a sachem of eighty summers," Kryn said in delight. "Tell me of this!"

"With pincers the crayfish protects himself; yet he must
lash the mud and dart away when he spies the heron bending."

Kryn cried out in delight. "You have locked such beautiful words in your stitches." He threw his arm around her
shoulder. "My little one, you shall teach the keepers of the
memory belts new patterns! More eloquent by far are your
pictures. And this last one?"

"Out from his shell the turtle thrusts to snap at the bait.
Never in his dreams has he seen the noose that strangles
him, nor has he dreamt of his shell as the sacred dancing
rattle."

"I hope this bodes no ill for the Turtle Clan," Kryn
joked. Tekakwitha dropped her eyes, and wrung her hands in
embarrassment behind her back. Kryn seized her by the
arms and lifted her off the ground and hugged her. "I thank
you, little one, for the rare gift and for the words locked into
the patterns. I shall ask Karitha to sew this into a quiver for
me, and it shall carry my hunting arrows."

Tekakwitha heard these words resonate through his chest,
through his jaw and cheekbone as he held her to him, and

the strong embrace surprised her so, she went limp in his arms. She heard a laugh rumble far down within him, then burst out through his lips. She wriggled then to be put down. As Kryn set her on the ground, she ran off to sit by the mossy boulders and relish the new joy she could neither understand nor control.

9

With much care she plaited her black braids with wampum and dyed porcupine quills, and she oiled the braids with golden bear grease to make them shine. She dressed in a new buckskin skirt and vest decorated by her bone needle. On her moccasins she'd embroidered mountains capped with fog, such as she'd seen on the fishing expedition, for she was journeying this summer to the Onondaga, the People of the Mountain.

It was now midsummer; the corn stood to the height of a man, and pumpkin and squash were yellowing in the sun. The tobacco, too, had spread its great leaves, and sunflowers towered lazily over the sleepy plantation. The crops required little care—half the village was departing for the yearly council and festivities at the middle of the five nations. The women had been packing corn meal and dried meat and smoked fish for days; the men had been lashing bundles of their ceremonial dress, sleeping robes, the hide tents they'd erect with saplings in the shadow of the council house. Early one morning with the sun at their backs, they departed in twenty-six canoes from a landfall above the white water.

They paddled upriver to Tionnontake, village of the Bear Clan, and then they paddled farther to Andaragon, the village of the Wolf Clan. At each village they collected chiefs, matriarchs, warriors, wives, and children. As guardians of the eastern gate for the Great Longhouse, the chiefs of the Turtle Clan delivered an address welcoming the other clans on their journey to the council. Then the three Canienga clans left their Land of Flint for the Land of the Oneida in a colorful flotilla of eighty-one bark canoes.

The Onondaga, middle nation of the League, occupied

the headland above a crystalline lake. Mightier than Kanawaka, the fortifications—breastworks, trenches, bastions, and a triple wall—showed the influence of the French. Within, a full sixty longhouses stood in orderly lanes. The Onondaga welcomed their brothers from the east, the Canienga and Oneida, in solemn ceremonies, and the Canienga erected their wigwams on the headland near the large council house. Days later, the Seneca and Cayuga arrived from the west. Old Garacontie welcomed them with the solemn Consolation Rite for the dead chief, Elk Horn. With much ceremony, Garacontie accepted the antler bonnet from the Seneca, then placed it upon the head of Elk Horn's successor, Brown Bear.

Soon the festivities began. Dancing, feasting, gambling—the lanes of the makeshift villages of each nation filled with activity all day and most of the night. Women shared hearth fires, catching up on news from other clans and other nations. The men joined in hunting and fishing parties to supply fresh game and fish to the large population, and they dispensed their game freely among the wigwams. Children banded together in games and contests. Quiet and more serious by nature, Tekakwitha observed the bustle and the joy in the assembly, but she also watched the progress of the council with a foreboding sense.

At midmorning each day, the fifty sachems in their ceremonial furs and antler bonnets—moose, elk, deer, and ram—filed into the council house. All day they delivered orations, deliberating upon important matters. They settled blood feuds among the members of clans, between the clans of a nation, and they agreed upon territorial claims of the different nations. They weighed proposals for monopolizing trade, for attacking and subjugating other nations down the watercourses in every direction from their high land, for punishing upstart war chiefs and renegade bands of Algonquin, Abenaki, Mohegan, and the Cat Nations who had begun trading directly with the whites—in defiance of the Iroquois monopoly. For twelve long days the chiefs met, sitting cross-legged on their fur robes, smoking pipes in the dim longhouse, adjourning in the evening to return to their clans with news of various agreements. For twelve days all went smoothly. Then they debated on their relations with the three nations of whites: Dutch, English, and French.

So hot did tempers grow over this heated issue that occasionally unseemly displays of emotion broke through the formal, paced, and grave delivery of the orators. Some council chiefs blamed war chiefs for the failure of the expedition to annihilate the French. Many blamed Kryn for setting out in winter—by the first thaw, blood had cooled for the fight, they said. The gravest criticism, though, was aimed at all war chiefs. The previous year, the council had urged all five nations to put aside plans for an autumn war. Kryn, viewed as an upstart and a half-breed besides, had entered into improper negotiations with the Dutch for muskets, and then had called warriors to join him on the unsuccessful campaign. Because he had ignored the rule of the council, Kryn was called into the council house to clarify and justify his actions.

Tekakwitha watched as Kryn arrayed himself in his finest wolfskin robe. She noticed the disdain, almost disgust, in his voice as he spoke to his wife about the council. Proudly he left the wigwam and walked through the lanes of the Canienga village to the central fire where the first pipe was lighted each morning. Garacontie, the host, lit the pipe, offered it to the sunrise, to the direction of the sunset, to the north and to the south, to the earth and to the sky. Then with folded arms, eagle feathers fluttering from his elk's robe, he led the fifty sachems into the council house. With apprehension Tekakwitha returned to Tonedetta's wigwam and silently worked on embroidery, awaiting the outcome of the council.

Within the council house, the fifty chiefs sat upon their robes. Kryn stood before Garacontie.

"The People of the Great Longhouse long ago decided to separate their ruling chiefs from their war chiefs," the old man began. "A chief who makes policy for a nation must keep a clear mind, while a chief who wages war must inflame his warriors into a battle fever. I joined the expedition of last winter, even against the wishes of the council, because my tired blood longed for war. I see now by its outcome that the campaign was foolhardy and ill-advised. I offer my condolences to all the assembled chiefs for their warriors that went under the earth."

Kryn bowed in respect to the chief's age and wisdom. "I likewise am sorry."

"Rarely do we invite a war chief into these councils, for important matters must be carefully considered dispassionately, and too often a war chief longs only for action and has no patience for deliberation. Explain to us, please, how this campaign was conceived." Garacontie replaced the pipe in his mouth, and his eyes lapsed into a trancelike gaze.

"I have found," Kryn began, gesturing with dignity, "it far better to look ahead than behind. With due respect to the sachems here"—he bowed to all corners of the longhouse—"the problems still exist that caused me to enlist a campaign last winter."

"You will please answer the question, Chief," Iowerano said, hardly masking his annoyance.

"The French even now build a fort at the mouth of the Lake of the Gar-Pike. They range through our forests and soon will build wooden ships upon the lake to hold it against us. Powerless will be the bark canoe and our muskets against their cannon. Seeking to surprise them in their stone cities, I mounted a winter campaign. Yet, when we met upon the island of the northern lake, no one wanted to proceed. All but myself agreed to wait until the thaw would unlock the rivers and the Seneca and Cayuga could join with us."

"I myself originated this plan," Garacontie said. "It was a good plan."

"With due respect, Chief," Kryn retorted, "a good plan is a plan that works." This impertinent remark set the assembly murmuring, yet Garacontie only nodded and motioned Kryn to continue. "By waiting, we received the surprise rather than delivered it. The chief is correct—many warriors have gone under the earth. But the French still remain. This is what the council must agree on this summer—how to attack and drive out the French."

"What of the other nations of whites?" a Cayuga chief, Wolf Tooth, asked.

"The English and Dutch war with each other," Kryn said. "As long as they do, they will not look toward the Land From Which All Rivers Flow with greedy eyes."

"Perhaps the French, too, will join one side, and the white men will kill each other and drive each other from the land," suggested a Seneca chief, Red Star. Other chiefs nodded.

"No," Kryn said. "One nation among the whites will conquer all, and then the People of the Great Longhouse will be forced to agree to demands, perhaps even give up our land. The strongest nation now is the French. The English hug the seacoast in fear. The Dutch clear land and build trading docks and warehouses—they want only their gold wampum and care little about us. The French, however, boldly explore far into unknown lands among hostile peoples. Their blackrobes make women out of warriors. They have penetrated the freshwater seas far to the west, as far as any Canienga has ever traveled, and they have paddled down the mighty western river of the Missipiacs. In a few seasons they will establish towns up all river valleys, creeping always toward the source of the rivers, and ultimately they will attempt to take our highlands. This year we must attack again."

"Pardon me, Kryn," Garacontie spoke, "but it is not your place here to suggest actions for our consideration. We have called you only to bring us information."

"Our League weakens year by year," Kryn said, gesturing impatiently. Then, with a great effort, he composed himself. "The meeting each summer to make laws and policy strengthens each nation when it returns home. However, we must see with the same eye. We must see with the eye of the eagle in the great pine tree of peace planted by Hiawatha. We must view the surrounding lands with vigilance, and we must show our might to those who say, 'The League is weak from disease and liquor.'"

"Again, Kryn, I remind you it is not your place to make these suggestions," Garacontie said.

"I apologize," Kryn bowed. "The dead tree in the forest takes many years to rot," he said, "but a bolt of lightning can splinter and burn it instantly. I have seen the French. I have fought the French. Some of them show courage as great as the Canienga." He looked around the hall. "—courage as great as all the nations of the Great Longhouse. Even now they prepare the lightning bolt. Our peace, the peace of Hiawatha, must be spread with the tomahawk. We serve no one, waiting like women for them to strike a blow into our vitals."

"Again Kryn is out of order," Iowerano said. "We must ask him to remove himself from this council."

Kryn glared at Iowerano who sat judiciously smoking his pipe. Saying nothing at all, Kryn bowed respectfully and turned and left the council house. Back he stormed to the wigwam, threw off the wolfskin robe, took up his bow and arrow, and headed toward the forest to calm himself with hunting.

"What has happened?" Tekakwitha asked Karitha.

"Nothing good," the woman said, shaking her head.

Later in the evening, Iowerano called a meeting of the Turtle Clan to acquaint them with the decisions of the day. The council decided to offer terms of peace to the French, to invite blackrobes again among any of the five nations that wished, to trade with French traders as well as Dutch. The Turtle Clan heard this new policy with mixed feelings, yet because it had been decided by all the sachems, no one argued.

When he returned long after dark, Kryn spoke with his wife, then quickly sought out Iowerano. He found the chief in his wigwam with Tonedetta, Tegonhat, and Tekakwitha.

"What is the meaning of this?" Kryn demanded.

"We wish to establish friendly ties with the French," Iowerano explained. "Why persist in useless warfare? We can negotiate with them to keep them from greedily eyeing our land."

"Never!"

"You must learn to hold your tongue, half-breed," Iowerano said.

Kryn scowled so fiercely, Tekakwitha feared to look at him.

"Though my father was white, my blood is all Canienga," Kryn whispered hoarsely.

"You flaunt your pale skin by not painting as we do," Iowerano said.

"I do not paint to remind myself that I must achieve twice the normal lot else someone say, 'There walks a half-breed,'" Kryn said. "Yet, you go into council and allow the western tribes to sway you. Canienga, the People of Flint, guard the eastern gate. We will be the first victims of French treachery. We do not have the luxury to watch storm clouds rise and darken. The lightning will strike without warning."

"You defeat your purpose," Iowerano said. "You should not have come into the council house. Many of the elderly chiefs thought your impertinence should be punished."

"Punished?" Kryn cried in disbelief. He made a supreme effort to control his rage. "The League has fallen upon sad times," he said, shaking his head regretfully. "Not wisdom, but cowardice guides our sachems. Garacontie caused the delay that cost our defeat at the hands of a few whites. Now he wishes to parley with these arrogant French?"

"More is to be gained through trade and treaties than through war."

"More what? More liquor? More hatchets and kettles? More muskets so we can turn and slay the Dutch? We who rule this land are being used by the whites, and we go along blindly and allow this to occur."

"Your blood is far too hot, Kryn."

"That is the decision, I suppose, of the Women's Council?" Kryn gave a derisive laugh. "In the legend of Hiawatha, the Entangled One had a head of snakes. The Entangled One lived here among the Onondaga. The Entangled One still haunts this place, for no agreement, no action comes out of the council house, only entangled purposes and talk from many forked tongues."

"The strength of the League allows that many opinions enter a single decision. Are you so headstrong you consider yours the only opinion of worth?"

"The weakness of the League is that no one leads. Like a herd of bison on the western plain when the wolves attack, we huddle head to head, horn to horn. I can no longer remain at this council. I can no longer watch the Turtle Clan retreat before the whites. I can no longer watch the League make decisions based on weakness and fear rather than courage. It surprised me when so few French held our warriors for so long, but it surprises me no longer." Kryn turned on his heel and left the wigwam.

"He will learn to regret his rash behavior," Iowerano said. Tekakwitha stood to leave.

"Where are you going?"

"I must go into the forest, Uncle."

"Very well."

Into the darkness she pushed, and she dashed to Kryn's wigwam. "Where is he?" she asked Karitha.

"He has departed in anger," Karitha said. "He wished that I remain here so he can be alone."

Without answering, the girl turned and ran for the lake. Kryn was stepping into his canoe. "Kryn!" she called, as he pushed off, "Kryn!"

He did not turn. With a strong stroke of his paddle, the canoe lurched ahead.

"Kryn!" she cried, tears suddenly blinding her eyes. "Kryn! It is I, Tekakwitha!"

The form, bending to take another stroke, straightened, and slowly the paddle entered the water like a rudder, turning the canoe halfway about. "Why do you follow me?" the deep voice asked across the water.

"Do not leave me here!"

Kryn dipped the paddle and with one stroke brought the canoe's prow softly upon the sand. "Little one," he said, "these are matters you do not understand."

His words stung her. "I do!" she pleaded. "Take me with you! Please!"

"Many forces are struggling these days," he said. "The struggles within each of us are dividing us. We must have a single purpose."

"I do," she said. "I want to accompany you."

"Why?"

"You speak true words. Our League has fallen upon evil days. I see no hope for the People of Flint without you. Iowerano is weak. He will allow the evil magicians of the French, the blackrobes, to journey through our land so they may reach the Oneida. I have no desire to dwell with him any longer. Please! I shall be useful to you. I will build the fire and cure the skins."

This amused Kryn. "You have a noble heart, little one. In my pride and anger you cause me to reason things out. Where should I go? Into the forest alone. Why? To draw strength from the trees and the creatures. Why? Because I feel weakened by being so long among men. Yet, I should stay and abide by the council's wishes and work within their pronouncements as best I can." Kryn stepped from the canoe. "It is good you have called me. How can a man hope to master the French if he can't even master his own anger?"

Kryn beached his canoe and walked with the girl back to the Canienga encampment.

VERSAILLES, FRANCE

Under the Rule of the Sun King
Spring, 1664

1

Even before Adam Daulac took his heroic stand at Long Sault, letters and emissaries beseeched the king to send a regiment to support the priests and nuns, the farmers, and few tradesmen who comprised the colony of New France. Though Iroquois attacks, massacres, kidnappings, tortures, and murders were often viewed as punishments for sins, a detachment of French bluecoats would ease many minds. The king, building the most ostentatious palace in the western world and passionately in love with a new mistress, Louise de La Valliere, turned a deaf ear to requests from such an obscure corner of the earth. Yet his chief minister, Jean Baptiste Colbert, saw merit in investing in the New World.

During "Pleasures of the Enchanted Island," a week-long celebration for six hundred guests to show off the new Versailles, Louis XIV rode into the gardens wearing gold and silver armor encrusted with jewels and a scarlet plume atop his golden helmet. For his new mistress, he had costumed himself as Roger, Charlemagne's paladin, just arrived from the Enchanted Island, followed by Apollo in a glittering chariot. To entertain her, he'd commissioned two new Molière plays, promenades in the garden, and lavish feasts. He did not wish to be bothered in the midst of such revels. He granted an interview to Colbert only after Colbert doggedly insisted.

"I am in receipt of a letter from Avaugour, former Governor of New France, and it bears out the claims of the Jesuits," Colbert said. In answer to the king's raised eyebrows, he explained. "Avaugour was provincial governor until he fell foul of Laval, Bishop at Quebec, for his stand on the brandy question."

"What is the brandy question?" asked the king impatiently. He was petting the hawk perched on his gloved hand, and he viewed Colbert's talk as an intrusion.

"It seems the natives of New France have an inordinate passion for liquor, and the brandy causes them to murder each other, to neglect the simple hunting and agriculture they conduct to sustain themselves. Liquor debilitates them, turns them into animals."

"That is hardly a staggering metamorphosis."

Colbert flashed an obsequious smile. "Perhaps not, Your Worship, but Laval and the Jesuits have hope to redeem their souls. The brandy makes this impossible. When the Jesuits insisted he pardon a woman convicted of selling brandy to the natives, Avaugour threw up his hands and said he'd no longer enforce the prohibition anywhere, anytime. The Jesuits schemed, and he has been removed. Still the others write in the same vein."

"Who removed him?" the king asked curtly.

Colbert cleared his throat. "You did, Your Majesty, upon advice of Père Auguste Chauchetière, the Jesuit. The Jesuits continually try to run the colony, and to this end they use the royal confessional."

"Is this contrary to your wishes?" The king stroked the hawk in an attitude of boredom.

"Of course not, your Majesty." Colbert barely concealed his true feelings. "And yet, I think the sway the Jesuits hold over the colony is not in the best interests of the subjects of France or of Your Majesty's long-range policies."

The king eyed his minister suspiciously. "Define those policies for me."

"You, yourself, Your Majesty, often remark how all disciplines of the arts and sciences, commerce, and the military must tend toward one goal. The Jesuits, I believe, have such narrow vision, they keep the colony as a testing ground for their spiritual creed—if they can convert the heathen, the theories of Loyola will reign triumphant. They discourage settlement. They thwart the building of mills. They have even been accused by civil authorities of encouraging the torture of captured natives simply so the prisoners' souls will enter heaven."

"Do you object to focusing sights upon a heavenly reward?"

"No, Your Majesty." Colbert feigned humility, but his eyes glittered with cold disdain. "Yet, I believe France can expand its influence in the New World as Spain has done, as

England has done, as Holland and Portugal have done. The New World holds vast riches we may exploit if we encourage colonists to settle. We can add vast tracts of land to your empire—tracts many times the size of France."

"Your plan seems to have merit. How do you see it being undertaken?"

"Allow me to defer to the former governor, Your Majesty. He writes that the St. Lawrence River is the entrance to what could become the greatest state in the world. He advises, and I agree, that the brandy trade must be increased. This debilitates the savages and makes them far easier to conquer. We must also forbid the Jesuits any jurisdiction over the brandy trade—let them care for the savages' souls; we'll care for their bodies. Avaugour further suggests dispatching three thousand soldiers to the colony to make Quebec an impregnable fortress, to lay waste the ferocious Iroquois—particularly the easternmost tribe, the Canienga—and to build a fort upon the river where the Dutch have their Fort Orange. These heretics are meek and may easily be driven from the land, thereby opening the great port of New Amsterdam to us. This should take three years to accomplish, he says. And afterward, the soldiers may be discharged and turned into settlers by granting them the lands they've subdued."

The king nodded. Colbert unrolled a parchment.

"I have taken the liberty, Your Majesty, to draw up a charter for a new company, the Company of the West. Ever since the dwindling fur trade caused the collapse of the Company of New France, the religious sects of Quebec and Montreal have been quarreling as to who controls the colony. I suggest we give this new company authority to name the governor and intendant of the colony and to be the sole body to whom appeals for decisions are made. I propose putting the colony on a secular, economic footing by encouraging the migration of women, the importation of livestock, and the stimulation of trade and industry. Under your far-thinking reign, we have accomplished so much at home since the civil strife of the Fronde, indeed, even since Cardinal Mazarin's death. Let us carry this prosperity into our acquired lands."

"The Company of the West, then, would be on a footing with other trading corporations?" The king considered, then nodded. "Yes, Colbert, I see much merit in the plan. And among my generals, who strikes you as most capable to subdue these heathens?"

Colbert bowed deferentially. "Your general in Croatia, where our troops are defending the ramparts of Zrin from infidels is Marquis Prouville de Tracy, as able a commander as France has. Should we recall him and press him into service in the New World, he could accomplish this plan within three years."

"And yet, he has passed his sixtieth year. Those are harsh regions."

"With your leave, sire, he is as vigorous as a man of forty."

"Very well, the Turks are nearly vanquished. Recall him and name a successor."

"Yes, Your Majesty." Colbert bowed and began backing from the room.

"We shall put in your hands the management of our colony of New France," the king said. "Inform the valet of my hunting plans."

"Yes, sire." Colbert backed from the chamber, gently closing the mirrored doors behind him. And he set off at once to put his plans into operation, leaving the king to more important matters—his mistress, dancing, and hunting.

Twelve days later, May 24, 1664, King Louis XIV signed an edict creating the Company of the West. Any loyal subject who invested not less than three thousand francs became a partner in the company. The company controlled not only Canada, but also trade from West Africa from Cape Verde to the Cape of Good Hope, South America between the Amazon and the Orinoco, Cayenne, the Antilles, and all the expanses of New France from Hudson's Bay to Florida.

According to the edict, the glory of God was the company's chief objective, and stipulations were made so the company provided sufficient priests to planned settlements. The company could build forts and warships. It could cast cannon, wage war, make peace, establish courts, appoint judges, and enjoy a monopoly of trade for forty years. Sugar from Antilles, slaves from Africa, and the beaver and moose skins of Canada were its chief sources of income.

Marquis de Tracy was named lieutenant general for America. Daniel de Courcelle was appointed governor of New France, and Jean Baptiste de Talon, Colbert's cousin, became intendant—the king's controlling agent for finance, courts, public works, and also the king's spy upon the governor.

And each man, Tracy, Courcelle, and Talon, with his train of attendants, servants, young nobles, soldiers, valets, and priests, fitted out ships to sail westward into the unknown with the fleur-de-lis fluttering.

And standing among the priests who clung to the taffrail of Tracy's ship and looked their last upon French soil was Père Claude Chauchetière, determined to flesh out his romantic missionary dreams, and to win, if such was his destiny, a martyr's death in New France.

2

Immured in the seminary at Montmarte since his shocking visit to Versailles, Père Claude Chauchetière had continually pondered the thorny, rocky road to salvation. So subtle were the ways of Satan that a demon in the guise of the Virgin Mary had infected his dreams, blending erotic desire with his hunger for spiritual peace. From Loyola's spiritual exercises lingered a horror of hell, the infernal region of noise and stench and eruption of flame, as well as a reverence for sacrifice and suffering—"Your will, not mine, be done." Avidly Père Claude reread the letters of Isaac Jogues, who had found martyrdom in New France.

> It is not easy to detail all the miseries of the voyage, but the love of God who calls us to these missions, and our zeal in converting these poor savages renders these sufferings so sweet we wouldn't exchange these pains for all the joys of earth. Our food is a little Indian corn pounded between two stones and boiled in water with no seasoning; our bed is the earth or the frightful rocks lining the great Ottawa, which rolls by in the clear moonlight.

How different from the stone vaults and cloisters! How stirring was Jogues's conduct when captured by the same Iroquois he wished to convert! On a mission of peace, he offered his life to the Lamb of God who takes away the sins of the world, and for this and only this he was brutally tortured.

Père Claude imagined the rectitude, the certainty, the sublime joy Jogues must have felt following Christ unto death. He'd only wanted to teach, to help, to reduce the common misery of humankind, and for this pure motive he was tortured and mocked.

> On the eve of Assumption (August 14, 1642) we reached a river that flows by their village—Ossernenon. Both banks were filled with Iroquois, clamoring for our blood. They received us with clubs, fists, and stones. As they despise a bald pate, in a tempest their fury burst upon my bare head. They tore out my remaining two nails with their teeth, and with their nails they stripped off the flesh underneath to the very bones.

"Father, take from me this bitter chalice," Christ had said. "Let Your will, not mine, be done." How like Christ's passion was Jogues's ordeal!

> They next hung me between two poles in a hut, tied by the arms above the elbow with coarse bark rope. I thought I was to be burnt, for this is a preliminary to burning at the stake. So far, I had kept a grave silence. Now, alone in this torture, I groaned aloud for 'I will glory in my infirmities that the power of Christ may dwell in me, and I begged them to ease my bonds. But God justly ordained that the more I pleaded, the more they drew my bonds. I thank thee, O, Lord Jesus, for I learned by some slight experience how much Thou didst deign to suffer on the cross for me when the weight of Thy holy body hung not by ropes, but by Thy hands and feet pierced by hardest nails.

The pain! The despair! Life in a heathen land with no hope of delivery, dragged out day by day with no mass, no sacraments, no glimmer of an end. How revolting to the body! How withering to the soul! And yet Jogues endured. And the temptations!

> I lead such a truly wretched life where every virtue is in danger: faith, in the dense darkness of

paganism; hope, in so long and hard trials; charity, amid so much corruption, deprived of the Sacraments. Purity is not, indeed, endangered here by delights, but is tried amid this promiscuous and intimate intercourse of both sexes by the perfect liberty of all in hearing and doing what they please, and most of all, in their constant nakedness. For here you must see, willing or not, what elsewhere is shut out, not only from wandering, but even from curious eyes.

Hence daily do I groan to my God begging Him not to leave me without help amid the dead—begging Him that amid such impurity and superstitious worship of the devil to which he has exposed me, naked and unarmed, 'My heart may be undefiled in his justification,' so when the good Shepherd shall come 'who will gather together the dispersed of Israel,' 'he may gather us from among nations to bless his holy name. Amen! Amen!'

How Isaac Jogues wished to bring the savages under the mantle of a forgiving, all-understanding Jesus! Yet his efforts had been rebuked, insulted, vilified. How Claude envied his suffering for his beliefs. More than a decade he himself had paced the stone corridors, living in frigid intimacy with hundreds of men. Quirks became manifest—excessive penance, a desire for corporal punishment, overeating, scrupulosity, intolerance, a dearth of compassion—as the intellectual and spiritual dimension of each personality became exaggerated. Where were the true tests of endurance, the true tests of faith? Claude grew impatient endlessly shaving down subtleties in the manner of Aquinas. The abyss between spiritual thought and heroic action widened as he compared his own life with the life of Jogues. Would he ever be able to endure, to submit to God's will, to triumph over the weakness of his flesh? Would he ever be tested?

Jogues's last letter comforted the young priest each time he returned to it, for it showed the martyr, after two years of torture, after his escape to France and his return to the howling wilderness, after superhuman endurance and unfailing courage, still questioning his own motives, his strength, and the depth of his faith.

Alas, when shall I begin to love and serve Him whose love for us had no beginning? When shall I begin to give myself entirely to Him, who has given Himself unreservedly to me? Although I am very miserable, I do not despair. He will make me stronger by giving me new occasions to die and unite myself inseparably to Him.

The Iroquois make presents to our governor. Peace has been concluded to the great joy of New France. I have reason to think I will be sent again among the tribes, as I know their language and their country. Pray for me. I will be among them without liberty to pray, without Mass, without the Sacraments, responsible with my life for every accident their superstitions fasten upon. What do I say? My hope is in God. We must not spoil His work by our shortcomings. Obtain with your prayers this favor, that having led so wretched a life till now, I may at last begin to serve Him better.

My heart tells me if I am sent, I shall go and not return; but I shall be happy if our Lord completes the sacrifice where He has begun it, and makes the little blood I have shed in that land of strife the earnest sacrifice I'd give from every vein of my body and my heart. The Canienga are "a bloody spouse to me...in my blood have I espoused them to me." May our good Master, who has purchased them in His blood, open to them the door of His Gospel, as well as to the four allied nations near them.

Adieu, dear Father; pray Him to unite me inseparably to Him.

Eighteen years before, Jogues had been killed by a tomahawk buried in his skull as he entered a longhouse to sit down for supper. The Canienga impaled his head upon a pike at the northern gate to the village of Ossernenon as a warning to any intruding French, and they threw his body to the dogs. Words upon paper, words upon birchbark, words upon the hide of deer, the skin of sheep, words in Iroquois, Flemish, and French penned with ink and berry juice, with ashes and bear grease, words as varied and insubstantial as air were all that remained of Jogues's heroism.

Yet for the young priest, Jogues was very much alive. Every word the martyr wrote started from the page as if written in blood, conditions of a convenant with the Almighty. The picture of Jogues, taunted and suffering at the hands of the savages, became for the young priest a modern crucifixion scene—a tumult of screams and laughter, firelight and shadow, mangled flesh, and the courageous spirit saying, "Forgive them for they know not what they do."

By midsummer, news of Adam Daulac's heroic stand at Long Sault reached Paris. A whole generation of young nobles and gentlemen had come of age reading thrilling accounts of New France from the yearly *Jesuit Relations*. By saving Montreal, Three Rivers, and Quebec from the Iroquois hordes—knowing in advance his death pact had been signed—Adam Daulac arose as a popular hero, the epitome of Franco-Catholic chivalry. Ballads were penned, tragedies staged, a mass in the Cathedral de Notre Dame celebrated, a holy day called by the cardinal. Out of the forests the news had come on the lips of an Algonquin survivor, and all of France thrust out its chest in pride and rededicated itself to raising its lily flag over forts and trading posts in the wilds.

Nor did Minister Colbert hesitate to exploit this fervor in enlisting men to sail westward in his new Company of the West. Applications to accompany Tracy, Courcelle, and Talon poured into the ministry offices. Sons of nobles used old political connections to gain berths on the ships heading first for the Antilles, then to Quebec. With the excitement of a crusade, the waterfronts of le Havre, Brest, Bordeaux, even the Huguenot town of la Rochelle busied to outfit the westward fleets.

Père Claude Chauchetière, due to be assigned to a parish, a seminary, or a mission in the far kingdoms of the globe, saw in this holy enterprise the workings of his personal destiny. As Jogues had a score of years before, Chauchetière would sail westward to the uncharted continent and work to dispel heathen rites and superstitions with the light of Christ's word. Fervently he prayed. Daily he dropped hints to his superiors. Constantly he asked about his assignment, hoping by applying pressure he could realize his most sacred and secret desire. His surprise, then, proved unbounded when the assignments were made—Claude Chauchetière, S.J., was dispatched as a Soldier of Jesus upon the next armada to

Mindanao, Philippines, to assist in converting the natives from Buddhism! And like a refrain, mocking his ardor for New France, conjuring dream sequences of servitude and obscurity in the tropical kingdoms of yellow-skinned emperors, these words played through his mind: "Your will, not mine, be done."

3

"I wish to implore the Provincial Superior to change my assignment," Claude explained to his uncle. "I fear all the zeal and fervor that are mine will be lost should I venture among the Philippines."

"You seem pale and overwrought, Nephew," Père Auguste Chauchetière observed, sitting in a lavish Versailles salon. "I'll ring for brandy." A bell summoned a servant, and brandy was ordered. "Should this dismal rain let up, we might take a drive around the grounds. Much work has been done since you were last here, and the king's gardens rival all of nature for luxuriance and splendor."

"I am reluctant to ask outright," Claude said to keep his topic foremost. "I wondered, perhaps, if you could say a word or two?"

The old priest narrowed his eyes, and a smile played at his lip. "Once you criticized my political influence. Now you wish me to meddle?"

"I do not seek a post with influence!" Claude blurted impatiently. "My motive is not ambition! I wish to follow the steps of Jogues! Should that be scorned?"

"Jogues. I see," the elder priest said, and placing his fingertips together, he thought for a long moment. "He and I were ordained together."

"I never knew that," Claude said with great interest. "What sort of man was he?"

"A small man, delicate, a man of meek temperament and simple tastes. We who knew him as a young man were much surprised by his hold on life during such inhuman tortures. You have chosen wisely in following Jogues, but you needn't be assigned to the same corner of the world. Opportunity for holiness exists in all kingdoms of the earth and in all walks of life."

"But the work I might accomplish in New France!"

The elder priest held up his hand. Just then the brandy arrived, but Claude, his cheeks now flushed with excitement, ignored it.

"I have heard nothing but praiseworthy reports from your instructors and superiors at Montmartre," the older priest said. "Yet in this matter of your assignment, you exhibit pride."

"Is it pride to desire to serve God in such a wilderness as New France?" Claude pleaded.

"It is pride to deem yourself a better judge than your superiors on where your efforts may be best employed."

"I have examined my motives for many long months, Uncle, and I know them to be faultless. I have sought through many long nights the guidance of the Virgin, and my destiny lies in New France. Would I risk eternal perdition by putting my own will above Father Superior's?"

"Why, then, do you attempt to?"

"I believe, Uncle, that insufficient thought was expended in making my assignment. I have hardly dared to breathe a word of my desire to go to New France, lest my desire jeopardize such an assignment. Now, before all is lost, I must take a bold step."

"Ah, Claude," Père Auguste groaned. "Your faith was begotten by guilt. You only embraced this life after the disgrace and dishonor of your liaison with the gypsy banished you from my brother's house. Since then, you have shown remarkable spiritual growth; but like love sprung from gratitude or loyalty founded upon duty, the foundation of your faith—atonement for a carnal sin—is not sound enough to support such a grand edifice as you plan."

Claude squirmed, having his shortcoming so openly discussed. "My soul is tormented night and day," he said. "Do you not believe men can change their hearts? My faith may be imperfect, but it is also untested. Instead of examining old scars like the soldier who has finished fighting, I wish to venture forth as a soldier of Jesus and win victories over the heathen superstitions and ignorance. I do not see why this impulse should be stifled or punished."

Père Auguste dropped his chin into his hand and considered. "You reason well, Nephew. However, the colony is no longer the place it was twenty years ago. Efforts to increase industry and commerce have begun, and an army has been assigned to subdue the savages. Your desire to follow Jogues may prove a vanity."

"With respect, Uncle, I think not. The Iroquois are as unruly and pagan as in Jogues's time, perhaps even more so."

"I can speak to the appropriate people. As an equal to your Father Superior, I can even petition Rome."

"Will that be necessary?"

"It may. The extent of my effort, though, is not important. Your spiritual growth must be the prime concern, for what profits it for a man to gain the whole world if he loses his soul? I have sounded you out on this matter, and have found your desire hardly tainted by hope of worldly glory. However, I caution you"—he narrowed his eye and pointed his finger—"should I be successful, you must be ever vigilant. You must guard against the subtle snares of the demon, for he appears in the least suspicious guise and at our most vulnerable times."

Into Claude's mind flashed the image of the blond woman he'd fantasized as the Virgin, and this vision pained him. "I know this too well, Uncle."

"And remember, too, that it requires more than zeal to forge a missionary of Jogues's stature. You must grow to love your tormenters; those who ceaselessly insult you will be the lambs you wish to save."

"I know this," Claude said. He looked up then, and stared his uncle full in the eye. "You saved me a dozen years ago from a disgrace that might have sent me wandering the world, a broken man without any purpose in life. I have examined the lives of others and have seen some of the world as an outrider for the Society. I know in my mind, my heart, and my soul that my fate lies in New France. This is not the mere whim of a young man, Uncle. I have grown and have been tested for these long years at Montmartre." Claude stood. "I must return now." Père Auguste also stood, and Claude embraced him. "I thank you for your help. Know that in the spirit of our order, my assignment to Quebec will be for the greater glory of God."

"I hope it will be so," Père Auguste said, regarding the young man sharply, "and I will pray it will be so."

4

Such pomp as Quebec had never seen attended the arrival of Marquis de Tracy. On the thirteenth of June, 1665, his flagship anchored in the basin of Quebec, saluted by cannonades and musket salvos, which echoed from Point Levi, Cape Diamond, and far-off, misty Cape Tourmente. All of Quebec lined the ramparts high upon the crag, shouting, waving hats and handkerchiefs as the ship emptied hundreds of soldiers into small landing boats. Bold with victory from their winter campaign against pirates in the Antilles, the soldiers stepped onto shore as saviors of New France. Though he'd been stricken with fever upon the voyage, the great Tracy insisted on walking alone. He was followed by young nobles, bold, chivalrous men in full regalia of ribbons and lace and powdered wigs. With the French applauding and Huron converts staring in disbelief, Tracy climbed the steep path to the city. He scowled as he passed the dilapidated fort they called Castle of St. Louis. He passed through the applauding folk with much self-possession and grandeur. Following him were twenty-four guards of the King's own livery, four pages, and six valets. At last he came to the cobblestone square between the Jesuit college and the cathedral. Bells rang furiously. And in his retinue, among the soldiers and priests, walked Claude Chauchetière, drinking in the cold, clean air of the New World.

Bishop Laval waited on the cathedral steps in red, pontifical robes, surrounded by priests. He greeted Tracy warmly and offered him holy water. The general blessed himself with the sign of the cross. Laval motioned the general to a kneeler; Tracy refused. The priests at hand offered him a cushion; again he refused. Still trembling from fever, the large old man knelt on the pavement and uncovered his head. All knelt and did likewise. The bells ceased. Fervently spreading his arms, the general intoned *Te Deum*. Laval and the Jesuits nodded to each other as the old man sang and the fleur-de-lis snapped smartly over the ramparts. The King's interest gratified them—piety and zeal would be defended with gunpowder.

5

Marquis de Tracy's arrival in Quebec threw the Onondaga Council into disarray that summer. The chiefs of the eastern tribes, the Canienga and Oneida, urged banding with the Dutch and attacking Quebec. The central Onondaga, and the two western nations, Cayuga, and Seneca, argued that peace should be maintained. Kryn had attended again this year despite his rebuff the year before. With measured, solemn eloquence, he again urged attacking the three forts on the Richelieu River. More chiefs listened to him this summer because the growing strength of the whites, as proved by Daulac's defense at Long Sault, had come to pass as he'd predicted the year before. Yet so confused was the assembly by exaggerated tales of soldiers and cannon and battleships and horses, that Kryn's appeal for action was lost.

Old Garacontie brought a captured Jesuit into the council house. "Tell us," the Onondaga chief commanded, "what this arrival signifies."

Father Charles Lemoyne stood in their midst, his hands bound with bark rope, and he answered: "The arrival of soldiers shows that our king, whose power emanates as do the rays of the sun over the entire world, will continue dispatching soldiers until the Great Longhouse of the Iroquois is a smoking ruin. More men are coming than live in your villages, more men than there are deer and bear and elk in your forests, more men than stars in the heavens stand ready to embark in the great winged canoes. They have countless muskets and cannon on wheels that can blow apart your palisades, even as the strong wind scatters the leaves of autumn.

"You must make peace," Lemoyne stated categorically to the assembled chiefs in antler bonnets. "There will be no quarter for any man who defies the French. Return me to my people, and I will negotiate the peace for you. All men must live as brothers. Ask the chief of the whites to send the blackrobes into the Great Longhouse, and he will be much appeased."

After the prisoner was escorted out, the chiefs argued far into the night and the entire next day as to the correct course of action. For once, Iowerano and Kryn agreed: The Canienga, guardians of the Great Longhouse's eastern gate, must remain vigilant and defend all incursions into the Land From Which All Rivers Flow.

As she tended the fire and cooked the sagamite and looked after the children, Tekakwitha kept her eyes and ears attuned to the signs and whispers of the men. She listened as Kryn and Iowerano debated, smoking their pipes after the day's meal, and their concern conjured a vague fear in her. The entire League, she sensed, was poised at a brink, and an ill-considered move, either to make peace or to refuse peace, could plunge her people into an abyss of obliteration or slavery. Tekakwitha's vague fear turned into alarm, almost panic, when shouts were heard in the council house the next day. Suddenly Iowerano and Gandegowa, chief of the Oneida, and twelve other chiefs of various Canienga and Oneida clans stormed from the council house.

"Begin packing!" Iowerano yelled in the midst of the Turtle Clan's wigwams. "We leave for Kanawaka this afternoon!"

In a flurry of activity the tents, bed robes, kettles, dried meat, and sacks of cornmeal were lashed into the canoes, and with no further ceremony, no farewell to the other three nations, the Canienga and the Oneida left the sacred council hill. Through the valleys and lakes they paddled and portaged, the individual clans leaving the flotilla one by one until the Turtle Clan alone was left to journey on to Kanawaka.

It wasn't until many days after they reached home that the girl learned the cause of their abrupt departure. In a motion before the entire body of fifty sachems, Garacontie had proposed signing a peace treaty with the French, turning their warfare on the Dutch, and inviting the blackrobes into the Great Longhouse to teach of the white man's *manitou*. Tekakwitha sat in Kryn's longhouse, pretending not to be eavesdropping on the talk between Kryn and Karitha.

"Garacontie grows old and feeble of mind," Kryn said. "He turns to the evil blackrobe captive, and that magician promises him he will live forever if he allows more blackrobes among us. Rather than lead the League against these French who now so boldly muster soldiers and threaten attack, rather than meet them in the forest where we can fall upon them and kill them to a man, Garacontie seeks to make peace." Kryn spat disgustedly into the fire. "This notion of his and its acceptance by the western nations breaks our League in half. We live in the worst of times, I fear."

And Kryn's words caused Tekakwitha to grieve. She grieved because the peace of Hiawatha was threatened, because the League had fallen apart, but most of all, because Kryn could do nothing about it.

6

Fitted out with feathers and the tails of foxes, squirrels, and racoons, the canoes of the Onondaga, Cayuga, and Seneca caused a great stir as they passed Montreal and Three Rivers on their way to Quebec. Glad to see the Iroquois flotilla pass, the residents nevertheless were alarmed at what it could portend. As the twenty-four canoes of white birch bark and gray elm bark landed below the cliff of Quebec, hundreds of muskets and four cannon were trained upon them. With his ceremonial staff of eagle feathers, Garacontie chanted a greeting and an offering of peace to the soldiers along the rock. Then he brought forward Father Lemoyne, bound by the wrists.

Just finishing his daily breviary, Père Claude Chauchetière heard a commotion, a rattle of muskets being seized and orders barked by lieutenants. He ran to the battlements and looked in wonder at the colorful array of three Iroquois nations. He later described the scene in a letter to his uncle.

They climbed the escarpment with a slow and dignified pace. Like grave Roman senators, their robes of skins taking the place of togas, they filed through the streets of the small city. Most had painted their faces with white clay, with ashes, with an ochre or a blue dye. The chest plates they wore were decorated with attractive patterns of red and white and green and yellow. Designs of beads and embroidery were sewn upon their garments, leather leggings, vests, and long robes. Their hair was plucked, all but a rooster's comb in the center that grew long and was greased straight into the air. All the men were beardless.

Often had I read of their savagery, their cruelty, their fiendish dances and torture. Yet, seeing them come to sue for peace in so dignified a manner, so colorfully arrayed, so grave and solemn, I hardly believed them capable of brutality. Far from the savages I had pictured, these men seemed civilized. Their weapons were primitive—spears and arrows pointed with chips of stone, a few ancient Flemish muskets—and their costumes were fashioned from the skins of the animals they hunted, and their boats seemed fragile. Yet their noble bearing, like that of our ministers and bishops, showed that intelligence and reserve guided their steps. They were among enemies, and they showed respect without fear. How different from the Algonquins and Hurons that befriend us! The difference precisely between the nobles who rule France and the rude peasants who till the soil.

Hurriedly, the bishop donned his crimson cassock, the general his armor and plumed helmet, the governor his robe of scarlet brocade. Soon, as nuns and priests bustled from the convent and the college, an assembly opened under the afternoon sky, the French sitting in chairs of state upon the cathedral steps, the Iroquois arrayed in three ranks in the square with soldiers eyeing them suspiciously.

"Brothers, we have come to you to drown the war hatchet and the musket in the waters flowing from our land to yours," Garacontie began, striding and gesturing dramatically. "Like two stags meeting in a death battle have our people met—you to stop our attacks and avenge our massacre of the Hurons; we to defend our Land From Which All Rivers Flow."

About the square, stalls in the marketplace still stood, and faces of farmers and farmers' wives craned over ranks of soldiers to see the ancient chief whose voice rolled forth.

"We must separate our antlers, so entwined in claims of ownership, and live, each in his own land, in peace. To show

our good faith, we bring a captured blackrobe along with us."
The chief turned grandiosely and a warrior brought Lemoyne
forward. "Look at him!" the chief exclaimed. "Not one of his
nails has been torn out. He has all his fingers and his eyes.
Not once have we entertained him with burning brands."

Marquis de Tracy whispered to Governor Courcelle.
"Says that like a true orator!"

"Heathen bastard!" Courcelle cursed. "We should fire on
him now."

"There will be time."

"Now, before the chief of the whites," Garacontie called
with the translator following, "I will cut the bonds and restore
this blackrobe to you." The old chief pulled a horn-handled
knife from his belt and in a grand sweep sliced the bark rope
from the priest's wrists. The assembled priests and nuns, the
habitants and traders shouted in joy. The soldiers brought
their muskets to present arms. Gravely Garacontie nodded,
and he turned with satisfaction to the Seneca and Cayuga
chiefs. "We bring other gifts as well."

Ceremoniously Garacontie, with brief descriptions of
their significance, bestowed a wampum memory belt, a robe
of white elk, an ornate tobacco pipe, cakes of maple sugar,
the bark model of a longhouse pledging the good faith of the
People of the Longhouse, a tortoiseshell drum, and a copper
bracelet inset with a large garnet mined from a cleft in the
sacred mountain of Onondaga.

After Leaping Salmon and Brown Bear presented their
gifts, Bishop Laval called the Jesuit interpreter, who deferred
to Lemoyne, and asked the chief, "Why do the brave Iroquois
send only three chiefs? Where do Canienga and Oneida hide
their emissaries of peace?"

"My brother, the red robe, asks a most difficult question." Sadly Garacontie shook his head. "Our longhouse
shelters five nations, it is true. But if the rain and sleet pour
only on one hearth fire, it will be that family who repairs that
portion of the longhouse. The League feels secure in its
longhouse holding the Land From Which All Rivers Flow, yet
two of our nations have remained at home to make repairs
they feel are needed."

"Then, they feel no danger from us?" the bishop asked,
waving toward all the soldiers.

"My brother, like the north wind, like the rain and sleet
and snow, they believe you threaten our Longhouse, for they

are closest to you. Thus they fortify their portion of the longhouse instead of coming north."

"If they fear us, why then do they not sue for peace and avoid our attack?"

"They shall fix their portion of the Great Longhouse in their own way." More than that the chief would not divulge. His wise, placid face closed inscrutably. "Send the blackrobes to the Onondaga, the People of the Mountain," he said, waving toward the sky, "and we shall learn anew of your God who lives beyond the stars."

7

After the chiefs of the three nations departed, Courcelle argued heatedly to punish the Canienga and Oneida. More than any other nation, the Canienga had harried the French. In the council chamber, Governor Courcelle howled against their arrogance in not coming as supplicants. He planned a winter attack.

A rash, impatient noble, anxious after glory, Courcelle would not listen to men who'd lived through twenty and thirty Canadian winters, who strongly advised against exposing soldiers to winds and snow. "The rivers will be smooth as French highways," Courcelle argued. "The lakes will be broad plains. Winter is the season to march as soldiers and subdue the savages, not paddle in their flimsy canoes."

Marquis de Tracy granted Courcelle five hundred soldiers for the expedition, and after Mass and Communion, praying that Adam Daulac's courage might guide them, the army set off on the ninth of January. Courcelle declared his campaign as great as Hannibal's crossing the Alps to conquer Rome, but his words of pluck proved little comfort to the infantry. Gales bent them double, sent them skidding upon the windswept ice of the St. Lawrence; the wind tore at their clothing, scattered weapons, packs, and snowshoes as they fell. They paused at Sillery and prayed to Archangel Michael that his sword of vengeance attend them. "Onward!" urged the governor.

Blizzards hid men from each other, and they groped

blindly to keep in line. The frost bit their hands, their feet, their ears, and hung from their mustaches and beards in long white icicles. Men fell in exhaustion and were dragged by companions into shivering camps each night. Reaching Three Rivers, with barely a third of the distance covered, eighty-two soldiers were disabled and left behind. Yet from that garrison, other men who were anxious for adventure joined. Courcelle ascended the Richelieu River toward Lake Champlain. From fort to fort they staggered—Fort Sorel, Fort Chambly, Fort Ste. Thérèse—past frozen cascades, through forests where trees split with the cold, over drifts higher than three men. On the first of February, the blank expanse of Lake Champlain lay before them.

Awed by the vast emptiness, Courcelle paused to pray to Isaac Jogues, the first white man to travel into the heart of this enemy land. Then he plunged onward, vowing to conquer the heathen territories where even the weather was his foe. Winds from the west swept snow into mammoth drifts; it burned and blistered the men's flesh as they struggled along in the scanty shelter of the leeward shore. At night, they scooped snow from the high drifts and sprawled together for warmth on beds of spruce and hemlock. Above, the northern lights flickered some nights; feet of snow fell others.

By the twentieth of February, Courcelle reached the lowland farms of the Dutch. His thirty Algonquin guides had drunk themselves senseless at the last French outpost, Fort Ste. Thérèse, so Courcelle had left them behind. For three days, he followed the river, not knowing where to go. Instead of falling upon the three villages of Canienga, Courcelle happened instead upon the Dutch settlement of Corlaer, and the news he heard there greatly disturbed him. The English had seized all of New Netherland! The British agent of the crown demanded to know why a French army had invaded territories of His Royal Highness King Charles II!

"I am the unluckiest man in the world," Courcelle confided to his aide-de-camp.

Hearing their plan to conquer the Canienga and Oneida, the British agent forbade it. "We are on friendly terms with the Mohawks, the nation you call Canienga, and your attack would severely displease the governor."

Courcelle balked. His army needed provisions. The agent invited them to lodge until spring in the barns of Corlaer, yet Courcelle feared his men would desert if allowed such comforts, and the spring thaw would prohibit a retreat for men unaccustomed to building canoes. With disappointment, frustration, and failure on every side, Courcelle purchased salt pork, dried beef, and biscuit from the Dutch, and with a heavy heart he turned his army northward and struggled back the way he had come.

The campaign to subdue the two eastern Iroquois nations proved a dismal failure, yet it accomplished much that was not immediately apparent. Iowerano and the other chiefs of the Canienga and Oneida had grimly watched the British seize Fort Orange from a sputtering Pieter Stuyvesant. Redcoated soldiers, new stone breastworks, and cannon now protected the settlement, renamed Albany to honor the king's brother, Duke of York and Albany. When the river thawed that year, a warship sailed into port. Like the Dutch, the Canienga had no recourse but to make peace with the English. And now, with an army of five hundred French regulars marching in the dead of winter from the stone citadels of the north, debate raged in the village of Kanawaka as to what diplomacy should be employed toward the French.

8

When Iowerano ordered her to embroider the robe, Tekakwitha had terrible misgivings. "The robe will be a gift from the Canienga to the chief of the French," Iowerano said. "It will seal the peace that we seek."

It was the first time her prowess with bone needles and porcupine quills had been recognized by her foster father, but that was not what unsettled her. News of the British taking New Amsterdam and Fort Orange threw the village into turmoil; far more warlike than the Dutch, the British posed a threat to the League, particularly to the easternmost nation, the Canienga. Now five hundred soldiers had invaded from the north, all the way to the eastern porch of the Great Longhouse. Many of the warriors had been hunting when Governor Courcelle reached Corlaer. If the British hadn't stopped them, Kanawaka would have been a smoking ruin.

But what troubled her the most was her feeling she was betraying Kryn.

"We should make no pact with the French," Kryn insisted to Iowerano. "Let us aid the redcoats in driving the French out of this land. You should not abandon the plan you framed after we left last summer's council."

"Rather than go away," Iowerano said, "the whites invite more and more of their brothers to our land. Let us make peace with both the redcoats and the bluecoats, then neither can enlist us to attack the other. It does not suit the purpose of the League to act as the white man's tomahawk."

"Your reasoning meanders like the creek through a swamp, Cold Wind," Kryn said. Tekakwitha, in the shadows, thrilled to hear him address Iowerano with such disdain. "The Canienga must reason like the broad river that flows through the heart of our land. We have a treaty with the British. Far off in their land across the sea they are at war with the French. They will also soon be at war in this land. We cannot remain neutral."

"And yet, Kryn, it is possible to make peace and afterward to catch the French off guard."

"I know the value of a surprise attack," Kryn nodded. "But why make the overture of peace? By making pacts and giving our word and telling each one what he wishes to hear, a net is being woven of cross alliances," Kryn said, knitting his fingers together to demonstrate, "a net that will catch us up. Let us ignore Garacontie and his journey to the French city. The bluecoats' attack failed. So will all attacks upon us."

But despite Kryn's plea, Iowerano ruled that the Turtle Clan would join the flotilla headed by old Garacontie that summer, and peace would be made between all five nations and the French. With the sense each stitch was an irrevocable step toward confrontation, Tekakwitha sewed the ceremonial robe of buckskin, careful to keep it and herself out of Kryn's sight.

9

Quebec bustled with activity that spring. With no battles imminent, soldiers built barns, cleared fields, graded roads, and in general radiated civilization out from the hub of the town. Chapels and shrines went up along roadways. Church bells tolled. In May, when Gallic hearts thought of home, remembering Normandy and Bordeaux and Provence and Paris, a maypole rose outside the town, and yeoman's daughters wove colorful ribbons in an age-old dance, accompanied by pipes and tabors. Athletic contests among the soldiers and even a few swaggering, drunken nights spoke more eloquently than any royal edict that France had taken possession of what had been before a desolate, forbidding wilderness.

Brown Bear, the new Seneca chief, arrived first, followed in two days by Leaping Salmon, the great Cayuga, and then Garacontie. A week-long festival was planned. Early in July the Oneida, led by the Scarred One, and the Canienga, led by Iowerano, climbed the twisting path to the top of Quebec's escarpment. Solemnly, in council dress, the chiefs entered the square to embrace their brothers in the League.

"Many have asked if the Flemish Bastard will join you," Garacontie said to Iowerano. "His reputation from the Huron raids has caused the French to hope he will join in smoking the peace pipe."

"Kryn, the half-breed they know by that name, is rebellious by nature," Iowerano said. "He has not joined us. Nevertheless, I do not fear that he will be one to break the peace. If he becomes sullen, he journeys off by himself into the woods to hunt and fish. He will abide by the wishes of the League."

"That is good," Garacontie said.

For a week French and Iroquois lived harmoniously together. On the last day of the Iroquois' visit, a great banquet and peace-making ceremony was planned. Warriors ranged through the forests and returned with deer and bear and elk. They fished trout and pike and bass from lakes and streams. The French baked pastries and prepared gravies and sauces. Tables were set up in the square and loaded with game and poultry and fish. The French carefully avoided giving wine to the Iroquois. As the sun set and torches were lit, Bishop Laval, Governor Courcelle, Marquis de Tracy, and Intendant Talon, all wearing their robes of office, sat in chairs on the steps of the cathedral.

Garacontie, wearing his embroidered skins, paced and gestured and solemnly addressed all. "This summer, all five nations of our Longhouse have come among you as brothers.

Together we have eaten the flesh of the fleet-footed deer so our mutual love may bound and run swiftly." He reached into a pouch. "To you as brothers we give the gift of maize, kernels from our finest ears, so the sun, the rain, and the land we share may sustain us both." Garacontie handed the seeds up to Marquis de Tracy. He motioned Iowerano to bring forth the ceremonial robe.

"From the land of the People of Flint, the Canienga, closest to you, offer you a robe," Garacontie spoke. "It has been sewn by their finest seamstress. You see embroidered here the longhouse of my people, and within, the five families warm themselves at their separate hearth fires. Outside, the wind and rain and sleet demand entry into the warmth and comfort of our longhouse. So do the three nations of whites press to gain entry to the Land From Which All Rivers Flow. Our house is strong, and all five families will seek to keep out the rain and sleet and wind. By presenting the great chief of the northern river this robe, may he find shelter in it and not seek to enter our longhouse."

Through the interpreter Tracy responded. "I am most grateful, Chief Garacontie, for this gift. Know that as long as your people dwell in peace with us, we will not enter your land. Brothers must trust one another. Let us, therefore, clasp hands, hands that have no weapons, and seal the peace."

The old marquis held out his hands, and the old chief clasped them. A cheer rang out from the soldiers and the priests and nuns watching. The Iroquois warriors, however, respected the gravity of the ceremony with silence.

"And lastly," Garacontie said, "to assure the peace, we will give you twenty-four men to hold as a pledge. They will lodge with you, teaching you such secrets of the forest you wish to know and learning from you such things that will be useful to our people. I grow old, Great Chief, and my eyes have seen much bloodshed, my ears have heard the screams of much suffering, my hand has dealt many death blows. May the pact we seal here bring at last the peace of Hiawatha to our land. There is much in common in the words of Hiawatha and the victim of torture who died on the crossed poles, your Christ. I have learned much from the blackrobe we freed last year. Such knowledge, I believe, will help my people. I ask you, Great Chief, to send blackrobes among us now, even as we leave our twenty-four youths with you."

In the throng of Jesuits watching the ceremony, Claude Chauchetière had been listening carefully, trying to understand the guttural Iroquois tongue he had been studying, trying to compare what the chief said with what the interpreter spoke to Tracy. When he heard the chief's request, his eyes glistened with tears, he shuddered with emotion, and he bowed and made the sign of the cross. "Praise be to Jesus," he whispered.

The marquis held up his hand and Garacontie bowed, allowing him to interrupt. "Your people have killed blackrobes and massacred the Hurons whom they were teaching. Your treatment of the blackrobes has been more severe than the treatment of other white men. Why now do you wish them to journey among you?"

Garacontie bowed, then cast his eyes upward. Though his physical sight had failed in his dotage, his spiritual sight had grown keener, and he suspected the peace of Hiawatha and the peace of the blackrobes' Christ were the same. He saw in his deepening blindness beyond mere objects, and he now chanted to the evening sky. When finished, he spoke slowly. "The blackrobes, I have found, possess magic far more powerful than the magic of our people. The blackrobes show bravery far greater than the Dutch or English. The blackrobe Jogues returned to the Canienga, even after he had been tortured and had escaped. I have seen the blackrobes heal our children. They learn our tongue and inquire about our customs. They speak of a happy place where ghosts journey when the body goes under the earth. I believe the blackrobes, who never ask for land as do most whites, will be proper envoys between us."

"The chief's words," Tracy said, "make the bishop, the governor, and myself happy men. Now the blackrobes can journey out from their stone cloisters to your land of the Great Longhouse from which rivers flow in all directions. And great will be the mutual respect and understanding we will reach."

"Let us then smoke the pipe of peace," Chief Garacontie said. He produced a long iron tomahawk with a pipe on the reverse side of the blade. From his pouch he took tobacco, lit the pipe from a nearby torch, passed it to the Scarred One who puffed on it, then to Leaping Salmon, Brown Bear, and finally to Iowerano. Iowerano held the pipe a long minute, glaring at the row of French officials in their scarlet robes, and at the soldiers in blue uniforms. Reluctantly he placed the stem to his lips, drew in a small puff of smoke and exhaled with the sound of a spit. A warrior carried the pipe to the Frenchmen, and they smoked in succession. When at last Tracy drew long upon the pipe, and exhaled a great cloud of smoke, the soldiers and nuns and Jesuits cheered loudly.

Iowerano spoke to Agariata, chief of the Canienga's Wolf Clan, "Let us gather the Canienga and return to our homes. The conditions of this peace do not please me."

"Nor me," Agariata said, narrowing his eyes.

As the leader of the Canienga delegation, Iowerano had authority to refuse the treaty. Yet he'd felt compelled to follow Garacontie. Now he turned to Yellow Cloud, chief of the Canienga's Bear Clan. "Let us leave this place."

"I wish to stay," Yellow Cloud said.

"Agariata and I find a surprise in this agreement. Garacontie has invited the blackrobes among all nations. We do not want them."

"I will also open Tionnontake to the blackrobes," Yellow Cloud said.

"Yet to reach your village, they must pass Kanawaka," Iowerano protested.

Yellow Cloud nodded with tightened lips, and with the hint of a threat in his voice, he said, "And you will assure them safety."

This infuriated Iowerano. "I will not answer for what may happen."

Yellow Cloud corrected him. "You and the entire League will answer."

Enraged, Iowerano stormed from the square. "See how the white man's peace divides us?" he fumed. Together he and Agariata collected their warriors and descended the escarpment to the riverbank. They slept a few hours in the open, and when the sun rose, they pushed out in their bark canoes and paddled upriver. Rather than subside, Iowerano's anger heated with each stroke of the paddle. He felt betrayed by Garacontie since no provision for inviting the blackrobes had been discussed this year. He remembered the hated Jogues who had buried the silver cup and plate in the ground, and he remembered the worms that had devoured the maize crop so that the Turtle Clan had to revert to a nomadic life, hunting like bark-eaters in the mountains.

"The blackrobes are fools!" Iowerano told Agariata. "They

tell us we can have only one wife, and yet they say it is wrong to kill. How then can we dispose of the others? Tell me! No," he scoffed, "it is impossible to obey both laws at the same time."

"You speak the truth, Cold Wind," said Agariata, hauling his canoe from the river to carry it around a cascade. "The blackrobe says all men are the same, but we do not know how to make coats like theirs or guns or iron hatchets."

Sullenly they journeyed on. At each of the three forts on the Richelieu, French soldiers greeted them and asked about the ceremony. Some warriors spoke, but Iowerano watched the French suspiciously, htis hand on his musket. No occasion for retaliation presented itself, and this angered Iowerano even further. He longed to fall upon the whites, burn the forts, and return to Kanawaka with a collection of scalps on his belt.

As he launched his canoe into Lake Champlain, shots rang out in a nearby wood. "They fire upon us!" Iowerano cried.

"Today," Agariata spoke, looking at the overcast sky, "the whites shall learn a lesson."

Quickly both chiefs turned their canoes toward shore, and the other warriors in their party followed. All the Canienga, whooping at the top of their lungs, took up the chase, beached their canoes, spilled over onto the sand, and ran full speed into the forest, screaming and brandishing tomahawks.

A hunting party of French officers from Fort Ste. Thérèse had been stalking a bull moose. Wounded in the shoulder, the moose had bellowed horribly, and other soldiers had shot at it to bring it down. Yet, hearing the Iroquois war whoops, the French abandoned their moose and ran pell-mell through the woods. Fear spurred them on as the war whoops grew nearer. Screaming to each other, "Iroquois!" they fled over fallen trunks and rocks, twisting ankles, heedless of the branches that slapped them as they ran. Nearly two leagues separated them from the fort. The Iroquois were gaining. Finally François Chasy, a young gentleman who'd led the group, halted. He called to the others, "Peace has been made. Let us stand and talk to them." The others, disheartened by the nearing shouts and the difficult path, stopped and gathered about Chasy. "I shall speak to them, Pierre, if you will translate." Chasy's cousin nodded.

On came the Canienga, bounding through the forest,

and soon fifty evil-looking warriors surrounded them. "Brave chief," Chasy said to Iowerano, frightened at the horrible looks of the Iroquois braves, "we did not fire upon you. We were hunting. We brought down a moose."

Iowerano advanced, trembling with rage. "You lie!"

"I shall take you to it," Chasy offered.

"Is this the way the white man keeps his word?" Iowerano cried, glaring at the French. "We shall take hostages." He pointed his hatchet at Chasy. "I shall enjoy entertaining this one upon the scaffold."

Pierre Leroles muttered the translation.

"No!" said Chasy. "We were only hunting! We shot the moose!"

"Silence!"

"You must believe me!" Chasy pleaded, his arms outstretched. "We have no evil thought against you! Go! Go to your homes!" Pierre conveyed these words.

"Silence!"

"You must leave us here! The peace!!"

Agariata grinned cruelly. "We shall leave you here alone," he said, "but the rest will come with us." And he swung his hatchet and buried it in the skull of the young man. Chasy reeled and fell, blood streaming down his face. The other whites looked on, horrified. Fearing the same fate, they fell silent and docile.

Iowerano howled, "Bind them! Old Garacontie returns with a useless peace. It is war trophies we bring home." The others sprang to their task and bound the men with thongs and bark rope, and led them to the canoes.

Two officers had escaped, and the news spread quickly: The Canienga had broken the peace only days after it was made. Search parties were sent from the fort to comb the woods. François Chasy's corpse was found. News reached Quebec three days later. Marquis de Tracy was plunged into mourning—François Chasy had been his sister's eldest son. He did not kill the Iroquois hostages, but he dispatched three hundred soldiers to retrieve Pierre Leroles and the others.

Down through the network of waterways and portages the Canienga brought the whites. Runners announced them at Kanawaka. Yet, when Iowerano's party broke from the forest, no column of villagers met them. No fires had been kindled to burn the prisoners. No rattles or drums sounded with anticipation.

Kryn stood at the gate to the palisade with folded arms. "These prisoners will be returned," he said firmly, barring the gateway.

"Step aside, Kryn!" Iowerano said threateningly.

"If you will not return them, I shall."

"We took these men as they fired upon us."

"You have broken the peace you set out to make," Kryn countered. "I wanted no peace with the whites, but old Garacontie framed it and all the People of the Longhouse pledged their word. Our entire Clan of the Turtle and Yellow Cloud's people of the Bear Clan wish these prisoners returned."

"Impossible!" Iowerano cried.

"You have only to consult your mother, the eldest matriarch."

"I shall."

While Iowerano entered the village alone, Kryn remained by the gate, glaring at the bloodthirsty band and the terrified, half-naked whites. After a time, Iowerano returned.

"It is so," Iowerano said to Agariata. "My two cousins are held by the whites as hostages. No matter if the peace is broken, the women of my *ohwachira* wish the prisoners returned. Kryn has been named to accompany them."

"Give them food this night," Kryn ordered, "and allow them to rest. Tomorrow we shall depart."

Sullenly Iowerano's party entered the palisade.

Days later, passing along a rocky path, on a portage, the three hundred French soldiers in boots slipped and slid, their legs buckling under the loads of canoes and weapons and food. Determination to rescue their fellow soldiers spurred them on, yet the sombre quiet and the shrill cries of jays and crows caused them to scan the forest warily. Suddenly, above them on both sides of the pass, Iroquois materialized as if from air. Loaded down as they were, the French soldiers couldn't reach their muskets. The long line of Frenchmen halted, looking from side to side at Iroquois guns trained upon them.

Kryn advanced to the captain of the company. "We do not wish to capture you," he said. "This ambush is to prevent injury to anyone. We have the men who were taken captive, and we wish to return them to your stone city, Quebec."

Hastily the captain spoke with the interpreter, then

replied, "Peace has been broken. A man has been slain. We do not accept these terms."

"Many more shall be slain," Kryn said, scanning the Canienga who lined the defile. "Today. On this spot."

"Not seven days after peace was made, a war party killed a young gentleman!" the captain protested. "We are sent to bring the others back and to chastize those who broke the peace."

Kryn considered. Agariata nodded. Kryn spoke thoughtfully. "Water that foams and boils in the rapids grows placid in the broad river. Do not think of rapids behind. They have been passed. We shall deliver the men into your hands. We shall make full payment for the young man's death, and we shall accompany you in good faith."

Entering Quebec, the young officer boasted, "I have captured the Flemish Bastard." As they smoked their pipes after supper, Kryn and Agariata were seized, manacled, and flung into prison with the twenty-four hostages. Cathedral bells rang in joy for the returned men, and in his Sunday sermon, Bishop Laval preached that though ninety-nine remained in the flock, the good shepherd would risk all peril to rescue the one sheep who'd been lost.

In the dark cell that stank of nitrous mold and excrement, Kryn continually demanded of the jailer that he see the Great Chief. The turnkey laughed at his superior airs and was quite pleased that he had the legendary Flemish Bastard in custody. Constantly Agariata chided Kryn. "See now the white man's treachery?"

Two weeks passed. In confession one Saturday, a lieutenant whispered the true story of the campaign—how Kryn had ambushed them, delivered the prisoners into their hands, then accompanied them to Quebec to reestablish peace. The priest, Claude Chauchetière, immediately presented himself to Tracy. The marquis summoned the captain, threw him in chains, and threatened execution. He then issued orders that the four chiefs be made presentable and join him at dinner the following day.

Candelabra cast gentle light upon goblets of cut glass, wine decanters, delicate china, and silver utensils as the four Canienga, in ill-fitting sailors' clothes, were ushered in. Wild flowers, arranged by nuns, decorated the center of the table, and fifteen servants in livery stood strategically about the room, waiting for the marquis. Shown to their places, the Canienga sat uncomfortably in the white man's chairs. Like astonished children, they folded their hands, afraid of disturbing anything.

The door swung wide and the great, bulky Marquis de Tracy entered. Two boys advanced, pulled out his chair, and he sat grumpily down. "Welcome, chiefs," he growled and his whiskers shook. Arranging his napkin, he turned to the head of the servants. "Bring soup," he ordered.

The door opened again, and a slender, dark-haired Jesuit entered and sat at the marquis's right hand. The Jesuit sat bolt upright and maintained a reserved expression, even when the marquis said to him, "Pretty devils, aren't they?"

"I am sure in their homes they are loved and respected," Père Claude responded.

"Bah!" The marquis ladled soup from the silver tureen and motioned for Kryn's dish. Kryn peered around the room as if sensing something not entirely right. His soup arrived and he paused for all to be served, as he'd seen whites do before. The marquis called for the wine steward to fill all glasses. Kryn counseled the Canienga not to drink, but Agariata held up his glass to be filled. They began the meal with a toast, and the Canienga put the bowls to their mouths and emptied them in one gulp.

Next was served pheasant, then racks of spring lamb. The Canienga ripped the bones apart and ate hungrily. Although the spices and sauces of French cuisine did not please them, they'd been living on oat gruel in the dungeon for the past two weeks. With each course came a new wine, and Agariata gulped his glass, outdoing both the Jesuit and Tracy. The marquis ate with zest, savoring each bite, swallowing it with wine, talking animatedly with the Jesuit. After the meat, he called for apples and cinnamon. Finally, an interpreter entered. Warily Kryn watched the entrances and exits of servants, sensing something not at all right.

"So, you come to reaffirm your bid for peace?" Tracy said, picking his teeth with a wood sliver.

"The peace of Hiawatha extends to all men," Kryn said, hands folded. His blue eyes gleamed in the candlelight. Père Claude Chauchetière listened intently to the interpreter.

"For a score of years your people have attacked and carried off and massacred Frenchmen, yet now you sue for peace. Do you tire of war?"

"No!" bellowed Agariata, flushed with wine. Kryn placed his hand on Agariata's, cautioning him, and spoke to the general. "The Great Chief must know the land is broad enough for all."

"Yet, you fear our soldiers will invade your land," Tracy suggested.

"Canienga fight like *okies* in the land of others, and doubly hard in their homeland. Yours is a mighty army, yet we too have many guns and many brave men."

"Peace seems impossible with the People of the Longhouse," Tracy said, smiling cynically. His purpose was to anger Kryn.

"And yet, that is all we want." Kryn opened his hands frankly.

"The half-breed lies like all Iroquois."

At this, Agariata sprang from his chair, but Kryn wrestled him down.

"Such fire and rage cannot be cooled with reason," the marquis said, sitting back, idly picking his teeth. The other Canienga watched a battle of wits that only Kryn seemed to understand. "No agreement will ever be honored, so what does it matter the words we use?"

"Our chief, Iowerano, made a bad mistake," Kryn said, his blue eyes glaring in the candlelight, "and I take steps to set things right. Yet I am imprisoned, then insulted."

"The thief always tries to cover his tracks," Tracy sneered.

With a cry, Agariata grabbed a knife and lunged at Tracy. Behind the door, clattering noises were heard, yet Tracy cried, "No! Stay out!" Alarmed, Père Claude left his chair and huddled with the servants by the sideboard. Again Kryn restrained Agariata, and with angry words ordered him to remain seated.

"Come, Père Claude, resume your seat," Tracy invited, ridiculing the priest's fear. "These are fine dinner guests, and they shall teach us much about digestion." Cautiously the Jesuit again took his chair, and the marquis continued sarcastically. "And as soon as the peace was made and both sides parted brothers, not seven days passed until Chasy, my nephew, was murdered by a tomahawk."

Agariata leered at him, held up a clenched fist. "And this is the hand that split that skull!"

"Now!" called Tracy, and both doors burst open. Armored soldiers trained muskets upon the Iroquois. They seized the four chiefs and hauled them from the room down into the courtyard, where they bound them with tarred nautical ropes.

In the glare of torches, soldiers ran back and forth calling to each other. Jesuits from the college convened with the town's officials. From the cathedral steps, Marquis de Tracy supervised the operations.

Quickly all was prepared. Over the crosspiece of a tall wooden cross, they slung a noose. Beneath the noose they placed a table, and upon it, an empty powder keg. Roughly manhandling Agariata, they stood him upon the keg. A soldier fastened the noose around the chief's neck. Alone, teetering on the keg, Agariata laughed at them. Then, as the marquis called his men to attention, from within Agariata rumbled his death song.

"Against the Hurons I led the charge. When we scaled walls, I was first. We tortured blackrobes with coals and knives, and in the morning, the women wailed. In the deep forest I hunted bear. The red eyes I never knew before suddenly growling, upon me sprang and clawed raw wounds where the blood flowed free."

"Witness, you they call the Flemish Bastard!" Tracy cried. "Take back to your people what you see tonight. Know your raids and your lies will be tolerated no longer. I will burn your villages and scatter your nation to the winds."

"In the raging water I steered my craft," howled Agariata. "The boulders sprang at my frail canoe. I plunged over falls with no more of a cry than the old chief makes when filling his pipe. In the month of the wolf, while on the hunt over the frozen lakes where the old ones died, I chased bison—" There was a sharp rush of breath, a gagging sound, and in the thick summer night in the ruddy light of torches, Agariata danced in the air like a child's doll, legs thrashing, head lunging back and forth. Slowly life subsided, and his twitching corpse came to rest.

"Carry this back with you!" Tracy called triumphantly. "I've executed Dutch heretics, Turkish infidels, Spanish pirates, and even Frenchmen deserting my command. Soon I will execute the Canienga and burn your towns for the murder of my nephew."

With his jaw set firmly, Kryn glared up at the marquis. Humiliated by two weeks in the dungeon, insulted at the table, now forced to watch the execution, he vowed revenge for himself and his people against the old marquis and all the French.

Already the Jesuits knelt, praying for the dead man's soul. Yet the soldiers did not cut him down at once. Standing at attention, they watched with great satisfaction as the body turned slowly in the summer wind.

10

On the Feast of the Exaltation of the Cross, Tracy, Courcelle, and thirteen hundred men left Quebec in three hundred large canoes to chastise the Canienga. The vast flotilla passed Three Rivers, entered the Richelieu, and with a steady progress alternately paddled and carried their craft. At last they launched their navy upon the placid surface of Lake Champlain. October had painted the wood with luxuriant hues of crimson, purple, rust, and gold, and overhead, loud flocks of geese passed in formation.

By night, the French camped upon islands and sandbars, and the stiffening autumn wind blew campfires bright, casting shadows upon pine backdrops. By day, they threw their backs and shoulders into the painful paddling. Up through the inlet they wended, into Lake of the Blessed Sacrament, then down the eight leagues of that clear lake through the labyrinth of islands and narrows, finally beaching their navy of canoes upon a headland. Twenty leagues of forest, swamp, rivers, and mountains lay before them—a narrow, broken Iroquois path.

A hundred and ten hardy Montreal natives blazed the trail led by Lemoyne, the Jesuit whom Garacontie had freed. Five hundred Canadians followed with six hundred Europeans, and a hundred Huron and Algonquin converts ranged in the forest like hounds in front, flank, and rear. All carried great packs of shot, powder, and provisions. The aged Tracy, seized with gout, bore up as best he could. When a Swiss soldier tried to carry the marquis across a swift stream, his strength failed, and barely did the soldier get him to a submerged rock. Hurons came to their aid, struggling and splashing, and soon ferried Tracy to the other side.

Provisions gave out as they struggled along through the forest. Faint with hunger, the men chewed the leather of their straps. At night, exhausted, they stretched out upon the barren ground only to awaken to the delirium of trudging onward. Four days after leaving the lake, they stumbled upon a grove of chestnut trees, and they boiled chestnuts in kettles to stave off their hunger.

11

Terror seized Tekakwitha when Arosen ran through the lanes crying, "The whole world is coming against us! Quick! We must flee!" All the villagers rushed out of their long-houses and assembled in the center of the village. Kryn cautioned Arosen against alarming the people. "I have seen them!" Arosen cried. "More men than at Onondaga in the summer!"

"How far away?" Iowerano asked.

"One day's journey! They all have muskets and swords and pistols! We must flee!"

Hastily Iowerano and Kryn conferred. Tekakwitha approached Arosen.

"What will happen if we decide to stay and fight?"

"We all will die!" Arosen cried. "The army reaches far along the trail, nearly as far as Ossernenon lies from here." He threw up his hands. "This is what comes from angering the whites. The League is destroyed, and now we'll all be slaughtered!"

"Will they hang us by ropes from trees as Kryn described?" the girl asked.

"They will drive spikes through our flesh for they worship a man who died that way!"

Anxiously Tekakwitha watched Kryn and Iowerano argue. Iowerano wished to send for the Bear and Wolf Clans to surround the army and massacre them to a man. "This is our homeland," Iowerano argued. "We must guard the eastern gate! We must stand here."

"Let us pack quickly and retreat to the Bear Clan's

village, Tionnontake," Kryn said. "There we can make our stand."

"Fear is like fire—once kindled it burns higher and higher, consuming what engendered it."

"Farther upriver," Kryn said, "lies Andaragon, the village of the Wolf Clan. Andaragon is the strongest fortress of our nation. Let us gather the Bear Clan and all of us—Turtle, Bear, and Wolf—will join in protecting Andaragon."

"No," Iowerano said. "Once the back is turned, the enemy pursues with renewed strength. Their army is weakened by the journey. White men cannot survive in the forests. Let us fall upon them here."

Throughout the village, rumors, fears, and accusations, fanned by many tongues, burned like a forest fire. In panic, the people turned to the Women's Council. "Nothing as large as this army has ever been seen in our land," the women ruled. "Let us retreat and our scouts can watch its progress up the river valley and report about the chances of an ambush."

Everyone hurried into the longhouses and hastily packed belongings and food into leather bags. With great apprehension, Tekakwitha gathered her sewing materials and followed the refugees in a line out of the western gate.

12

The evening Huron scouts reported Kanawaka lay in striking distance, a storm broke. "We will push on all night!" decreed Tracy, and the men, envisioning food supplies they might pillage, took heart. Fallen trees, bogs, beaver ponds slowed them. Soaked and chilled to the bone, they stumbled on as if sleepwalking. After the dark, interminable night, a blustery day dawned. The vanguard emerged from the forest downriver from the Canienga corn plantations. Bleached cornstalks rattled in the October wind. High upon a hill rose the palisade of thick, pointed logs, its gates closed. Canoes of gray elm bark lined the mudbanks of the river. The quiet was suspicious, ominous.

The marquis's captains drew the men into orderly rank,

and with the drummers beating a tatoo, the men fixed their bayonets and charged. Quickly the infantrymen ran toward the breastworks, expecting a shower of musket fire and arrows, but they met no resistance. Forcing the gates, they spilled into the narrow, deserted lanes of Kanawaka, finding only a few dogs and a half-skinned deer carcass. They swarmed through the longhouses, ripping the tapestries of dried corn from bark walls. Some of the men kindled a fire from the bark and poles of a longhouse, and soon they had a stew cooking of dog and deer and corn, yet this only whetted their hunger.

By midmorning the troops were mustered, and with the drums beating a quick march, they covered the two leagues to the next village, Tionnontake, home of the Bear Clan. Along the route, Canienga scouts were spied on hills, firing muskets out of range. Like Kanawaka, the second village stood on a knoll high above the river. Cautiously, the soldiers flanked the battlements, then to the quick beat of the drum they charged. Bursting through the gates of the second village, they encountered a similar sight—all had fled.

A quick search produced two old men who reported, under torture, that the Canienga were hiding in the forests, unwilling to fight. Some baskets and bundles of pelts attested the flight had been quick.

"There is no use pursuing them," the marquis was told by his advisers. "They are scattered like leaves in the wind, and once in the forest, theirs is the advantage."

Tracy considered. "We will sleep here tonight and search for maize. Tomorrow we will burn this village and the lower one as well, and winter can accomplish what we have been unable to do." But as they pitched camp outside the walls, a woman was brought to Tracy. The old general, gout swelling his ankles, lay on a bed of pelts. Through the interpreter, the woman, an Algonquin who had once been captured by the Canienga, told of another village farther upriver.

"The third village is the largest of this nation," she said. "It is very well fortified and sits on a crag that can't be approached except by a narrow path."

This news brought a quick call to arms. Word spread down the chains of command to the infantrymen. Exhausted, hungry, fearful of an ambush in this alien land, they nevertheless fell into rank and file and stepped out. Holding a pistol in one hand and Courcelle's sleeve in the other, the Algonquin woman led them on to seek revenge at Andaragon.

13

In a frenzy White Adder spun and leapt. "Tawiskaron! God of serpents! Strike with venom and spite! To Aireskou we will offer all the whites we take today!"

As a sacrifice to the war god, eight Algonquins were roasted on spits in the center of the third village, Andaragon. Joined by other medicine men, White Adder prayed for the destruction of the French army while the chiefs met in council to decide between retreat and a night ambush.

Tekakwitha sat with Tegonhat and Karitha. The uncertainty and commotion frightened her terribly. The League had been shattered. No other nation could come to the aid of the Canienga upon such short notice. Descriptions of the white army unsettled the bravest of the men. Where would they go? Would the butchery and the blood-letting begin before nightfall? The three clans filled Andaragon with squalling children, fearful mothers, wary old people, and grim warriors. Food would be in short supply within a week. If surrounded, where could they get water? The great pine tree of Hiawatha's peace was tottering and about to fall. Worse than the liquor, worse than the weapons, even worse than the disease, the white man himself was marching unchallenged through their land, raining death upon the people.

In the council house the debate raged. "We must stand here and fight," Iowerano insisted.

"We should scatter into the forest where we'll never be found," Kryn countered. "The white man cannot survive in our land. He will leave soon, and next year we will build our villages stronger."

"What of the winter?" asked Yellow Cloud, chief of the Bear Clan.

"We have been homeless before," Kryn said. "I participate here because I wish that my strategy will save the lives of others. But when we hear the drums of the white man, I will leave with my household."

"Coward!" Silver Fish, new chief of the Wolf Clan, called.

"Words and names are of no use to a corpse," Kryn said. "Iowerano and Agariata provoked these whites. No land has ever seen such an army massed. With sheer numbers they will overrun our palisades. It will be like our forces falling upon the yellow-haired Frenchman who held out so heroically against our six hundred. No, we must flee."

Heated argument met Kryn's words.

14

Twilight was descending when Tracy's forces reached the headland of the river and the third and final village of the Canienga rose before his army. Large, well-fortified with four bastions, the fortress showed much Dutch influence. Gun ports riddled the walls. Yet not one shot met them.

"It could be an ambush, waiting for us to get close and overconfident," a battle-hardened aide counseled Tracy.

"We'll storm them and take the fortress coup de main."

The command ran down through the ranks with lightning speed. Affixing their bayonets, checking the dryness of their powder, the men nervously talked of victory and of death. Bristling with nervous energy, the troops flanked the black rock where the fortress stood and readied themselves for the command. No sign of warriors met their expectant eyes. The fleur-de-lis fluttered from the guidon's pole. All fell quiet for a long moment. All stood at attention, adrenalin pumping through their limbs, empty stomachs complaining and tense. Then Tracy's sword flashed in the dull light. "Charge!" sounded from fifty captains' throats. "Charge!" repeated twelve hundred men, and in a screaming blue wave, the army charged up the black rock, seventy feet above the river, and burst through three gates simultaneously. The fourth gate soon fell, and the men ran through the lanes, empty except for discarded baggage.

Marquis de Tracy toiled up the slope behind his men, assisted by his Jesuit confessor, Père Claude Chauchetière.

"Go in, enter this place of the devil, Father," Tracy told him, "and bless the ground."

Père Claude entered the town and walked among the bark huts as he had in the lower towns, considering what manner of people could live so simply. The stenches of dung and putrified meat and ash mingled in horrible testament to superstition and ignorance. Père Claude remembered sharply the gypsy camp so long before, so far away, when he lost his innocence. In filth, this far outstripped the camp of those pariahs. Mud, excrement, slaughtered beasts, lingering smoke... Distracted by his reveries of the gypsy camp, he turned a corner. The sight he spied brought him suddenly to his knees, and uncontrollably he doubled up and retched upon the ground.

Eight corpses upon spits, half-roasted, charred and naked, remained as unfinished offerings to the war god. Père Claude retched and retched. Now a new stench invaded his senses—burning human flesh, burning hair. Beneath the corpses, fires burned low, and drips of human fat sizzled on the coals. One corpse's head hung down at an impossible angle. Another's chest cavity had been hacked open and lungs hung out. Another had been disemboweled, and the spit entered between its buttocks and proceeded out its mouth.

As he crawled away to escape the sight, Claude saw before him the swollen, gouty feet of his general. Looking up, he gagged, tears streaming down his cheeks. "Devils!" he gasped. "Devils!" More terrible than any of his imagined sights of hell, more putrid than a Paris sewer or the hold of a ship, more sickening than any plague—the encounter, when he looked again, caused him new spasms.

The marquis spat into the dust. "Baptize them, Father." And Tracy turned away, shaking his head.

Marquis de Tracy's manner calmed Père Claude somewhat. He swallowed, wiped away the tears that streamed from his eyes. He stumbled to his feet, swallowing his gorge that rose from moment to moment, and his head swimming, he proceeded to the scene of sacrifice. With a gourd cup of water, he went then from corpse to corpse, making the sign of the cross. *"In nomine Patris, et Filii, et Spiritu Sancti, Amen."*

The troops found two old women, one man, and a small

boy who had hidden under a canoe. The boy talked to Tracy through an interpreter.

"Here all clans of the Canienga amassed. Here the Canienga resolved to fight to the death. The men lined the scaffolds and the towers of the bastions with loaded guns and quivers of arrows and piles of stone and full tanks of water. The victims had been burned; Aireskou was appeased. Then seeing the army marching in pursuit, all cried as one, 'Let us save ourselves, brothers! The entire world is coming against us.' The Canienga fled into the forest, scattered as leaves in the autumn wind."

"That is good," Tracy said with great satisfaction, "and in a like manner, we will dispel the demons here." He instructed his men to erect a cross where the victims had been roasted, and at its side there also rose a standard emblazoned with the crest of the Sun King, Louis XIV.

As evening fell upon that blustery autumn day, the marquis arrayed his men, drawn up in rank and file through the large town. He advanced among them, sword in hand, to the central compound, and he raised the sword to the cross and to the royal standard. In a loud voice, he intoned, "In the name of King Louis, I take possession of all lands of the Canienga!"

"Vive le Roi!" cheered the troops.

"And I claim for the crown, too, all land they hold in subjugation."

"Vive le Roi!"

"And I claim the chain of lakes and rivers from our land to this, to hold evermore, to settle, and to raise the cross of Holy Mother the Church above this land of Satan!"

"Vive le Roi!" the men cried, ecstatic in triumph.

That night, a mighty bonfire lit the tall primeval forests of the Canienga, reflecting hellishly in the river and against the leaden clouds. Two old women found in the village pitched themselves onto the pyre rather than be taken. Higher, higher the flames burned, crackling and spitting, purging for the Europeans the evil of the place.

In the morning, the great town of Andaragon was a smoldering heap of ash. Père Claude Chauchetière set up an altar near the entrance to the village, and with the corn from storage pits heaped about, he offered Mass and blessed the food. Thirteen hundred soldiers knelt in the mud and ash to hear Père Claude's impassioned *Hoc est enim corpus meum* ring out over the great ash heap, over the harvested cornfields and the painted backdrop of an October wood. Claude's hands trembled with emotion as he raised the host into the damp air. Then, for a benediction, the men intoned *Te Deum*.

Collecting corn from underground pits, they touched off the cornfields and burned all corn they could not carry. Then the vast army turned, and to the steady drum, marched back down the course of the river, burning the remaining villages, the hoards and stores of corn, and all canoes and fields. Not a shot had been fired, not a man injured or killed. If his army hadn't annihilated the Canienga, Tracy reasoned, destruction would be visited by famine, snow, and the relentless winter wind.

PEACE IN THE VALLEY

The Land of Flint
1666

1

The three clans of Canienga retreated to a high tableland a league north of Andaragon. From the brink of the cliff that very night, they watched the bark huts and the palisade burn. Joined by other medicine men, White Adder implored the heavens to rain and extinguish the flames. Helplessness and dejection, sorrow and rage filled the homeless ones.

Tekakwitha and Tegonhat stood together watching sparks erupt and flames roll into the night sky. "Each time we fled upriver, Tegonhat, sorrow pierced my heart. Each flight meant the Canienga lost more. Like cowering dogs we allow the whites to force us from our land, and we growl, but we do not bite. What will become of us now?"

"It was Iowerano's rash act in the northern wood that brought this army upon us." Tegonhat was very concerned about their homelessness and her brother's role in it. "The League has fallen upon evil days, and the peace of Hiawatha has been shattered. While the Canienga are resourceful—we can enter the forests and spend the winter hunting—our return to the valley will only return us to the intrigues and buffetings of the three white nations."

"Kryn is wise," the girl offered hopefully.

Tegonhat smiled and stroked her hair. "My poor little one. You were orphaned before you knew your parents. Now your people must prowl the forests like the bark-eaters. Our nation is strong no more, and you turn for comfort to the half-breed Kryn."

"He is braver and wiser than all other men," she protested.

"But he will never be allowed to make decisions. He can try his influence and he can carry out the wishes of the chiefs, but he cannot make policy."

"I am only half-Canienga," the girl said, "but each decision affects me, too."

"And close friends were your mother and myself." The woman sighed. "You, Tekakwitha, are a daughter of these troubled times."

In three days the Canienga broke camp and wended as refugees back into the valley. Clan by clan they took possession of the headlands where the proud palisades had risen—now smoldering heaps of ash—and they pulled down the crosses, the hated symbols of the French. The Turtle Clan camped near Kanawaka. Everything had been burned—canoes, longhouses, storage pits of corn, plantation fields—and fire had even reached here and there into the pine forest.

The wind grew colder day by day. Old men smoked pipes, tobacco relieving their hunger. Warriors ranged in the forest, but game proved sparse as the herds migrated. Boys fished in the river and streams and lakes. The women nursed their infants and boiled acorns and roots to feed the children. Hunger, a cruel master the clan had known often in small ways, now threatened every life. Quietly, with no complaint, Tekakwitha turned to her quills and bone needles and skins, concentrating on her work to ignore spasms of hunger.

When Kryn returned from a hunting trip with a bear cub, the village feasted until all, even the entrails, eyes, and bone marrow, had been eaten. He announced he was taking his wife and others into the north woods to pitch a nomadic hunting camp. Tekakwitha pleaded with her foster parents, and they, seeing value in the loss of one hungry mouth, granted permission for her to accompany Kryn's band.

Into the howling wilds with Kryn, Tegonhat, Karitha, three young braves, and an old woman, Tekakwitha ventured. On snowshoes they plodded through vast, silent forests, over endless expanses of frozen lakes, looking for signs of the migrating herds. Day and night, cold and hunger gnawed at them. For ten days, the party struggled along, surviving on the smallest provisions of cornmeal and dried meat. Yet during the quiet time of night, wrapped in her robes of deer and elk, the girl felt safe so near to Kryn.

On clear nights the stars dazzled her. She lay awake in shelters carved from snowdrifts watching her breath mingle and vanish, feeling comforted by the steady, streaming starlight upon the treetops. She watched, too, the aurora borealis lighting the sky with fantastic greens and roses and yellows.

At last Kryn ordered them to pitch camp. Downwind

from a deer run, they threw up a bark teepee in the snow and kindled a fire within. The old woman slung her kettle, nearly empty of any food, stirring it with veined hands.

Tegonhat, Karitha, and Tekakwitha set snares each day to catch rabbits and squirrels. The eight of them survived on one or two of these small animals each day while the men stalked the herds in vain.

On the tenth evening in this camp, Kryn appealed to the two women. "Journey with us tomorrow, and together we shall bring down a buck."

"Have you found the killing place?" Karitha asked.

"Yes. As yet the snow is not deep enough to slow the deer for us to shoot. But today we located a small cliff, and there we will drive one over and make the kill."

The morning dawned overcast. Snow would fall before sunset. Crawling from the shelter, Tegonhat and Karitha strapped on snowshoes. So did Tekakwitha.

"Where are you going?" Kryn asked her. "Do you fetch more wood for the old woman?"

"I will accompany you today," the girl said.

Kryn laughed at this notion. "Will you carry a spear or bow and arrow?"

"A spear."

The young braves laughed at her audacity.

"The chase becomes dangerous when the beast is cornered, and we used all our powder during the white man's raid."

"Hunger," she answered, "has cornered us all. We shall have good luck today."

"Very well, then, you shall be our talisman, little one. You shall draw the deer to us." Kryn gave her a spear of ash, and wrapped in their robes, they turned into the biting wind, leaving the old woman to tend her thin blue column of smoke.

Half the morning they trudged along on snowshoes. They reached at last a pass between two outcroppings—a mountain on one side, a precipice and stream on the other. Along the trail, the tracks of many deer still faintly showed in the windswept snow. Kryn placed two young men up the pass to stop the herd, and he placed the girl and two women farther down to prevent its retreat. He and the other brave, Cawing Jay, hid behind a ledge in the middle.

Against the relentless wind they pulled tight their fur

robes. Near its zenith, the sun peered briefly through the clouds, orange as a dying ember. Then the clouds obscured it, and the wind stiffened. With stoic patience they waited in ambush, limbs cramping, faces squinting in the dull glare, eyes filmy with hunger. A light snow fell gently, then stopped. Light faded, then grew as clouds passed.

Late in the afternoon, Tekakwitha shook her head, squinted, then elbowed Kryn's wife. Far down the pass a dark spot moved. No one spoke. As it moved closer, they saw it was a large buck cautiously sniffing and listening. Behind him came his does and fawns. The buck held his large rack of antlers high at each step. He paused, listened, sniffed the wind, then proceeded on past the women into the ambush. As the buck reached the place below Kryn and Cawing Jaw, he drew up sharply, listened. His nostrils quivered, then he continued on. The does and fawns ambled along behind.

Suddenly the two braves ahead of the buck jumped up, shouting and waving from their blind. The buck cried, spun on his hind legs, and leapt back toward his does. Kryn and Cawing Jay vaulted the rock ledge and ran screaming, strewing snow, spears raised, into the herd of does. Tekakwitha, Karitha, and Tegonhat leapt up and raced through the snow. With raised spears and shouts, they closed off any retreat. Panic seized the does and the bleating fawns. The sleek bodies of the deer spun this way and that, hooves pawing in the air. The buck lowered his antlers and charged Kryn. Deftly Kryn stepped aside and planted a lance in the deer's shoulder.

Two does raced at the women, but they screamed, "Aiiiii! Aiiiii!" driving them to the center. Other deer tried to escape up the trail, their fawns close behind, but the two men closed in from above. The buck rose up on his hind legs, his sharp hooves threatening. Cawing Jay rammed his lance into the buck's chest. Again the deer lowered his head and charged. Cawing Jay was too slow. The antlers lifted him high in the air, and he fell among the thrashing bodies of does and fawns.

Plunging and stamping in panic, the deer turned this way and that as the humans closed the circle. Kryn seized a spear from Handsome Lake and goaded the rearing buck toward the edge of the cliff. Up came the women again, crying, "Aiiiii! Aiiiii!" Watching the deadly antlers high in the air, Kryn skillfully dodged the sharp hooves and jabbed with the lance.

Steaming blood ran down the buck's sleek coat. Arosen joined Kryn, but a hoof grazed his head, and he fell back among the frightened does. Two does escaped up the pass with their fawns, quick and graceful in flight. Furiously the men pushed the buck toward the edge. It turned its body this way and that to avoid their prodding lances. Then at the edge, it peered over its shoulder, snorted, and sprang at Kryn. Kryn grappled with its antlers, pulling the head and strong, rippling neck downward into the snow. The buck planted its back legs firmly and pulled Kryn upward to a standing position. Kryn relinquished neither hand, but screamed for Arosen to slit the buck's throat.

Arosen planted his spear into the deer's back, but it missed its goal—the heart. The buck cried out, heaved Kryn aside, spun on its hind legs, and saw the chasm too late. Tucking its forelegs, it leapt from the ledge, but misjudged the depth. It landed, crumpled, on the frozen bed of the stream. Up rose its hind legs, then its forelegs, but its left foreleg buckled, and the hooves slid helplessly on the ice.

Down the chasm spilled Kryn, Handsome Lake, Karitha, and Tekakwitha. In clouds of snow, stripping branches from bushes, they landed waist-deep in snow. Calling to each other, they struggled from the drift to the buck, now lame on the ice. The buck raised its antlers in defiance, but naked bone showed in the left leg. Blood streamed down its back and belly, and it bleated helplessly.

Kryn reached it first. With fierce eyes it swung the deadly antlers to keep him at bay. Tekakwitha reached it next, and she prodded the buck in the hindquarter with her spear. As it turned upon her, Kryn sprang forward, grabbed its lower jaw, and slit its throat. Gasping, frothing at the mouth, the buck fell upon the ice, blood streaming in a growing pool. Deeper still, Kryn slit the throat. The bright, intelligent eye of the buck blinked, its mouth opened to suck for air, its hot and steaming blood melting the snow.

Screaming in pagan triumph, Kryn slit the buck open from the throat down the belly, and a steaming mass of entrails spilled upon the snow. He felt between the lungs, then pulled the heart forward and cut it free. A quivering shook the body and spasms trembled along the beast's legs. Blankly then the eye stared up, and the warm blood continued to spread.

Arosen, Handsome Lake, and Tegonhat clambered down

the escarpment and struggled through the snow. Quickly Kryn carved the palpitating heart, and handing portions around, they ate greedily, drinking the warm, sweet blood that quenched both thirst and hunger.

Gored by the antlers, Cawing Jay breathed noisily as he joined them. Kryn butchered the buck. Snow began to fall. He gave a hindquarter to each of the women. He gave the forequarters to the two braves. He severed the head, then he and Cawing Jay bore up the trunk. Tekakwitha grasped the antlers and dragged the head behind her in the snow.

In the blinding snowstorm they made their way to the hut. The old woman still tended the fire, and the hut was filled with harsh smoke. They dragged the carcass and limbs and the head inside, and Kryn swept their trail with pine boughs to put wolves off the scent.

Because they had gone without a kill, without food for so long, custom dictated they now eat every morsel of the deer in an "Eat-All Feast." Drunk with fatigue from the kill, they carved and threw large morsels of venison on the coals, and the redolent smoke pleased their nostrils and taste buds. Before anyone could sleep, to guarantee good luck on the next day's hunt, they set about eating the entire carcass.

"Ah, little one," Kryn said, dishing the girl a slab of venison. "You bring us luck. Eat this; there will be more."

The three braves and the women ate hungrily. Even the old woman with no teeth pressed the meat between her gums and sucked at blood. Though thin, the carcass provided quite enough meat for them. Each had eaten his fill, but still a hindquarter and a loin remained.

"Before we sleep," Kryn said, "we must finish this." He butchered the hindquarter and handed around steaks. To gain breathing time, most of them cooked the steaks in the fire. "I have seen a man die trying to finish a deer he'd slain," Kryn said. "None of his relatives would come to his aid."

"I care for no more," Tekakwitha said, handing back the steak.

"But you must."

"I cannot, for I will be sick."

"Then you will be sick. Eat." Kryn dished it back to her.

"Please, chief, so long have I gone hungry, the rich blood and meat cause my head to spin. I must lie down."

"You must help us finish," Kryn said. "It is not what you want, but what is custom. Eat."

Sullenly, Tekakwitha took the meat, and with much chewing, she slowly ate it. Then there was more. Again she took meat and slowly consumed it, and still there was more. All the others likewise had slowed in their eating. Karitha had already gone outside to vomit. Kryn handed the girl yet another slab of meat. "I must go outside," Tekakwitha announced, and all the others laughed and jeered at her, as they had at Karitha. She struggled to her feet, and bending over, crawled out of the shelter. The blizzard lashed her face as she struggled away from the hut, and falling upon the snow, she disgorged the meat in spasms. At last she lay gasping, and she bathed her forehead with snow.

When she reentered the smoky confines of the shelter, the others ridiculed her. "You have the stomach of a squirrel," Cawing Jay said.

"Come, have more," Handsome Lake said. "You must help us finish."

"Let us instead leave some meat for morning," she suggested.

This brought much laughter from the rest. "We cannot. We must finish all the meat tonight, and then crack the bones and suck the marrow."

"Why is this necessary?" she asked, wrapping herself in her robe. "So long have we starved. Why now must we consume all the meat?"

"Ah, little one," Kryn said, "you do not observe custom."

"I do," she said quietly, "when it is wise. This custom is foolish."

"For this reason," Tegonhat teased, "does her foster mother call her 'The Pouter.'"

Tekakwitha pulled the robe about her head, ignoring them.

"Come, Pouter, here is a tasty morsel," Arosen said. The others laughed.

"After your visit outdoors, your belly must be empty. Here, fill it with good red meat."

"That is enough," Kryn intervened. "The buck is almost finished. If the orphan will disgrace herself, we cannot help that."

These words stung her, caused her eyes to burn and moisten. Though she wanted to cry out in anger, she huddled instead in the robes, hurt that even Kryn turned against her when she did not follow custom.

2

She did not accompany them again. She gathered wood and sat with the old woman tending the fire, and she daydreamed as she embroidered. "The proud buck rears in anger to protect his does. Yet his blood stains the ice, his eyes film when men from the ambush attack. Then off bound the does and young ones to find another."

She watched the old woman suspiciously. That was how she'd be, wizened, alone, despised, begrudged the share of food she ate. And in her daydreams Tekakwitha again saw the proud, noble buck rearing, lashing out courageously, finally reduced to a crippled tangle of bone and gore. This was a sad lesson to her. In the legend of Hiawatha's league, men joined together to live in peace and harmony. But that legend was a lie. Men—her own Canienga as well as the whites—joined only to murder, butcher, and burn. Kryn's courage, she saw, was only the measure of his cruelty.

To counteract this disturbing knowledge, she sewed more hopeful pictures as well. "In the pouch lies the dried corn we must not grind for eating. Whole will it be kept till melting waters bring green life. Then in mounds will we bury it near the ashes of our home, and from the earth will spring new maize."

Soon another disturbing lesson was hers. The dark pleasure stirred within. On the hunt, morals loosened, and in the dark she lay awake listening to the laughter and the moans of Karitha and Tegonhat as they shared the sleeping rugs of Kryn, Arosen, and Handsome Lake.

Cawing Jay's wounds from the buck's antlers festered. Unable to hunt, he lay day after day looking silently, stoically at the inner skins of the wigwam. The old woman prepared a salve from the antlers of the buck, and she chanted spells to draw out the pain and the suppurating pus. Tekakwitha sat with him day after day, communicating only with her eyes. One morning, Handsome Lake discovered his body outside the wigwam where he'd crawled to die. Cawing Jay's complexion was nearly snow white, his lips blue, and his large brown eyes open in horror. Rigor mortis and the cold had hardened his body like stone. While the three men and two women hunted, Tekakwitha and the old one dug in the snow to hide the corpse from wolves.

When all was quiet that night, the girl heard a voice. "Open your robe, little one. I shall comfort you for our brother's death." It was Handsome Lake. Tekakwitha allowed him under her sleeping robe, and he lay behind her, embracing her with his strong arms. This new sensation of warmth and comfort caused her flesh to tingle, and Handsome Lake's regular breathing lulled her to sleep. She felt, then, his hot lips upon her neck.

"No, my friend," she whispered, "do not do that. Lie still."

Again she drifted into sleep. In a dream she saw wolves, large, bony wolves with ragged yellow coats and red eyes creeping over the snow toward Cawing Jay's body. A hand upon her buttocks awakened her with a start. Impatiently she flounced the robe. "Do not do that! Lie still next to me."

"Let us comfort each other, little one. Our friend is dead."

"You provide much comfort when you allow me to sleep."

Once again she drifted into sleep. Another dream, the dream of the turtle began. This dream had recurred often since the northern fishing trip. She was on the path to Quorenta's hut, and the hot, humid air was suffocating. A stirring in the brush at the side of the path caused her alarm, and she began to run. She ran, chased by an invisible *okie* that tugged at the hem of her buckskin skirt. As she rounded a corner, a mound rose before her with iridescent plates set in patterns. The mound moved on four scaled fins, and suddenly, from underneath its shell, a great scaled head and a long neck, thick as a tree trunk, appeared. The swollen head and neck extended itself like a terrifying phallus. "I am the great Turtle upon whose shell the world was founded," the turtle said. It was Iowerano's voice. Tekakwitha tried to cry out, but her voice stuck in her throat. Kryn, only Kryn could save her. She called, but he was not near. The turtle gasped, moved forward sluggishly to devour her. The hot, swollen air pressed upon her, then suddenly she was awake, with Handsome Lake's hand upon her nipples.

"Stop this, or you shall leave my bed."

"You must learn of the dark pleasure. I shall comfort you."

"No," she said firmly. "I am not yet a woman." She turned away and pulled the robe tightly about her. In the dream, Kryn was the one who could save her, but in the wigwam, he was coupling with Tegonhat this night. Noble Kryn was groveling like a beast. Again Handsome Lake's hand had found her breast and the warmth pleased her, yet the pleasures caused her unspeakable dread. She pulled it away. "No!" His other hand reached up between her thighs. "No!" she said firmly. A warmth she had never known spread through her lower regions. "Please!" Of their own accord, her thighs parted, and his hand circled ever so gently.

"You feel the dark pleasure now," the young man whispered. "I shall show you more."

"No!"

He wrestled with her. Cawing Jay's death! A fear of wolves! The dark pleasure! It all terrified her. This tussle with Handsome Lake conjured horrible dread in her, and she remembered vividly the towering oak along the path to Quorenta's hut. She heard again the girl's horrible screams, and helpless, she remembered turning and running away. "No!" she protested, struggling as much with the memory as with the young man. "I can't! I mustn't!" Usually this dimly glimpsed memory was accompanied by a paralyzing, suffocating fear, but this night she thrashed and fought to free herself.

Handsome Lake sensed a game. He pulled up the hem of her skirt, and he laughed and playfully bit her ear. Tekakwitha clawed at his eyes, and she bit his jaw. With a muffled cry, the young man rolled away, and she pulled the robes tightly about her.

Scanning the wigwam to see what disturbance her refusal had caused, she saw Kryn with Tegonhat, and Karitha with Arosen, the robes bristling as they gave each other pleasure. She looked toward the old woman. The embers glowed brighter just then. Tekakwitha saw the old woman, her eyes squinting in the ruby light. With a stick in her veined hands, she stirred the coals alive, trying to kindle heat from her dying fire.

3

Into the ice citadel of the high country, spring stole at last. Snow fell heavily from evergreens, the heaving ice of lakes groaned slowly, ponderously, and freshets broke through, running freely into creek beds and streams. The sun climbed and grew warmer day by day. At the equinox, Kryn broke camp. With bundles of pelts from their hunting, they strapped on their snowshoes and journeyed along gushing streams down to the lowland river.

Out from the forests on every side, nomadic bands of Canienga joined again on the banks of the river near Kanawaka. Some men had begun to fell firm, tall trees to erect a palisade. Four bark huts stood already on the high ground. The river groaned with ice floes, flooding its banks, and everywhere men and women were working to lash canoes, erect longhouse frames, rebuild their town.

Again Tekakwitha joined the house of Iowerano, yet it wasn't as before. The spring this year brought a change in her, an aching, a new tenderness within. Like ice breaking up, this new tenderness brought a warming, jagged upheaval, and swift, gushing emotions. She listened to the women pounding corn, a gift from the unmolested Onondaga. She listened to women scolding the children. She listened with new ears to the evening laughter and talk, for her flesh was awakening to new pleasures and pains.

Just before the full moon in the month of planting, cramps seized her. Groaning, doubled up, she pleaded with Tonedetta to send for White Adder, yet Tonedetta and Tegonhat knew better. They walked her beyond the stumps of the cornfield into the forest, and they built a hut of bark and pine and spruce boughs.

"It is now," said Tegonhat, tenderly smoothing her forehead, "that you will experience the first bleeding."

They laid her on a bed of fragrant spruce boughs. "Dreams will visit you and *okies* will speak during your silence of seven days. From these dreams you must select

177

your special talisman, your medicine, the special force or creature or object that will reveal your secret nature to you. Once you find your medicine, much of life that was a mystery will be explained to you. And to the medicine you will appeal in times of difficulty. You should fast during this time so your dreams will be pure, untainted by digestion. You should talk to no one. The men will not molest you while you bleed."

Even shrewish Tonedetta showed understanding. "When you return from this ordeal, Tekakwitha, you will offer a young man the bowl of sagamite, and you shall become a wife. Think of a good hunter, one who will provide well for our longhouse. Rest here; open your mind to the *okies*, and they will speak to you of future things."

They left her in the hut. Tekakwitha lay all afternoon groaning with cramps. Warm, tingling pain spread from below her stomach, gripping her, then easing. During calm moments, she listened to the thrush piping, to the cries of jays and crows. The wind in the pines soothed her. She allowed her mind to roam among thoughts and memories when the cramps abated. The Festival of the Dead, the torturing of Mohegans, the failed campaign, the fishing expedition, the white man's siege, the hunt—all these memories returned with the clarity of her embroidered pictures.

With evening came a feeling of utter helplessness. Against her will, blood flowed from her loins and smeared her thighs, warm, sticky blood. Tekakwitha thrashed upon the pallet of pine boughs. Blood, her own blood, betrayed her. She felt polluted. Unlike the girls who allowed boys and men to fondle and penetrate them in imitation of their mothers, she had held herself away from them. Blood like the blood of torture victims; blood like the blood of the buck upon the snow; blood like that day upon the path in the shade of the oak tree... she could hardly remember except for the blood upon the grass; blood like all the other women of the village. How she'd hoped to avoid the blood! She felt despicable, incontinent, beastly. She wept long and bitterly, pausing now and then to hear the soft, clean wind in the pine. If only she were clean!

Tekakwitha slept fitfully. The recurring dream of the grotesque turtle on the path to Quorenta's hut troubled her. Its armored head, its long scaly neck extending from the shell. Blood, slaughter, the monstrous turtle. The path to Quorenta's in the shade of the oak tree. She thought about that path. Long ago, a child's scream; golden hair, the color of corn silk; Kryn and Iowerano arguing; blood. The horror of that slow moving turtle, as if the entire hill had come alive, and the head and neck extending—

Suddenly Tekakwitha bolted upright. Someone was approaching. Keenly she listened, her mind racing, conjuring images. The full moon streamed an eerie light. She pulled the robe to her chin and tried to make herself small. Then she wondered if she had heard correctly. Far off, the owl hooted again, the forest reverberating with its predatory calm. Perhaps it was simply a racoon.

Then her heart stopped. Another footfall. Stealthily someone came. Her voice caught in her throat. No escape. Moonlight quivered. The crickets chirped. She sensed another human nearby, breathing, listening as intently as she. No, no, no, her heart pleaded. She was helpless, alone in the forest, then a wave of adrenalin shivered through her—she had no weapons! Her lips snarled and her hands became claws as she crouched back, waiting to spring. Infuriatingly quiet the forest had become, and with astounding clarity she heard pine sap fall upon the forest carpet.

Then she saw the outline of a head in the entrance. Her blood froze.

"My child," a voice whispered, "do you sleep?"

Over years of dreams the voice returned, familiar, soothing, and all her tensed nerves came undone. "Quorenta?"

"Yes, child, yes. I have come."

Tekakwitha gulped at the air, sighed, then settled back upon the bed of spruce boughs. "Enter, please."

The old woman crept into the shelter and held the girl's face in her hands. "How do you fare?"

"You frightened me."

"And yet, you knew I would come."

"In my pain I had forgotten. How did you find me?"

"Many things are known to us who venture out at night. I bring medication to ease your pain. I have food also." The old woman embraced her, and the young woman buried her face in Quorenta's breast, smelling the familiar bear grease and the scents of potions. "Uncover yourself."

Tekakwitha pulled up her long skirt. Quorenta's gentle hand felt her belly and thighs. "Ah, it is the moon's pull. I shall help you clean yourself." From a pouch she brought sawdust from a rotted stump, and she gently applied it to absorb the blood. She next anointed the girl's belly with a fragrant balm that infused her abdomen with warmth.

"That is good," Tekakwitha moaned, relaxing to the massage.

The old woman brushed off the sawdust with ferns.

"I know how it is you feel," the woman said. "I have administered to many, yet none ever for whom I hold the affection I hold for you. Ah, my child! Long ago did I rescue you from the plague, and your laughter brought sunshine to my cabin. Now you enter womanhood, and I am able again to aid you. Let us talk of men and the dark pleasure, and I will teach you." Quorenta settled back. "Even as a girl you possessed such inner strength that others envied and ridiculed you. Yet, these qualities, oddities, and burdens to children, are distinctions in adults. You shall marry the bravest of the Canienga, and you will bear first a daughter, strong-willed and wise as yourself, and then bold, strong sons. You shall become matriarch to a proud *ohwachira*, foremost in the Turtle Clan, and you will rule with wisdom and pride."

"Quorenta," the girl whispered, "I fear men."

The old woman laughed quietly. "Oh, you must not. The pleasure they give while they take their own is compensation for much pain, the pain you now know and later the pain of bearing children."

"And yet, I have seen their eyes, like wolves' eyes, fierce and hot."

"As children, many things frighten us—thunder, serpents, deep waters. Yet, learning what is harmful and where pleasure lies, we soon see our fears were without cause." Quorenta stroked her hair. "So it is with men. When pleasure has been given and received, their ferocity falls peaceful. After you bear a child, the man begins to share your sleeping shelf every night. It is then you learn his secrets."

"No young hunter interests me, Quorenta. They are rough and selfish and vain."

The old woman smiled kindly. "But in the dark they can be tender."

"It is all so confusing," Tekakwitha complained. "I do not know what to do."

"For now, you must rest." Quorenta patted her arm maternally. "I shall remain with you and counsel you in selecting your special medicine. Do not talk like a shadow person, like one who lives apart from the village. Do not wish to be as I am, old and alone. You shall learn the benefits of submitting to men, and you will enter the village after this first bleeding to begin looking for a husband."

Tekakwitha hugged her old friend, and together they lay upon the bed of spruce and slept.

4

During one of the many conversations about life and love and the girl's most secret feelings, Quorenta asked, "What manner of man do you consider ideal?"

Tekakwitha thought. "There are many qualities in men I admire, yet I have never met one who possessed them all."

"Let us put these qualities together and see who most resembles him."

"A man must first of all be kind," Tekakwitha began, sitting up on the spruce boughs. "He must treat all people— women, children, and other men—fairly, patiently, respectfully. He must therefore be wise enough to see that what is best for everyone serves him best. Men of mean disposition, men who see only their own side to a question are far too common, like Iowerano. They sow arguments and reap only anger, frustration, and strife."

"This is good."

"The man I consider ideal must be gentle. He can take no pleasure in killing for its own sake—whether on the hunt or in the treatment of prisoners. He will avoid violence at all costs and will seek a solution with words, not by matching strength and brutality. He will possess true courage—the courage to believe and live by his beliefs—and will require no proof that he is right."

"You have given the matter much thought. This is good, but I have never seen a bear with wings."

"Do not scoff. The man I consider ideal would never treat me as a beast, a drudge, or a possession. He would never try to force his way to my sleeping shelf. Of course, I'd till the fields and grind the maize and dress the skins, and he would hunt and fish. But we both would perform our tasks in the spirit of giving, not of fulfilling debts."

"What of his power in bargaining with the whites?" Quorenta asked. "His status in the council house of the League? Your father, for instance, was a chief of great reknown."

"The opinion of others is unimportant," Tekakwitha said. "So are hereditary ties."

Quorenta frowned. "Unimportant so long as a man possesses them. Only when they are lacking do they become important."

"These are merely ornaments," Tekakwitha said. "Just as our maidens embroider their skirts and headbands and moccasins so they will attract the wandering eyes of the strong, young hunters, so are these things ornaments with men— position in the Turtle Clan, ability to trade, ability to sit in council. All are outward things that distract. Your thinking is like the thinking of whites—valuing an otter or deer for the hide only."

"And what of age?" Quorenta asked.

"Age is unimportant except for one thing—the older the better. There are youths in our village who believe they can alter the course of the river; they think they can speak words and the mountains will move. This boasting and all the promises they make are so much wind. Men who have seen many summers see also what changes and what remains the same. They learn to change the things they can and to live with the things they can't."

"As I have long said," Quorenta remarked, "you are most wise, Tekakwitha. You have exactly described a man I knew when I was a girl."

"Yes?" Tekakwitha asked with some excitement. "And did you marry him?"

"No."

"Why not? I would have."

"Yes, I believe you would have. Yet we weren't as wise as you are. We were merely silly young girls who wanted to explore the dark pleasure. We wanted braves with strong backs and rippling arms, men who'd kill the bear and the deer, who'd drive away the wolves in winter. We wanted men who'd defend our village during attacks. We wanted all the trivial things, and in addition, we wanted children, many strong, joyful little ones to fill the longhouse with laughter and singing. We wanted children so we could watch how they made silly mistakes, so we could witness their wonder and their awe, so we could tell them the legends. Life was much happier then, before the whites, and we were far less critical in the choice of men, for there were far fewer causes for criticism."

"But what of the man I describe? Who married him?"

Quorenta smiled. "He was married already and had been three times before."

"So he was a favorite?" She folded her arms with self-satisfaction.

"Oh, yes," Quorenta said. "He wasn't as strong or as young as the man I married, but he was far kinder. He had no distinction in the clan, but he was wise. He possessed none of those things you call ornaments, but he had a generous heart, and he was gentle to everyone."

"And what was his name?"

"I never knew. We called him The Wheezer."

"The Wheezer?" Tekakwitha frowned.

"Yes, he sat indoors but for the warmest days of summer when he limped upon a crutch all the way to his porch. He never removed his tobacco pipe from his mouth. He was wise in proportion to his silence, which was very great. He never expressed anger or impatience. Truly he had learned patience, for he was ninety summers in our village when I first knew him. He was gentle and had never engaged in war. My father had held him as a coward, worthy only of ridicule, but he was too old to hold accountable when we came to know him. Yes, Tekakwitha, you would have brought him the bowl of sagamite to marry him before others stole him away."

"You joke with me!" she cried.

"And he, fearing death," Quorenta kept on, "would never have shared your sleeping shelf."

"You mock me! I am in earnest, and you make sport!"

"You must be more truthful," Quorenta said.

"I have told the truth!"

"No, you have not. Not to me. Not to yourself. You shall find a strong warrior of high standing who will fill your belly with many children. Great will be your *ohwachira* among the Turtle Clan and much will be the respect of your children and your children's children and yet again their children when you are an old woman such as I."

"This will never be," Tekakwitha said impatiently.

"And yet it must," Quorenta said with confidence. "For

the Canienga to remain strong, it must. Do not follow my
path, young one. A wiser voice within you will soon speak,
wiser than your foolish fear of men. It is the voice of the flesh
that cannot be ignored. You will heed it, as your mother and
her mother and her mother heeded it. To do otherwise is a
great misdeed against our race."

Tekakwitha fell silent then, considering—and fearing—
that the old woman might be correct. But soon, relaxing in
the luxuriant afternoon sun, with birds calling high in the
trees, she and Quorenta talked of other things.

5

With questions and advice Quorenta plumbed the thoughts,
the dreams, the hopes and fears of her young friend in the
search for her medicine.

"What makes you despise this time of living away from
the village?"

"I do enjoy the peace and freedom from chores and the
time to contemplate, Quorenta. But I hate being unclean."

"It is natural and normal. What troubles you about it?"

"The flow of blood. It is as if I were wounded. It signifies
I may marry, that I am eligible, yet I am not ready to share a
man's sleeping shelf."

"When I was a girl," the old woman said, "each nation
had one longhouse where women not wishing to marry lived
together. That custom ended with the arrival of the whites."

"Oh, I wish that custom were still practiced. There I
would go immediately."

"But let us find your medicine. The blood troubles you;
you have fears. If we look long enough there, perhaps we can
find the cause, and thus your medicine. For when the mind
projects fear, beneath the surface of that fear lies a past
incident most important to us, one that changes our thinking,
our actions, and causes dreams. My medicine was the female
hare for I wished many offspring. Yet, when I was found to be
barren, then did I leave the village of men and burrow like
the hare in my solitary ravine."

"It is not merely the blood that flows now," said Tekakwitha introspectively. "It is the blood of a noble buck that Kryn slew this winter. Instead of walking proudly, the buck hobbled upon the ice of a stream, then gasped when its throat was slit, and its eye peered up so horribly as the blood ran out upon the snow. Its very life ebbed with that blood surging upon the snow."

"You feel a kinship with that buck, and you sympathize with its pain, even though its meat allowed you yourself to live. Do any other incidents come into your mind?"

She thought, and slowly said, "Y-y-yes. With Iowerano— two times in particular. Once was after Kryn's defeat on the northern river when the warriors brought back the white man's liquor. Instead of torturing prisoners as victors do, the men turned upon each other and upon women, and chaos reigned. Iowerano visited his anger upon Tonedetta and two concubines."

"It couldn't have been the time of their bleeding or they would have been sent from the village."

"No, it wasn't then." She thought. "It was watching Iowerano mount them, the viciousness of forcing himself upon their backsides or into their mouths. There was no blood."

"Such is the fear, normal in a child, of the dark pleasure. But why does the thought of blood remind you of this?"

Tekakwitha examined her thoughts. "There was another time, too. It was soon after the Festival of the Dead. Iowerano selected a young girl only my age for a concubine, and Tegonhat bound her to his sleeping shelf. It sickened me."

"Was she wounded in a struggle?"

"Not very badly. It was her eyes, not her wounds, that terrified me."

"I see no connection between the buck's slaying and these two."

"Nor do I," Tekakwitha said, shaking her head. "And yet, there was a third time, though I cannot remember it fully. I was on the path to your hut and in the shadow of a towering oak there were screams and blood, blood everywhere, on the grass, on the tree, smeared across the sky, and I tried to cry out, but my voice stuck in my throat, and I turned and ran and ran and ran . . ."

"Do you ever dream of this?"

"Often, but the dream ends strangely. In the dream as I pass the tree, blood springs from the earth, and as I turn to run away, in front of me a hill rises, taking the shape of a turtle, and in Iowerano's voice the scaly head of the turtle speaks of the creation of the world."

"Ah, you see," Quorenta said. "The dreaming points the way to your medicine. Iowerano is chief of the Turtle Clan. It is proper that he should speak of the origin of the world. Yet, think upon that tortoise. What does it bring into your mind?"

"The mud of the swamp where I caught turtles once with Moneta and we talked about the dark pleasure. But this makes no sense."

"Yes, yes, it does. Think, little one, of your favorite legend."

"You know what it is, for we have spoken of it many times. It is Hiawatha establishing his peace like a blanket of snow over the land of the five nations."

"And why did the sight of the buck slain by Kryn disgust you?"

"Because its blood stained..."—her eyes widened—"...the snow!"

"Yes, we have something here."

"Snow is my medicine?"

"Perhaps, but let us consider further. You told me yesterday that you felt much happiness returning to the village this spring from the mountains, that you followed the course of swollen creeks to find your way to the river."

"Yes," the girl offered. "It was like my heart was thawing after the anguish of the whites' burning our nation's villages and after the frozen solitude of winter. I felt much joy in descending from the mountains to the riverbank just as the melting snow rushed and tumbled along. And like the lakes that groaned and cracked as the ice split, my entire being came alive."

"This, then, is your medicine, Tekakwitha."

"The melting snow and ice?"

"Yes," Quorenta nodded. "The water that springs from the winter's cold, that falls from the great storm clouds, that streams through the five nations of our league in every direction and gives our home the name Land From Which All Rivers Flow. You mentioned you hated being unclean. It is water that cleanses us by washing without and by drinking within."

Tekakwitha closed her eyes. The quest through her memories and her dreams, through her hopes and her fears

for an appropriate medicine to inspire her in times of trouble
had ended—water, the clear element, dazzling in the sun was
her very sacred and secret medicine. The correctness of this
swept over her with a joy and security she had never known.
Just as blood coursed through the veins of her own body, so
did the water stream through her homeland.

"Though women should not wash when this time is upon
them," Quorenta said, "since water is your medicine, it will
be good for you to bathe. Let us go to the stream nearby so
you may immerse yourself and commune for the first time
with your discovered medicine."

The two followed a shady forest path to a brook where
soft moss covered huge boulders and wet, tangled roots. "You
do not want to risk polluting the water supply of the village.
You must never perform this cleansing near the village, or
where men might drink," Quorenta cautioned as Tekakwitha
stripped naked. With Quorenta uttering charms, the young
woman entered the pool. She ducked her entire body under
the surface of the water and remained in the cold green
depths as long as her lungs allowed. Then, rising into the air,
she plucked some moss and washed her loins and her thighs
clean of blood.

6

Returning from her seven-day ordeal, Tekakwitha saw
the village with new eyes. The sturdy pikes of the palisade
wall, the ordered ranks of longhouses with lanes between,
the central compound, the layout of the village within its
circling maize fields—it wasn't happenstance that caused the
village to be so built, it was custom and wisdom accumulated
through many generations. Her solitary meditations made the
laughter and arguments and scoldings welcome as she stepped
through the gate. After the ravages of war, the long winter
hunt, and her puberty rite, it was a time for building and
putting things in order.

Both Iowerano and Kryn had departed, the council chief
to an orgy dedicating the new village of Tionnontake, and the
war chief to the forests to fish. Many warriors had accompa-

nied Iowerano to the five-day orgy. Kryn had left alone. Passing through the lanes of the village, Tekakwitha met her cousin Linawato who explained what had happened. When the orgy was announced, Iowerano decided to attend. Three blackrobes had arrived, and despite his hatred, Iowerano ordered the Turtle Clan to be hospitable, for he wished to keep the priests at Kanawaka until the orgy was over. This angered Kryn, and he had left.

"And where do these blackrobes lodge?" Tekakwitha asked.

"In your longhouse," Linawato said. "At the hearth fire next to you and Tonedetta."

With great apprehension, but with a sense of curiosity, Tekakwitha continued home. Often had she heard of Jogues and his bravery in returning two summers after his escape. She had heard of the five brave blackrobes who had been tortured and slain in the land of the Hurons. Three now had come among her people—one to journey west to Tionnontake and two to journey to the People of the Hill, the Oneida.

She pulled aside the bearskin robe over the door and entered the dim, smoky longhouse. Three white men sat upon a sleeping shelf, and they ceased talking and looked at her. "Hello," one said to her in tolerable Iroquois. Tekakwitha dropped her eyes and walked past them to her own hearth fire. She busied herself preparing the kettle and reacquainting herself with the position of things while keeping a suspicious eye upon the whites. They talked quietly, moved slowly, and appeared as gentle as a new mother to her baby. Their magic must be very strong, she decided, for them to have such a bad reputation.

They left before supper. Tegonhat, returning to the longhouse with Tonedetta, told about their ceremony in the forest, a ritual they performed each day. "They use the silver cups and plates," she said, "to hold their cakes made of wheat and their wine to the sky. They say it is the body and the blood of the torture victim, Christ, that they eat and drink."

Some charm, some spell, some mystery occurred to the young woman—the blackrobes conjured up the dead torture victim, and just as the warriors of her clan, they ate his flesh and drank his blood. They did this, too, not when victims were captured or war was announced, but every day! Did it give them courage and strength as the torturing of victims did the warriors? Did they, in secret, torture and burn living victims and eat them when they could? Many said the blackrobes' magic was far stronger than White Adder's. Were their customs and healings, then, more brutal?

Tekakwitha was fetching wood one evening when she heard singing. Down the path through the forest wended a line of people—three blackrobes and seventeen Hurons who had been captured and adopted into the Turtle Clan. The young woman hid herself. If Iowerano and Kryn had been here, the Hurons would not have dared join the whites. Singing happily, they passed her and slowly crossed through the fields of corn, then through the wooden gates back into the village.

Each night the priests ate with her and Tonedetta. They ate slowly and talked much in their strange tongue. They smiled pleasantly at her, yet she felt they were disarming her so they might work some evil spell. Their magic in the forest had put them in a friendly humor, and unlike Canienga warriors, they helped in serving the supper and in cleaning the bark plates and the kettle. After kneeling by the sleeping shelves and murmuring chants, they slept each night without women.

During the next three days, she watched them closely for evidence of their evil magic. One episode caused her to reexamine all she had heard about the blackrobes. Foaming Brook, a lad of twelve summers, had caught his foot in a badger's hole while hunting. The bones of his leg had snapped, and though he had not undergone the puberty rites and had not searched for his medicine, he tried to keep the solemn demeanor of a grown warrior as White Adder administered a cure. Summoned by her cousin to watch the blackrobe's magic battle the medicine man's, Tekakwitha saw Père Claude, the tallest of the priests, the one with soft brown eyes, bending over the boy.

Chanting spells, shaking rattles, dancing about the young hunter, White Adder prodded the leg with a pole of elm that had been peeled of its bark to resemble a shinbone. The boy grit his teeth and winced with pain. When the priest stepped forward, White Adder slapped the boy's foot at an impossible angle to the leg, then rubbed the pole up and down the shin. The boy nearly fainted.

"Does it show signs of healing?" the priest asked.

White Adder leapt at him, his face painted blue, and screamed, "Your evil magic will cause him worse pain! Leave now! Look, he suffers worse!" The medicine man shook the pole in Père Claude's face. "You take away his courage! He whimpers!"

"In my country we have a cure."

"What is your country to us?" the magician cried in ridicule, looking to his audience for approval. All laughed with him. "Do you compare your brittle French bones with the Canienga's?" Again, laughter.

"When the shaft of the spear breaks, what can be done?" the priest asked.

"It must be thrown down. Nothing can be done."

"And yet, are we like the dead wood of a spear or like the living tree?"

"Your riddles snare you," White Adder said haughtily, pointing the wand at him. "This boy will be crippled, but he shall live. No poisons may enter since his skin has not been split."

"But will the child grow into a tall and strong warrior?" Père Claude folded his arms, calmly and sincerely examining the problem with his questions. "Will his bones remain small?"

"No, they will grow," White Adder admitted. "But when the tree is splintered by lightning, it never mends. Do not speak nonsense."

"When building the longhouse," Père Claude pointed overhead, "how is the curve of the roof achieved from two straight poles?"

"The blackrobe seems very stupid," White Adder laughed. "The trees are bent together and lashed to remain that way."

"When the women cut gashes in the maple tree to collect sap, do these gashes remain open all summer?"

Intently the crowd listened, all answering the questions by moving their lips.

"No."

"What becomes of the gashes?"

"They heal as do wounds."

"Yes, and in this way, too, bones can heal. If bones are lashed together like the arch of this longhouse or like the ribs of a canoe, being still alive, they can knit back together." He demonstrated with his fingers.

"This is impossible." White Adder spit upon the dirt floor. "Bones are made of stone. They do not rot in the earth."

The priest appealed to the crowd's sense of honesty. "And yet the magician White Adder just observed that a man grows from an infant like the tree from a sapling."

Opinion now stirred in the crowd against White Adder. Seeing himself cornered, he bragged, "I have saved the young one's life. Your magic will undo mine. Leave us alone here. You will kill the boy."

The crowd was divided, many persuaded by Chauchetière's argument.

"Let me place the broken bones together," the priest asked in a humble, quiet voice, "and they will knit and heal, and Foaming Brook will walk again. Is it not better to run and hunt than spend a life hobbling upon a crutch?"

White Adder threw up his hands in disgust. "I will not answer for what becomes of the boy, blackrobe. We have seen your evil spells. The water you place upon the foreheads of infants kills them."

"I only place water on infants who are dying, so they will go to Rawanniio, father of us all. Yet this boy will not die. I shall make him well."

"I see his parents believe your lies." White Adder pointed the pole disgustedly at the parents. "Very well, I shall stay no longer. Do not call me when the boy is near death. I will not answer for the blackrobe's evil magic." Collecting his rattles and charms, he left the longhouse for the forest.

With the help of two men who held the boy, Père Claude set the leg, then securely tied it between splints and quietly instructed the parents to keep him in bed for many days. Tekakwitha returned to her longhouse behind the priest, convinced the blackrobes possessed very powerful magic and fearful that White Adder would seek revenge.

7

Kanawaka
June 14, 1667

Père Auguste Chauchetière
Versailles

My Beloved Uncle:

I write you from the heathen land of Jogues and Goupil. I must use juice crushed from berries upon

the white, papery bark of a birch tree. My letter
will be transcribed at Quebec.

The Iroquois savages of New France possess a
pride and dignity I find surprising. In a pitiable
state of nakedness, hunger, and superstition they
drag out their lives. Their villages are squalid collec-
tions of bark huts, and the lanes smell of rotting
meat and excrement. Yet, ignorant of civilization,
they seem especially like children, carefree and
joyful.

Pagan gods and demons govern their thinking;
they continually pray to the devil. Their superstitious practices are of two kinds. The first involves
touching. By laying hands upon a person or a person's belongings, they consider their magic can be
conveyed to that person. If a man has a grudge
against another, he will attempt to gain possession of
a garment or tool of the other, and by tearing the
garment or breaking the implement, he hopes to
cause the other injury. It is very much like the black
heathens of the Antilles, about whom I wrote, who
fashion little clay effigies of their enemies and stab
them with needles.

The second sort of magic involves imitating a
desired act. For a plentiful harvest, the savages
stage an orgy and copulate freely in the cornfields.
To conjure rain, the medicine man urinates in the
frenzies of his dance.

To increase their courage before setting off on a
campaign, the warriors dance a pantomime, fighting
their own shadows and embedding their hatchets
into a pole.

Just now an orgy rages at the village where I
shall dwell—Tionnontake, the next village upriver
from Kanawaka. This clan, the Turtle Clan, holds
the tortoise as its father. The clan at Tionnontake
believes it has been sired by the bear. The strange
logic they employ, the ungoverned passions and
rages, the employment of pain as a test of courage—
young warriors pierce their nipples with bone
needles, and laugh at the pain—illustrate the
sway of the demon. Much like hell is the heathen
land.

I ask for your prayers as I open my mission upriver. With the grace of God and the strength of Loyola, may I lead these children out of their pagan darkness.

Yours in Christ,
Claude Chauchetière, S.J.

8

Tekakwitha was saddened when the blackrobes left. A new manner of men, their gentleness, concern, and charity had been appreciated greatly by the entire village. During their seven-day stay, they cured a man of blood poisoning from a tatoo. They bounced young children on their knees. They never turned to watch Crying Lynx when she tried to capture their attention by walking suggestively.

With great respect and reserve, the blackrobes discussed all things with all men and women from the oldest matriarch to the youngest concubine, from the wisest chief to the laziest hunter. They kindled fire with flint and steel. Their oratory and reasoning equaled Kryn's, Tekakwitha felt. And their magic in the forest, holding high the silver cup and plate, their magic that she watched from a hiding place, provided her with a delicious mystery to ponder.

Iowerano returned from the orgies, cursing the blackrobes who had entered Tionnontake and disrupted the pagan festivities. Sullenly Tekakwitha retreated from his sight, and her heart sank when she heard him say, "Oh, the girl went into the forest for the bleeding? It is time she married."

So final, so offhanded, so immutable were his words that Tekakwitha despaired. If only there were some escape! Only the Kryn she had known before the hunt understood the hunger of her spirit. Lately Kryn was always away trading or hunting. He cared no more for the village he'd defended, the people he'd protected. He wanted to acquire something—a profit, a trophy, a prestige—that he could not achieve at home, and Karitha, when she didn't accompany him, remained in her longhouse, saddened by his solitary trips. What other could compare, Tekakwitha asked herself. All other men were tyrants who subdued their wives and made them breeding, laboring beasts. She felt she must find a man who'd treat her with respect and dignity.

Each time a plentiful kill signaled a feast, Tonedetta and Tegonhat plaited her hair with wampum shells and Dutch ribbons and dressed her in the finest embroidered buckskin dress and moccasins. They urged her to talk with the other girls, to flirt coyly with the young hunters. With curious eyes wandering over her, though, Tekakwitha felt terribly uneasy. The dancing was complicated, the small talk trivial, the entire courting ritual stupid. Why were not intentions made clear and reasonable agreements made, she asked. The laughter and joy of courting proved hollow if anyone examined most of the married couples in the village. Yet, with a grim sense of duty, she went through the motions.

Summer passed with no choice made, then autumn, then winter. When spring came once more, Tonedetta said, "You must narrow your choices this year, or we shall choose for you." Yet, the girl's ears remained closed. She danced only the *genoshotè*, a dance where the partners did not touch each other. She spurned any advance with shyness until a cutting remark became necessary. She longed for the times when the blood flowed, for then she could seek refuge in the forest and be alone with her thoughts.

Toward the end of summer, Tonedetta began choosing mates for her foster daughter. "We shall entertain Sleeping Bear at supper," she said one afternoon. "He is very well regarded in the clan and knows how to trade with the whites. Rich are the hangings of his longhouse. I believe he will make a fine addition to our home."

"He is fat," Tekakwitha said, "and dull. He speaks about nothing but his bargains with the whites. Scarcely has he ever been in the forest. He knows nothing of the hunt. He is well beyond his years only in the skill of smoking a pipe." And she endured an entire evening of Sleeping Bear's bragging.

"We shall acquaint you with Bobtail," Tonedetta said a few weeks later. "He knows well the secrets of the stream and brook and will bring us plenty of fish. Also, he has the keenest eye with a musket, so Iowerano tells me. Marry this hunter, and we shall be well-provided for."

"He has a dignity as small as his body," Tekakwitha replied. "I have seen him torturing a puppy. He inflicts pain for sport so he can feel superior. How will he treat a wife? Probably as his father treats his mother—with cuffs and slaps and insults. True, he is skilled in hunting and fishing, but what is the use of food when each morsel is begrudged and endless thank-you's demanded?" And she endured an evening of his sheepish flirting.

"I have wonderful news!" Tonedetta announced as the leaves turned scarlet. "Golden Stag will sup with us tonight. Long has he been an admirer of your embroidery. He despises silly girls and seeks a woman of more serious purpose. Although young, he is a man in all things—strong, virile, accomplished. And he is the most handsome young man of our village. Think of the warriors and maidens he'd sire!" Tonedetta suggested she herself would enjoy sharing his sleeping rug.

"All these things you say are true," Tekakwitha agreed. "He would make any woman a fine husband—any woman who appreciates a sullen, complaining mate, always worrying and fretting. He complains about a blue sky because it means rain will be but a few days away."

"But think of the pleasure he'd bring!"

"I care nothing for the dark pleasure."

"It is because you don't know it. You will."

Tekakwitha shivered with disgust at this. Never, she thought, will I submit to being mounted like a concubine, and the thought of that deed with Golden Stag immediately thrust him out of her mind. She endured a supper of his morose complaining, and she watched with interest the attention Tonedetta shamelessly paid him.

The Iroquois traced ancestry through their mother's family, so paternity was of minor importance and marriage was fairly casual—easily done, easily undone. A marriageable girl's family invited a young hunter and his family to the longhouse. All wore their finest buckskins. The young woman handed the young man a bowl of sagamite, signaling she wished to nourish him as her mate, and he accepted it to say he agreed. The married couple slept together infrequently— both remaining with their own families—until the birth of the first child. Then they set up housekeeping by occupying a vacant hearth or by adding another section to the longhouse. Divorce occurred when one partner removed his or her sleeping rug.

"Dress in your finest robes," Tonedetta ordered Tekakwitha one morning the following summer. "I have invited Flattened Nose and Laughing Bird to dinner."

Their son, Foaming Brook, had been cured by the blackrobe of his broken leg two years before. Tekakwitha took more than her usual interest in these dinner guests. She allowed her hair to be braided, and she donned her embroidered skirt and vest and moccasins. At sunset, Flattened Nose and Laughing Bird entered the longhouse with Foaming Brook. The young man, now with no sign of a limp, entered proudly wearing an embroidered vest and loincloth with an eagle feather in his hair. Bashfully he regarded Tekakwitha.

"Sit near me," the young woman said. She had no intention to marry, only to discuss the blackrobes. "The blackrobe's cure has been truly wonderful, and we can talk about them."

"No talk of blackrobes is allowed!" Iowerano said, and he welcomed the parents. "We have much else to discuss."

At her invitation, Foaming Brook took a seat beside her. Uncomfortably they listened to the adults talk. Along the longhouse, other families watched the ceremony with great interest—Tekakwitha's refusal to marry, so unusual in the nation, was well known.

"Bring the bowls so we may eat," Tonedetta ordered her foster child.

Tekakwitha picked up the bark plates and held them out.

"Help me serve," Tonedetta said. She ladled a large portion of sagamite, tonight laced with fish and bear bacon and strawberries, onto the first plate. Tekakwitha handed it to Flattened Nose. "No, do not give it to him," Tonedetta said impatiently. "Give it to Foaming Brook."

The boy's parents both smiled. Foaming Brook held out his hands for the marriage bowl. Tekakwitha held it back.

"Hand it to him!" Tonedetta commanded.

"She seems so very shy," Laughing Bird whispered.

As the trickery became apparent, Tekakwitha peered into each of their faces with disbelief. "You consider this a marriage?" she asked hoarsely.

"Hand him the plate," Iowerano ordered.

"What can an empty gesture like this mean if I do not consent?" she asked.

"Give me the sagamite," Foaming Book said. "I accept you as my wife."

"No!" she cried.

Iowerano's brow clouded.

"Do not disgrace us!" Tonedetta hissed.

"I will not marry even as fine a hunter as Foaming Brook!" she cried. She dumped the plate into the fire, and steam and choking smoke issued from it. "Trickery cannot make up for what I do not feel!" She stood and scanned all the astounded faces in the longhouse, then she dashed out. Blindly she ran through the lanes of the village, out the southern gate, through the fields of maize, and into the forest by the river. "I will never go back!" she vowed, her face flushed with anger and rage. "I will journey far from here." She walked along the river to compose herself, to make plans. She slept that night in the forest, and her sleep was troubled by dreams of White Adder and the great scaly tortoise and women yelping in the dark.

9

She gathered roots and berries next morning and drank deeply from a creek. She continued westward, away from the sun; she was hurt, confused, angry, yet resolved to stay away from Kanawaka.

As the sun reached its zenith, she passed through a grove of birch, and entering again the hallowed shade of pine, she heard a voice. She crept nearer and peered over a rim of rock.

"And here I repair to be alone and think of you." A young man knelt in a clearing and spoke to the air in an awed, respectful, loving voice. He stretched his arms out to a cross of two lashed branches. Tekakwitha watched and listened with much interest. ". . . for a new age dawns among the Canienga, and the traditions of our fathers are vanquished by your word. No longer must I live in doubt, in terror, dreading the future, despising the present. Among us you have come, bringing peace and truth and love."

"Whom do you speak to?" Tekakwitha asked, suddenly forgetting herself.

The youth jumped to his feet, whirled about, plucked the cross from the tree and hid it behind his back. "Who are you?" he demanded angrily. "Why do you come here? You have no right to spy upon me!" He looked quickly in all directions. "Is this an ambush?"

"Whom did you talk to just now? I saw no one. Were you speaking to *okies* in that piece of wood?"

"Where do you belong? I do not recognize you from Tionnontake."

Tekakwitha climbed over the ledge, dropped to the floor of the hollow, and approached the young man. "I am called Tekakwitha. I live downriver at Kanawaka among the Clan of the Turtle. Who are you?"

The young man dropped his head and looked at the ground. "I am called Eagle Claw. I live upriver at Tionnontake."

"What do you do here? Certainly you do not hunt, for game would flee from the talking you do." She had recognized the blackrobe's crossed symbol and now enjoyed the youth's discomfort at being discovered praying. She sat upon a fallen tree.

"It is no business of yours. Why does a young woman such as yourself venture into the forest alone? Evil things might befall you."

"What is that you hold behind your back?"

"It is nothing. Nothing."

"Then why were you speaking to it with the respect we reserve for chiefs?"

"I do not have to justify my actions to you." He turned away, holding the cross in front of him now.

"It is the blackrobe's symbol," she said accusingly.

"What do you know of it?" he asked, turning back.

"I kept house for three blackrobes when they stopped at Kanawaka two summers ago while orgies raged in your village."

"There are no more orgies at Tionnontake."

"There are no blackrobes at Kanawaka," Tekakwitha said.

"Yes," Eagle Claw agreed with a slight superiority. "The priests tell us Kanawaka still lives in the sway of pagan devils. Only your Huron slaves will reach their final reward."

"Reward?" Tekakwitha frowned. "What reward?"

The youth turned away again. "If you do not know, I won't tell you."

"Tell me!" she said, reaching for his arm. She turned him back, facing her. "What reward?"

"The final reward—heaven."

"Is that why the Huron slaves go so happily about their chores?"

"Yes. Gaining heaven is the reason we are placed upon this earth. The blackrobes open heaven for us. It is far grander than the place brave warriors go. Those at Tionnontake who have listened to the blackrobe have found a wondrous peace. We sing hymns each day, and one day in seven there is much joy and celebration. It is on that day we eat of the body and blood of Christ the Lord."

"The blackrobes burn victims?" Tekakwitha asked in disbelief.

"We do not eat flesh and blood. We eat bread and wine that has been changed into flesh and blood."

"But how can this be done?" she asked suspiciously.

"The blackrobe's magic performs it."

"I would like to see such a feast."

"First you must take instruction and change your name."

"Change my name? Why?"

"The blackrobe sprinkles water upon your forehead, and you take up a new name, the name of a saint."

"A saint?"

"Yes, someone who lived virtuously before and who now dwells in heaven with Rawanniio, with God. One who can produce favors when asked."

"What saint are you called after?"

The young man blushed. "By Christians, I am called Jerome."

"Very well, I shall call you Jerome," she said promptly. "It suits you far better than Eagle Claw."

"Why are you in the forest?" Jerome asked. "I have told you my reason."

Tekakwitha scuffed the pine carpet with her moccasin. "I grow tired of the tricks and the customs of my longhouse." She looked up in appeal. "I wish for escape."

"Escape from what?" He seemed sympathetic.

"My foster parents wish that I marry. They tried yesterday to trick me into marrying a young hunter."

"You want another?"

"I want no one!" Tekakwitha said firmly. "I have examined the question from all sides. I have watched how married ones act. I do not wish to marry, to become the possession of some warrior."

"But it is unheard of a girl not marrying!" Jerome protested. "Who will provide for you?"

"I do not care. I shall provide for myself. To a resourceful woman marriage is not the last word."

"You are headstrong. That is not a valuable quality in a woman."

"And I see that even though Christian, you still think like Canienga. Very well, I shall leave you to your wooden sticks." She turned and climbed up the side of the hollow.

"Wait!" Jerome called. He scrambled up beside her. "What you say interests me greatly."

"Yet you speak the thoughts of others."

"Your choice in this matter is fixed . . . forever?"

"Yes. I will not marry no matter how they press me. I will not be enslaved. I have a mind of my own and a heart that guides me." She considered him, judged him to be understanding. "So vast have been the changes in our world that those who rely upon the old laws and customs do so only because they fear change. Our league has little strength left. We cannot pretend we do not see. Our villages have been weakened by war, by the white man's diseases. If our times are so bad, what future lies ahead for our children? I cannot close my eyes to all this."

"And so you refuse to marry," he said, considering for a long, silent moment. "I, too, have refused to marry," he finally announced, uncertain of her reaction.

This news greatly interested the young woman. "Why?"

"I imitate the blackrobe. He takes no wife so he may come among us and bring us news of the man who died for us upon crossed poles."

"Who is this man?" she asked. "I have heard much about a man who died long ago. People die every day. Why is his death special?"

"This man called Christ saved the world by His death."

"Saved the world from what?"

"From the fires of hell." Jerome frowned, wishing for the blackrobe's eloquence. "If we follow this Christ, we will avoid the fires that punish evil ones, and we will enter heaven after death."

"Like Hiawatha who ascended to the sky in a white canoe?"

"Yes," Jerome said skeptically, then he warmed to the comparison. "Yes!"

"Did Hiawatha find the reward you speak of?"

"No."

"Because he had a wife? To go to this heaven you must not marry?" she asked. "Like the blackrobe?"

"You may marry. Many do. But Hiawatha never received the cleansing waters. I have chosen not to marry so I may be free from a wife and children, so I may bring news of Christ to our people as soon as I complete my instruction. I never knew a woman could refuse marriage in this way."

"I do, but for different reasons," she said curtly. She refused marriage because it would stifle her creativity with the bone needle, it would intrude upon her meditation with a thousand domestic drudgeries and would limit the horizons of her waking thoughts to a man and his children. Jerome refused not because he feared losing something, but because he would gain much. Tekakwitha saw the difference and it annoyed her—his seemed far better.

"Perhaps your reasons are not so very different," Jerome remarked. "But I see you become impatient. I have enjoyed discussing these things with you. Will you come here again?"

"What for?"

"That we may continue talking of these concerns."

"I see no use. You are a Christian and I am not."

"But we are both Canienga." Jerome took her hand. "I see you are resolved to live as you will, free from a husband. Perhaps I can help you. I shall be here each afternoon praying—for such is this called. If you wish to talk further, visit me here. I, in turn, will take your greeting to the blackrobe in our village."

"I will consider these things," she said. She turned from Jerome and walked toward the river and Kanawaka. Meeting him, talking, she had gained courage and could now return home. The encounter thrilled her, for someone shared her most cherished thoughts.

10

Père Auguste Chauchetière
Versailles

My Beloved Uncle:

Praise be to God that He in His infinite wisdom
has sent me hither! And my most heartfelt thanks
for the part you played in arranging my assignment.

For nearly two years I have been ministering to
these children—for they are children, so great is
their innocence. Demons and hobgoblins fill their
nights, and luck, both good and bad, is the sole
ruler of their lives. They were fierce in the time of
Jogues, yes, even until two years ago when Tracy
chastized them. But among themselves, when they
learn of Christ, they become kind, considerate,
generous, and dedicated family men and women.

Know that when an Iroquois, properly instructed and received into the church, takes up the cross
of Christ, not a more inspiring convert is there in all
Christendom! Their purity and innocence of heart
inspire me constantly. Their resolve brooks no second-
guessing or skirting of moral issues. They make over
their hearts fully and become reborn in Christ.
While occasionally their morals may relax, as upon
the winter hunt, their zeal never flags.

Still, the demon holds a sway in this land.
Many and fierce are the enemies of my converts,
seducing them from the right path, whispering of
pagan gods unappeased. Brandy undoes much of
our work with licentiousness and debauch. Yet, I am
not the voice of one crying in the wilderness, for we
have a new praying wigwam or chapel, and I have

two acolytes who vow they will study among the
Jesuits at Quebec.

Frs. Fremin and Pierron convey their best wishes
from farther to the west. Know that I am happy in
doing service for the order, for the Church, and
above all *ad majorem gloriam Dei*. In the honest
hearts of these Canienga lives a fervor and sincerity
to rival any mystic of civilized Europe. Please, I beg
you, intercede with Minister Colbert to turn the
King's mind from soaking this land with brandy.
Although it fetches pelts more cheaply, it does so at
a cost of souls.

> Your most affectionate nephew,
> Père Claude Chauchetière

11

"You shamed our house last evening. Only at a terrible
cost will we win back our dignity." Iowerano sat cross-legged,
smoking his pipe. "Even now the villagers say, 'Look at such
a fool that cannot control the orphan girl of his house. Is he
able to lead us as chief?' And the half-breed Kryn incites such
talking, and he gloats."

"Uncle, I did not wish to shame you." She was humble,
but not contrite. "I wished only to be left alone, to have my
will respected."

"The will of a girl of thirteen summers? What is that—a
thrush flitting from tree to tree? Your will!" he scoffed. "You
consider nothing but your own whim. What of our family?
We have no children. Who will provide for us when I become
infirm? Who will provide for you?"

"A new season is upon us," Tekakwitha said.

"A new season?" Iowerano spat. "What nonsense is this?
Does the wind not blow from the west? Does the corn not
ripen, the fish seek the shade of rocks, the deer fatten on
grass sprung from the burnt hills?"

Modestly Tekakwitha dropped her eyes. "I speak of the
whites."

"The whites?" The chief grew animated. "What of them?

We shall undo them soon enough—both French and English. We shall regroup when old Garacontie goes under the earth. Strong hot blood shall command us. Our tomahawks will spread the peace of Hiawatha."

In a quiet voice, Tekakwitha said, "I speak only of how things are now, today, not of what may be tomorrow."

"And how are things today?" Iowerano asked with sarcasm.

"The whites have shown they can obliterate us, and this causes much concern among all our League. Some turn to liquor to hide the bitterness of this knowledge. Some think back and cloak days gone by in false garments and cry for a return to them. Others turn to the god of the blackrobes and find peace and contentment."

"I will not allow you to mention the blackrobes!" Iowerano cried out. "They bring worse than the other whites. Other whites bring liquor and guns. The blackrobes bring evil spells that make women of our men, infect the minds of our wives. . . ."

"And yet the Onondaga, the Oneida, the Seneca—even the Wolf and Bear clans of the Canienga—have welcomed blackrobes."

"The Turtle Clan never will! I have spoken with White Adder; our minds are one. First come the blackrobes to fill us with lies about another world where we shall go if we follow them and give up our ways. Then come the traders who cheat us to make their profit. Then come the settlers who clear our hunting grounds, build their houses, and call the land their own. Then come the soldiers to punish us for burning the farmers' homes and reclaiming our land. If the snow on the high peaks is not allowed to melt, the streams will not fill, the river will not swell and flood. The Turtle Clan guards the eastern gate. I shall remain as cold as these peaks toward the whites."

Tekakwitha fell quiet. She thought of the young man on his knees praying toward another world. Was it an illusion?

"So . . . when will you marry?"

She looked up with trembling eyes. "The blackrobe's manner of thought is not so sinister as you believe. When they visited here, many were the helpful deeds they performed, seeking nothing in return."

"I ask you, when will you marry?"

"I am sorry, Uncle." Her voice wavered. She feared angering him, yet knew she must. "I do not wish to marry."

"What you wish does not matter," he said curtly. "What I wish is what will come to pass. You will marry this winter."

Tekakwitha hung her head, averted her eyes. Her determination, she knew, would never falter. She regretted the confrontation. She did not wish to be impertinent, so she remained silent.

"You make no answer."

"I have answered, Uncle. With every respect for your wishes, I will not marry, not this winter, not ever." Though she did not say it, her talk with Jerome had opened new possibilities.

"It is the mad woman, Quorenta, who has cast a spell upon you," he said impatiently. "She was barren, but instead of bearing it like Tonedetta does, she hides away from men and now enlists you to be barren like her."

"It is not Quorenta," the young woman said.

The chief's eyes narrowed, anger smoldering. "It is the blackrobes, then?"

"No, Uncle. It is my wish."

"It is the blackrobes!" He hammered his fist upon the earthern floor. "See their infection spreading? What deer or bear or elk or marten does not seek a mate and bear offspring? See how blackrobes poison minds? And yet my word is stronger!" He folded his arms and drew back. "In this land I am chief. No one will dare challenge my word. You will marry this winter. You will not speak with any blackrobe or any Christian. I have tried to reason with you, but you rebel. If I hear of your speaking to a Christian, any Christian, he or she shall perish by my hand."

Sick at heart, confused and saddened, Tekakwitha met her uncle's gaze. "Please do not test me," she pleaded, her lip quivering. "I shall cast the sagamite into the fire as I did before."

"Go!" the chief commanded, pointing his finger to the door. "You will learn not to trifle with me."

12

Often that summer, to seek comfort and to avoid her uncle, Tekakwitha ventured into the forest and talked with

Jerome. He gladly interrupted his prayers to discuss the new faith, the new way of thinking with her.

"Rawanniio holds each of us accountable for our deeds," Jerome said. He and Tekakwitha sat in the dappled shadows of an early autumn wood. "He places in each of us a knowledge of right and wrong, and like the seed of maize, we must water and cultivate it."

"But what of the customs of the League?" she asked.

"Hiawatha established the League to unite men in peace and brotherhood. Our chiefs have used it instead to conquer tribes and monopolize trade. This is not peace; it is slavery and commerce. Especially since the whites have come, the aim of the League has been toward warfare. The burning of captives, the drunken feasts, the Festival of Dreams—all these are condemned by the blackrobes. Excess, they say, is the devil working with us to keep us from seeing the true way."

"And the blackrobes allow each of us—even women—to choose a path to follow, even though it might conflict with traditions of the League?"

"Not only do they allow it, Rawanniio demands it."

"When two wills clash, which one must win?" she asked, hoping to hear the answer she wanted.

"The one with right on its side."

"Must I marry if I do not wish to?"

"No. In that matter, the blackrobes teach it is the individual who determines his own action."

"Then what of custom, what of tradition?"

"They are fine so long as they do not lead us from the path of goodness. Each of us has a free will, and that free will, that conscience, must seek out goodness and truth. We must all be responsible for our acts, for we all will be judged and accountable for them after death."

Tekakwitha sat back, pleased to hear what she herself felt.

"Why do our people enjoy the liquor so much?" Jerome asked, holding up his finger. "I will tell you. Because they can say, 'The demon in that cask caused me to do this.' Why do whole villages run riot during the Festival of Dreams when each man and woman seeks out what he or she dreamed? Because they can say, 'I dreamt this and so I must gratify my wish.'

"In each instance, the blackrobe teaches, they use liquor

and dreams as excuses. They place responsibility upon the liquor or the dream. But Rawanniio, and Christ his son, teach nothing can be blamed but the will of men and women."

"I have been called stubborn, unyielding, twisted because I refuse to marry. And yet my heart counsels me wisely." Tekakwitha looked longingly at him. "I wish I might receive instructions from the blackrobe, Jerome. I followed him and spied upon him all the days he was among us, and even though it was two summers ago, I remember so very well. If only I might speak to him and find the peace you have found!"

"Yes. The blackrobe wished to come among you, but your chief refuses any contact with him."

"I know, I know." She hung her head. "My uncle tries again to force me to marry. He invites another brave to sup with us tonight. I cannot do that! I cannot! I could only marry someone like you, Jerome. Someone with whom I'd live as a sister and helpmate, never as the wives of our village live."

Jerome smiled. "That is a fond thought—to live as brother and sister. Yet I shall soon depart for Quebec to study among the blackrobes, and not even the luxury of a sister do they allow themselves."

"What?" she asked in dismay. "You are leaving?"

"Yes." He looked at her with much emotion. "Next spring when the rivers thaw. I will study to become a donné and work with the blackrobes at a mission."

"But what of me? What of these times we spend in helping each other see more clearly?"

"I must go. I am sorry. I love you dearly, Tekakwitha, more dearly than my own sister." He looked into her eyes and she was terribly, utterly saddened.

"And I love you more than I have ever loved anyone, ever." Sadly she hung her head thinking of Kryn. Yes, Kryn was a man and Jerome was a boy, but Kryn had grown distant and no longer did she enjoy his favor.

"But I must leave. It grieves me very deeply. However, the Lord Jesus calls me and it would be selfish to stay."

"I hope I can maintain my resolve not to marry," she said.

"I do not leave until spring." His face brightened. "Hear me! Why don't you seek out others who believe as you do and we'll all go together?"

She turned away. "It is not that easy."

"Of course it is! The forest and the streams belong to us all."

"Yes," she said, "but my uncle would kill me."

She looked again at him. The gentle contours of this face, his limpid brown eyes, and sensuous lips comforted her. "I long for greater peace than a simple freedom from warfare," she said with much emotion. "I long for a peace that brings certainty and contentment to my heart. Is such a peace possible, Jerome?"

13

Peace affected Kryn oddly. He'd witnessed the French marching through the eastern gate with impunity, burning crops and villages, boldly claiming the land for a far-off king. The Canienga did not even raise a tomahawk! Blackrobes brought their new magic to Tionnontake, an effeminate magic that unmanned warriors, yet converts from Kanawaka wore a path through the forest to the priest. Despite his rantings against the blackrobes, Iowerano pretended not to see.

Gone were the scalping parties, the campaigns and conquests. Kryn believed the lethargy, the purposelessness, the uneasy calm held a suppressed violence that needed expression. He grew disgusted and embittered. He left the village often on solitary hunting and fishing trips, and alone in the woods, he communed with forces grander than the daily frustrations that drove villagers to bickering.

Something, though, soon sparked joy in the war chief's brooding thoughts. Kryn had long considered his wife barren. Many women, Tegonhat and Tonedetta included, had contracted the white man's gonorrhea and could not conceive. Kryn often viewed this with irony—a white carelessly begat him, but because of the whites he might not know fatherhood himself. White Adder often tried to remedy Karitha's sterility by rubbing rich soil from the cornfield upon her belly, by slicing open the soles of her feet to encourage bleeding so her menstrual blood would be staunched. Karitha urged Kryn to take a concubine—Tekakwitha, the orphan, had been mentioned—yet for the same reason he did not paint his skin, he preferred to live with his curse and let all men witness what he endured.

In the third summer since the whites' siege, the summer of 1669, Karitha announced she was pregnant. Kryn's joy knew no bounds. In the forest he opened his heart, and he intoned songs in his rich bass voice when paddling on the lake. The mountains, the rivers, the very sun, reverberated with his happiness, and he reflected upon each ordinary act. Mending his weir nets, whittling arrows, tracking deer by footprints and droppings—these were lessons he would teach his son.

A cloud obscured his happiness during Karitha's sixth month. The serenity of her condition had pleased him, and he praised her often and openly. Still she labored in the fields of the plantation as the summer ripened the corn, and in the evenings, their section of the longhouse was filled with young women visiting the expectant mother. Kryn usually avoided such gatherings, but one rainy evening he sat smoking his pipe as the rain pattered comfortingly against the bark of the house. A chance remark of one of the girls set him musing.

"I journeyed to Tionnontake yesterday," the maiden said. "He was quite interested in your condition, and I told him the babe will arrive when the leaves blaze with color."

Karitha shot a look at Kryn, a fearful look, then she scolded the girl. "Do not speak such nonsense! I know no one there! Who should care about me?"

Yet, after the young woman returned home, Kryn regarded his wife solemnly. Karitha hid from his gaze, busying herself with straightening her hearth side. Kryn, smoking his pipe, spoke at last. "Often barrenness is blamed on a wife when it may be caused by a husband."

She looked up, startled. "What are you saying?"

"For sixteen summers we have shared the sleeping shelf, and never did you bear a child. Now you do. How did this come to pass?"

Karitha shrugged, turned away from him. "In the usual way."

"And yet certainly it is not my seed that ripens in your womb."

She turned, shocked. "Of course it is!"

Kryn placed the pipe thoughtfully in his mouth. "I have often considered how this wonderful thing came to pass. The girl's remark has solved the riddle."

"She is a loose-tongued fool!" Karitha's eyes flashed with anger.

"And yet, the path we take in life is better lit by the sun than cloaked in mists and fogs. Who is the father of the child?"

"You are!" Karitha said, yet the fear in her voice remained.

"Then who did the maiden speak of that caused you such concern?"

Sullenly the woman dropped her head. She whispered, "The blackrobe."

"Ah," Kryn nodded. "And so this son of a half-breed shall be a half-breed himself."

"No!" Karitha protested. "This is your child! I have lain with no other man! The blackrobes do not know women!"

"Then what did the girl speak of? Why should the blackrobe care about the child?"

"Truth is something only the courageous pursue," Karitha muttered to give herself confidence. Then she said aloud, "Iowerano's sister Tegonhat, who loves you nearly as much as I, came to me last winter. 'The blackrobe's magic proves stronger than White Adder's,' she said. 'Let us go to Tionnontake and visit him.' You were in the forest hunting, and you brought a moose and two elk on that occasion."

"Tegonhat puts stock in the blackrobe?" Kryn asked in disbelief.

"Much stock. She was fond of the orphan's mother who told her much about the blackrobes. Secretly Tegonhat talked with the blackrobes when they passed through here two summers ago, and she has been journeying to Tionnontake twice each moon. I accompanied her. The blackrobe would not admit me to the secrets of the praying wigwam until I took many lessons, yet neither would I submit to that faith until I had tested it. I asked Rawanniio—their god, Father of All Things—to allow me to carry a child. I told Tegonhat that if I conceived and bore a child, then would I take lessons in the blackrobe's faith."

"I see," Kryn said, very disturbed.

"But who can argue that the blackrobe's magic is not stronger?" Karitha paused. "The praying has eased my anxiety. A wise woman, a Christian, taught me the proper time for conceiving, and I invited you to the sleeping shelf then."

"And Tegonhat, is she receiving instruction?"

"Yes. And I will join her after the child is born."

"And the child?"

"Oh, Kryn, do not look so! Long have we wanted a child, and now we shall have one. What matters how it came to pass?"

"The blackrobe has used trickery to turn your mind and that of Tegonhat to his religion."

"How can you label this trickery?" She patted her belly. "This child shall make us very happy. It will fill the longhouse with laughter and with song. Do not scowl so, my husband!"

Silently Kryn smoked his pipe, his arms folded.

"Why has this news removed your joy?" Karitha knelt at his side and threw her arms about his neck.

Kryn said nothing.

"Please do not be angry! I made such a vow only to benefit us!"

He fixed her with steely blue eyes, but said nothing.

"I was curious!" Karitha protested, pulling back. "The white man's army proved so strong, I longed to test the power of his magician!" She placed her hand upon Kryn's wrist. "Oh, why do you scowl? Is not reaching a destination more important than the turns and the steepness of the path?"

"And yet," Kryn said hoarsely, "I sense a net being woven, a net of fibers we cannot see, a net that will one day haul the Canienga from our true element and leave us gasping, suffocating like fish upon the riverbank."

"Oh, do not think so!" Karitha cried, sitting back on her heels.

"And I sense, too, that I shall be most unfortunately caught, for I am the son of a white man and all these things were fated at my birth."

And Kryn rose from his reed mat and walked from the longhouse. He passed slowly, thoughtfully down the path to the river and launched his canoe in the moonlight. With strong strokes he paddled alone downriver.

14

In the lanes between longhouses dogs stretched awake, gnawing idly at bones. Trails of smoke curled into the resplendent sky as women blew alive hearth fires, preparing a small repast before harvesting the corn. Children sprang awake and ran naked into the autumn morning, excited at the day's play ahead. Slowly, with much care, braves arose and tended to their nets, preparing for a fishing expedition. Tekakwitha, cooking breakfast for her uncle, smiled to think she'd meet Jerome in the forest today. A sudden, loud, terrified scream snapped all reveries. "I am slain!" a woman screamed. "Help!!"

Out from the bark huts ran braves holding muskets, war clubs, spears, and hatchets. Out ran women, collecting and herding children back inside. Out ran young boys, clambering upon the scaffolds inside the walls, whipping arrows from quivers and drawing back bowstrings. Gates to the village slammed shut behind the woman who'd screamed. She stumbled and fell; blood from the tomahawk wound in her skull spilled upon the dust. The village was surrounded. From the cornfields and the underbrush came volleys of musket fire, burning arrows, war whoops.

"Take Red Wolf and climb along the northern wall!" Kryn cried to a warrior. "They seek to divert us with fire to the south." He turned to Tonedetta. "Fetch Karitha and Tegonhat, and together carry the keg of powder to the western gate. There will be an attempt to force it. You!"—he hollered to three young men, running toward the gate— "Aid Diving Otter and Handsome Lake with stones."

Behind the walls, warriors' bodies strained, aiming muskets, thrumming bowstrings, hurling cobblestones upon the attackers, dousing burning arrows with water from mossy tanks of bark. Women ran with powder and shot and quivers of arrows, handing these up to men on the high platforms.

"Who attacks?" demanded Iowerano, strapping on his oaken chest plate.

"By their arrows, Mohegans," Kryn cried.

"How many?"

"Many."

A burning arrow sailed over the palisade and fastened in the roof of a hut. "There!" Kryn called to women, and immediately a ladder went up, the arrow was pulled out, the fire doused.

"Let us open the gates to the outer palisade," Iowerano said. "We can lure them and massacre them between the two rings."

"No, there are too many. They will overrun the village." Kryn glanced to the western gate. "With a battering ram they attempt to force the gate." And calling for braves to mount the scaffold and pour heavy fire upon the attackers, Kryn ran to enter the battle.

At places around the perimeter, bark ropes lassoed the tops of the palisade, and brawny Mohegans scaled the walls to be met by war hatchets and burning torches. Behind them scrambled others until iron hatchets of the Canienga cut the ropes and sent warriors falling back into their attacking bands.

Kryn rained down fire on the battering party at the western gate until the men dispersed. Fourteen lay mortally wounded. A cry went up to the east of the palisade as the attack shifted there. "Quickly," Kryn cried to Handsome Lake, "vault the gate and run to Tionnontake and Andaragon. Summon the Bear and Wolf clans! Otherwise, all of Canienga will be destroyed."

Armed only with a war hatchet, Handsome Lake flew over the wall. As soon as his feet touched the ground, he broke into a run.

All morning, pagan screams, war whoops, shouts of encouragement, and cries of pain filled the air as the battle raged. Incited by the English who greedily sought the Land From Which All Rivers Flow, five hundred warriors led by Chickatabutt, House Afire, the Mohegan chief, had come to attack the Canienga in their weakened state. Five hundred warriors—twice as many as in all the Canienga clans combined—assaulted the sturdy palisades. All morning, Mohegans equipped with English guns shot at the rooster combs of Canienga moving along the walls. But as the sun reached its zenith, different shouts rose from the cornfields and the underbrush. Behind Chickatabutt's five hundred warriors, Canienga from the Wolf and Bear clans now poured hot fire while a steady repulse continued from the palisade. Caught in the crossfire, the Mohegans retreated through the brush trying to regroup. Yet the forests behind them bristled with Canienga. Finally the Mohegans abandoned their siege and fled to the river.

Within Kanawaka, drums resounded louder, and still louder. Hastily a council was called. Chiefs of the Wolf and Bear and Turtle clans assembled in the council house. "We shall pursue them," Kryn announced, battle fever in his voice. "Not with impunity do these homeless dogs attack us in our homes. We shall pursue them as far as necessary and cut them down." All chiefs concurred.

Meanwhile, women ranged through the corn plantation and dragged wounded Mohegans back to the village. Some they tied to stakes upon the scaffolding, some they staked to the ground. Out came the children with cudgels and iron rods. They placed burning coals on the Mohegans' flesh. They gnawed their fingers, slashed their skin with knives, and beat them senseless.

"Boil the war kettle!" the braves cried, hauling a great iron pot into the center of the village. "Tomorrow shall Aireskou feast until he falls sick from gorging on the flesh of these curs!"

Toward evening within the smoky council house, the chiefs designed strategy. Two war parties were dispatched to the mountain pass far to the east. When the Mohegans reached the pass, the ambush would be sprung.

The men smeared themselves with bear grease, armed themselves with weapons and pouches of shot and gunpowder. Then quietly like shadows, they stole through the eastern gate, away from the center of light and heat and the cries of victims and their streaming blood, into the cool dark of the forest where the sparkling river threaded into the lowlands through the valley that was peaceful no longer.

15

Tekakwitha stumbled through the forest three nights later, seeking a cool refuge. Screams and drums and rattles echoed in her mind. Frenzied dances and licking flames conjured hot, agonizing thoughts that drove her deeper into the wood. For two nights the torture had continued. She came at last into a clearing where starlight streamed. "I must find Jerome," she said, pausing, out of breath. The attack had frightened her uncontrollably. The torture revolted her. "I shall go to Tionnontake and find him." She longed for the understanding of his eyes, the quiet comfort of his words, his softness, his gentleness.

With resolve, she crept along the river path that joined

the two Canienga villages. She passed around a great outcropping of black rock and high upon the headland rose the palisade of Tionnontake. The gates were open: All warriors had run to assist Kanawaka and had not yet returned. Now the women and children and elderly people slept. Tekakwitha crept through the quiet village, passing among the huts, wondering how to locate Jerome. At the south wall as the eastern sky grew pink she saw a bark hut topped with a cross. That is the sign of the blackrobe, she thought; perhaps I may find him there.

She pulled aside the heavy bear rug hanging over the entrance and entered the praying wigwam. A light burned at the front upon a table where another cross stood. Wild flowers adorned the altar and a metal box stood as tabernacle. The place seemed mysterious, tranquil, strangely forbidding. At the sound of a voice, Tekakwitha jumped and whipped around.

"Who is it that comes to pray?"

She saw the tall, thin blackrobe with the black beard and soft eyes. She stammered, "I-I-I do not belong. I come seeking a friend. I-I am sorry to intrude."

"How are you called?"

"Tekakwitha."

"You are not of this village?"

"Kanawaka. I have fled my village for returning warriors have brought many Mohegan captives and liquor from the Dutch," she blurted out. "I am very afraid."

"You may stay here until it passes," he offered, smiling kindly.

She sighed and sat upon the floor.

"Do you wish to talk?" asked Père Chauchetière, sitting upon a bench.

She regarded the priest. "I thought it all had passed," she said with sorrow. "I considered after the great army burned our towns three autumns ago, no more would war drums sound, no more would our villagers torture captives for Aireskou."

"You are daughter to the chief!" Chauchetière said, recognizing her. "You kept house and cooked meals when we passed through your village."

"This is so, but I am not his daughter. My parents have gone under the earth." Timidly she peered into the priest's face, and saw there great sympathy and compassion. "My mother was a Christian from the stone city where three rivers meet. She died of the plague."

"And are you a Christian?"

She looked warily at him, calculating the consequence of her answer.

"Have you received instruction?" he asked.

"Only from a friend, a young man of this village."

"How is he called?"

"Jerome." Suspiciously she searched his eyes. "This is his new Christian name." She grew worried at the sadness in the priest's face. "I have come to see him," she persisted. "Often he has comforted me in the forest."

The priest offered her his hand and helped her from the floor. "A woman of your village is nearby preparing breakfast. Let us eat, and you may talk with her." Père Claude led Tekakwitha out of the bark chapel, across the yard where long shadows fell in the pale dawn, then into a small bark house. "Anastasia," the priest said to a woman bending over the kettle. She turned.

"Tegonhat!" Tekakwitha cried.

"Ah, Tekakwitha!" They embraced.

"I did not know you had become a Christian!"

The woman smiled. "Yes." She stroked the young woman's hair. "I receive instruction here."

"Have you forsaken Kanawaka?"

"Not completely. Only until the torture ceases and all is peaceful again. So long have our braves been at peace without prisoners to entertain that they redouble in the cruelties."

"You are correct," Tekakwitha said. "Just yesterday morning they led more than forty men and women up the path to the gate with bark halters around their necks. With much joy our people formed the gauntlet. I watched only until I saw my uncle begin to burn a Mohegan woman who was with child. Then I fled unnoticed."

Père Chauchetière sat Indian-fashion upon the ground. "What became of the other Mohegans?"

"Massacred," Tekakwitha said. "Every Mohegan warrior upon this earth. Now their name is nothing but a memory, Kryn told us. The old woman, Quorenta, followed our war party and observed the ambush. She told me how she lurked outside the village walls, how they fell upon them, how the braves of our Turtle Clan followed the large Mohegan band and engaged them in skirmishes to slow them down, while warriors of the Bear and Wolf clans raced ahead through the forest. At a pass through the eastern mountains, one hundred Canienga fell upon the five hundred marauders. They severed Chickatabutt's head from his body and killed every last Mohegan, except for the prisoners they took. Quorenta composed a dirge about the battle. The next morning, the very rocks wept. Iowerano now has named this pass The Pass of the Weeping Rocks."

"You are trembling still!" Anastasia Tegonhat embraced Tekakwitha.

"I have wandered all night filled with fear of evil *okies*. I had thought such tortures had come to an end." Her voice fell. "As long as these customs continue, I do not wish to live at Kanawaka."

"Oh, Father," Anastasia Tegonhat said to the priest, "such scenes of torture are exactly like pictures you show of damned souls burning in hell. Once you have heard these death songs, once you have smelled the roasting flesh and burning hair, once you have seen the skin blister and burst, you will know intimately the hell of which you teach."

The priest stood. A look of great sadness had come over his features as he remembered baptizing the roasting victims three years before.

"Where do you go, Father? Let us eat."

"I shall enter the chapel and offer prayers for the souls of these poor victims that, passing through hell on earth, they may be saved from the eternal flames. After you break your fast, take this young woman to see Jerome in the longhouse of the faithful ones."

The priest passed through the bearskin door. In the quiet of the bubbling kettle, Tekakwitha and Anastasia Tegonhat sat silently, each with her own vision of the torture, bloodletting, and cannibalism taking place at Kanawaka.

"Jerome has spoken often of the Christian heaven and hell," Tekakwitha said at last. "If burning and torture meet evil ones after death, what can heroic warriors and matriarchs expect who are not Christian?"

"They will go to a place of peace and contentment, but they will not enter the presence of God."

"Why not?" the girl asked.

"Because courage and skill in fighting—virtues of the Canienga—do not cause one to enter heaven," Anastasia said quietly. "Neither does the bearing of many children who become leaders of clans and nations. Christians have different measures of virtue."

"What are those, Tegonhat?"

"Please, Tekakwitha, call me by my new name—Anastasia. With the new name I took on after the water was poured, I put aside my former identity of Tegonhat, the pagan." She spooned sagamite upon two bark plates and offered Tekakwitha one. The young woman ate with great hunger, listening avidly. "Christians measure virtue by the love and kindness we show each other. This love is far different from the duty the Canienga call love—duty to our father, our husband, our *ohwachira*, our children. This love is an elevation of the spirit, of the inner self, allowing us to see with new eyes, to seek the happiness of all around us, not merely our own selfish pleasures."

"Jerome has spoken to me of these things."

"Ah, poor Jerome!" the woman sighed. "He knows now." The tone of her voice troubled Tekakwitha. "The reward, then, for following the path of Christians is to journey after death far up beyond the clouds and to sit in the presence of the Great Spirit—Rawanniio, the Father of all things." Anastasia waved her hands. "There will be great light and softness and much singing—as we do at the Christian service—and a greater peace and happiness than we have ever known on this earth, than we can ever achieve."

"But will there not be war between the evil god of the fires and the good god of the clouds?"

"No," Anastasia said. "This earth is the battleground for good and evil. What comes after death is decided by our conduct here. So it is with Jerome."

"Let us go see him," Tekakwitha said, sensing something amiss. "He and I have met in the forest often, and we have discussed these things. I wish to speak with him."

Anastasia frowned. "You do not know what has happened?"

"No. What has happened?" Tekakwitha frowned, suddenly filled with alarm.

"You shall see," Anastasia said.

They stood up, left the bark wigwam, and walked through the lanes between the longhouses. Singing came from a house by the palisade, and they went toward it. Entering, Tekakwitha saw fifteen or twenty Christians standing by a sleeping shelf, singing a hymn.

"I do not see him," she whispered into Anastasia's ear.

"There." The woman pointed to the sleeping shelf, and in the light of candles, the young man lay in a monk's hood, his face placid as if in sleep.

"Do they sing to awaken him?" she asked, her voice quavering, hoping beyond hope it wasn't as she feared.

"He will not awaken to us," Anastasia said.

"He is not . . . ?"

"Yes," Anastasia nodded, and she smiled to comfort the girl. "A party of Mohegans, scouting ahead to our village, fell upon him as he prayed in the forest. The hood about his head hides his missing scalp."

"No!" Tekakwitha cried.

Many turned, but the singing did not stop.

> *The Lord is my shepherd;*
> *I shall not want*
> *He maketh me to lie down in*
> *Green pastures . . .*

Tekakwitha rushed forward, fell to her knees, and embraced the corpse. Slowly Anastasia advanced and stroked her braided hair. "Rise, Tekakwitha," she whispered. "Stand and sing."

"I loved him," she said, looking up, tears streaming from her eyes. "I loved him as a brother. Oh, Jerome! Above all men you were the most gentle and kind! They have murdered you!"

"Be happy for him," Anastasia said comfortingly. "Though his body has died, his soul lives with God in heaven. This is why we rejoice."

The others continued singing.

> *He leadeth me beside the still waters.*
> *He restoreth my soul: He leadeth me*
> *In the paths of righteousness*
> *For His name's sake . . .*

"But he is dead!" she cried.

"He has entered into a new life, a life far greater than we have ever known."

"No more will we share our thoughts!" Tekakwitha moaned, burying her face against the robe.

"You must pray to him," Anastasia said, embracing the

young woman. "He lives with God now, and he listens and sees all we do upon this earth. He will bring you much comfort if you pray to him."

"Please, Anastasia, teach me the prayer!" she implored.

"He understood. He wanted peace, and he has been scalped! Many were the thoughts we shared. I shall never meet him again!"

> *"Yea, though I walk through the valley*
> *Of the shadow of death, I will fear*
> *No evil: for thou art with me;*
> *Thy rod and thy staff they comfort me.*

"He died while praying in the forest," Anastasia whispered. "His reward is assured. You must feel no sorrow, Tekakwitha. He has gained what we are placed upon this earth to gain. You must seek your own heavenly reward."

"But my uncle!" she moaned. The final verse of the hymn drew all their voices high into exaltation, and in the dark, smoky recesses of the candle-lit longhouse the words of the hymn stirred their hearts with visions of soft white clouds, streaming sunlight, the peace of a summer day.

> *"Thou preparest a table before me*
> *In the presence of mine enemies:*
> *Thou anointest my head with oil;*
> *My cup runneth over.*

> *"Surely goodness and mercy shall follow me*
> *All the days of my life:*
> *And I will dwell in the*
> *House of the Lord . . . forever."*

THE PRAYER

Kanawaka
1669-1676

1

The day Karitha delivered a child, Kryn stormed into Iowerano's longhouse. "For once we agree, Cold Wind," he said with much anger. "The blackrobe has worked his evil."

Tekakwitha looked up from her embroidery with alarm. The mention of anything Christian sent Iowerano into a rage. Kryn wore only a loincloth and moccasins. His supple limbs trembled with anger.

"The woman has changed her name, adopted the *okies* of that cursed blackrobe, and now has borne me a deformed babe!"

"I am most sorry to hear her pain has been for naught," Iowerano said.

Tekakwitha groaned. Tonedetta expressed sympathy. Kryn fumed impatiently. "That," he said, "is why I seek your help. Great is the sway our women have, but I never heard a case to equal mine."

"Sit," Iowerano offered. "Enjoy a pipe with me." He signaled to Tekakwitha to bring tobacco.

"I am too upset," Kryn said, waving the pipe away, refusing to sit. "The babe possesses a withered right arm—he will never hold a bow or tomahawk, even a musket will be beyond him!—but Karitha will not allow me to place him upon the rock. Instead of offering this deformed babe to appease the wolf or the eagle, she wishes to nurture it, to feed it at her breast, to raise it as anyone would a whole child."

"I understand your anger," Iowerano said, motioning the war chief to sit upon an elk skin. "Alas, the law of the wampum belts is quite clear. A woman may elect to keep such a child so long as it can walk."

"Even now she names it, not a name of the forest or of the river, but a name the blackrobes have taught her—

223

Matthew. What insanity possesses these women?" he cried. "Tegonhat calls herself by another name and calls my wife Marie. It is an outrage!"

As she stirred the embers, Tekakwitha timidly asked, "May I address the chief?"

"What do you say?" Iowerano snapped.

"I only wish to suggest that this child may grow wise in the ways of men. A withered arm is no terrible shortcoming. Isn't it what a man holds in his mind that puts him above others?"

"Curb your tongue," Iowerano scolded. Kryn glared at her.

"How can a young man possess self-respect if he cannot paddle a canoe?" asked Kryn. "Have you, too, been listening to the blackrobe of Tionnontake?"

"She has not!" Iowerano said firmly. "I do not allow any talk of blackrobes in my longhouse! Punishment for listening to these evil magicians is removing the ears, cutting out the tongue."

"I join you in this belief," Kryn said firmly. He motioned for the pipe, lit it, then puffed angrily upon it. "I see no other course than to divorce this woman. Let her rely upon another hunter for meat. I shall disown this son. To me he is dead, exposed upon the rock as an offering to the wolf or eagle."

"That is a wise course," Iowerano nodded. "Let us abandon all those who heed the blackrobe. Hunger can turn the mind to see things with reason." He glared at Tekakwitha who still refused to marry.

"There are other hungers," she murmured, "than the hunger for meat."

"What do you speak of?" Iowerano scowled at her impertinence.

"I speak nonsense, Uncle." She looked boldly from chief to chief. "So have you always accused me."

"Divorce her immediately!" Iowerano said. "This upstart of a girl refuses to marry. At least she possesses a kind aunt and uncle to keep her. Karitha has no one but you to support her. Let the woman see how it is to proceed husbandless through life."

"Yes," Kryn said. "Let her go to the blackrobe for his small pieces of bread when she is hungry." He spat. "May her milk sour and poison the child!"

Kryn's stubborn anger deeply troubled Tekakwitha. Since

glimpsing the conduct of Christians, she had concluded the more intelligent and sensitive among the Canienga embraced this faith of gentleness and submission while the dissolute, ignorant, and intractable villagers kept on in the old ways. Dominated by her uncle, she gave no sign she longed for instruction, yet she watched The Prayer polarize her clan. Since the winter hunt when he had rebuked her, Tekakwitha had found Kryn less wise and kind. He had grown aloof and quiet during the long peace. Kryn, always more aware, more sensitive and considerate, had possessed, she thought, qualities of an ideal Christian. Now, with a Christian wife and a malformed child, he took pride in a savage conduct. He ridiculed the child. He criticized Karitha, ordered her about more brusquely than the most arrogant young warrior. He never missed a gibe at the blackrobe. Tekakwitha was pained by his behavior. Still, though, Kryn did not divorce Karitha.

Because of Iowerano's protests against her faith, Anastasia Tegonhat lodged now with Marie Karitha and Kryn. Tekakwitha enjoyed visiting the household and playing with the infant. The babe had inherited his father's blue eyes, and had such a happy disposition that his laughter cheered everyone in the longhouse. Marie Karitha showed a vast change in temperament. Once gloomy and quiet, she was now filled with a great serenity, and her joy in the babe was unbounded. She called Tekakwitha Little Mother and allowed the young woman to carry Matthew in his cradleboard, to clean him, as Iroquois mothers did, with sawdust from rotted stumps, to rock him in her arms and sing the Song of the Owl and the Song of the Squirrel.

One evening, as snow flurries filled the air, Tekakwitha entered her smoky longhouse. Iowerano and Tonedetta were eating.

"Where have you been?" asked the chief.

"I have been to Kryn's hearth."

"He has yet to divorce that woman," Iowerano said to his wife. "A year it has been. I do not understand." He turned to the young woman. "And what did you do there?"

"I helped Marie and Anastasia with the child Matthew. I wrapped him in a robe of otter I have been embroidering, for it grows cold and he is so delicate."

"And did you speak at all of the blackrobe?"

"I may have. I don't remember."

"You don't remember," the chief said with sarcasm. "So

prevalent is talk of whites and blackrobes that it becomes like the air we breathe, something we do, but do not remember." He pointed his finger at her. "Yet you shall remember this!" He lowered his eyes and his expression unnerved her. "You will not return to Kryn's hearth. You will not speak anymore with Tegonhat nor with Karitha. They are no longer Canienga."

"Why?" the young woman protested, showing more emotion than she wished to.

"It is not for you to ask!" the chief said firmly. "They are my friends no longer, not even Kryn—at least not until he divorces her."

Tonedetta explained. "The Women's Council met and voted today, over the chief's refusal, to invite a blackrobe here to Kanawaka. Already word has been sent to the stone cities of the whites. We shall have a blackrobe among us when the lakes thaw."

"Enough!" said Iowerano, greatly angered. He pointed his finger at Tekakwitha. "I caution you to have no communication with Christians. That is the end of the matter."

Tekakwitha fetched her bark plate and spoon and dished herself sagamite. And as she ate, she thought about a blackrobe in Kanawaka. She remembered the gentle eyes of the blackrobe at Tionnontake. She thought of the joyous songs at Jerome's bedside. She thought of the serene calm of Anastasia Tegonhat and Marie Karitha even while Kryn raged and stormed and threatened divorce. This news thrilled her. Dread stole into her heart, dread of the confrontation the blackrobe would bring, but she also felt a delicious excitement that even she might learn The Prayer.

Kryn took the news with silent gravity. After being informed the blackrobe would build a praying wigwam inside the palisade, Kryn simply said, "The whites infect us now worse than ever. I must leave this land. I must renew my spirit in the northern mountains, hunting the elk and bear."

"You will enlist a hunting party?" Iowerano asked.

"I shall go alone," Kryn said.

"That may be dangerous," Iowerano said. "Alone, you may starve."

"And yet, what good can life be here with the blackrobe turning our warriors into women?"

2

With inward rage Iowerano watched converts build a praying wigwam inside his palisade. When the frost left the ground, six men planted poles in the earth and bent them into an arch. Women, including Anastasia Tegonhat and Marie Karitha, peeled bark in long sheets from the elm tree, and lashed it to the building frame. In ten days the chapel stood ready. With his transfer ordered by Father Superior in Quebec, Père Claude Chauchetière journeyed downriver from Tionnontake to open the Mission of St. Peter in Kanawaka.

Children laughed at the accent with which he spoke Iroquois. Saucy women flirted wantonly with him to cause him embarrassment. Young warriors challenged him to arm wrestling and foot races. Père Claude took all in good humor. He visited the aged ones who rarely left their hearths; he befriended young mothers by treating infants for many minor infections; he treated the matriarchs with due respect.

Père Claude held instructions each morning in the praying wigwam. He taught how days were collected into groups of seven—the first day in each group was different from the other six. His pupils—all ages, both sexes—showed an eagerness, a curiosity to investigate and consider and reason out the various matters he placed before them.

"Father," Sleeping Bear asked one morning, "if the Lord said 'the meek shall inherit the earth,' why is it the French make muskets with such care, build stone forts, and sail the waters in great war canoes?"

"You are right. Conquering and owning things of this world prevent us from seeing the true light," Père Claude explained. "Many among the French are greedy. The Iroquois, by holding lands in common, by sharing the hunt no matter how scanty the portions, show a great example to the French. It is necessary, though, for you to be instructed so you can share these matters with them."

"It is good to know The Prayer," Sleeping Bear concluded, "but it is good to know how to fight as well."

"But Christ said his kingdom was not of this world," Claude persisted.

"But we haven't entered His kingdom yet, and we must live in this one."

"You teach us," a young woman said one day, "that the mother never lay with a man before she bore the Lord. Did God Himself enter her sleeping shelf and mount her?"

"God the Father has power over all of nature," Claude explained. "He willed that she bear His son, and it was done."

"Why then does He not will that corn grow as plentiful as the pine tree, that deer in winter be as abundant as spawning salmon?"

"Through original sin," Claude answered, "man lost the Garden of Eden and now must earn his living by the sweat of his brow." They had been fascinated with the story of Adam and Eve.

"You say the Father created us in His image and likeness," Marie Karitha asked him one morning. "Why does He never come among His children? Is it because we appear deformed to Him and He won't own that we are His?"

The pointed questions they put to him proved a challenge for this student of theology. Claude found their curiosity, their manner of associating one thought with another, their demand for truth, and for proof, indications of the fertile soil for his spiritual seeding. As prickly as the questions became, he tried to provide answers or suggest mysteries and miracles beyond his understanding as explanations. Never did he retreat behind pious platitudes.

"You teach that torturing war victims and eating their flesh is wrong," a young warrior said. "Why do Christians then worship a victim of torture and change bread and wine into His body and blood so they may eat of it? Are these not the same things?"

Père Claude was hard-pressed to answer. He pointed out the difference between the sanctity and grace emanating from communion and the enraged war behavior associated with eating human flesh. He contrasted the contemplative sacrifice of the mass with the orgiastic and brutal torture feast. But he sensed he was skirting the question. Were they not very much the same thing? Perhaps it was this savagery, this human sacrifice that intrigued Jogues and brought him back to this wilderness after the intricate theological abstractions of

Paris. Perhaps Jogues needed to fulfill a pact more sacred than ordination. Striving to understand theology, journeying to the far corners of the world to bring the light of Christ's message, laboring as a minister against devil-worship, cannibalism, fornication, and polygamy—this, at last, proved insufficient. Perhaps Jogues had reached the limits of his priesthood, Claude pondered, then spiritually progressed to the ultimate step beyond. Instead of presiding over the sacrifice, of offering the sacrifice of Christ's body and blood, he needed to become its victim. Jogues placed his own body and blood upon the altar, and the sacrifice was consummated.

"Could I follow Jogues to death?" Claude asked himself, and his flesh withered, his will shrank from the ultimate sacrifice, and he grieved to know his faith was so imperfect.

Resentful of the priest's authority over many, White Adder continually challenged him to battles of wits.

"You say your Lord had power to rise from the dead," the magician said. "No one ever rises to walk again after the last breath." The priest had just administered the last rites to a young warrior who had died of blood poisoning from a tattoo. The stench of gangrene nearly made Claude retch. "Say your words over him," White Adder taunted, "and make him rise and be well."

"He would not want that," Claude replied, "for he is with the Lord right now, and we are still here. He is safe and happy, yet we are prone to disease, hunger and pain."

"If that is true," White Adder snarled, "why don't you shoot a musket into your face, or dive over the waterfall and embrace the rocks? Why continue in a world that is so troublesome?"

"Suicide is cowardly and plunges us directly into hell," Claude answered. "Don't you value courage?"

As he came to know the villagers, Claude saw, as he had at Tionnontake, how unique each one was. He often caught sight of the young woman, Jerome's friend, but she turned quickly away each time, apparently terrified of speaking to him. Claude remembered that she was Iowerano's foster child, and he understood.

He recruited some men and women for a choir. The intelligent Canienga learned things remarkably fast, and used to intoning the Consolation Rite for departed chiefs, the battle litanies, and various other elegies and panegyrics, they now turned their fine voices to hymns. They practiced in the praying wigwam, while Claude marked time with his hand in the air, and each Sabbath the village marveled at the sound from that quarter. Tekakwitha, whose longhouse was nearby, often lay upon her sleeping shelf listening to the Sunday morning service.

Claude's presence gently changed Kanawaka. Men receiving The Prayer washed paint from their bodies, became reasonable, purposeful, and refrained from beating their wives. Women ceased gossiping maliciously at the corn mortar and grew modest, more dutiful, and quietly happy. A serenity stole over Kanawaka, punctured only occasionally by non-believers. Iowerano considered it all very ominous.

As days shortened, during the autumn of 1671, activity in the chapel busied. Hymns rang out morning, noon, and evening. As the snow fell and the river froze, Claude supervised a grand project. The men fashioned carvings from logs, carvings of the dull beasts of the Dutch—cows, sheep, and horses—and carvings of people. Children placed hemlock and spruce boughs about a small structure, and a rumor spread through the village that a wondrous happening, a miracle, soon would occur.

Three days after White Adder performed his frantic dance to call back the sun from its lowest spiral in the southern sky, all Christians assembled in the praying wigwam at sundown, singing and murmuring prayers. Tekakwitha lay on her sleeping shelf, anxious to glimpse the ceremony where the baby Jesus would be placed upon the hay in the corn mortar. She'd widened a crack between two plates of bark, and far across the yard she saw the sheen of candlelight upon trampled snow and a throng of villagers pressing to the door of the chapel. The melodic strains of the choir echoed in the still night.

"Not at all do I understand the great attention in reenacting the birth of an infant," Iowerano was saying, wrapped in a thick elk rug. "In all seasons do our women give birth and no fuss is made. Do these Christians wish to increase births and so petition their god with this rite?"

"The babe whose birth they reenact grew up and was tortured upon the crossed poles," Tonedetta explained.

"Why do bold warriors who have caught and scalped and tortured many, now kneel in the snow to worship a torture victim?" Iowerano said puffing upon his pipe. "I will never comprehend these Christians—they respect all the wrong things."

Beneath her bear rug, Tekakwitha watched as many villagers, Christian and pagan alike, knelt in the snow, piously imitating those inside. She was thrilled when a bell rang, and a solemn and respectful silence spread over all. Iowerano's talk at the fire profaned this sacred rite. "When will he sleep?" she murmured to herself.

Soon hymns of joy rose from the chapel, and the large gathering that knelt in the snow parted and bowed. Out from the chapel walked Père Claude with a wooden effigy of the Christ child. A procession followed him, singing, carrying candles and holy water, and the priest led them through lanes of the village. Many who had not assembled to kneel in the snow peered from porches of their longhouses as the procession wended by. Dark corners of the village where screams of war victims had echoed before, now rang out with the hymns celebrating Christ's birth. With a solemn purpose the large assembly followed the priest between the huts, through the central compound where torture stakes and scaffolding still stood, then back to the southern wall of the palisade. A band of children, shouting gleefully, had joined the procession. Four acolytes in red robes from Quebec raised their arms as the priest approached the nativity scene. Then silence fell.

"Tonight, dear Christ Jesus," Chauchetière called, holding high the wooden effigy, "you take on mortal flesh and come among us once again." Solemnly, the multitude knelt when the blackrobe genuflected. "Yet our celebration becomes so much more meaningful since tonight is the first time you have come among the Canienga at Kanawaka. Dwell here for evermore, O Lord, and spread your peace and love among these noble people, that through your grace, they may follow the path of virtue and holiness."

Gently the priest lay the Christ doll upon the hay. A sigh of awe escaped from the kneeling Canienga. Acolytes ranged their candles about the crèche, and the priest turned and led the choir in "O Come All Ye Faithful."

Still Iowerano and Tonedetta talked at the hearth fire. "When will you sleep?" Tekakwitha murmured silently, as the comforting melody of the carol drifted over the trampled snow.

Far into the night, Iowerano finally began to snore. Tekakwitha peeled back her bear rug, carefully, quietly, and tiptoed along the center of the longhouse, past hearth fires with embers glowing, between shelves where men and women and children lay in contortions of sleep. Outside, the moon cast a faint blue sheen upon the drifts of snow and the tall pines, and when the breeze changed, she heard the river gurgling beneath its icy crust.

Stealthily, lest she be discovered, Tekakwitha passed over the snow to the crèche. She had watched carefully as the forms were sculpted, dressed in clothes of the Canienga, then placed about the corn mortar acting as a manger. She walked among the wooden figures, and by the light of the moon, she peered into the manger. The wooden doll stared blankly up at her—black shells had been fixed for eyes and it was wrapped in beaver skins. Tekakwitha stroked its cheek and hair. She remembered with much sadness the little doll she'd buried during the Festival of the Dead. The Christ doll drew the attention, the respect, the honor of every Christian in the village. Tekakwitha envied the woman who'd cut her hair to furnish the babe with such a small amount as he required. She envied the men who carried candles and the choir that had learned such wondrous new songs. She envied Anastasia Tegonhat and Marie Karitha, grown women able to embrace this new way of life with no tyrannizing man controlling their behavior. When would she be free? She tried to control her thoughts, yet her envy of Anastasia Tegonhat and Marie Karitha soured into self-pity. Her lip quivered, her breath quickened, her eye grew moist. She knelt and placed a hand upon the doll and wept.

Next morning, Tekakwitha traded her cousin Linawato a string of glass beads for a dressed otter skin. And while the Christians passed back and forth calling greetings of the first Noël in Kanawaka, Tekakwitha stayed in the dim reaches of her longhouse with the smoky fire burning and fashioned a pattern on the skin to give form to her sorrow. She stitched an old woman crouching behind a wall, peering in at a throng of villagers assembled around a bright fire. The fire gave much light and warmth, yet the old woman of the embroidery crouched froglike in a marsh of reeds and lily pads.

Tekakwitha composed as she stitched her frustration. "Bat-Feeder watches beyond the walls, envying the warmth and light and fellowship of our clan. And like old Quorenta, I must stay, hidden among dark customs, watching, envying those who know the light of the blackrobe's prayer."

3

Dogs met Kryn as he stumbled through the blizzard. Four days had passed since he last tasted food. Day and night he had trudged on snowshoes looking for the settlement that hunters had told him about. Dogs yipped and pranced at his side. He followed them through the blinding snow to a cluster of huts. He needed food—his powder and shot had given out, and the few deer he spied leapt from his bow and arrow. He needed fire, too. But having hunted alone for more than a year, Kryn above all needed fellowship. He knocked upon the door of the first house he approached.

"Please!" he called. "Allow me to sit by the fire! Is anyone within?"

A woman's face, swollen with sleep, appeared at the door. "Who is that?"

"I am called Kryn. I am of the Canienga. Allow me to sit and warm myself at your fire."

"Enter." She shuffled aside.

Numb with cold, Kryn entered the hut. Carefully the woman placed pine knots upon the embers and stoked them until flames rose. In the ruby light Kryn saw she was an old woman with a round, flat face and a flat nose. Her black hair was streaked with gray. "Sit," she said and motioned toward a bison robe. He did not approach too near the fire. Gradually he brought warmth back to his flesh by rubbing. The woman lowered a sack from the rafters and removed a leg of venison. Deftly she cut a large steak and handed it to him. "Eat." He accepted the gift and sank his teeth into the chilled meat. Blood ran into his mouth, rich and delicious, and he chewed it with great hunger.

"How are you called?" he asked when he finished the meat. He wiped his hands in his long hair, and drew nearer the fire.

"Monica," she replied.

"Ah," he nodded, "a Christian." She said nothing. Her face was impassive. "What place is this?"

"La Prairie. The mission." She folded herself in a shawl.

"Have you no questions of me?"

She stared into the fire. "No."

"Do you not wish to know how I happen to be alone in such weather?"

"Many are the wayfarers we see each winter." She did not look up.

The woman's manner puzzled Kryn. "Every Christian I have met wishes to convince me of the great worth of it. Why do you keep silent?"

"The wish to convert everyone soon passes." The woman spoke slowly, patiently, firmly. "I am secure in my faith. I needn't convince others."

"That is as it should be," Kryn said.

"Yes." Still she stared into the flames. In silence they sat for a long while, the pine knots spitting.

"What is your tribe?" he asked then.

"It is of no account." She peered at him then and her steady, even gaze unnerved him. "I am of the mission now."

"Many are the rewards, I suppose?"

"Yes," she said, "many."

"Tell me, then."

Again she fixed him with a steady gaze. "You do not wish to know. You only wish to humor me. I sleep now." And backing from the fire, she lay down on a large bison robe and rolled herself into it. For a long time Kryn sat, gazing into the fire, bewildered and curious.

The woman Monica allowed him to stay as long as he wished. Though she asked nothing of him, Kryn chopped wood for her and for her neighbors. He trapped hares and raccoons. He left for two days and returned with a young buck of four antler points. The woman gave no sign she approved or disapproved of his presence. Neither did the neighbors. Kryn's pride prevented him from asking any questions.

One morning, he entered the hut with an armload of wood as Monica knelt in prayer. "What is the reason the Christians kneel like beggars?" he asked in a mocking voice. She made no answer. "Do you speak to the blackrobe if he interrupts?" Again no answer.

One afternoon as Kryn lay smoking his pipe, the Angelus

bell rang in the chapel. Monica, taken by surprise, ceased from dressing the skin and knelt. "What is the control the bell exercises?" Kryn asked. "I have seen it often in the towns of white men. Its tongue speaks to them, commands their actions." She did not answer, but murmured the Angelus prayer. "Is it more important," Kryn asked with sarcasm, "to speak with one who is not here than with me?" Monica continued praying.

By accident the wanderer had stumbled into this mission seeking food and warmth and shelter. He had found that. Often, though, he felt more lost than he had in the forest. Monica treated him with disdain.

One evening, as they finished eating, Kryn asked, "You pray before taking meat. Why not after?" Monica ignored him. "It seems to me," Kryn persisted, "that you do not care very much about saving me from the evil one."

Monica stared at him and her eyes burned. "No, you err, Kryn. You do not care to be saved, so there is nothing at all I can do."

"And yet you make no effort to show me the correct path."

"You do not make it clear where you wish to go."

"You are very wise."

"Flattery produces the same effect as mockery."

Kryn pulled out his pipe and packed it with tobacco, slowly, thoughtfully. "And if I ask you about The Prayer?"

"I would tell you."

"Have you a husband?"

"No longer."

Kryn nodded. "I have a wife . . . to the south. She, too, is a Christian." Monica said nothing. "Perhaps she should be here, and I there."

"We all are where we are." Monica seemed annoyed, impatient.

"When will you inform me about The Prayer?"

"When you ask. The dog chases the badger and barks at the door to its lair. The dog wishes evil upon the badger, doesn't he, else he would simply ask for entry?"

Kryn nodded and puffed thoughtfully upon his pipe. "Has the blackrobe taught you this method of answering?"

"I have sufficient eyesight to see my own way with my own people."

"Tell me, then, what effect this prayer produces."

She looked at him, scrutinizing his sincerity. Somewhat satisfied, she nodded. "You know of the peace of Hiawatha uniting all Iroquois in the Great League. The peace is like a soft blanket of snow, yet blood stains the white snow. It is not peace, but war and killing and brutality that the five nations crave. Just now they are peaceful, but when will fighting erupt again? The five nations vaunt their pride; they seek tribute and admiration; they are happiest when villages burn, creeks are sweetened with blood, and victims scream and writhe in pain. This is not the peace Hiawatha sought. This is not the path of wisdom. This is the path of pride.

"The Prayer of Christ was taught by the victim who never showed pain when spikes entered His flesh, who forgave his torturers even while impaled upon the cross. The Prayer teaches a way that reaches far higher than merely enduring pain. The courage it lends allows men and women to laugh the cruel, prideful torturers to scorn."

"It is similar to the death song we all compose for the moment when we withstand the torture?" Kryn wondered.

"No. I erred saying they laughed. They do not. They feel pity. They forgive the deluded ones who must burn the flesh with hot irons, who gnaw fingers, who place live coals in the eye sockets. They forgive them and call them brother."

"But isn't this foolish?" Kryn asked.

Monica waved toward the wall where shadows flickered. "Foolish instead are those who cannot see this life is merely a shadow cast upon the wall, merely a dream. This life is ever fleeing from our grasp, slipping through our fingers like grains of sand."

"I have heard about a dream of Christians that a place awaits them after death, a place far greater than the hunting ground of the brave. Indeed, that is all my wife can speak of. Yet, she does not take her own life."

"And yet there is the other place, the place of ceaseless burning."

"She has spoken of that, too."

"That is where men and women go who die by their own hands."

"This hell is like the tortures we administer—far worse than the foggy realms of serpents where our cowards lurk after death?"

"Consider Jogues, the first blackrobe murdered by the Iroquois," Monica said. "Consider his courage. He came again to the Canienga even after returning to his home. He sought to teach the ignorant, persuade the stubborn, save the prideful from hell. So, too, did the blackrobes Brebeuf and Lalemant also submit to the flames when your five nations obliterated the Hurons. The blood of these blackrobes cries out from the earth, not for vengeance, but for the Great League to take heed, to forget pride and magic and superstition, to look away from shadows cast upon the wall, to see at last the forms that cast shadows, to see at last the shining light."

"You speak in a way I understand," Kryn agreed. "Yet why do the soldiers and those who clear the land and build cities, why do they press us and seek to run us from our land?"

"Some of these have evil hearts. Greed, a sin our people do not know, drives them. The whites amass things of this world, hoping that by surrounding themselves with lands and riches, the uncertainty will vanish. Yet they err, too. They infect the land and cause strife and bloodshed, and the mantle of new-fallen snow becomes stained once more." Monica held out her hands. "It is for each man to reckon with himself. When the true path is found, he shall know it. He will turn to others. He will warn them, but they will not listen. Still he is certain, and his heart is content."

"Has the blackrobe explained all these things to you?"

"Many of these things he has put into words. But only by questioning and seeking truth do each of us find peace. Another may guide, but no magic can produce it."

Kryn smoked thoughtfully for a long while. Then he said, "I have stumbled through many forests alone. In the mountains did I wander through all seasons, chasing beasts as if chasing my dreams. My confidence in the Canienga and the Great League has been shaken. Certainties I once knew have fallen." He narrowed his eyes. "Your words hold forth hope. Yet what if they prove hollow?"

"It is for each of us to choose and to evaluate," she said, staring at him steadily. "I have found what I yearned to find. I need look no further. You are seeking a way, else you would not question my certainty so, nor would you have left your village. Yes, I have heard much of you, Kryn. You are a great chief. You are called The Great Mohawk by the English and The Flemish Bastard by the French. You are respected for your courage and skill in warfare by all men. Yet at night you are alone with yourself, and the opinions of others provide little comfort."

Kryn nodded. "You have very keen eyes."

Gazing into the fire, Monica spoke in a slow, hypnotic voice. "I have only just learned not to be distracted by shadows. After looking for so long to see the true objects that cast the shadows upon this earth, only now do I begin to discern the light that shines into the dark recesses of our superstitions and our souls."

Over the next months, Kryn continued to question Monica about the special prayer and about Christ. And rather than stem his curiosity, the answers opened richer and wider realms of thought than the wisest sachems ever entered. Kryn came to recognize the tricks of White Adder, the magician he'd long despised, as preying upon the fears of the villagers.

Under the tutelage of Father Cholonec, priest of the mission, he learned of the kindness and compassion of Christ, and he saw how wisdom and courage and inner strength could be exercised away from the battlefield.

The Great League of Hiawatha, decimated by disease, corrupted by liquor and trade, bled by perpetual war, was only a ghost of its former self. Morale and enthusiasm hardly existed within the palisades. Factions and the bickerings of families filled the village with strife. Iowerano symbolized the Canienga for Kryn.

Kryn saw now that the teachings of Hiawatha in the memory belts and the teachings of Christ in the book of the blackrobes were not far different. Both sought peace, both sought brotherhood. What was war, if not the sum of frustration and rage? Perhaps some integrity, some native honor and dignity could find expression through Christian instruction. Memories of Marie Karitha and the son he'd wanted to execute stabbed him at night in his sleeping robe. He saw his error, saw why he'd wandered through the forests for a year; saw what he must do. When the river thawed, he built a bark canoe and paddled upriver into the chain of lakes that led homeward.

4

"Have you heard the news?" Tekakwitha asked excitedly, entering the longhouse of Anastasia Tegonhat, Marie Karitha, and the child Matthew.

"You should not be seen here," Anastasia Tegonhat whispered, casting her eyes about in fear.

"Oh, it is all right today. Many are the runners who go from house to house telling that Kryn is returning."

"Kryn?" Marie Karitha's expression showed hope, then dejection.

"Yes. He tarried long to the north, and many say he has passed this last winter near the whites at Montreal. They say he is much changed."

"Yet, how much changed could he be?" Marie Karitha asked. "Still he will breathe war and campaigns. His time among the whites could only have been to scout and determine the weaknesses of their fortifications."

"We shall see," Anastasia Tegonhat said.

Indeed, that afternoon, an overcast spring day with a smell of summer in the wind, Kryn entered Kanawaka, followed, like a conquering hero, by the youth of the village. Instead of haughty pride though, Kryn showed reserve as he smiled and embraced many. "Yes," he told them, "I have been away a very long time, two winters and the summer between." He proceeded into the compound where the torture stakes still stood. Extending his arms, he called the villagers forth.

Iowerano came, and they embraced. "It is good you have returned, Blue of Eye," the chief said. "Now may we bring some sense to the Turtle Clan, and together we shall journey to the summer council at Onondaga."

"I shall not remain here long," Kryn said, and he called to the villagers to draw closer around him. Their curious jostling created excitement. Raising his hands into the air, Kryn spoke in a loud, deep voice. "People of the Turtle Clan! I return to you for a brief visit before I depart again with my wife and son." The blackrobe, Père Claude Chauchetière, hastened near as whispers of surprise went from mouth to ear. "Know that I do not wish to be called Kryn." Many gasped in surprise. Marie Karitha, holding Matthew, looked to Anastasia Tegonhat and whispered, "Can it be?"

"Long have many held me in respect, I am told, for my deeds in waging war. Together have I fought with many of you, side by side, in the heat of battle. Yet I tell you the war clubs and tomahawks are not one-tenth as difficult as is the war that wages within each of us." Cries of surprise filled the air. Kryn quieted them. "Bravery and courage and vigilance of a far different sort are required. Many of you now shaking your heads are as skeptical as I once was. I was wrong. Kryn, the war chief that mocked the blackrobe and the Christian, erred in his judgment. Soon I will be called Joseph Kryn, after the water is poured upon my forehead and the words spoken over me."

Marie Karitha and Anastasia Tegonhat embraced. Radiant with joy, they pushed to join Kryn in the center of the assembly.

"I have renounced my former ignorance," he called, "my superstitions, my ridicule of the new path open to us through The Prayer. Yes, I have received instruction from the blackrobes of the northern river. I urge all of you to listen. Many and deep are the secrets he knows, secrets of the human heart and mind and soul. Far better does he administer to us than does White Adder."

Heads turned, looking for the magician, but at the first mention of Christianity, he'd fled.

"I wish to tell you of a wondrous place upon the northern river," Kryn smiled. "It is called the Mission of St. Francis Xavier at La Prairie. Together live our brothers and sisters from all nations. Though founded to house the homeless Hurons after we massacred their nation and burned their towns, it now welcomes all people who will go and live in peace.

"In the shadow of the cross on top of the chapel, these people live in contentment and harmony. They attend the mass each morning, and they carry their thoughts and prayers into the fields. Here men call each other brother, but there they understand brotherhood—each man working for the good of all. Here we argue. There they sing. Here we plant and harvest. There they plant and harvest, then consecrate the bounty to the Lord who allows the corn to grow. Here we beget children. There they rear children in joy and security, instilling in the children the values of duty, hard work, and worship. Here we laugh if we outsmart the whites or the Algonquin. There all men live and die, profit and lose by how each man or woman acts, and so all men and women care and contribute to the total happiness. Here we embroider the maize stalk upon our leather. There they paint pictures of Him who died for us all, and so these pictures gain an integrity, a significance our seamstresses' efforts never enjoy.

"Yes, there I will return, and I will bring my wife and son so we may live in peace, following the ways of the Lord. I offer now to lead to the mission as many of you who wish to follow me there. We shall build our longhouses upon that northern river. We shall clear fields and plant our maize. We shall pray together and counsel each other and heed the words of the blackrobes. Please consider my words. I shall leave in ten days, and you should make yourselves ready by then."

Kryn now embraced Marie Karitha. He lifted his son high in the air, and with a joyful step, he moved off toward his longhouse. Tekakwitha's face burned at this news. Kryn, the mighty war chief, had learned The Prayer and would soon change his name and lead many of the Christian converts from the village. He was abandoning her and the ones who would stay, she felt. Only the Christian converts had planted regular fields of corn hills that spring, had encouraged fishing and hunting expeditions that brought in meat and smoked fish. The rest of the village relied on the beaver pelt trade and whiskey to bring immediate profit, momentary hilarity, then so much suffering. As she turned back toward her longhouse, she felt frustration, impatience, sorrow. She longed to leave with Kryn.

Iowerano's brow was clouded that evening, but he spoke no words to Tonedetta or Tekakwitha. After the evening meal, Iowerano sent a boy to fetch Kryn. The war chief came readily, and with a wide smile, entered the longhouse. "Greetings, Cold Wind," he said. He walked to Tekakwitha, saying, "And greetings, stitcher of skins." He placed his hand on her cheek, and she felt his rough, calloused fingers upon her ear. "What does the chief wish?" he said, sitting down. They produced pipes and shared tobacco.

"You have abandoned the ways of our fathers," Iowerano said, lighting his pipe.

Kryn smiled. "Ah, Cold Wind, you amuse me. Long have you counseled others not to listen to me because my father was a white trader from among the Dutch."

"Even so, you now abandon the ways of the Canienga. I cannot help that, nor can I dissuade you from leaving Kanawaka. Yet, I wish to warn you not to ask others to join you."

"I may do what I please."

"Yes, with yourself and your family. But your authority no longer extends over the Turtle Clan. You have no right, Kryn, to seek companionship upon this journey. Our clan has been weakened by war with the whites and with the Mohegans. Our clan has been weakened by disease. I cannot allow it to be weakened further by the spells and charms of the blackrobes."

"Our clan," Kryn said with frank good will, "has been weakened by wars that we have instigated. It has been weakened by rum and brandy that we have not had the discipline to deny. It has been weakened by forgetting the peace and the brotherhood of Hiawatha, by reverting to the arguments and confusion of the Entangled One, the chief with serpents for hair. I now offer what could have been ours since Jogues, the first blackrobe, but which we refused. Other blackrobes have attempted to save us, not from hunger, not from cold and want, but from ourselves, from our ignorance. It takes much honesty, Cold Wind, to face these things, more honesty than you possess."

Tekakwitha thrilled to hear Kryn talk so. Yet she averted her eyes and pretended not to listen.

"And so, what shall become of the People of the Longhouse if you and the blackrobes counsel them to put aside the tomahawk and the war club?" asked Iowerano.

"When the seasons change, the Canienga always adapt. The season for war and resistance is no longer upon us. The whites build cities of stone. They will not leave this land. It is now the season for peace. Any great chief must recognize the developments that will affect his people. The true chief leads his people into new things, teaches them to adapt; he does not blind his eyes to occurrences and imprison them in old ways."

Iowerano scowled.

"Do not think I hold anger in my heart against you, Cold Wind," Kryn continued. "I only wish you to open your ears and your eyes and witness what change is sweeping over this land. You must recognize you are powerless to stop it. Investigate it, search out its faults if you must, but do not pretend it does not exist."

"Since you were a child, Kryn, you have resented my authority, my birthright in the *ohwachira*, and you have employed every trick and method to gain control. Now you use this Christian faith to delude our people and lead them from their land." Iowerano scowled mightily. "I regret your selfish desire for power will cause our village to suffer. I cannot stop you. Take those who will go with you. But"—he held up his finger—"I caution you never to appear again at our gate, for I will treat you worse than the wolf who prowls when the snow is high."

"Perhaps someday you will change your heart," Kryn said, standing. "I will not be long in preparing to depart." He stepped over to Tekakwitha's sleeping shelf, and the young woman hardly dared to breathe. She longed to throw herself into Kryn's arms and plead with him to take her along. Yet she held her tongue, dropped her eyes, and shied away.

"Farewell, Little Owl, I shall miss thee."

That was all he said. She watched as Kryn left through the open door, her heart aching, tears pressing at her eyes. She swallowed a sob, then looked toward Iowerano who was watching her with a narrow, smoldering scowl.

5

In the monotonous cycle of seasons, the river thawed, swelled, slowed and froze; cornstalks sprang from the earth, ripened, then bleached and fell under the weight of snow. One half of Kanawaka converted, and the other half kept their pagan ways.

New France saw a change in 1673—Count Frontenac replaced Daniel de Courcelle as governor of the colony. Marquis de Tracy had long since returned to France. To put his colony on a profitable footing during the next year, Frontenac imported vast supplies of brandy to stimulate the fur trade. Though Jesuits protested in long epistles to Minister Colbert, the brandy flowed, debilitating all Indian nations of New France: the Algonquins, the Nation of the Cat, the Tobacco nation, the Ottawas, and the Iroquois.

Though at peace, villages of the Canienga, now soaked with brandy, became living hells. Plantations were overgrown, hardly cultivated; hunting and fishing expeditions were neglected in favor of trapping—an enterprise that brought more brandy. Drunken orgies replaced long-established traditions and festivals. Men swilling brandy roamed the forests and butchered each other, clan against clan. The summer councils were long, complicated affairs sorting out feuds among the clans and the nations, as sachems attempted to keep civil war from splintering the League. Trapped in great quantity, beaver and raccoon and otter populations fell. Difficult times lay ahead for Iowerano's people, and in periods of lucidity between binges, he mourned the Canienga's lost greatness.

Tekakwitha lived virtually as a prisoner after Kryn's departure. Forbidden to talk with Christians, compelled to embroider skins to please the traders who stalked at will through the village, Tekakwitha remained indoors much of the time sewing by the light from the chimney hole in daytime and by the smoky fire at night. One afternoon in the autumn of 1674, she peered up as a form darkened the doorway. She squinted to see who it was.

"I come to see Iowerano." By his accent he was a foreigner, perhaps a trader.

"He is not here."

"Are you the niece?" the man asked stepping inside.

"Yes." Her heart jumped. It was the blackrobe!

"Why do you not harvest maize in the fields with the other women?"

"I am required to stitch upon these skins. Besides, I have injured my ankle, and it is difficult to walk."

"Allow me to see," the priest said. He approached, but shyly she backed away.

"I am supposed to have no word with you."

"Why not?"

"That is what Iowerano orders."

"Let me see the ankle." Gently the priest unlaced her legging, and he turned her ankle in his hand. "You have sprained it, nothing more. I shall tie it for you to give support." He rearranged the leather stocking and the straps to provide support. As he worked she watched him, marveling at his gentleness, his kindness. "That should help," the priest said at last.

She said nothing. She wanted to say so much. She considered. She looked to her embroidery. The priest turned and walked toward the door. Before she knew what she was saying, she blurted, "Father? Father? May I learn The Prayer?"

Père Claude Chauchetière turned. "What did you say?"

Tekakwitha rose and hobbled to him and clasped his arm. "Father, long have I desired to learn what brings such comfort to others. Please will you teach it to me despite my uncle's orders?"

Père Claude reached out and gently touched her shoulder. "Of course," he said quietly. "Why have you not asked before for instruction?"

"My uncle forbids it absolutely. In the two summers since Kryn and Marie Karitha and Anastasia Tegonhat left, I have been alone in my desire. The Christians of our village keep away from this longhouse, as you know. Yet, I watch and listen. Jerome of Tionnontake taught me a great deal about the babe, the victim of torture who died heroically upon the crossed poles, and I wish to know so very much more."

"Come, then, to the chapel with me."

Fearfully she turned away. "I do not dare! My uncle would punish you severely."

Père Chauchetière smiled. "I do not fear him. I shall speak in your behalf. The Women's Council has ruled anyone who wishes to accept The Prayer may. Do not fear him." The priest led her out of the longhouse and across the yard to the shadow of the palisade, then into the chapel.

In the following weeks, Père Chauchetière numbered Tekakwitha among his catechumens, and he taught her basic tenets of Christianity. So struck was he by her progress, he wrote to Père Cholonec at the northern mission of La Prairie.

My Dear Pierre:

Praise be to the Lord! Often has it been said the blood of martyrs is the seed of the Church, and you have written of the astounding spiritual gifts of Joseph Kryn, the half-breed. I have begun instructing a Canienga maiden of the same clan, the clan that tortured Jogues thirty years since, a maiden of nearly twenty years. My words fall as the rain upon parched soil. This young woman drinks in lessons of the gospel with a spiritual thirst I have rarely encountered. Constant are her questions about the mysteries of our faith. Fervently she prays. Anxiously she inquires how to atone for the evils of her clan and her past life.

More than any other native that I have instructed, this young woman grasps abstract tenets of faith. Her questions, always asked with great humility and reservation, rival theological issues our professors put to us. Just yesterday she perplexed the medicine man, an albino of ferocious appearance and temperament. He skulks about our bark chapel seeking to waylay our catechumens and outsmart them. I listened to their discourse.

"How will you live in the blackrobe's heaven," he asked, "when there are no spirits of deer or bear to hunt?" She spoke quietly, but firmly. "No need will there be for meat in heaven." He persisted, "But in the Canienga afterlife many will be the deer and bear and moose and elk, and our warriors will feast upon this game." "And yet," she said quietly, "your place of hunting is impossible. According to you, the deer and bear and moose and elk will be present as spirits. Yet how will the men kill them? Do arrows and spears harm our shadows? And if they do, is there yet another hunting ground where the spirits of these spirits go?"

You may guess my delight in hearing this, for often, under the shaman's persuasion, our devotees begin to question The Prayer as something only white men can comprehend.

A change came over Tekakwitha as she received instruction. Her embroidered pictures had long been her only expression. But now the questions she framed surprised the priest, and he expressed his answers so she'd understand.

"If God gives all men free will, but not the same intelligence in seeing His design, why does He punish ignorant men the same as men with wisdom? Isn't the ignorance that He created the cause of their sinning?"

"Men who choose not to follow the Lord blame all sorts of causes and will do so at the Last Judgment. Blaming is simply a denial of responsibility. After Christ's word has been offered as a gift to us, if we choose not to accept it, we ourselves are to blame. Consider how many have heard us sing, have witnessed the many kindnesses we extend, yet continue to ignore or ridicule us."

"If we must love our enemies, why must we hate the devil?"

"Our enemies upon earth are other men and women with whom we disagree. The devil is a fiend who seduces us from the path of the Lord. Showing love for our enemies triumphs over the anger and rage and selfishness that are tools of the devil. The devil is the enemy of all—even of those we call our enemies. We must join together to resist him."

"If the white man's chief loves us so that he sends you to teach The Prayer, why does he also send liquor to addle men's minds?"

"I am sent by my superior, not by the chief of Quebec. The ruler of Quebec regards your people with hate and jealousy. He wants your land and the pelts you trap. He must learn to listen to my superior who sends me here, and we should pray so that he will."

Because she now had a vent for her doubt and her speculation, Tekakwitha's presence in the longhouse changed. The challenge of discussing her thoughts with the priest and the satisfaction of finding answers made her joyful in Iowerano's home.

"One day in seven you refuse to work?" Tonedetta asked with scorn. "That is a teaching we should all starve from if we followed it. It teaches laziness, no wonder you enjoy it."

"You know it is not that way, Aunt," Tekakwitha answered. "I will be happy to do double my share tomorrow."

"The blackrobe counsels you not to marry?" Iowerano asked. "Is it to keep you as his concubine?"

"You know that is not possible," Tekakwitha said. "He cannot marry and I do not wish to marry. He shows me how we must all bear the responsibility of our actions, and being unmarried is a responsibility I choose to bear. The blackrobe teaches that we must respect each other's decisions, as I respect yours not to study The Prayer."

Yet as great as the comfort of new teachings was for her, as clearly as it explained the world and provided an outlet for her wondering, Tekakwitha still wrestled with her dreams. The dream of the large, scaly, tortoise rising upon the path to

Quorenta's hut still troubled her. One night she awoke in terror when the disgusting scaly head and long green neck appeared from under the shell, for the accent was Pere Claude's saying, "Come closer. I shall eat of your flesh, and that will save you from the fire." She cried out that night, awakening in the dark longhouse, and she caught her breath and tried to discover the dream's meaning.

Chauchetière asked her one day to embroider a cross and a lily, a fleur-de-lis, upon a small piece of doeskin. She did so and presented it to the blackrobe. The priest stitched Dutch paper to the leather cover, and began a journal.

Account of a Spiritual Progress among the Canienga Nation of the Iroquois League

begun February 26, 1676
Claude Chauchetiere, S.J.

I begin this book to chronicle the progress in spiritual enlightenment of a young Mohawk woman named Tekakwitha. Among the filth, brutality, promiscuity, and ignorance, she has led a life of quiet and purity.

She possesses the forthright willfulness of her race. She can see a principle in all its manifestations far quicker than trained logicians. Her thought is not sterile or useless, as much of theirs seems to be. She takes things extremely personally, and to each thought she weds her feelings. It would be interesting, myself as her counselor, to take her through Loyola's spiritual exercises. And yet, that is a humbling thought, for she has lived through scenes of hell that we in the spiritual exercises have only imagined.

Tekakwitha prayed fervently for the light of Christ's teachings to dispel the dark superstitions that still lurked in corners of her mind. So long pent up and solitary, her heart poured forth emotion in a flood of passionate pleas to her confessor that the way be shown. Christ replaced Hiawatha in her thoughts as the bringer of peace; indeed, she came to see Hiawatha as a forerunner of Christ, readying her people for the message of the blackrobes. Pere Claude employed Hiawatha's pine tree image. In the earth the wood of Christ's cross had been planted, and it flowered and grew, towering above all nations. The blanket of snow spread over not only the five roots of the Iroquois nations, but also all nations of the world. Yet it was not an eagle that perched on the highest limb, it was a dove. Not fierce revenge, but wisdom of the Holy Spirit watched vigilantly.

I wonder no longer how Jogues came to love these people. Sober and serious, they grasp theological issues immediately and weave them into their thinking. The girl, Tekakwitha, grows ready for baptism. Sprung from a Christian Algonquin mother and a Canienga father, she possesses the best qualities of gentleness and forbearance of the one, and the stoic courage and unmoveable will of the other. Daily she defies her uncle who still forces her to live in his longhouse—her departure would prove an embarrassment, a disgrace—and she defies him with such tact and consideration even that misanthrope cannot object.

Her instruction continues, yet it is far from usual. Most often, catechumens accept the teachings over long periods, then the desire to convert grows until the will decides to renounce lurking traces of the old ways. Tekakwitha, however, daily and gladly sheds the old customs and teachings to embrace Christian ways. It is as if she were waiting, waiting all her short life for this way to be shown her, and now her spirit leaps up and follows wherever I lead.

It is not odd, but significant, that upon this wild continent among this brutal savage race a young woman holds forth hope for conversion and civilization. Wasn't it Mary, the young Jewess, who brought our Savior into the world? Wasn't it Joan of Arc who embodied the triumphant spirit of the French and led our armies? Wasn't it holy Theresa whose visions inspired the Spanish Carmelites? No less than they, this Iroquois maiden possesses the will and spiritual gifts far above the common course of her people. Truly these maidens were blossoms in their times and in their lands, and no less is this maid a flower in the Land of Flint. It is humbling to witness her spiritual growth, yet I thank God for entrusting the care of her soul to my hands.

6

A procession wended through Kanawaka—a cross bearer, two acolytes, three young women, then a choir of twenty, silent until the beginning of Mass. And last came Père Claude wearing white vestments for the Easter service.

At the door to the bark chapel, decorated today with dogwood and violets and tiger lilies, the procession halted, and the priest proceeded to the entrance. He asked the young women, "Whither do you come and why?"

"We come to the house of the Lord," they answered, "to receive Him into our minds and hearts and souls."

"Very well," he answered. "Enter and dwell with the Lord."

Into the chapel he led them. The altar was decked with wild roses and dogwood and cherry blossoms, and a font of holy water had been placed before it. With Tekakwitha leading, the three young Canienga in festive dress—yet free from the pagan wampum they usually plaited in their hair and free from the dyed eelskin headbands—walked with bowed heads to the priest. Tekakwitha looked up into the priest's eyes; she saw comfort and quiet joy radiate from his face. He nodded to her and smiled. She bowed her head, overwhelmed by the solemnity of the occasion. The lighted candle she carried trembled in her hand.

To each question, she delivered the answer in a hushed whisper, afraid if she spoke too loudly the spell might be broken. Then Tekakwitha inclined her head over the baptismal font.

"Having received the necessary instruction and having shown your sincerity and readiness to receive the Lord Jesus Christ into your mind, your heart, and your soul," Père Claude said, dipping his hand into the water and running it over her forehead, then making the sign of the cross with his thumb, "therefore do I baptize thee Kateri in the name of the Father and of the Son and of the Holy Ghost."

She had chosen Kateri as a name to embody the virtue of

250

St. Catherine of Alexandria, an obscure, quiet saint, her favorite among Père Claude's lives of the saints. Catherine had lived among Egyptian pagans, cherishing the light of Christ's word alone, privately, among the depredations of a heathen culture and animal gods. How Tekakwitha identified with her, admired her! Baptism, a first threshold, had led Catherine to sainthood, had made her an example to emulate, a mediatrix to pray to in time of need. As the water ran over her face she remembered that the medicine, the sacred entity she had found during her puberty rites, had been water. Now the water in this Land From Which All Rivers Flow was cleansing her spirit.

As she peered again at the blackrobe, her eyes moistened with tears, and the smile that spread across his face gave her great joy. Kateri Tekakwitha walked to the front pew, her mind feverish with many thoughts, her spirit swelling with emotion. Soon the two other baptized catechumens joined her.

The priest in white vestments proceeded to the front of the church. "I will approach the altar of God," he sang in Latin, "the Lord who gives me strength..."

And the joyous melody of resurrection rang out.

> *"Christ the Lord is risen today*
> *Christians make your vows to pay*
> *Offer ye your praises meet*
> *At the paschal victim's feet."*

Tears of joy scalded her cheeks, and a prayer trembled upon her lips. Kateri Tekakwitha bowed her head, thrilled at the song of triumph and the sacrifice of the Mass that was beginning.

She heard the Easter gospel with joy: the body not found, the Lord risen from the dead. Jesus, the Lamb of God, slaughtered as cruelly as any torture victim in her land, triumphing over the flesh and returning to life. Greater than Hiawatha ascending to heaven in his white canoe, Christ returned to earth to assure his work was carried out. And like her meek, beloved Christ, tortured in her mind by the evils of the time, Tekakwitha this day felt her soul rise from the dead to reenter the world. As she gazed upon the candles and the flowers and listened to the choir swell, how radiant was that world!

For his part, Père Claude considered Kateri Tekakwitha his own protégée, his special charge. Each day he watched her pass in a veil from the chief's longhouse to the chapel. He observed her silently working in the fields among the women. He noticed her joy in tending to the young ones of Kanawaka. Fear of hell did not enter her motives.

"Why do you carry sagamite to the old widow?" Père Claude asked her one day.

"Because I love Jesus, and Jesus is in her."

"How much do you love Jesus?"

"Oh, Father!" She shuddered and a transcendent look came into her face. "Much more than I can ever say!"

She told him, too, that she loved the Lord as a babe in the manger, as the teller of parables, as the miracle worker, as the crucified Savior, and as the glorified Christ ascending into heaven. Her spiritual growth after baptism was met with cruelties heaped upon her by Tonedetta and Iowerano, and even by some of the children of the village. "Here, Christian!" they called in the same voice they called their dogs, and they pelted her with stones and clods of earth as she passed to daily services in the chapel.

Because bold Canienga feared nothing so much as ridicule among their own people, Iowerano encouraged the villagers to heap criticism upon Kateri. They refused to use her Christian name. They allowed her no food on Sundays when she did not work. They would stop the young woman on her path, and say, "Aren't you ashamed rushing to the chapel every day?" "You disgrace the memory of your father, the great chief." "Weak is your Algonquin blood."

Patiently Kateri followed the priest's instructions in offering up her humiliation to ease the suffering of those who'd gone under the earth. Yet one crowning insult Kateri Tekakwitha was not able to bear.

During the summer of 1676, she accompanied her aunt and uncle and members of other *ohwachiras* to the fishing grounds at Tawasentha below Albany. Upon the riverbank they erected their wigwams of skins and the men fished all day while the women filleted the catch and dried it over smoking fires. Away from the blackrobe and daily services, Kateri rigged a cross in a thicket in the forest, and there she ventured each morning and each evening to offer prayers to Rawanniio.

One twilight as she returned toward camp, she met

Otken, husband to her cousin Linawato. "Hello, cousin!" he called. "Where do you come from?"

"Long have we been friends," Kateri said, joining him on the forest path. "I ask that you call me by my new name."

He grinned affably, "Only if you call me by my name."

She blushed. Referring to a man in one's own longhouse by his first name showed familiarity, intimacy.

"Doesn't your faith allow the relaxing of the old ways?" he teased.

"Some of them, cousin." She smiled bashfully. "But it isn't allowed for me to say 'Otken,' for you are my cousin's husband, not mine."

"You have just said the word you mustn't."

"These are foolish old ways," she agreed. "Christians call everyone by their names." She looked at what he carried.

Otken adjusted his satchel of four hares. "Sit at our fire this evening and enjoy a portion of these fat hares." He fondled one by the belly.

"I will," she said.

As they entered camp, Tonedetta pointed at them and whispered in Linawato's ear. Otken cooked the hares on spits over the fire, and he carved them and doled out portions. The day had been a fine one for fishing—overcast and muggy— and the catch lay upon ferns waiting to be cleaned after supper. Otken had already described how he had snared the rabbits, but Linawato continued to ask questions about how long he had waited and in which place.

"Do you care for more, Kateri?" Otken asked, playfully using her Christian name.

"No, thank you, Otken," she replied, returning the gibe.

"I knew it!" Linawato cried out as if someone had slapped her. "I knew it! I just knew it!" and she buried her face in her hands and burst into tears. Kateri Tekakwitha and Otken looked at each other. All faces about the fire watched them suspiciously.

"Whatever is the matter with you?" Otken asked his wife.

"You and her! I knew she was not to be trusted!"

Hearing this, Kateri Tekakwitha blushed deeply. Her shock was seen as guilt by those about the fire.

"You don't think..." Otken said, blanching. "Kateri and me?" He attempted a laugh.

"Her aunt warned me!" Linawato cried. "Now it has

come to pass! My own cousin seducing my husband. A Christian! What a hypocrite!"

Mortified by the accusation and seeing all raising their eyes in knowing looks, Kateri Tekakwitha stood and hurried from the fire.

"Look at her flee," Tonedetta said loudly so all might hear. "And these Christians pretend to be above fornication! Ha!"

Returning to Kanawaka, Kateri Tekakwitha immediately sought Père Claude. "Rumor has accused me of impurity with Linawato's husband," she told him with a quivering lip. "I do not see why they try so hard to discredit me." She recounted the innocent way the accusation had occurred.

"Did anything, any touch or kiss or impure suggestion pass between you and Otken?" the priest asked, sitting upon the sleeping shelf he employed as a confessional. Seeing her anger, her frustration, he qualified the question. "You know how morals relax when on hunting and fishing trips."

She looked into his eyes for a long moment. Tears flowed down her cheek. "Father," she implored, "do you not believe me?"

"I do," he insisted, looking away, "I do." He regarded her again. A strange, haunted feeling took hold of him. With a start, Père Claude realized that jealousy had infected him with suspicion. Searching for the wellspring of his jealousy, he knew with profound and sudden insight that he loved Kateri Tekakwitha in a more possessive way than was safe. He grew sick at heart when turning his own suspicions upon himself.

"Please, pay no attention," Père Claude said quickly, apologetically. "I had another matter on my mind. I was not concentrating upon your words."

Kateri wiped her tears. "I know not why," she said sorrowfully, "the others ridicule me so."

"In this world of imperfection, Kateri, such goodness as yours is scarcely believed." Père Claude sighed. "Like the looking glass the girls obtain from traders, your virtue reflects back images of others who look at you. They see all their own faults. Yet, who can blame the looking glass for his own imperfections?" The blackrobe inclined his head into his hand.

"And how is this, Father?" she asked, bewildered by his metaphor.

"Your aunt, Tonedetta, longs for ease from her chores, and so accuses you of laziness. The chief, Iowerano, harbors jealousy for Joseph Kryn's integrity and influence among the Canienga, and so he resents any Christian rite or ideal you hold. You, Kateri Tekakwitha, are a looking glass to each of them. It is not you who have erred. It is their wayward thoughts. You must not fear their evil accusations."

"And yet, Father, I do not wish to be a looking glass, to show others any faults they might possess. I am terribly faulted myself." Again tears flowed, and she shuddered and turned away from him. "I long for admission to the sacrament of penance, Father, so I may confess my sins and have them forgiven."

"In time," Père Claude said, placing his hand on her shoulder. "In time. You must receive additional instruction to ready yourself."

"And yet," she murmured, "I feel there is not much time."

Kateri Tekakwitha stood and left the chapel. Père Claude watched her go, afflicted with a profound doubt about his ability to administer to his flock. He loved her, he knew, in a worldly way. He saw danger ahead. His faith was challenged by this Canienga maiden, and he had erred in becoming so personally involved with her.

7

Kanawaka
August 6, 1676

Father Superior:

Praise be to God! I write you from among the savages that I have labored so long to convert. For nine years—since Marquis de Tracy's triumph—I have lived with the Canienga and brought a ray of the Christian faith into this dark land. It is easy to draw lines of demarcation on maps, yet territory of the Lord and the sway of the demon are not always so easily separated.

I beseech you, Father, to allow me a journey to
Montreal or Quebec. It is not frivolous, nor is it the
fellowship of my own race that I seek. My spiritual
well-being demands a renewal of the Spiritual Exercises. I cannot accomplish it here for many reasons.
It is with a terrible hunger and thirst that I long to
receive the sacraments and hear Mass said by members of the Society.

Be assured the Mission of St. Peter in Kanawaka
prospers. Still do I minister to the Mission of St.
Mary at Tionnontake, though many converts have
migrated north to the mission or westward to live
with pious Oneidas under the direction of Father
Pierron.

I place my petition before you, knowing
Christ Jesus will guide you in your decision. I
can journey north before the rivers freeze, and
there are many pious Canienga who will act as
my guide.

Yours in Christ,
Claude Chauchetière, S.J.

8

When she heard of his plan to journey northward, Kateri
Tekakwitha hastened to the priest's home. The long, dim hut,
deserted by most of its families when Joseph Kryn escorted
them northward, echoed with her call. "Father? Are you
here?"

"I am here," he said. She made her way through the
hut, and came upon him packing his chalice and patten and
ciborium in a leather case.

"They tell me you are leaving."

"Yes," he said, trying to appear unconcerned. "I will
journey to Quebec before the rivers freeze, and next spring I
shall receive a different assignment."

"You will not return?" she asked sadly.

His eyes met hers. "No. But . . . but another of my order

will arrive in spring to take up the mission and the counsel of souls."

She stared at him with an inscrutable, expressionless, unnerving stare, a Canienga stare. She said nothing.

"You will continue your instruction under my successor," he rattled on. "I shall write him, too, about the backsliders who fall occasionally into the old ways."

"I wish to accompany you," Kateri Tekakwitha said quietly, but firmly.

"I am sorry. That cannot be."

"Haven't you always spoken of our avoiding the occasion of sin?"

"Yes, Kateri." Père Claude sighed and pulled tight the straps of his leather case. "We must all avoid the occasion of sin." His words echoed with peculiar hollowness. His personal journal, his occasion of sin, was securely packed.

"Then I wish to accompany you. My uncle and aunt continue to press me to marry. They see your departure as an opportunity to turn my eyes from the true faith. Take me with you only as far as the mission where Joseph Kryn lives. There shall I find true happiness and contentment."

"I cannot," Père Claude said impatiently. "If I abduct you without your uncle's permission, he will send braves to ambush us and massacre us before we reach the northern lake."

"Then I shall have to escape by myself," she said firmly. She turned to leave.

"Kateri?" He spoke before he realized it.

"Yes, Father?" She turned hesitantly.

Père Claude shook his head. "Nothing. I just want you to be well. Obey your uncle and aunt as far as you are able. And listen well to the counsel of the blackrobe who succeeds me."

"But I shall not be here," she said. The odd tone to her voice and her abrupt turning away unsettled him. Viciously Père Claude shoved leather stockings and moccasins into his bag.

He did not see her again. Two days later, he embarked in a canoe. Many of his converts and catechumens lined the riverbank to wave farewell. He looked among them for Kateri Tekakwitha, but she had not come. Shrugging and telling himself it was for the better, he turned his eyes to the lower river and struck out with the paddle to help his guide. Yet that night in the forest and many, many nights afterward, he

thought of her, her wisdom, her kindness, her frank innocence, and above all, her purity.

She did not plan her escape. The Sunday morning afte
Chauchetière's departure, Kateri Tekakwitha walked to the
chapel and found it empty. Instead of returning to the
longhouse of her uncle, she simply walked out the north gate
of the village and kept on walking.

Leaves, falling from the trees, and chill gusts of wind
caused her much sadness of heart. With the speed of thought
she longed to fly northward to the mission where Joseph
Kryn, Anastasia Tegonhat, Matthew, and Marie Karitha all
lived. Yet the wild, difficult trail posed a great obstacle, and
the chill weather numbed her willpower. Nevertheless she
kept on.

For twelve days she wandered alone, eating such roots
and bark as she dug and peeled, eating frogs and mud turtles
she caught in ponds and meandering streams. At an abandoned campsite she found a stone hatchet, and this allowed
her to fashion fire-producing sticks to warm her nights. She
had worn only the leather dress, leggings, and moccasins,
and shivering each night, she curled upon the bare ground
close to the dying embers. In the morning she carefully
doused the fire so no telltale smoke would signal anyone who
might be pursuing.

Often she knelt and cried out to Rawanniio for help so
she might reach the mission. And she rose from her knees
after the prayer, understanding this flight as a test of her
fortitude. On the evening of her thirteenth day as she walked
through the tall pine forest, a man suddenly appeared. Kateri
Tekakwitha ducked behind a large tree trunk, and her heart,
accustomed to solitude, beat doubly fast, fearing who he
might be and what he might do.

The man, however, had spied her. He circled the tree
and dragged her out, writhing in his grasp. "Handsome
Lake!" she cried, recognizing him. He gave a shrill whistle
and soon from all directions braves assembled. "Iowerano
sent us to find you," he explained. "He is very angry. I did
not want to accompany this search party, yet I felt it was
better to seek you out than to allow you to perish in the
forest."

"I will go with you now," Kateri Tekakwitha said boldly,
scanning the ring of braves, "but I will not remain long."

9

In a cell in the stone cellar of the Jesuit seminary of Quebec, Père Claude Chauchetière again progressed through Loyola's spiritual exercises. Dangerously close to worldly love, he'd allowed masculine emotions to pollute the spiritual counseling of the young Canienga woman, Kateri Tekakwitha. Tormented by carnal desires, he feared his faith was flawed, flawed from the tryst with the gypsy and doomed to be flawed evermore. He brooded that dark women held a sway over him. He longed for the innocence and purity of his first retreat in Montmartre—the vision of hell, the agony in the garden, the image of the virgin. Yet, hadn't that deluded him with an impure vision? Did dwelling upon the sway of evil, guarding against its progress, searching everywhere to find it lurking so it could be expelled, did that jade men?

During one of his more violent spiritual battles, New France supplanted the biblical world of his first retreat. The brutal cannibalism and murder of the Iroquois held more horror and terror than hell, for it was actual and immediate. The meek, uncomplaining Jogues reenacted the passion and sacrifice of Christ, and his agony, his suffering, and his forgiveness were precisely those of the Lamb of God. The quiet, meditative young woman, Kateri Tekakwitha, radiated the pure, saving, unquestioning love of the Blessed Virgin. In the dead of night in the stone cell, his soul tormented with doubt of his faith, Père Claude saw a pattern being woven, a pattern to his destiny, a pattern begun in the first spiritual exercises, perhaps even during his grievous sin, his fall from innocence and grace. Wasn't it his sin that caused him to seek out this brutal hellish land and to follow in the bloody footsteps of Jogues? Wasn't it his sin that caused him to search everywhere for an uncorrupted and uncorruptible woman?

He saw during this month-long retreat that his life in the New World was living out a scheme, a pattern begun during his first spiritual exercises—passage through a hellish land, the guiding example of a martyr, and the saving, unsullied love of a young woman. While the biblical realm was far more common to the meditation of all Christendom, Père Claude clasped New France to himself. It was personal, actual, his own.

Still one doubt carped at him late at night. The virgin of his first meditation was based upon the image of a courtesan. What if, at some future time, this devout and loving young woman Kateri Tekakwitha proved unworthy of his reverence? This question gnawed at him, yet he was blind and could not see his doubt for what it was—a creation of his ego, his pride, and therefore, the prime flaw in the fabric and texture of his faith.

Emerging from the spiritual exercise, he asked to be reassigned in New France, but sought a mission closer to the French cities. Having taught among the Iroquois for so long, Père Claude was assigned a post at the Mission of St. Francis Xavier at La Prairie, directly across the river from the island citadel of Montreal. Under his direction and to find more arable soil, the villagers soon moved the mission a league upriver to the base of a falls and designated it Mission of St. Francis Xavier at the Sault. There he settled to counsel these natives, finding comfort in the austerity, the regimen, and the simplicity of his life.

10

Tonedetta and Iowerano made Kateri Tekakwitha's life unbearable after her escape. The most burdensome, undignified tasks devolved to her. They refused to call her Kateri, and ceased even calling her Tekakwitha. She was 'The Christian,' spoken with sarcasm. Quietly, patiently, Kateri Tekakwitha performed her tasks, holding within herself her sorrow, her love of The Prayer, and her hope of escape.

The long, dark winter crept on. The light of the new faith had been extinguished. Iowerano threatened to murder any new blackrobe resuming Chauchetière's mission. Sometimes Kateri Tekakwitha passed former members of the congregation in the village lanes, but their joy faded as the dark months wore on, and they avoided each other's eyes. Large quantities of brandy were hauled into the village by French traders anxious for thick winter pelts, and nights of screams and lust were frequent.

The spring seemed as though it would never visit the Land From Which All Rivers Flow. Yet, at last the river groaned, ice split and clogged the river, and meltwater flooded the lowlands. Slowly the sun climbed in the southern sky.

Anxious to escape her uncle's stern gaze, Kateri helped the women prepare and plant the fields. She prayed quietly each morning and each evening, and she watched sadly as the chapel was slowly dismantled by one *ohwachira* after another to provide bark and poles to repair damage done by winter snows.

Seeing canoes of pelts sent north to Quebec, the English made overtures to the Canienga that spring. More rum than the brandy they now received would be supplied for each laden canoe, the English promised, and to discuss the deal, they invited Iowerano and chiefs of the Bear and Wolf clans to Corlaer for a treaty signing. Debilitated by a winter of licentiousness, the clan, Kateri felt, would now sink further into dissolution. The life at Kanawaka disgusted her. She felt helpless; rather than try to change minds, she withdrew further and further into herself. At the first opportunity, she vowed, she'd make her escape. With the planting nearly completed, the village was suddenly astir with news of Joseph Kryn's visit. Kateri Tekakwitha's heart was thrilled. Perhaps he'd take her with him!

The morning after runners brought news, a long canoe with three men landed on the mud flats below Kanawaka. In bristling fur robes, Joseph Kryn and two companions, Jacob and Onas, strode up the path, through the southern gate, and into the compound where the torture stakes stood.

"Pull those down!" Joseph Kryn called by way of greeting. "The era of burning victims is over."

Canienga braves came running into the compound where Joseph Kryn stood, his arms folded.

"I wish to see Iowerano," he announced. "I have heard of the drunkenness and debauchery, and I see for myself how low the Canienga have fallen. I have come to invite my people to accompany me first to the Oneida, then to the Onondaga, then by way of the great lake and rivers to the blackrobe's mission at La Prairie. I know you have no blackrobe now."

Diving Otter spoke. "Iowerano is at Corlaer negotiating a treaty with the English. We shall not see him for five days."

"Well, then, I will appeal directly to the Christians. There is no future living in filth and squalor as you do here. I can see the effects of the brandy. The sacred traditions of our League have been forgotten, trampled under. No one hunts. No one practices the least discipline." With hatchets Jacob and Onas hacked through the bark flooring of the scaffold. A creaking groan resounded and the tallest of the torture poles tottered and fell. "Come now, who is going to help these Christians destroy the old ways?" Joseph Kryn called.

Sullenly the warriors watched, and Joseph Kryn ignored their mutterings. Kateri Tekakwitha longed to go to him, yet she dared not.

"A new blackrobe will be here as the corn ripens," Joseph Kryn announced. "There must be Christians among you who will help these men rip down the hated torture poles."

Kateri Tekakwitha stepped forward, then stopped when she heard Otken say, "Iowerano will surely punish you for this outrage, Kryn."

Joseph Kryn leaned back and a laugh erupted from deep in his breast. "Iowerano? What is he to me? He is like the Entangled One of our legend; his thinking is like a writhing mass of snakes. He cannot lead for he argues with himself. No!" Joseph Kryn shook his head. "The new way lights a clear path through all dark and misty places. No longer can men and women blame each other for their misdeeds. No longer can White Adder trick us. The new way makes each responsible for himself. This is what the blackrobes teach. Now, who will help pull down the torture poles?"

Inspired by Joseph Kryn's courage and the appeal of his speech, Kateri Tekakwitha pushed between two braves and stepped toward him.

"Noble chief," she said. "I am called Kateri Tekakwitha now. Since you went north with Marie Karitha and Anastasia Tegonhat, I have been baptized by the blackrobe. I wish to journey to La Prairie and to live with my people who have accepted The Prayer."

"There!" Joseph Kryn cried, holding forth his hand.

"There's an honest woman worthy of imitating. Where are more? Come forth!"

"Kind chief," she added, cautioning him, "my uncle forbids me to leave, as he forbids any of these who still hold him in high regard. For myself, death is preferable to another year in Kanawaka. Yet my uncle is a powerful man. What guarantee will you promise any who accompany you that their safety will be assured?"

"None, but that I will do battle myself to the death with anyone hindering us, for to fight for the Lord is the most sacred challenge we can accept. And to win is the sweetest victory possible."

This caused talk among the villagers. As the last scaffold now groaned and fell, Joseph Kryn began enlisting men and women to accompany him westward to the Oneida. Kateri Tekakwitha waited patiently on the periphery of the crowd, then invited him to share a meal in her longhouse.

"Good Joseph Kryn," she said, dishing out the sagamite. She placed it before him on the ground. "Both my aunt and uncle have persecuted me for my beliefs since first I heard the word of the blackrobe. I wish now to escape. However, accompanying you westward toward the Onondaga keeps me in the land of the Great Longhouse, still subject to the orders of other chiefs."

Joseph Kryn mused and stroked his chin. "A blackrobe who ministered to the Mission of St. Peter here in Kanawaka," he said, "has recently joined our mission of St. Francis Xavier and has helped us move to the Sault. His name is Père Claude Chauchetière."

"Père Claude?" This news quickened Kateri's heart. "Let us leave immediately!" she said, her eyes flashing. "Let us go while my uncle is still negotiating the treaty."

"I have a plan," Joseph Kryn said to calm her. "Both Jacob and Onas now return to Three Rivers. Why don't we ask them to take you along with the pelts, then go upriver to deposit you at La Prairie?"

"You say our blackrobe has come to La Prairie? Oh, I will endure any hardship," Kateri said imploringly. "Let us leave in the morning."

"There are considerations."

"No, there are no considerations!" Kateri said with finality. "My heart, my soul know the path. Considerations will only waste time. Let us tell Onas and Jacob of this plan, and we shall leave. We must! Before my uncle returns! Oh, Joseph Kryn, I have longed so often to be with you and Marie Karitha and Anastasia Tegonhat and Matthew! Kanawaka is like the blackrobe's hell when all are drinking brandy. I will pack. Let us begin loading tonight!"

Joseph Kryn laughed. "Like many quiet natures, you appear as the frozen creek in winter. When the sun breaks the bonds that holds you, you gush forth. Shall we load the boats by torchlight, and thereby hide our plan?"

"Oh, please do not take back your offer!" she said fearfully. "In this longhouse, in this village, in this Land From Which All Rivers Flow, my soul has been like the dried seed of maize, a husk with no life stirring. Yet, were it to be planted in the soil of La Prairie, high would sprout the stalk in the warm sun of The Prayer."

"I do not take back the offer," Joseph Kryn said. "The new faith teaches that each man, woman, and child will live according to conscience. Freeing you from your uncle's house frightens you, not me. Yet your judgment is sound in escaping the drunkenness and disorder of Kanawaka. You will depart with Onas and Jacob at first light."

Kateri Tekakwitha cast her eyes to the ground, a shudder passed through her body. She looked up, tears brimming in her eyes. "Oh, Joseph Kryn! So long have I prayed for you to rescue me!" And chastely, as a daughter, she threw her arms about his neck and embraced him.

That night her sleep was troubled. The actuality of her escape blurred the boundary between sleep and waking. She dreamt of Hiawatha's daughter seized by the Thunderbird. She dreamt of Hiawatha himself, paddling into the burning clouds of a sunset, the white canoe leaving the river far below. She dreamt, too, of the path to Quorenta's hut, the hillock rising on scaly feet and the ugly, green scaly head thrust out from beneath the shell, the long neck extended, and the voice of Iowerano—"I am the turtle upon whose back the world was formed." She woke, sweating and panic-stricken. Iowerano! Thank Rawanniio, she'd soon be free from her uncle.

At first light, Jacob, Onas, Joseph Kryn and Kateri Tekakwitha carried corn satchels, bundles of robes, a kettle, and the young woman's belongings to the riverbank and lashed them securely into the canoe. Returning to the village, Kateri walked through the lanes momentarily reliving occurrences and events of her life there—the Mohegan attack, the blackrobe's first encounter with her, her baptism. She tried to ignore memories of the many insults and abuses she'd suffered. Her heart ached, and she found herself fighting back tears. Naked children ran freely and shouted and danced. Girls decked in wampum and ribbons and embroidered patterns giggled, peering around a longhouse at a young warrior. Women ground maize in a hollowed stump, and on porches of the longhouses, old men squatted, smoking their pipes.

The sense was keen in Kateri that she was a spirit, invisible, watching everyday tasks of her people from a great distance. The affection she felt for the old traditions and the love she still had for many of the villagers melted the severe disdain, the disgust she felt for the Kanawaka alive before her. She did not regret leaving, but she was saddened by the ignorance, superstition, drunkenness, and squalor her people would continue to live in. Heaving a sigh, she turned and walked out the southern portal down to the river.

"Have you made your farewells?" Joseph Kryn asked

"I had none to make," she replied. "Only with myself."

"And yet, your departure is even like a death," Joseph Kryn observed. Jacob, an old, wiry Oneida, stepped into the front of the canoe. Onas, a bulky lad with powerful arms, stepped into the back. "It is like the death of someone who has survived all the members of her *ohwachira* and now travels to heaven to be with them. You will find the mission so, Kateri Tekakwitha. I wish you a swift and safe journey."

Kateri's eyes moistened. "Joseph Kryn, no one has ever shown me such kindness. We are much alike—both half Canienga, both leaving the Canienga behind. I thank you. I will pray that you gather many souls among the western tribes." She cast her eyes once more to the top of the hill where the strong palisade rose among the cornfields and clumps of scrub pine. "I look forward to meeting you again at the blackrobe's mission."

"The men grow impatient," Joseph Kryn said. "Step in. I shall calm your uncle when he returns." The chief helped her into the middle of the canoe, and Kateri picked up her paddle. Joseph Kryn shoved them along the gravel into the river. With a strong stroke of the paddle, small whirlpools forming, the bark canoe leapt ahead into the current and was soon gliding swiftly toward the morning sun. Now, with exhilaration, with a delightful sense of freedom, Kateri presented her face to the wind and sunlight. The fragrance of pine, the songs of birds, the soft rippling of the water cheered her. Soon she would be among her loved ones in a safe haven, free to practice The Prayer.

Yet, when Linawato learned of her cousin's departure, she dispatched two young runners to alert Iowerano. The runners reached the river town toward evening, but the canoe of the three Christians had already passed unnoticed below the stockade.

Iowerano raged when he heard the news. The young woman who'd disobeyed him by not marrying, now defied him. His face burned with anger, and he sputtered at the runner. He would comb the forests to drag this disobedient maiden back. This time he'd humiliate her, force her to marry; if not, he'd plant a tomahawk in her skull and send her to her cherished heaven. When he heard of the torture poles being dragged down, he cried out, "They pull down our poles of torture and replace them with their cross? We shall learn their method of torture and nail the next blackrobe to it!" He collected his pack, his food satchel and his musket. "Three bullets will be all I need: one for each of the men, and one for the girl." That very night he set out alone.

Cold determination showed in Iowerano's face as the strong strokes of his paddle pulled the canoe closer to a confrontation. Hadn't he captured the one they called Jogues? Hadn't he massacred the Hurons? Hadn't he alone sought to keep alive the integrity of the Turtle Clan? Kryn, the half-breed traitor, had used his arts of persuasion to call Canienga away, to diminish the nation. Now the French threatened to send another blackrobe among them. The English would aid him, he'd see to that! White Adder and himself, two against many, would cry out. With each stroke, Iowerano pulled himself toward the moment when he'd murder the rebellious woman who mocked his authority even in his own longhouse. And the next blackrobe sent among them would be crucified.

Meanwhile, Kateri Tekakwitha's sense of freedom infused the river, the placid lakes, the mountains and cliffs, and the tall pine forests with a new elation. She prayed each morning before setting out and each evening after they ate. She knelt with Jacob and Onas murmuring the "Hail Mary" and "Our Father." They sang the Angelus four times each day, paddling through misty lagoons, over broad, glaring stretches of lake, among the far-flung islands. Even when the thunderstorm spoke with wrath and vengeance, no longer did it frighten her. Now she marveled at its power, not its ferocity. Like a heaven on earth the mission beckoned, ruled by the ringing bell, guided by the gentle voice of the blackrobe, and holding in a tight community the good Joseph Kryn, Anastasia Tegonhat, Marie Karitha, and so many others of her village. Yes, as Joseph Kryn had said, she had died to the old ways, and the canoe carried her swiftly to a blessed place, a new beginning.

One morning, rising early, Kateri knelt upon the sand. Scanning the lake of sweeping mists, she offered a prayer of thanksgiving to the One above all clouds. Suddenly her heart froze. Had she seen a canoe? She darted up, her flesh trembling. Did her mind conjure it? Did she imagine the man looked like Iowerano? Perhaps it was a demon that the blackrobes said disguise themselves and appear on earth. Hiding behind a tree, she watched as the fog parted again. Every fiber of her flesh tightened. Iowerano's grim face, his shaggy rooster comb of hair, his painted, tattooed flesh, his brawny arms, leapt suddenly out of the fog in a canoe of elm bark.

There was no time to awaken the men. Iowerano had spied their canoe and their camp. Kateri Tekakwitha darted further into the forest and watched. Iowerano beached his canoe many paces downwind. Stealthily he crept toward the camp, his musket pointed, a war hatchet in his belt. Suddenly, though, Jacob stirred. Iowerano stopped, crouched. Jacob arose and shook Onas. They both looked about for Kateri. Not finding her, they strolled together to the lake. They made water, then ambled along the shore. Kateri crouched in her camouflage watching her uncle watching her saviors. What if he killed them? Yet, to warn them would signal her whereabouts. Upon the sand the two Christians knelt and offered their morning prayers. They extended their arms and loudly intoned a hymn. Then, scanning the shore, Jacob spied Iowerano's canoe. He tried not to show his surprise, yet Iowerano saw his reaction, and Kateri saw her uncle's. Birds fell silent. The forest itself bristled with nervous anticipation.

Jacob and Onas started toward the strange canoe. Cautiously they scanned the forest, but saw nothing. Kateri watched helplessly as Iowerano crouched lower. The two reached the canoe and, by its workmanship, saw it to be Canienga. This surprised them. Slowly through the brush Iowerano advanced, his musket pointed at them. He lay full length upon the sand and raised the musket, resting his elbow upon the root of the pine tree. Just as he took bead upon the men, Kateri cried out, "Flee to the lake! Jacob! Onas! Flee! It is me he wants!"

Iowerano turned, shocked at being discovered. Kateri spun on her heel and dashed into the forest. She heard no shot; she heard only the splashes of Jacob and Onas diving into the water. "Where will I hide?" she cried. "The Lord must hide me!" On she ran, faster and faster. She leapt gurgling streams, and mossy, rotting trunks and banks of fern and smooth gray boulders. Branches lacerated her face and arms. She thought she heard her uncle behind her at each step. "Where will I hide?" And her eyes darted back and forth looking for refuge.

When Iowerano heard the girl cry out, he turned quickly and aimed the musket at the sound. Yet he glimpsed only her skirt entering the forest. He then heard splashes and turned back to see the two men escape by diving into the water and swimming beneath the surface. Resolving to capture the girl, Iowerano sprang to his feet. Swiftly he pursued her into the forest, blind to everything except finding and killing her. On he ran as birds cried at the rising sun. He spied broken twigs and occasional footprints, but suddenly all traces of her flight ended. In the middle of a clearing he stopped. Toward one edge of the clearing was a beaver pond; the rest was hemmed in by heavy undergrowth and creepers. Iowerano put his nose to the facing wind and attuned his hearing while his eyes carefully scanned each square foot of briar and brush. She was nearby—his hunter's instinct told him so—yet to flush her from the bog, he'd need dogs and many more men.

Iowerano sat while the long shadows cast by dead trunks shortened, then languorously grew longer in the afternoon sun. With no twitch of a muscle he sat, stone-faced. By sunset, when not so much as a briar had moved in the clearing, he began to mistrust his instincts. As twilight drifted in, he stood, stretched his cramped limbs, and called out.

"Tekakwitha! Hear this! You have always been weak, and your life in my longhouse has been a worthless one. Go to the mission where the traitor Kryn is chief! But know that the Canienga will overcome this exodus of its people, and one day the French will fall beneath the hatchets of our warriors, and we shall drive them from this land."

Iowerano prayed aloud to Aireskou, calling vengeance

down upon Kryn, then he turned from the clearing and headed toward the lake. The Christians' canoe was gone, yet his still lay where the water lapped upon the gravel. What strange warriors, he thought, to leave his canoe intact! He stepped in his canoe and pushed out upon the moonlit lake. He wouldn't sleep at their campsite because they might be lurking nearby. He'd find an island to sling his kettle and unroll his bear robe. Iowerano soothed his anger and worked out his cramped muscles by paddling back down the lake.

At the clearing, still no briar moved. Owls perched in the limbs of the dead trees, which had been rotted by the beavers' flooding, and waited to pounce upon frogs and water rats. Moonlight sparkled on the still water. The moon set in the west and the chill night lengthened beneath the stars. The eastern sky brightened. Birds cried and beat the trees alive. The sun rose and dispelled the fog. Suddenly a movement at the beaver dam sent ripples across the pond, and the cattails and swamp grass waved. Kateri Tekakwitha surfaced and swam to the edge of the pond. She waded through the muck, listening cautiously at each step. She fell at last upon a bed of moss. All day and all night she had watched, submerged to the neck under the thatch of the beaver dam. Now she peeled off her deerskin skirt and vest to warm her shivering flesh in the sun. Naked, she knelt and stretched out her arms, and looking to the clear summer sky, she offered thanksgiving for her deliverance to Rawanniio.

THE PASSING OF THREE WINTERS

Mission of St. Francis Xavier, La Prairie
1677-1680

1

Upon the broad flats of the St. Lawrence valley, south
across the river from the island city Montreal, a cluster of
bark huts was ringed by fields of waving corn. When the
wind shifted, bells of the Ursuline and Recollect cloisters
might be faintly heard from Montreal. But the mission had its
own bell and its own priests—Fathers Fremin, Cholonec, and
Chauchetière. The mission housed native converts from all
nations—Abnaki, Montagnais, Nipissing, survivors of the Huron massacres, Micmac, emigrants from the Cat and Tobacco
Nations, Algonquin, survivors of Chickatabutt's Mohegan army,
and Christian converts from the five fierce nations of Iroquois.

Her first view of the mission gladdened Kateri's heart.
The chapel occupied the center, a position of prominence,
and as Jacob and Onas beached the canoe, the bell rang for
Angelus. These converts kept their huts clean and orderly—
one family to each. They dressed themselves and their children modestly, shielded their passing of water and excrement, and hid their mating from other's eyes. Yet what
cheered Kateri most was what she did not see; there were no
palisades, no bastions, no spears or muskets. These peaceful
Christians attacked no one, and so required no walls of
defense.

Anastasia Tegonhat, Marie Karitha, and Joseph Kryn
greeted her warmly. Matthew had grown into a cheerful lad.
The family accepted Kateri Tekakwitha into its hut. Though
she had been baptized, she had not yet received First
Communion, and sharing the Bread of Life with these fervent
Christians was now her strongest desire. Immediately she
sought out Father Chauchetière. Père Claude received her
with guarded joy, happy in her faith and conviction, wary of
again drawing too close to her. After a month of instructing

273

Kateri, he resumed his "Journal of a Spiritual Progress," til
then all but forgotten among his belongings.

Many are the harrowing tales these natives tell
of surviving adversity. Kateri has thrilled me, though
I did not display my wonder, with her account of
waiting through the day and night submerged in a
beaver pond. She said her first piece of embroidery
after visiting the whites at Fort Orange depicted a
frog waiting through the cold night, while the eye of
the wolf burned red. This surely is a remnant of her
superstition. I questioned her about the significance
of the embroidery with which she decorates her
clothing, and she willingly uncovered a hidden side
of her nature—she is a poetess. She brought some
samples of her work.

With no sentimental or flowery language, as we
witness among young French women, she set forth
the poetry she'd depicted in each of her embroidered pictures. Some of the images proved quite
striking: 'Loud roars the wild pig who eats roots and
berries. But the wolf, silent and watchful, feasts on
the flesh of the noble stag.' This picture depicted a
boar rooting in the earth and a wolf viciously tearing
meat from the hind of a stag. And yet, I observed
she had no religious pictures. A tear filled her eye
when I asked her about this:

"My uncle refused to allow any cross or any
picture of the bearded Christ upon my clothing,"
she said with much emotion. "Yet, I stitched this
Christ in His cradleboard." She showed me the
babe, not in swaddling clothes, but in deerskin.
This greatly touched me.

"Kateri," I said, "you must give up decorating
your clothes with pictures of the forests and creatures. Better by far would be turning your talents to
the life of Christ our savior, to the Creator of all
things, and to the saints, to the rewards of heaven
and the punishment of hell, to the radiance God the
Father sheds, and to the mystery of the Trinity." She
nodded, and agreed at once. I showed her my
paintings of the rewards of the good life and the
punishment of the bad. She observed:

"Such agony you show upon the faces of these victims. You must have witnessed captives burning upon the spit." This was my picture of hell. Then she observed the one of heaven. "And the peace upon these people's faces shows. It is exactly as we are here at the mission of St. Francis Xavier." This comparison of the afterlife and her own life pleased her greatly.

"Further," I said, "since you have arrived, you have continued plaiting your hair with wampum. This vanity, like the vanity of your stitching, must cease." Again her eyes moistened, and she looked so hurt, I feared I had spoken too harshly. She takes the least criticism to heart, and her fear of sinning is overwhelming.

"I will no longer plait my hair, nor stitch upon the deerskin unless it be pictures for the chapel," she said humbly. "Father, since I have arrived, I have felt such happiness that I am afraid I act foolishly." She peered up at me, and her eyes were filled with emotion. "I long for Confession so I may be forgiven. My nights are beset by terrible dreams—wolves, snakes, owls, and foremost among them, a great turtle. I long only to learn what pleases God most so I may do it. Please show me."

I cannot express the look of joy that passed over her features when I agreed. Among these people, I have never witnessed such sincerity. I believe her years of concentration upon the embroidery have taught her the disciplines necessary for abstract thought. I shall guide her in allowing this capacity to bloom. She possesses extraordinary humility. Her piety is inspiring to all who watch her. Many have begun sitting close to her in chapel. But she shrinks from such attention. After conferring with Père Cholonec, I have decided to allow her to receive Holy Communion at Christmas Mass rather than waiting out the usual year's instruction. If I am any judge of zeal, Kateri Tekakwitha will be no backslider.

Chauchetière, however, did not write about what troubled him alone upon his pallet each night. His doubt grew at the same pace as his curiosity about the young woman of the forests. His doubts about her virginity stemmed from his own lack of courage, and this doubt crept into his heart like a frost, numbing, deadening. He doubted his own motives. His missionary zeal seemed nothing but misplaced vanity. And in the dark night of his soul, he cried out for spiritual light, and he despaired when none came. Telling himself a temporary loss of faith occurred to others of the order comforted him in no way. His faith had been profoundly shaken by this recurrence of his fascination with women. At last he vowed to vanquish passion once and for all or else return in defeat to his father's château.

And yet, when in Kateri's presence, hope shone like the sun bursting through clouds. Hers were no imaginings of hell. She had lived in hell. She had witnessed the bloodlettings, the torture, the screams, the stench of burning victims. Witch doctors and dream readings had provided the only guidance for her soul. She had lived among the seething, turmoil of all lusts in the pandemonium of her village—constant war parties, bizarre superstitions, copulation, sodomy, drunken brawls. She had entered the mission with a far different attitude than most of the natives. Most sought escape and refuge. Kateri Tekakwitha sought true spirituality. "Tell me, Father, how I may best please God so I can do it. That is my only desire." The simplicity of her faith overwhelmed him. Yes, counseling and guiding her in the path toward perfection renewed Chauchetière's own spiritual vigor. He vowed to help Kateri achieve a holiness that he, for all his theology and training, could not.

2

"Bless me, Father, for I have sinned most grievously in thought, word, and deed. This is my first confession, and I wish to cleanse my soul and heart to receive the Lord through Communion."

Kateri knelt upon the earth of Chauchetière's hut, her eyes imploring, her hands folded. Winter had arrived. The shortest day of the year had dawned to a severe blizzard. Winds ripped the thatch off two homes in the mission and sent those families, cowering from its roar, into the homes of others to huddle by the fire.

"Father, my whole life long I have plaited my hair with shell and I have worn headbands of the brightest dyed eelskin. I have been most vain. I have sewn patterns of all colors into hides and robes, moccasins and skirts, and so have encouraged my people to pride and vanity.

"Often, Father, while living with my uncle and aunt, I wished them injury and death. With Quorenta, I conjured spells against them when they ridiculed me."

Outside the chapel, half-buried in snow, a crèche depicted the Nativity scene—wooden figures of Mary and Joseph carved lovingly with hatchets once used to split skulls. The wind rattled the bark plates of the wall, and snow blew through the chinks of Chauchetière's hut. In a slight whisper Kateri enumerated small sins—hoarding of glass beads, refusing to share sagamite, coveting Linawato's necklace of wolf teeth. Then she paused, and the priest asked her the one question that when confessing to another priest always made his own heart sting.

"Kateri Tekakwitha, have you committed sin through impure thoughts or deeds?" He bit his lip nervously.

"Yes, Father," she hung her head. Tears streamed down her face. A great sob wracked her body. Chauchetière longed to embrace her, to offer her comfort. He refrained. A cynical idea slithered into his imagination like a serpent. Had he once again enthroned a woman only to have his ideal dashed?

"Tell me," he said with a dry throat, looking at the ceiling. The wind howled.

"Once in the forest, with curiosity I watched a buck mount a doe." She buried her face in her hands. "I took much delight in watching their muscles ripple beneath sleek hides. After the kill, I used the buck's forehooves to whip my back and sides as I had seen him paw and clasp the doe."

A long pause followed. Père Claude swallowed hard and asked: "Have you committed impure acts with men?"

Shocked, Kateri shook her head and looked at him with streaming eyes. "Oh, no, Father!" she whispered. "Oh, no! When men even touched me, I quickly discouraged them. And because my uncle had such high standing in the clan, they did not persist."

"Have you watched men and women copulate with the same delight as you took in watching the beasts?"

"Oh, no, Father!" Kateri poured forth a succession of sobs. "Oh, no! No! I can't bear to see that! I have hidden my eyes in horror. Only when stunned by fear such deeds would be done to me I watch."

This perplexed the Jesuit. "What is the difference between the deer and the villagers of Kanawaka?"

Kateri bowed her head. "Men and women have faces."

The priest moaned. His mind raced. He imagined such horrific expressions—straining, sweating men, teeth grinding, eyes clenched; and the women, open-mouthed, groaning in brute passion, throats stretched, tongues out; and then the dull, selfish, sated smiles, the sneers of young braves, the grief of young squaws. This woman had, in one simple sentence, reduced the loftiest theology to a principle: God made man in his image and likeness. Père Claude saw again the silk and satin masks worn in Versailles masquerades, and he saw the crude tribal masks carved by African slaves in Martinique and tribes of the northern woods. Veils, cosmetics, portraits, gargoyles, icons, the busts of kings and generals, costumes of the theatrical stage—in a single breath, Kateri had shed spiritual meaning like a piercing ray of light upon all motives of men to embellishment and disguise.

"Quorenta, an old woman—" Kateri stopped, frowned. "I do not mean her. I mean Anastasia. Why did I say Quorenta?" She shook her head. "Anastasia Tegonhat has told me, Father, how my mother was raped by my father. As long as I lived at Kanawaka, she never mentioned it, but here, among Christians, she tells me." Her voice faltered. She cleared her throat. "And I think of this often." She paused, then murmured, "I cannot help myself."

"Kateri," the priest said comfortingly, "great does the Lord love you for your purity. Do not think of your mother being seized and forced that way. Turn your thoughts instead to God. Think upon His goodness and love. In this way, within you the Christian hope and love of your mother will triumph over the fierce passions of the Canienga."

It was with great wonder that Chauchetière looked into her eyes, and as her confessor, he administered the absolution he felt she did not need.

On Christmas Day, the blizzard ceased, but a gray pall hung over the frozen river. The chapel bell tolled and Christian converts in moccasins, leggings, and fur robes knelt at the nativity scene while the three blackrobes placed the babe

Jesus in the manger. Into the humble chapel they filed. Candles lit pine boughs that decorated the altar. With joyful hymns the assembled intoned a high mass.

At Communion, Joseph Kryn led his household forward. First Anastasia Tegonhat received the host, then Marie Karitha. Joseph Kryn protectively led Kateri Tekakwitha forward and nodded to the priest. With wide, imploring eyes, her hair unbraided, ungreased, flowing black to the hem of her long skirt, her hands folded, Kateri approached Père Claude. He picked a host from the ciborium, made the sign of the cross in the air, whispering, *"Corpus domini Jesu Christi,"* and with the choir intoning the carol "Adeste Fidelis" he placed the wafer upon her trembling tongue. Kateri closed her eyes, bowed her head. Then she looked up to the priest. Joyful tears brimmed in her eyes. The wheat host, so different from the corn cakes of Kanawaka, tasted foreign as it melted upon her tongue. Overwhelmed by possessing Jesus within her, Kateri hardly dared to breathe. She pressed her eyes closed in the delightful melody of the carol, and she swallowed carefully. She looked again at the priest and murmured, "At last." She moved aside, and Joseph Kryn, the powerful warrior, opened his mouth likewise to receive the Eucharist.

3

Crops had been plentiful that year at the Mission of St. Francis Xavier. During her first winter, Kateri saw few of the households leave the settlement for the winter hunt. Late the following summer though, a violent sleet storm ruined much of the maize. By first snow of her second winter at the mission, many of the family groups left to survive by hunting in the wilds.

Kateri, Joseph Kryn, Marie, Anastasia, Matthew and another family of six members trudged on snowshoes into the forest. With a few pouches of corn, they ate well until the first kill—a cow moose. Rather than squander it as in days of old on an Eat-All Feast, they buried both hindquarters in the snow, and the meat sustained them until the next kill. Joseph Kryn and Michael, the father of the other family, and his three sons, Luke, Peter, and John, proved a fine hunting team. Only two days that winter was the band completely without food.

Kateri prayed with the family each morning, but as morals relaxed somewhat, she avoided the gossip of the women as they discussed the previous night's laughter in the dark. Kateri felt embarrassed. Her hungers, her desires were beyond the carnal and convivial scope of the hunting camp. She wanted to share the intimacy of being together with them, yet she aspired to a private, sacred calling that grew louder and stronger each time she heeded it. Wary of committing the sin of pride in her own virginity, she carefully remained courteous to them all, yet she held herself aloof. The group remained monogamous, but away from the stern gaze of the blackrobe, it did indulge in playful suggestions. Kateri left the cramped, smoky hut each morning and trudged upon snowshoes a league to a hollow where she'd put up a cross. She was disappointed, angered by their backsliding. She tried to ignore them, to forgive them, to pity them. Yet, thinking about it, she became so confused, she prayed in her solitude for guidance. She prayed for them, too, yet their frivolity grew so nettlesome, she remained away from the hut virtually all day. On her knees with hands folded in stark winter sunlight or in blizzards, she prayed at her makeshift chapel each day until the sun began to wane. She felt pure and clean, alone with her God, away from occasions of sin. Then on her way homeward, she collected fallen branches to keep the fire alive through the night.

Toward the end of the Month of the Wolf, a catastrophe occurred that threatened her newfound serenity. Luke was separated from the hunting party when they encountered a herd of elk, and he did not return with them. They were all overjoyed with the kill of three elk and Luke's wife Beatrice tried not to show her concern when Luke hadn't returned by nightfall.

"Do not worry," Joseph Kryn told her comfortingly. "We will pray that he has brought an elk down, for he is a resourceful hunter and would never lose his way or freeze in the night."

Fervently the little band knelt in the hut and prayed for the well-being of Luke. They retired then, Beatrice sleeping by her in-laws for warmth. In the morning, she awoke and looked about the hut. She counted the forms under fur robes, then she crept from one to the other. She found Luke under Kateri's sleeping robe. She was filled with jealousy and bitterness, but returned to her own robe, her heart saddened by Kateri's hypocrisy. When the others arose, she told no one. The joy that Luke displayed about his kill filled the camp and caused no one to question where he had slept.

When the rivers loosened once more and the iron hold of frost was steamed from the land by the climbing sun, the band returned again to the mission. On the journey home, Beatrice shared her suspicion with Anastasia Tegonhat and together they designed a course of action. Beatrice would speak with Kateri's confessor, and Anastasia would speak with Kateri.

"I have watched John, the son of Michael, grow from a boy," Anastasia said to Kateri one afternoon as the two sat dressing hides. "If his father and brothers are any indication, he will make a daring and successful hunter. Have you thought of marrying since you arrived?"

"The question is closed," Kateri said quietly. "I will marry no one."

Anastasia sighed. "I had expected Joseph Kryn home long ago." She strode across the hut and looked out the door. "He has been dividing up the bear he and Daniel and Michael hunted. It is so difficult for him providing for us." She turned to Kateri. "I have not the heart to say it to him because of Matthew."

"What of Matthew?"

"He cannot hunt because of his withered arm. It is so difficult on Joseph Kryn providing for such a son and three women besides."

"Yes, it is. But we till the field."

"Think, though," Anastasia said, excitedly peering out the door, "if only Joseph Kyrn had someone to help him hunt! If he had companionship when the men fished, someone to double the portion he brings to us!"

"That would be very nice," Kateri said.

"Then consider marrying," Anastasia Tegonhat pleaded. "Please! You—"

"Speak no more about it!" Kateri said insistently.

"But what of the blackrobe? Doesn't he urge us to have children, to expand the mission? Doesn't he baptize the little ones born here? Didn't he discuss with you how matrimony is a holy sacrament in the church and much grace is attained?

Didn't he explain that the dark pleasure was created by God so many new souls would enter the world?"

"Yes, he did," Kateri said.

"Well, then, think of bringing a child into the world, for this is the greatest wonder a woman can know."

"I have much reverence for the blessed Virgin Mary," Kateri said. "I pray to her night and day to keep me from temptation. She, above all other women, was chosen to bear God's son. Virginity is a spiritual gift. Matrimony, babes, a family life are all things we enjoy upon this earth. I will never marry," Kateri said. "This is precisely why I wished to be a Christian—because the Christian faith allows each of us to live our lives in the manner we choose."

"But your situation is unnatural!" Anastasia protested. "I married young, to Shining Cliff, the bravest of all warriors. He died in battle before we had children. So peerless was he among our clan, I never could consider another for my sleeping shelf, and memories of him have sustained me these many years. But you! You have never wed, and you have never accepted a man as your husband, the father of your children. Like old Quorenta you will be scorned and cast aside."

"What do you speak of?" Kateri dropped her work. Anastasia's tone of voice greatly unsettled her.

"Sharing the rug with married men," Anastasia said.

"I never shared the rug with any man."

"Oh," Anastasia said, grinning slyly. "I see how things are. Kateri, whom everyone admires and nudges close to in the chapel; Kateri, the angel, more perfect in the white man's faith than anyone in the mission; Kateri, given Holy Communion four months after her arrival, received into the Society of the Holy Family without the preliminary steps; Kateri, the hypocrite and liar."

Kateri was shocked. "Of what do you speak?"

"Come now, you know!" Anastasia smiled broadly.

"Know what?" She frowned, bewildered and deeply hurt by the insinuation.

"You know of what I speak. Do not deny it!"

"What?" Kateri asked, growing more alarmed. She feared some ugly joke was about to be played.

"That I speak of you and Luke."

"Explain yourself," she demanded angrily.

"You and Luke, sharing the sleeping rug." Anastasia

forced a laugh. "You lured Beatrice's husband away on the hunt by devotion and prayer. Some are more honest—they braid wampum in their hair."

"Who told you this?"

"I promised I would not say."

"This is foolish, laughable..." Kateri protested with anger. She scowled, looked around for an explanation.

"You should marry, and then those needs would be met," the woman said pertly.

"Anastasia!" Kateri cried. She shook her by the shoulder. "Who has said these terrible things?"

"They are no more terrible than your feigned piety."

"I shall find out," Kateri said, pointing her finger at Anastasia. "And if you have dreamed this up, I shall forgive you only when I learn your motive."

"My motive," Anastasia said haughtily, folding her arms, "is saving you from greater sin than sharing a sleeping robe."

"I must see the priest," Kateri said, climbing to her feet.

"He has already been told."

The young woman's eyes widened in disbelief, in panic. "Who?"

"She told me never to say."

"Poor Beatrice!" Kateri cried, pushing out the door. She saw the matter fully now as she hurried through the lanes of huts to the chapel in the center. The chapel was empty. Kateri hastened up the aisle between the rough benches, and she threw herself prostrate before the altar railing. Tears flowed, anguish twisted and wracked her body. So abhorrent was the thought of mating and the scandal that was being spread, she retched and gagged. The path to Quorenta's! The dream of the turtle! Orgies in the firelight! "Dear Lord," she murmured, raising her face in the dark, "how can these souls still be so suspicious and evil-thinking after they know You? Certainly Your power cannot be to blame. Every fiber of my being is filled with love for You. These poor, deluded souls glimpse You occasionally, yet obscure Your love with their own wants and fears." She knelt up. Her anger, her bewilderment, her panic had subsided with the prayer. "I will go," she told the crucifix calmly, "and I will talk with the priest."

Père Claude Chauchetière called, "Enter," when she knocked upon the doorpost. The slender, bearded man with soft brown eyes moved not a muscle when she entered. He was holding an eagle quill and had been scratching with dark

juice upon paper, reducing language and oratory to black
marks.

"May I speak with you, Father?" she asked.

"Certainly." His lips were pressed tightly together, his
eyes were red. He seemed angry, disappointed. She felt great
pain, seeing him so distant.

Kateri sat cross-legged before the chair he used. "Father,
I have heard some terrible things."

"Yes?"

"Please, Father!" she implored. "Least of all did I expect
you to believe this evil gossip."

This took the priest aback. He scrutinized her. "Well,
Kateri Tekakwitha, is it true?"

"I know not what anyone told you."

"You know well enough; otherwise you would wait until
Saturday to confess small vanities and scrupulous failings of
belief. But you have come now." He sighed and turned away
from her.

"It is not true!" she cried. "And yet to protest too
strongly is to protest not at all." She looked up at him,
scowling. "Father, I see patterns in creation. I see the feeding
of beasts, deer upon grass, wolf upon deer, bear upon wolf,
and man upon all. I see the arrogance of the corn each
summer to sprout in the wind. I see, I see, oh, I see the
waters bleeding down from mountain snows, foaming in
tumult each spring, placid in the summer, crystal and still in
the dead of winter. I see, too, how men and women behave,
and it causes me great sadness."

"I understand behavior on the hunt," the priest said,
agonizing over the words.

"No!" she said, violently shaking her head. "No! You do
not comprehend anything if you believe rumors."

"Kateri, you should marry," he said. "Your holiness has
but one flaw. You should seek out a young hunter."

"No!" she cried. "Please hear me!"

He looked to her and his eyes held scorn. "You deny it
then?"

"I deny nothing, for nothing occurred."

"And yet, we who seek perfection, who set ourselves
apart from others, often our burdens become too heavy and
we must clasp others in the darkness."

"Father, you speak for yourself, not for me."

Chauchetière groaned and cast a look to the floor. Her

accuracy unnerved him. He closed his book. With a shock, Kateri recognized the pattern she had sewn long ago in her village, under far different circumstances, of a French fleur-de-lis and a cross. "Beatrice told me," he said, "how she discovered your hypocrisy."

Kateri nodded. "In my utter darkness I have come to you."

"What darkness is yours?" he asked.

"The darkness," she said carefully, in a measured, quiet voice, "the darkness that is all of ours—the darkness of men's minds."

Père Claude stared at her.

"The night comes on, the daylight wanes, and in the glow of the fire, suspicion breeds. One night, Luke returned from chasing a lone elk. He had buried his tomahawk in its skull, but had not enough strength to carry it to the camp. He crawled into the hut and awakened me, thinking I was Beatrice. Excited with his success he was, but I soon corrected him. 'Let us not awaken all,' he said. 'Let me climb beneath your robe.' I discouraged him. 'I have watched you receive the priest's bread, Kateri Tekakwitha. You are above gossip. I will not sully your reputation. Grant me the covering of your robe, and I will not awaken the entire camp.' I did so, Father, and we slept as brother and sister. Next day, much excitement was made over the kill, and the men set forth to bring it home. Nothing was ever said till now. Yet I understand the suspicion in Beatrice's heart." Kateri paused while Père Claude assessed all she said, then she added, "But I do not understand the suspicion in yours."

Père Claude closed his eyes and groaned. "What now?"

"Now? Now I grow tired of all eyes upon me, Father." She looked to the earth. "I want to pray to God, to please Him, to live apart. I feel like the old woman who fostered me as a child."

"Will you marry?"

"No!" She cried out as if wounded. "You understand nothing of what I say!"

"It would be the best course of all."

"But not for me!" she protested. "Don't you understand?" she asked in disbelief. "You of all people? Don't you?"

"Yes," he said. "But I think you must marry."

"Why?" she cried. "Is a woman without a man so threatening to men that they wish to pair her at any cost?"

"You must know," Père Claude said, "that great has been your effect upon our community. You alone refuse to marry. All eyes watch you. All eyes are upon you at Mass and when I deliver Communion. All women ask in the confessional how it is you can live without a man. What if other women tried to imitate you? How many sins would they commit?"

"But you, Father, you live without a woman."

"Yes," said the priest, "but I do that because of a vow."

"Then I shall take a vow," Kateri said. "I shall vow never to marry or submit to a man, just as you have vowed never to marry or submit to a woman."

"But you cannot do that!" he protested.

"Are not all creatures the same in God's eyes?" she asked.

"Yes," he said hesitantly.

"Then I am the same as you, and I shall pledge as you have."

"That cannot be!" Père Claude groaned.

"As my minister, my confessor, I must obey you." She stood. "Even though you will not sanction my vow with your blessing, I will keep this vow sacred and quiet. The church allows us to choose how we can best fulfill God's plan. I have made my choice. So have you. I hope I do not offend you by being so bold."

Kateri Tekakwitha walked from the hut and left the priest pondering her words. After much time, Pere Claude reached down and attempted to retrieve his journal. It was too far away. He pulled himself from the chair and he bent and picked it up. Ruefully, he read what he had written just before she had entered.

> And at last, all hope is shattered. She has fallen! She has fallen! And so it is that the most beautiful flower is but an attraction for disappointment. And so are hopes. The flower perishes for it springs from the earth, and the earth is base. The hope, the trust perishes, for above all else, man is flawed, flawed beyond mending. Oh, how quiet and long are the hours of despair! And she, she in whom I had such hope, the hope of this entire dark race, she who never brought superstition to the liturgy. And I loved her! I thought I had found at last the perfect

soul mate, the one being I might admire. And she has fallen, fallen.

Now, knowing her purity secure, seeing the pride and egoism of his own doubts that conquered his faith, the priest ripped the pages from his journal and carefully fed them to the flames.

4

When the woman spoke to her, Kateri looked into her eyes with great awe. She had not noticed her approach, and the raspy voice and the tone of familiarity surprised her. "Where will the women sit?" she asked.

Kateri had been watching the building of the new chapel, larger and more commodious, due for completion by the autumn. "It matters not where we sit in the chapel," Kateri replied, "as long as God is in our hearts."

"You are as beautiful as they say," the woman observed. Her eyes peered into Kateri's, and Kateri saw in them astonishing understanding and sympathy. "I have longed to meet you."

"How are you called?" Kateri asked. The immediate affinity she felt for this woman astonished her.

"I have heard of you. You are most direct. That is good. I am called Marie Thérèse."

"Let us talk together," Kateri said. "We can walk along the river."

"Very well," the other replied, and a smile brightened her face. A big-boned woman, her legs were stumpy, yet she moved with agility and speed. Marie Thérèse's eyes burned with a zeal Kateri recognized immediately. She had not heard before of the woman, but they each sensed great spirituality in the other. They walked along the river and talked of their conversions.

"It was years before my heart was opened," Kateri said. "I lived among the tortures, the constant war, and the hunger that always gnaws at our vitals. Yet, when at last I opened my heart to Jesus Christ, I saw the purposes of all men should be the same—to live unmolested, to obey His word, to adore God, and to live harmoniously with our sisters and brothers."

"Yet, you are of the Canienga, the fiercest of the five nations," said Marie Thérèse, herself an Algonguin.

"I see your meaning almost before you open your lips," Kateri said. "And you see mine." The other nodded. "The peace rumored in the days of Hiawatha has come at last. Hiawatha prepared our people for Christ's word, for the peace. But the peace is not spread with tomahawk and war club; it is spread with the cross and The Prayer. The meek shall inherit the earth,' so says the Lord. It is the ignorance, the shortsightedness, the impatience of men that cause them to hoard, to claim possessions, to argue and fight."

"I, too, have opened my heart to the Lord," Marie Thérèse said. "On the hunt last winter there were eight of us. We killed nothing. In blinding snow we stumbled, searching like barkeaters for food. Starving, unable to proceed, we cast lots, and it fell to me to kill and butcher the oldest among us, an old man. I killed him with a hatchet as he lagged behind, and like dogs we fell on him, ripped apart his flesh, and ate." Her quick looks into Kateri's eyes searched for understanding. "I vowed, eating the flesh of that old man, that if the Lord—for I had instruction as a child—allowed me to reach Montreal, I would commit my life to Him." Her voice grew more determined. "I will not go on the hunt this winter."

"Neither will I," Kateri said. An idea brightened her expression. "We shall live together!" She looked into the other's eye, and Marie Thérèse nodded. "I feel I have known you for a very long time."

"Yes," said Marie Thérèse. "We are sisters."

From that afternoon on, the two spent much time together. Their conversations ranged over a broad landscape of topics with nimble grace and supple logic—topics such as God and nature and Man. With a mysticism born of the blackrobe's instruction and native Indian pantheism, the two women talked of life and death and afterlife. Soon, though, they shared more than words and thoughts.

"Do you know of those who call themselves the secret healers?" Marie Thérèse asked one afternoon.

"No," said Kateri Tekakwitha, "are they a tribe nearby?"

Marie Thérèse laughed. "No, they are members of our

mission. They believe that only through punishing the flesh can the spirit thrive and grow."

"How do they accomplish this?"

"I will show you. You will be my healer, Kateri."

Marie Thérèse cut willow boughs from trees at the riverbank, and she and Kateri walked through the ripened corn to the far corner of the mission and into the cemetery. Neat rows of little wooden crosses marked the graves. In the center stood a hut where corpses were stored in winter until the frost left the ground. Here they came.

"Hold five boughs together such as this," Marie Thérèse said. She pulled off her tunic and stood bare-breasted in the dim light of the hut. "Whip me without mercy, Kateri. Each strike purges sins that my flesh has caused." Marie Thérèse placed the leather belt between her teeth, clasped the center pole and nodded her head. "Now!"

Unsteadily, Kateri raised the willow whip and brought it down gently upon the naked flesh of Marie Thérèse's back. "Harder!" the woman said, biting the leather bit. Again Kateri whipped her, but harder this time. She felt unsure of this, frightened, uneasy. Red welts started from the woman's flesh. "Harder!" Again and again and again Kateri whipped her until blood seeped from the red welts. At last, Marie Thérèse spit the leather thong out and said, "That is enough."

She and Kateri embraced. Kateri was sweating from the exertion. Tears streamed down Marie Thérèse's cheeks.

"Should I . . ." Kateri asked, "should I try the same way to atone for my sins?"

"Yes," said the other. She pulled back and stared into Kateri's eyes. The profound sadness Kateri saw in Marie Thérèse's eyes disturbed her. They embraced, overcome with emotion. "Our flesh," Marie Thérèse said, her lip quivering, "is so weak, so prone to seeking pleasure. We must not allow it to rule our souls."

Kateri stripped off her tunic and stood naked on the earthen floor. "I am ready."

"Place the belt between your teeth so you do not bite your tongue."

Kateri did so and leaned upon the pole. She heard the willow whistle through the air, and the first blow produced a keen pain that shook her involuntarily. A white explosion, like a gunshot, lit up her mind. The second blow nearly brought her to her knees. Lash after lash followed until she slumped. Suddenly the path to Quorenta's hut flashed before her mind... a muggy summer day... the turtle dream...

Another blow flashed white in her mind, and she cried out involuntarily. Iowerano, the turtle, was speaking... the ugly, scaly turtle's neck... Sssssoooooooowok! The willow branches bit into her flesh. The slow, lumbering turtle rose as if the hillock were animated... Kryn! Where was Kryn? Quorenta! she had cried that day, Quorenta! Then Kryn had lifted her high like the Thunderbird of legend, and kicking and clawing and biting, she had cried Sssssssoooooooowok! The willows bit again. She remembered now what had happened. On the path was Iowerano and a girl... Sssssssoooooooowok!

"Stop!" Kateri Tekakwitha screamed. "Stop it! Please stop it! No! Don't do it! Please!" She slumped to the floor, crying and shaking her head. "No! No!" she shrieked. "Don't do it to her! Please!"

"Kateri? Kateri?" Marie Thérèse said, dropping to her knees and pulling the young woman into an embrace. "I am sorry! I am so sorry!"

"He did it!" she sobbed. "She's dead!"

"Who did what?" asked the bewildered woman.

"Iowerano," she sobbed. "He killed her!" Her whole flesh convulsed with sobs. "Kryn tried to stop it! He tried! But he killed her with a war club in the shade of the oak tree. And I ran," she cried. "I ran and ran and ran!"

Marie Thérèse held her for a very long time, and slowly Kateri composed herself. She sat back at last, gasping, naked on the earthen floor. "It is evil to whip our bodies."

"The Canienga consider pain a test of courage," Marie Thérèse said.

"But it is our intent to put aside the old ways."

"What were you speaking about?"

Kateri shuddered, hugged herself, then pulled on her deerskin dress. "I remember now," she whispered, swallowing hard. "I remember now; now I see, and I know where a dream that troubles me comes from."

"Tell me, my sister, for we should hold nothing back." Marie embraced her.

"When I was very young, I traveled frequently to the hut of an old woman in a ravine." Kateri's voice assumed a trancelike quality. Her eyes looked off into the air. "It was just after a successful raid against the French when many captives were brought to Ossernenon. A young girl with white skin and blue eyes and hair the color of cornsilk had been taken, and Iowerano pulled her from the line of victims to adopt her. Many of the women of our village were stricken with a disease below so they could have no children. Such was my aunt. For the space of two or three moons the girl and I shared each other's company. I realized one day I had not seen old Quorenta, and I asked this girl to accompany me. Out of the gate we went." Kateri's voice grew more rapid, more insistent. Her breath came faster. "She began picking flowers, yet I hurried ahead for I had not seen my friend for a long time. Realizing the girl could become lost, I returned, and there was Iowerano!"

Kateri buried her face in Marie Thérèse's shoulder. "It was horrible! He had pulled her skirts high and had mounted her from behind. So terrified was she, she could not speak! The look on her face . . . !" Kateri cried out. "He pulled her by her long yellow hair, and he thrust into her with such violence! Such a look on his face! I screamed, and he turned. Just then Kryn, who'd been looking for him, called out. I ran to Kryn, and he lifted me up. I cried out what I had seen. He carried me there. Iowerano had finished, and his organ . . . long and swollen and red, angry, insatiable! I hid my eyes from it. I couldn't bear to look, Marie!

"Kryn and my uncle argued. Kryn told him to give the girl to him. My uncle accused him of wanting the girl for himself. He raged against Kryn, calling him a half-breed, saying that was why he wanted a white girl so he could breed white children. Then he cried that no one would have her, and pulling out his war club, he clubbed her again and again. The blood! Her golden hair! Her naked buttocks! Kryn rushed to stop him, dropping me. The war club crushed the girl's skull. I ran and ran and ran. Somehow I reached Quorenta's hut."

Marie Thérèse stroked Kateri's face. "It is with you, then, as it was with me. A horrible act of violence changed you."

"But it was worse!" Kateri said. "When I blurted the story to Quorenta, she ridiculed me. So it was with my mother, she said. My father had ravaged her during a raid on the French and returned with her to the village. If it weren't for that, Quorenta told me, I would not be in the world. 'In the Turtle Clan as everywhere, that is how the world begins,' she told me. 'Do not be so shocked or so proud.' I had forgotten. Oh, Marie, the whipping brought it back into my mind, though I believe my dreams have been trying to speak about it for many years. I feared to be as my mother had been, a concubine ravaged by warriors, and so I always turned to Kryn for protection."

"The workings of our minds are very strange indeed," Marie Thérèse said. "Yet now that you know, you may resume the whipping."

"I believe we should discuss this with the priest."

"Oh, no!" Marie Thérèse said quickly.

"Then it must be evil." Kateri lay back upon the floor of the charnel house. "It is evil," she said, the earth cool against her welts, "for it conjures up the horrible events we have forgotten. This explains much about Anastasia Tegonhat's memories of my mother and the harsh words always between Joseph Kryn and my uncle."

"It also explains," Marie Thérèse observed, pulling the young woman to a sitting position, "why you never married."

"Yes," Kateri said thoughtfully, "perhaps so." She dried the tears from her eyes. "There are many things of this world that will not be explained until the next." She stared for a long, long moment into Marie Thérèse's eyes. "I see many things now," she said. "I feel clean. Yet I feel the whipping is evil. Our bodies belong to the Lord; we must not abuse them."

Marie Thérèse remained unconvinced. "The Secret Healers are the most devout among us, and many wear the iron-studded belt into the fields."

"Until they give up enjoying pain," Kateri said, "they will not know the Lord."

The resurfacing of the submerged memory changed Kateri. Water had been her medicine during the puberty rites. Water had washed away her original sin at baptism. Yet it was reliving the vivid memory of the rape and murder that cleansed her soul and heart of any lingering paganism. The French girl had been her playmate, her alter ego, an orphan like herself, struck down by the lust and brutality so rampant in the village. Kateri now pitied those who had remained behind; she prayed for them; but so actively did she throw herself into adoration and worship of the Lord, even Père Claude, her confessor, watched in amazement. A quivering, transcendent zeal burned within her and, like a slow fire, seemed to consume the flesh it inhabited. Each prayer, each

Mass, each evensong fueled it. She fell silent for days at a time; working in the fields or hauling wood, she performed the work of two men.

A remark of Marie Therese to Anastasia Tegonhat struck a plan that autumn. "Kateri Tekakwitha conducts herself like white women I have seen in Montreal. When I survived the hunt and made my promise to God, I was taken into a house where white women live alone with no men. They fill their days with prayer, with denial of food, and they move silently through the halls, not speaking to each other. So does Kateri Tekakwitha live."

"I have an idea," Anastasia said. "Let us propose to her that we three live that way."

"But we cannot set ourselves apart from the village here."

"Certainly we may." Anastasia waved over the river. "Let us paddle to Heron Isle and live apart. We may have plenty of eggs all year, and we can return for such corn as we need."

When they approached Kateri, she seized upon the plan. "Yes, my sisters, that is wise."

"But what of Mass and Communion?" Marie Thérèse asked.

"We may paddle over once a week," Anastasia said. "And whenever we hear the mission bell, we will kneel upon the rock and alone to the sky with no interference, we will pray."

They paddled next day toward the island, an outcropping of rock covered with grass, stunted trees, and millions of heron.

"Let us," Kateri said from the bow of the canoe, "maintain silence upon the rock, even as we scout a suitable site for a hut. No human words have been spoken there. Let us make it our refuge of silent prayer."

The silence was agreed to. They beached their canoe, then climbed upon the uneven rock while herons whirled above them in the sunlight. Excited as children playing, they darted here and there, shielding the sun from their eyes. Kateri, pale and thin, nevertheless showed such intense excitement that her eyes burned, her pace quickened, her breath came more rapidly.

Anastasia Tegonhat tugged her sleeve. In sign language she indicated a grassy flat that would serve well as a campsite. Kateri and Marie Thérèse both turned quickly away from her. More intently Anastasia drew their attention. She ran in front of them, and in pantomime, she pointed out a place for cooking, a place for sleeping, a small grotto suitable for erecting a cross and praying. Kateri and Marie Thérèse refused to watch.

Quizzically Anastasia Tegonhat approached them. She shrugged in bewilderment. Kateri pointed to the canoe, and the three climbed over the rocks stepped in, and pushed off from shore.

"I do not understand," Anastasia said. "Why did you not watch me?"

"We decided not to speak while on the island," Kateri said. "Isn't signaling with the hands a form of speaking?"

"Yes," Marie Thérèse agreed. "You were mocking our holy silence by trying to get us to think of worldly things—cooking and sleeping."

"So you did watch me!" said the more practical Anastasia. "We must design some way to make our wishes known to each other. Otherwise it will be like three strangers living apart, not three servants of God living in communion."

The three paddled silently for a long while against the current.

"How do the white women perform this?" Kateri asked Marie Thérèse.

"I do not know."

"Let us ask the priest," Anastasia suggested. "He will know."

"Who will ask?" Marie Thérèse wondered doubtfully.

"I will," Kateri said. They made land and pulled the canoe up on the beach. Joseph Kryn was mending his nets.

"Where have the three sisters been?" he asked jovially.

The three stole looks at each other. "To Heron Isle," Kateri said sheepishly.

"You go and return with no eggs?" Kryn stepped closer. "Why did you journey so far? Some important cause took you there, for I have never known you three to waste your time with trifles."

"We . . . we wish to live there," Kateri said. "The three of us together." She avoided his gaze for a long moment, then summoning her courage, she looked up. Joseph Kryn stared down upon her with such sadness, she could barely return his gaze.

"And for what reason?" His tone of voice betrayed how badly the news stung him.

"So we can be nearer to God and less prone to sin," Kateri whispered, almost with shame.

"Our faith," Joseph Kryn said, "attempts to bring us together." He waved his arm over the mission, peaceful and orderly under the autumn sky. "Why do you seek more solitude even than the winter hunt provides?" His question hung unanswered in the air. "You three have been an inspiration to the entire mission. Why do you wish to leave us?"

Kateri sensed the hurt in Joseph Kryn's voice. She summoned courage. "The affection we feel for you and the rest of the villagers," she said, "is a worldy emotion. We wish to separate ourselves from that for it may pollute our praying."

"I see," Joseph Kryn said, turning away.

"Kryn!" she pleaded. "Joseph Kryn!"

He continued walking.

"Stay here," she told the other two. "I must speak with him."

Kateri ran across the sand and reached for Joseph Kryn's arm. He turned around and looked with keen interest at her. Kateri bowed her head. "I shall not live long beyond this winter," she said in a low voice. "I know my health wanes. I feel it daily, and I pray, Joseph Kryn, I pray for it to ebb so I may be with the Lord Jesus. I love thee," she said using the formal pronoun, "as a brother. I recently remembered a time long, long ago when you protected me from my uncle, the time he clubbed the girl with golden hair."

Joseph Kryn heaved a sigh. "The things we experience as children affect us forevermore. Even so, young woman," —her heart sank as he called her this—"as a child I knew the disgrace of being half white. To remind all men and to remind myself, I never painted my skin. Yet, I always strove to outdo the Canienga in courage, endurance, and integrity. I see now, since receiving The Prayer, that the tests I created and endured were not to prove anything to others, though I enjoyed their praise. Rather, these tests were simply proofs to myself. Even so, your desire to remove yourself from our midst is such a test." He smiled, and the warmth of his smile brought much comfort to her. "We only test ourselves, Kateri Tekakwitha, when we are unsure of the result."

"You speak wisely," she said in a whisper.

"It matters not how our skin is colored, whether we are

men or women, strong or weak. Look at Matthew, healthy and happy, a fine young man in the mission. It matters not where we live. It matters not what disgrace or sorrow or fears we knew as children. The new way, the way of Christ, allows each of us to make our separate peace. You have already done so by not marrying. Let that be sufficient, so you may continue to abide with us."

Kateri looked up and held his gaze a very long time. "I shall seek out the blackrobe, Joseph Kryn, and put the matter before him."

"Very well," he said, and he placed his hand upon her shoulder. She clasped it with both of hers.

"Impossible," Père Claude said when Kateri told him of the plan. "Why do you wish to leave the mission?" He could not control the pain in his voice.

"Father, two winters ago I left my home where you converted me. Here at the mission I have found the peace I craved to pray and please God. Here war does not come. Here regular hours and the progression of weeks order our lives. Yet here are all eyes upon me. Certain things I do are imitated by others. This tempts me to pride. I seek to hide from their eyes. Anastasia Tegonhat and Marie Thérèse and I wish to be as the white women who live apart."

"But I cannot allow that," Père Claude said agitatedly. "Your presence, Kateri, benefits the entire mission. What if others followed your example? What would become of the mission? In roving bands all would trail off into the forest. Gone would be the regularity and the community and the worship we now enjoy. It would not take long for all to revert to burning victims to Aireskou."

"Why cannot we tribeswomen enjoy the privileges of white women? Does the Lord have two laws, one for whites and one for us?"

Père Claude sighed. "Kateri, you are most wise. You above all others possess knowledge of the true way. Others here have been long in losing the darkness of superstition. Your wisdom and your piety are most pleasing to God . . . and to me. After one has progressed as you have in the faith, retreat from the community would benefit you, yes. But won't you prove far greater love of God if you sacrifice these plans and remain here to help lead your people toward heaven?"

Kateri pondered this a long while.

"Your entire life," Père Claude continued, "you have sought refuge in the dark longhouse or in the forest to be alone with your thoughts. Now you seek refuge again. Hasn't life at the mission taught you the value of putting aside one's own wishes, of working on behalf of others to guide them? You belong among us, Kateri Tekakwitha. Even by sacrificing this plan you shall please the Lord, for you will bring more souls than your own to Him. Can you do this?"

"So says Joseph Kryn, too." Tears ran down her cheeks, tears of doubt and sorrow. "I feel caught as a rabbit in a snare. My wish to please the Lord in any way I might often brings out my pride. Yet I still wish to please Him more and more. How can I choose correctly?" She hung her head. "I must rely upon your guidance. I will abandon the plan, provided you grant me a wish."

The priest cringed. "We can never bargain with such things. What is it?"

"You allow me to take a vow of perpetual chastity. By this I may accomplish all three vows of the white nuns."

"And how is this?" Chauchetière asked with surprise.

"I care for no possessions; therefore I have vowed poverty. I will obey your will not to retreat to Heron Island; thus I vow obedience. Chastity is the only one not accounted for."

The sophistication of her reasoning astounded him. "Very well," he said, "take three days to consider this step. If you still wish to make this vow, you may."

"I do not require three days. I wish to make it now." She knelt. "For God's glory, Father, I wish to consecrate my body. Never has a man violated my chastity, yet before, this was solely a selfish wish of mine. Now I place my chastity into the hands of the Lord as a gift, a spiritual gift, and I pray Him to help me keep this vow unsullied."

Deeply moved, Père Claude blessed her as she knelt. When he finished, she looked up with profound joy in her eyes. A question had been settled within her, and the comfort and the peace it gave her radiated from within.

"Return," the priest said. "Return to your people, Kateri."

"I thank you, Father, with all my heart and soul."

"Return and tell them of this."

"Oh, no, Father!" she said. "This must remain secret."

"Why then did you make the pledge, why keep it secret in your breast?"

"I needed to make the pledge with you, to have you

sanctify it. If it were to become known, many of the young women would also seek to make this vow without first looking deep enough into their hearts. And perhaps afterward, then sorely tested, they'd not keep it. A vow is better not made than made and not kept."

She stood and walked from the hut.

In writing to his uncle, Chauchetière ruminated about Kateri:

At St. Francis Xavier now lives that young native woman I wrote of before who possesses such piety that no abbess, no mother superior, no nun serving the poor and diseased of Paris is her peer. She has such faith, such an innate grasp of spiritual teachings, that each conversation with her leaves me more astonished. She possesses, too, the eloquence of the Iroquois and their stern, unyielding will. Oh, Uncle, all the hardships I have endured in this land melt away like ice in the spring sun when I consider the spiritual progress of this one soul. Like a delicate flower, like our beloved fleur-de-lis, this lily has sprung from soil sweetened with blood of scalpings, salted with the tears of massacre and war. It renews my faith to observe her, for her life proves that the great of heart dwell not only under gilded ceilings, but also in bark huts, and that our church can find piety in the humblest of hearts.

Kateri has taken the vows of poverty, chastity, and obedience. This daughter of the primeval forests wishes to live in a perpetual state of prayer. It is miraculous among her people, for few children beyond the age of seven have their virginity intact. Yet in spite of the orgies and the savage feasts, this retiring young woman has refrained from physical sin.

And, before relating the scene of her chastity vow to his uncle, Père Claude Chauchetière placed the quill to his lips and stared into the light from his rush lamp. He contemplated with an unsettling feeling that his love for Kateri Tekakwitha, in no way carnal, still was not completely divine.

5

The mission was nearly vacant that winter. With his family, Joseph Kryn left to hunt. The three women lived quietly together. Each morning at four, the bell rang to summon the few residents to Mass. By then, Kateri Tekakwitha had long been in the chapel, praying upon her knees. At ten o'clock another Mass was said, and again she knelt, watching—in wonder, but perfect belief—consecration of bread and wine into the body and blood of the Savior. And again at two in the afternoon, she attended Mass.

Her health ebbed away. Though never robust or hardy, Kateri had always been energetic in stitching, in performing domestic chores. Now a quiet, ethereal flame burned within. She answered questions slowly, carefully, as if hearing an echo after every word. She gazed meditatively into space or into the fire, as if insubstantial shadows were merging and parting. Frequently she cocked her ear and turned, listening to the silence. Was it Jerome whispering to her? Often she heard his soft voice describing in Iroquois eloquence the message of the blackrobe. Was it someone else? Her mother, perhaps? She heard her mother singing again with joy at the bounty the Christian Lord had supplied. And Kateri remembered the childish shame she'd felt when hurling her mother's bones into the common pit for outlaws. Now her mother of the warm flesh and bright eye and ready smile was in heaven, high above the clouds.

But other voices were in the wind, the wisdom of men, the joy of women, the laughter of children she had never known, and this made her curious. She yearned to speak with them, to tell them of her private joy, yet they were so insubstantial and fleeting, they evaporated like the mist above a lake when she turned her attention toward them.

Winter proved long and harsh that year. The cold blew into the huts, numbing those who huddled about small fires. On the hunt in the northern forests, game was plentiful. The families of Joseph Kryn and Michael shared a hunting camp on the Ottawa River. Joseph Kryn reckoned time by the phases of the moon so they'd descend the river in time for the Easter celebration. When the ice tore loose at last, the river swelled and ran, foaming with melting snow, and the hunting party left for the lowlands and home.

Joseph Kryn led the flotilla joyfully past the fort where he'd fought Daulac and the seventeen brave French lads. His big shoulders bulged when paddling to avoid the rocks, and his keen eye carefully scanned the foaming river for the true channel. Now after the dead season, they'd plant the maize and repair their huts and live in harmony with the regular tolling of the mission bell, the introspective sermons of the priest, and the comfort and grace gained from sacraments.

But when they beached their canoes, the mission seemed deserted. Bewildered, Joseph Kryn and Michael told the others to unload the canoes, and they walked through the grass swale into the mission. The first person they met was Anastasia Tegonhat, hurrying along the lane.

"Anastasia Tegonhat?" Joseph Kryn called out. "Has the priest's spell worked and all souls flown to heaven?"

"You would do well not to joke," Anastasia scolded. She turned and hurried along.

"What? No word of welcome? What impels you so?"

"I tell thee, Joseph Kryn, not to bring such drollery into the mission," she scolded. "Kateri Tekakwitha is dying. She is not expected to rise from her bed."

Joseph Kryn seized Michael's arm and they followed Anastasia. In the dim light of a hut Kateri, thin, gaunt, weak, lay on the elk furs of her sleeping shelf. Her eyes burned in the dim hut with an unnatural light. She folded her hands on her lap and slowly peered about the room. Around the bed clustered all the villagers. Some wept, some groaned, some attempted smiles as Père Claude knelt, administering the last rites.

"Hail, Joseph Kryn," Marie Thérèse whispered. "Kateri Tekakwitha is slipping from us. She has been talking to each of us."

"Silence, please," Kateri moaned. "Marie Thérèse, step over here." She did so. "I have seen what you did to purchase from God a peaceful death for me." Sobs broke out among the gathered converts. "I know you too well."

Marie Thérèse said: "I have done nothing. It is the lot of

each of us to pass through the vale of death. I cannot ease your suffering."

"And yet," Kateri said in a thick, clotty voice, "I know you and Anastasia did scourge each other with briars this very morning, praying the Lord to ease my pain." Kateri tried to sit up.

Embarrassed at the scolding, Marie Thérèse hung her head.

"Oh, the deeds we do, the things we hold dear upon this earth matter not at all." Kateri shook her head and spoke slowly, unhurriedly, yet her strength ebbed perceptibly. "Our lives are so short and fleeting. Like fragments of dream we live in each other's sight. My friends," she said, peering from each to each, waving her hand. "I have loved you all. I am not in pain. It is a soft weakness that comes over me." She dropped her hands and sighed.

At these words, new sobs broke out.

"Please stop that," Kateri said. "I will be present at the death of each of you, so please, please do not grieve! Instead, be happy. I see a beauty, a joy beyond any pleasure we have known, a peace and a contentment that flourishes like the corn in the summer sun. We all will be called to burst this husk and spread our leaves in the luxury and warmth and sweet rain of another world." She paused and held her ear attentively. "I sense that Joseph Kryn has arrived."

All eyes turned toward the door. The big man approached her bedside. "Ah," Kateri smiled. "It was in my prayers that you would arrive safely before I departed. I have lingered because I sensed you would return for Easter, and yet I felt God wanted me so soon, so very soon." She fell back upon the elk skin robe, her black hair disarrayed upon the pillow of skin. "He has sent you here," she smiled. "I am glad." She gasped. Pain tightened her face. "Now I may go to Him."

In anguish Anastasia Tegonhat cried out. The bearskin door parted and sunlight pierced into the smoky hut. Marie, Luke, Matthew and the others entered. Kateri summoned them to her and a smile lit her features.

"Why have you not brought her into the chapel as is customary?" Joseph Kryn asked.

"She was so very weak," Anastasia whispered, "and she prayed we not move her as she wanted to live to see you once again."

Père Claude Chauchetière's eyes were swollen and red

from weeping. He looked up imploringly, then took Kateri by the hand and wrung her fingers in his own. She hardly noticed.

"Do not grieve," Joseph Kryn said, kneading the priest's shoulder with his strong hand. "She is entering heaven soon. We shall rejoice."

The priest peered up humbly at this former savage whose faith seemed so much stronger than his own. "Though we all live together, yet we all die alone," he cried in anguish. The converts were disturbed: never before had the priest shown such emotion.

"I will be with you always," Kateri said weakly. Again she rose upon her elbows, and the thick curtain of her hair swung. "Oh, my friends, if you could see through my eyes how short and fleeting are the things of this world and how transient death is! You will join me one day. Do not be sad, please!" She extended her arm. A smile fluttered across her face, her eyes grew limpid. "I go. I go now to a greater peace and joy than can ever exist on earth. Oh, my friends, the poor struggles and the small desires that cloud our vision. Look into the sunset tonight. More brilliant, more peaceful than that is the merest glimpse of heaven." She closed her eyes to savor the vision, and she swallowed hard.

"What do you see?" whispered the priest, kneeling at her side, clasping her hand in both of his. "What is there?"

A smile quivered at her lips. "Joy!" she whispered. She opened her eyes, looked from the priest to the chief. "Good Joseph Kryn," she murmured, "bravest and most noble of the Canienga, watch over our people."

All were sobbing now, even Joseph Kryn. She shook her head. "Do not weep. Please, great chief. Lead our people in the path of goodness. And Marie Thérèse, my sister in Christ," she continued, "teach young women virtue. Abandon the whippings. Do penance by prayer and fasting and contemplation." She focused her eyes with difficulty upon the priest. "Père Claude, my guardian, you have taught me the way to the Kingdom of God. Continue your great labors to bring light into the forests and villages. Counsel all people to join in one brotherhood, to bring harmony and peace to this land."

She closed her eyes, fell back exhausted, and her black hair fanned upon the elk skin robe.

"Oh, my friends," she sighed. "Pray always to Jesus and

to Mary, ever virgin, for strength, for guidance, for comfort... Jesus... Mary..." The room shook with sobs. "I hear you crying. Do not cry!" she whispered. Then she gasped. "I go at last to Jesus and Mary." A deep sigh broke from her, and her body shuddered involuntarily. "Jesus and Mary," she whispered again, and then, as quietly as if drifting into sleep, she departed.

"Gone! She is gone..." The priest cried brokenly, dropping his hand which had clung to hers. Anastasia Tegonhat and Marie Thérèse began wailing as the Iroquois mourn the death of children. "Gone!" The priest clasped his hands in prayer.

At that moment a deap baritone lifted all their grief and sorrow, for a hymn broke forth in the voice of Joseph Kryn. Others joined in. They clasped each other's hands, and soon even Père Claude stood and joined in the singing. And out from the cramped hut, upon the fresh spring air, up over the untilled fields, over the chapel cross, out over the bristling river drifted their hymn of faith.

6

Père Claude still knelt praying. All the villagers had threaded out of the death chamber to prepare for Holy Thursday celebrations. He bowed his head over Kateri Tekakwitha in the dim light of the hut, murmuring prayers. As he concluded, he looked up. He gasped in wonder. He ran to the door and shouted, "Come here! Please! At once! Come here." Like a crazed man Père Claude ran into the yard crying for all to come, wringing and clenching his hands. "Come here! At once!" Father Cholonec and the villagers hurried again into the hut. A miraculous change had come over Kateri's features. Her skin, once marked by smallpox and emaciated by her consumption, was now imbued with a new earthly light and beauty.

"What does it mean, Father?" asked Joseph Kryn in a hushed voice.

The priest spoke in awe. "It is a sign from God to strengthen our faith."

"Even now does she enter heaven," whispered Anastasia Tegonhat.

"Praise be to the Lord," murmured Marie Thérèse, making the sign of the cross.

And over their shoulders peered other anxious villagers.

Next morning, two French farmers arrived at the mission for Holy Thursday services. They passed the open door to Kateri's hut, and entering the sacristy to help the priest, one remarked, "Who was that beautiful Indian girl sleeping so peacefully?"

"That is the fairest of our mission," Chauchetière said. "She has departed from our world, and today will be her funeral."

"She is dead?" The one frowned in astonishment.

Claude bowed his head to hide his tears. "She lives no more with us."

The two farmers hurried back to the hut to kneel at her bedside and recommend themselves to her prayers.

Lovingly that afternoon, Marie Thérèse and Anastasia oiled Kateri's hair and face and adorned her in a new tunic and moccasins for the burial, while the two farmers fashioned a coffin.

7

"Hello there, Father!" Joseph Kryn called as the priest passed meditatively along the shore that afternoon. Joseph Kryn was skillfully lashing the ribwork of his canoe. He dropped the greased cord and the bone implements and joined the priest.

"Ah, good Joseph," Père Claude said. "I hardly noticed you." He smiled faintly and placed his hand on the other's broad shoulder. "How are you faring?"

"Very well. Marie Karitha, Matthew, and I will journey downriver to Three Rivers soon to trade the pelts from our winter hunting." Joseph Kryn smiled and his blue eyes gleamed.

The priest attempted to return Kryn's smile. "You do not mourn her passing?"

Kryn's eyes narrowed and a smile played at his lips. "There is no need. She has received her reward. She looks down on us now."

The priest bit his lip and cast his eyes down.

"We were all deeply privileged to know her in life, and now we are privileged to pray to her in heaven," Joseph Kryn said.

"I know," the priest said. Tears brimmed in his eyes, and he clenched and unclenched his fists. "I know."

"She is very near us, Father."

The priest nodded, but did not speak, as if uttering one word would bring an outpouring of sobs and tears. Joseph Kryn placed a hand on his shoulder. "Why, then, do you grieve?" he asked. "Frame it into words so we both may understand it better."

The priest took a deep breath. "Her faith was so pure, so perfect and unquestioning," he said. "She truly believed, and her belief sustained her. Her faith sprang from the blood of Isaac Jogues. He prepared the way for her conversion. He has been my guide in counseling her. Yes, Joseph Kryn, she loved all things with a divine love, a love untainted by earthly desire. She loved you, Joseph Kryn, and she loved me." Chauchetière paused.

"So why does this cause you grief?"

The priest's eyes filled again. "You are correct. I should not feel sorrow. The maiden always inspired me to greater love of God. It is only that..." He heaved a sigh and fought to control his quavering voice. "It is only that by remembering her vast gifts that I see the flaws in my own faith."

"One of Kateri's piety is very rare," Joseph Kryn observed.

"Yes," the priest nodded. He smiled and he clasped Joseph Kryn's hand. "She has shown me my mistake. I fixed my sights upon things eternal and divine as a young man, and that was good. Yet I saw no possibility for truth and goodness in this world. Seeing evil everywhere, everything upon this earth was corruptible, and I despised the world, my home, the corruption of Paris and of Rome. Yet Kateri Tekakwitha saw poetry and beauty in the midst of unspeakable, unimaginable horror. No, she did not dwell on the ugliness or corruption, as I have. She held beauty above all things; beauty was her private treasure, and she tried all the time and everywhere to share it with us all. Ah, Joseph, I wonder if by sharing my view of evil with her, I might have been trying to corrupt her because I felt such goodness could not exist—temptation would pollute it."

"You were her spiritual counselor," Joseph Kryn said with a puzzled look. "You saved her!"

"Often," the priest remarked, "we lead others only because we ourselves have lost the way. It is among you, the Canienga, the people of forests and rivers, the sun and the winter ice that I have found such great zeal for my own faith. It grieves me that our white race hasn't this ability—our holy ones strive either as theologians or mystics."

"Be cheered then, Father, that you have known her." Joseph Kryn smiled, and his eyes moistened. He expanded his great chest in a sigh. "Be cheered that she blessed all our lives, brought us many spiritual gifts. Keep in mind, Father, that not only does she dwell in heaven, she dwells also in the forests. She dwells in the sunlight upon the lakes and rivers and will forever dwell among the echoing mountains, as she dwells here among us."

"Yes, Joseph Kryn," Père Claude said, "you speak with much wisdom." Again they clasped hands. "I shall keep your words foremost in my mind."

The priest looked out over the sparkling river, swollen with melted upland snow, and he fixed his attention to Heron Island, where flocks of white birds circled. "Yes, you are correct," Père Claude said. "She is not very far away. She is in our midst, and we must do everything we can to keep her here."

With a lighter step, the priest passed along the shore. Joseph Kryn returned to lashing the ribwork of his canoe, and as he worked, looking out over the broad river, he began to sing.

8

Claude sat in his cabin, listening to the hammering of the French farmers who were building her coffin. He reflected upon the Iroquois fashion of oiling the hair and face, dressing the maiden in new fur robes. The terrible grief of her departure had numbed him, obliterated all other concerns. She was gone. That fact, so simple, so unalterable, withered all other thought. Yet, as he sat there, as he remembered her shy kindness when he stayed in Iowerano's hut, as he remembered coming upon her and her passionate appeal to learn of Christ, as he remembered her baptism and her first communion, something occurred to him. A pattern, inexplicable but profound, as profound as the mysteries of his faith, began to take shape.

Yes, he remembered his spiritual exercises at Montmartre— the infernal regions of hell, the agony and submission of Christ, then the pure and saving love of the Virgin. So had his life been in New France—all a hell of heathen superstition, the warfare, scalpings, the march of Tracy, the burning of the Land of Flint. Then, remembering the agony and the submission of Jogues—*I shall go and I shall not return*, he had journeyed among them as a missionary. How imperfect and untested seemed his faith by comparison! But, he brightened at a thought: His destiny was not to be a victim! His destiny was to be a missionary! He has shed the light of Christ's word upon a poor, silent orphan who stitched her poetry into skins. He recalled her glorified features as she lay upon the pallet of fur, the smooth, radiant complexion, the look of peaceful slumber. And he knew with a confidence he'd never before claimed that her short passage upon the earth was a progression into holiness, sanctity, yes, even into sainthood, and this knowledge strengthened his faith, dispelled his carping doubts and cheered him.

Yes, even beset by doubts, by worldly love of her whom he so admired, his counsel was what had elevated her, guided her, channeled her passionate love of Christ into the right paths.

He would not follow Jogues unto death in this heathen land. Instead, he would live, and he would continue to minister to these people of the forest and lakes. He would guide them out of their superstitious rites, their ignorance, their violent, irrational ways. He would supplant their magic with a knowledge of good and evil, right and wrong. And in ministering to them, he would look toward Kateri Tekakwitha to be his guide and his sustaining strength.

He closed his eyes, at last feeling peace and serenity. He knew now; he was certain. Her death had sealed a pact for him. He was a true and worthy minister of God's word. From the depths and darkness of all his doubt, he had found the strength to live and teach the faith. This was his mission; this was his destiny.

Idly, Père Claude listened again to the hammering of the French farmers. No, it wasn't sadness, it was joy he felt. The momentary regret that she was gone gave way to a wonderful, sustaining joy. The blows of the hammer cheered him. They were not building a coffin to hide away a corpse. They were, rather, hammering together his wishes and his beliefs, building with these native materials his future and the fulfillment of his faith.

9

At sunset, in a purple stole and white surplice, with two acolytes in red cassocks, the other two Jesuits trailing with incense, Père Claude Chauchetière led the mission in a procession to the gravesite beneath the cross in the cemetery. And in a voice trembling with emotion, spreading his arms in prayer, Père Claude commended Kateri Tekakwitha's remains to the earth. And the other priests, the farmers, and the villagers from many savage nations bowed their heads, held each other's hands, and incense sweetened the spring wind from the river.

ABOUT THE AUTHOR

JACK CASEY first encountered the legends of the Iroquois, the Jesuit martyrs and the virgin girl Tekakwitha during childhood. After studying literature at Yale University, he traveled extensively and now lives in upstate New York. Mr. Casey is currently working on a novel about America's founding fathers.

The Days
of Eternity

by
Gordon Glasco

Here is a breathtaking saga of a passionate love so overwhelming that it defies war, betrayal, conscience—and time itself. One Sunday morning, Anna Miceli, a successful American lawyer, sits in church and sees a man—and her heart stands still. At that moment, time melts away. Once again Anna is the innocent girl of an Italian country village. It is wartime, and the time of her first consuming love—for the young German lieutenant who commands the occupying forces. But when he commits an unspeakable act, Anna's world is shattered, her life changed forever. Now, twenty-eight years later, he stands before her—a priest. And now, Anna knows the time has come to face an agonizing choice. For here is the man whose memory has been a cold cinder of hatred inside her, the man she has vowed someday to destroy—and the man her turbulent heart can never surrender.

Read THE DAYS OF ETERNITY, on sale September 1, 1984, wherever Bantam paperbacks are sold, or use the handy coupon below for ordering:

A TOWERING, ROMANTIC SAGA BY
THE AUTHOR OF
LOVE'S WILDEST FIRES

HEARTS
of
FIRE

by Christina Savage

For Cassie Tryon, Independence Day, 1776, signals a different kind of upheaval—the wild, unstoppable rebellion of her heart. For on this day, she will meet a stranger—a legendary privateer disguised in clerk's clothes, a mysterious man come to do secret, patriot's business with her father . . . a man so compelling that she knows her life will never be the same for that meeting. He is Lucas Jericho—outlaw, rebel, avenger of his family's fate at British hands, a man who is dangerous to love . . . and impossible to forget.

Buy HEARTS OF FIRE, on sale November 1, 1984, wherever Bantam paperbacks are sold, or use the handy coupon below for ordering:

THE LATEST BOOKS IN THE BANTAM BESTSELLING TRADITION